Barleycorn Blues

LEE DUNNE

POOLBEG

Published 2004 by Poolbeg Press Ltd.
123 Grange Hill, Baldoyle,
Dublin 13, Ireland
Email: poolbeg@poolbeg.com

1 3 5 7 9 10 8 6 4 2

A catalogue record for this book is available from the British Library.

ISBN 1-84223-212-6

Typeset by Patricia Hope in Sabon MT 11/14
Printed by
Litografia Rosés S.A., Spain

www.poolbeg.com

About the Author

Lee Dunne has spent most of his adult life as a writer. He burst to fame in 1965 with his novels *Goodbye to the Hill* and *A Bed in the Sticks* before the final part of the trilogy, *Paddy Maguire is Dead,* was banned by the Irish censor in 1972. By that stage he had long since escaped from a poverty-stricken Dublin background, working as a clerk, actor, singer and cocktail bartender in Jersey before spending one year riding a bicycle around London doing 'The Knowledge' to become a Cabbie so that he would have more time to write.

He has written 18 novels and 10 stage plays. Of his three movies, two were Hollywood productions, including *Paddy,* which was adapted by Lee for the screen from his novel *Goodbye to the Hill* and was banned by the Irish film censor in 1970. He has also written a large number of plays for both television and radio and has contributed 2,000 episodes of a radio serial to RTÉ. He has been published as a poet, has written columns for two national newspapers, and is currently a book critic for the *Sunday Independent*.

Lee also co-adapted and directed a drama based on the writings of Plato for the School of Philosophy in Dublin for six years. He has just graduated with an MA Honours degree in Screenwriting, is currently working on two novels and a screenplay and is intent on bringing his long-cherished dream, a musical called *Monto,* to realisation.

He lives in Bray with his wife Maura, walks the prom a couple of times almost every day of the year and declares without a blush, "if I knew where the madness came from I'd go back for another basinful." Lee will be 70 in December 2004 and is looking forward to middle age, while agreeing with Hubie Blake that "had I known I was going to live this long I'd have taken better care of myself."

Lee Dunne's new novel will be published in 2005 by Poolbeg.

Acknowledgements

Thanks to Philip McDermott and to Alice Horan. Thanks to my editor, Lucy Taylor, a total professional who worked with such love and care. Thanks to Paula Campbell, who can't help being special. And big time thanks to my best man, Mike Cunningham, who never quit encouraging me.

Part 1

Prologue

Dervla Devine, 300 Shrewsbury Road, Dublin
July 31st 1991

Joe Collins,
Tower House,
Whiterock,
Co Dublin

Dear Joe

I feel that I know you through your two autobiographical novels. I offer you heartiest congratulations on your well-deserved success. May I say how pleased I am that you have come home to Ireland, the land of the writers, to get on with as you expressed it yourself on television "the full-time job of being a professional writer".

Joe, I want to meet you to seek your help in relation to my drinking. Recently I reread your series on alcoholism in *The Irish Times* (my cousin sent them from New York when they were first published there in the *NY Times*) and your article *"I am an alcoholic"* in *The Evening Herald*. And I felt for the first time in many years, that it might just be possible for me to finally quit drinking.

I'm thirty years old and I have been drinking since I was fifteen. I have to admit right away that I took to booze like a duck to water. I allow that it took away whatever modesty a girl is supposed to have in these times, that I became a promiscuous teenager, and that this pattern of behaviour developed as I got older. I would think of myself today as a well-bred tart, masquerading as an upper-middle-class wife.

I have not sought help before and have never talked to anybody about what drink and I, as a team, could turn into – sometimes within minutes of taking those first few glasses. Joe, I have woken up with men I had never met before, people whose names I didn't know. Even as I got dressed in their bedrooms, I prayed to God they would not awaken. Is it possible you could be the answer to those prayers?

I know how busy you must be, due to receiving so much media exposure. But if you can see your way to meet me, to help me make a start on a life where everything doesn't revolve around booze, I will be forever in your debt.

The best time to get me at home is Saturday morning. Should my husband Gary answer the phone, please just say you want to talk to me about quitting the booze. The poor man will be all for that.

Sincerely,

Dervla Devine

PS My card, bearing my phone number, is attached.

I

Brooklyn, New York, June 1st 1988

The guy says his name is Telly and he says "I'm an alcoholic". This bunch of asshole guys, gals, and others chime in like some fucking Greek chorus with "Hi Telly!" It's like we're performing in a musical or something. And I hear this voice in my head crying "what the fuck am I doing here?" All right, I'm drunk. Sure! And I've got no control over my mouth. So now I hear me telling the guy to "shut the fuck up".

"You sound like every other asshole I ever heard at these fucking meetings. How can you kid yourself that a bunch of slogans, 'Easy Does It' and all the other 'One Day At A Time' bullshit is going to help you put the plug in the jug? Just take a look around you, pal. What a bunch of fucking losers! You could run a contest for Brooklyn's 'bum of the year' and you've got the winner right here in this fucking room!"

Telly turns to look at me and I can see he'd like to alter the shape of my mouth. But he holds it down. "Give me a break, will you, pal?"

Before I can tell him to sit on it, I'm moving. I haven't made any decision in this direction, but I am definitely moving. My feet are about two feet off the floor. Thanks to a couple of beefcakes who are not as tolerant as Telly was.

Moments later I am flying for a short time. Then I crash-land on the footpath at the bottom of the granite steps descending from the brownstone where the AA meeting I've just left is still going on. Like the song says, 'Something's Gotta Give' and in this instance it's me. I have just collided with an immovable force and I feel apple-green in my innards, like I've been kicked in the *cojones* by a mule. Later I realise that if I hadn't been as loaded as I was, I might have been badly hurt.

I'm lying there with no immediate plans to move, aware that people are stepping over me as though I'm a pool of dirty water. The torso of a man suddenly blots out the lunchtime sunlight and I'm looking up at the guy. It's Telly, who was trying to tell his story while I was shooting from the lip.

"Can I help you get up from there, sport?" he asks me. His New England drawl is at odds with his bloodshot eyes and the shakes in his manicured hands. "Give me a minute, will you. Something just occurred to me and I need to lay it on you."

My eyes are working better now and I can see that he has that kind of Ivy League polish dames find so attractive. His clothes could do with a trip to the dry-cleaners, but they didn't come off the rack.

"Take your time, sport. I've got no pressing appointments just now."

He lights a cigarette and hands it down to me.

I take a drag and almost spew all over myself. "What the

get rid of the aches and pains. I just sit there willing the coffee to stay down. I light another cigarette. Telly had offered to buy me food, but I wasn't ready to eat. Would I ever want to eat again, I asked myself?

"I feel like shit," Telly said, as though reading my mind. "But I'm glad I woke up alive." He smoked some more. "I'm grateful to the guy who discovered coffee."

I raised my coffee cup. "And to Sir Walter Raleigh, the gent who was crazy enough to smoke the first cigarette!"

Between us we found the remnants of a smile, and Telly joined me in a painful chuckle, fuelled by our collective defiance.

"Do you know anything about Bill and Dr Bob?" he asked, quaffing another cup of the java.

"I heard something about them. They founded AA, right?"

"That's right. These two hopeless drunks, educated guys, professionals, they couldn't quit drinking. Not until they met each other and started talking about booze."

"What're you saying? Two drunks talked about booze and they founded Alcoholics Anonymous?" He could tell I didn't readily believe this.

"These two hopeless cases," he tells me, "they started talking about booze. And they noticed they weren't reaching for a drink. So they kept on talking, talking about booze, and they didn't need to reach for a drink. And Joe, those two men, they never drank booze again. Can you believe that? They never drank another alcoholic drink. And yes, they founded AA in Akron, Ohio in nineteen thirty-five."

"That's some story," I said, surprised to find myself moved some by hearing how AA got off the ground. "They touched for some kind of miracle, I guess."

7

"Would you consider giving it a shot with me, Joe?"

"Giving what a shot?" My voice climbed a step.

Chuckling, Telly indicated to the waitress to bring more coffee. "Take it easy, sport. I'm not a fag. I'm asking you if you'd like to try getting sober with me. Two of us together, like Bill and Bob did it. They were even more hopeless than we seem to be. And I know I'm pretty sick of waking up and wishing I was dead."

Looking at Telly through the cigarette smoke, I just knew that this was a decent man sitting across the table. Admittedly he wasn't looking great right now, any more than I was. He was wearing that kind of bruised look we get when we're meeting withdrawal after a bender. But his olive dark eyes, as Greek as his name, hadn't had all the fight knocked out of them. Not yet. He looked uneasy, sure, not happy with himself. Just like the way I'd been feeling myself for the last hundred years!

When you drink long enough to get hooked on John Barleycorn, is it any wonder you might not be able to just walk away because he's no longer the friend you started out with? While I'm sitting there trying to figure out Sampras, my guess is that he's probably doing the same thing to me. We're real good at that, 'alkys'. Really talented at working out the other guy's shit, not so hot at seeing the way our own *merde* is coming off the fan. And anyway, how come we end up as alcoholics?

Like, I never met a guy yet who set out to be a drunk or made plans to be a drunken bum. I never knew any guy that set out to get alcoholism so he could wear it like a suntan. And the *beau* in my morning mirror never told me he had any intention of becoming all of the above. He wasn't that bright, bold or adventurous. He was just your average Joe –

a guy who drank booze so he could go and throw a few shapes in the dance-halls of Dublin where he was born. He needed the hit to be like the other guys. How could he have known they were probably just as scared as he was about stepping into the world where men are men, and women like it!

I know other guys who got dry at their first AA meeting and never took a drink again, the last I heard. Guys who walked in off the street and heard the magic can be there in those meeting rooms for anyone willing to go to any lengths to get sober. These lucky guys don't know they're up for going all the way, just as guys like me don't know we're only willing to go to *certain* lengths to get sober. It's like we're missing a gene or something. Somehow we can't make the shift into overdrive needed to go to any lengths.

On the train into Manhattan, Telly talks fifty and looks hung over-thirty-nine as he tells me about his boozing: "I drank because I thought I was an asshole. Pretty soon booze and me together, well I quit thinking I was asshole. I *knew* I was!" All of Telly's wit was turned against himself, like he never made fun of another person.

His story ran a predictable course. He began drinking because that's what guys do at a certain age. He didn't feel he measured up to the guys he hung out with, so he drank more than they did to help him feel better about himself. He needed help, just like me, to feel as confident as other guys seemed to be without doing anything to get like that. In this respect John Barleycorn didn't let him down and life was good. Life was fine, as long as he could afford the company of his buddy.

When he started working as a society photographer, often doubling as a photo-journalist, he was earning real money and living a lifestyle high on sensation and excitement. He was on the late-night circuit, personally and professionally, and it was dames, dames, dames, every night, most of them dolls wanting their picture in the paper. His own tastes were expensive and his bookmaker was really a luxury he couldn't afford. A run of bad luck with the ponies and his bookie begins talking in a way that suggests bad health is imminent for Telly – if a lot of bread doesn't change hands immediately.

"By the time I realised I was in serious trouble, the booze had me in a grip I couldn't break. I lost my wife, a decent woman, my home, and –" He stopped as though the memory had hit the brakes for him.

"Y'know sport, all the years working on the top magazines, I never stopped to think how privileged I was to have landed such a career. I just schlepped along when I should have been dancing in gratitude for the lifestyle that had landed on me like a beautiful rain-shower. I didn't do much to get where I was. I could always bang off a picture, and even a dolt with no education to speak of can write the caption for a picture of a lovely dame."

My surprise showed before I could hide it and he chuckled when I said I thought he was Princeton or Yale. He shook his head for what seemed a long time. "My father, a good man, he was a sergeant in the army. He did his best for me and my mother." He exhaled smoke like a sigh of chagrin.

I lit another cigarette myself and sat there, quiet, feeling he had more to say.

"I never forgave him, Joe, for not being a captain. Officer's kids got to ride the front of the school bus. Me and my kind, we sat at the back, just like the coloureds, before Martin Luther King and the Kennedys and those other guys helped change things."

He looked like he had a sour taste in his mouth. I guessed he was reliving the moment of those times, and maybe the flavour of whatever he was carrying about his father. Our silence spoke for both of us. I thought of Dublin, where my parents couldn't hold a public library card because they didn't own their home. In the land of the writers, the land of saints and scholars, the land my father risked his life for in the civil war, book borrowing was barred to the soldier returned from the dark night of the revolutionary, another sniper's bullet residing in his back.

At that moment on the subway I remember an AA slogan 'Don't Think! Don't Drink! Go to Meetings!' and I feel enough relief in my heart to stifle the power of those angry yesterdays. I realise it's happening because of the way Telly and me are talking to each other about the booze, and the baggage that comes with it.

"Hey!" I say, surprised at my own cheerfulness. "How about we go back out to Brooklyn to the evening meeting? After I find somewhere to get cleaned up, and maybe drink a little soup?"

Telly chuckles wickedly. "Only an Irish guy could think like that. And I say yes, let's go for it. We're about the same size. I can give you some duds. Chances are they won't recognise you after a shower and a shave. Are you first generation? Or were you born in the old country?"

"I was born in Dublin – came here when my mother died. I was nineteen. Uncle Ned, Ma's brother, he brought me over. He died since. Never been back, keep meaning to go, keep meaning to quit drinking, keep meaning to write my book, keeping meaning to get rich and famous, keep meaning to stop kidding myself."

Telly talked about the trouble he was having with the

'One Day At A Time' philosophy, which is the cornerstone of the recovery program offered by Alcoholics Anonymous. I had the same problem, feeling that no matter how they addressed the drinker's dilemma at the meetings, with suggestions like 'You Stay Away From One Drink for One Day', the truth was you were there in the AA room knowing you needed to give up the booze for life.

Telly said suddenly, "Bill and Bob, they didn't talk about AA or slogans or suggestions or rules. There was no AA yet. They hadn't come up with it. They talked about booze, booze and booze!" He got to his feet and I grabbed the support rail to stand beside him in the swaying subway car. "Next stop is ours." he said, with the energy of a guy who had just realised something that excited him.

As we left the subway, I told Telly again that I was sorry for my outburst at the meeting. We were passing Carnegie Hall on Fifty-seventh Street when I said, "You're throwing me a lifeline here."

He stopped and shook my hand. "It's a two-way street, Joe. We need each other, so let's just admit it, accept it and get on with trying to get sober. OK?"

"Suits me, man. But I have to tell you, I'm flat broke, I've got nothing. Been sleeping rough for a little while."

Telly's mouth shifted into a wry smile. "Then you got nothing to lose, right!" We walked on towards the corner of Ninth Avenue. "Fortunately I held onto this apartment, bought it as an investment when I was calling myself big shot. It's not Park, but it's a good spot. You'll have your own room, there'll be something in the refrigerator, and I keep the hot water hot at all times. It can be your home if you've no objection to living in Manhattan." He said this without irony, and I laughed out loud.

"Manhattan's the centre of the universe to me. I'll thrive here in this city. I love it. I call it the bright-lighted, star-studded centre of the world. Jesus, Telly! I'm getting hit with the fucking shakes." Even as I spoke my legs buckled so that I had to hold onto him, to stop from falling over.

Telly leans me against a wall and rushes in a store. He returns with a mess of candy and two cartons of milk. And there we stand, on the corner of Fifty-seventh and Ninth, cramming chocolate in and washing it down with cow juice until the need for sugar disappears. I let go a sigh you could photograph. Telly takes me by the arm, and I allow him guide me into the apartment block, very relieved that the hypo-glycaemia got zapped before it got settled by the fireplace.

Ten minutes later I am soaking in a hot-tub yelling out to Telly that I'll start paying my way just as soon as I can get myself a job. "That's got to be part of the deal."

"Suits me," he calls back. "All we need is the good fortune not to hit the sauce at the same time."

"I'll put in a call to St Jude. The Patron Saint of Lost Causes, right!"

Telly came into the bathroom and laid out a couple of towels and a dressing-gown. Before he went out again, he sorted out a razor and stuff I was going to need and he said quietly: "Y'know, I might not have made that lunch-time meeting." He shook his head in disbelief. "I stood right here, tossed a coin. Heads I drink, tails I attend the meeting. Imagine, a life, my life if you like, was hanging there for a moment. I was dangling on a thread while a coin got flipped by a guy in need of a guardian angel."

"I'm glad the angel came through," I assured him. "And listen, Telly, I won't say this any more. Don't want you throwing me out for being a pain-in-the-ass. I know I've said it already, but I need to say it again. I'm deeply sorry for my remarks at the meeting."

"OK," Telly held up his hand in surrender. "But that's the last time you get to mention that. We're going back to Flatbush Avenue. Lay it to rest there, right in the same meeting room where it happened."

A while later he brings me fresh coffee and a Danish which I dunk and chew slowly, not wanting to bring it all back up in the guy's bath on the first day in my new home. It sits OK and I feel good about that. At that moment I feel OK about being alive. This is evicted by the thought "I'm still a major fuck-up". I let go of this one right away.

Telly took the tub after me, but not before I cleaned it so you could see yourself in it. I lay on the bed in my room and took a nap while he soaked for an hour. When I woke up I found pants and a couple of shirts hanging behind the door. He had also left underpants, socks and a choice of shoes. And there was an unopened bottle of Brut on the bedside table.

I dressed in minutes, excited by the crisp feel of the duds. I riffled my mop of hair around, fixed a soft woollen tie into the collar of a Brooks Brothers' button-down shirt, and I had to admit I didn't look half-bad. I grinned ruefully into the bathroom mirror and said to myself, "You look like chips waiting on vinegar!"

This is how it began for Telly and me, each of us so desperate we were willing to take on a partner to help fight the fear that we couldn't make it alone. I know that when it comes down to the wire you're always alone, but as Telly and I took the subway back to that same AA room in Brooklyn I had hope. Impossible hope filled my heart, something I could not even have visualised just hours earlier as Flatbush Avenue impacted upon me for the first time.

Don't get me wrong. I was a long way from being out of the woods. My old enemy – this uninvited, live-in lodger with the power to undo me if I dropped my gloves – was perched on my shoulder, waiting to help me to fuck it up once more with feeling. In that moment at the meeting I refused him access, pulling out that slogan that had burned itself onto my recent thinking. "Don't Think! Don't Drink! Go To Meetings!" I sat silently with those seven words, asking some god somewhere to help me hold on.

Telly sat silently beside me and I felt the tension ease down. The truth was I hadn't had a drink for maybe seven hours, while Telly was close to being a whole day dry. OK, we were walking the high-wire again, but we pair were a willing safety-net for each other. We both knew it was never going to be a free ride. When you stop putting the booze in there to still the humpy-bumpy, the rollercoaster hitting your nerve-ends like a recurring acid trip, you hurt like hell. But so what? Hurt won't kill you. You're the guy who would have walked across a yard-full of red-hot coals to get a drink. So now you dance on the plate my man, you're a barefoot rube on a hot griddle. And you haven't died a winter yet!

The first two guys to greet me at the meeting were the dudes who had thrown me out of there at lunch-time. I don't remember their names, but I can still recall their decency as I apologised for my earlier behaviour. I practically smiled at their total lack of surprise that I had made it back to the meeting-room without having had a drink in the meantime. The chairman at the Flatbush meeting was just another recovering alcoholic, and I began listening to what he said. He was the chairman just for this meeting, just a guy who could admit he was sitting on a disease that could kill him if he fed it one more time. This guy was well-established physically, dressed like a guy who made money everyday. He had a wry wit about him that you often find in suffering people though. In his role as chairman of that meeting, he seemed to have put the pain behind him.

He gave us snippets of his own story. He answered questions truthfully, sometimes saying "I don't know" and I liked the guy. While I was wondering how long he'd been sober, he mentioned it was eight years since he last drank alcohol. I found myself listening more intently after this. Even though people bang on about "I'm just off it for today" you can't help admiring a guy who has years of sobriety behind him. And when it's obvious he is doing well in his life, making money and all that, it helps that glimmer of hope inside you to maybe grow a speck in a moment. It also struck me that this guy, Patrick, was honest without forgetting to be kind. For a big guy he had a gentle way about him, and he made me laugh like I hadn't done for quite a while. How long ago is that? Long enough that I can't remember when.

It happened because some guy in the front row claimed that he was seven years without a drink, but that he had felt like drinking all day because his wife had just left him. Patrick responded right away. "You're lucky, pal. When I was seven years sober my wife came back!"

As you might imagine, this line brought the house down. Finally, Patrick asked the guy to wait for him after the meeting ended so that they could chat about his situation.

By the time Telly and me left Brooklyn that night, we each had a bunch of phone numbers, every one accompanied by the offer "call me at anytime, day or night". One woman said something to me that I have never forgotten. "Whatever the time is, if you call me, remember this – I need to talk to you or we won't make the connection."

Not really understanding what she was saying to me, I started to thank her for her kindness.

"Hey hold it, Irish," she cuts me dead. "Cut the bullshit, right! I'm no kinda do-gooder. This is a two-way-street job. And don't you forget it, or you'll drink again."

As Telly and I headed back to Manhattan, I was conscious of some hint of change, some shift in emphasis. Maybe I was just feeling glad I'd been at the meeting. What did surprise me was the fact that I was looking forward to the next meeting, wherever it happened to be.

When I told this to Telly he connected with it. We shook hands again, feeling that since each of us was as keen as the other to get sober we had a real chance of making it. So thanks to him having thrown me a lifebelt, I was on the way out of 'shit city', with a chance at some kind of halfway decent life. I didn't know then that the power which arranges these things had already chosen my first assignment. Just as I didn't know that God had an odd sense of humour.

‐◅o▻‐

Dervla Devine, c/o Whiterock Clinic, Co Dublin
August 28th 1991

Joe Collins,
Tower House,
Whiterock,
Co Dublin

Dear Joe
Thanks a million for replying to my letter. I hope your UK trip was a successful one, and I look forward to meeting you.

I have tried to cut down on my drinking and the consequent wild behaviour, but I've not made any progress. Even when I go for one drink, I swear to you that as soon as it goes down the hatch my head seems to just flip-over like a coin and this "sure, what harm will one more do?" thinking slides into place. The next thing I know I'm jarred somewhere and most of the time I'm unaware of how I got to where I am. The next morning I have to haul myself up out of another hole I've dug myself into. Then there's the time and effort, and a lot of make-up, but even then I don't really come back to life. This doesn't happen until I've had a drink or two to help me stop shaking so that I can get on with my day's work.

I sell things, Joe, all kinds of things, though I was schooled to be a serious public relations person. Is there such a thing, I ask myself? I mean, when you consider the whole spin trip, how could anyone think it's a serious or worthwhile way in which to spend your working days? Yet, the PR geniuses and the great spinners are sought-after as though they have come up with the cure for cancer. Sorry. I'm waffling, something I hate in others so I'll stop it right now.

Just to say that my background is middle class. Daddy had the knack of making money, and I won't pretend it didn't make life a little easier growing-up. A good school, never hungry, holidays, presents at Christmas, a lot of stuff a lot of people don't have when they come into the world. I don't think I'm a very good person. I do think about what some people have to live with, put up with, and I feel shame that I am not eternally grateful for my life. But, the truth is, I am not grateful. I find I am critical of my parents who thought money was the answer to everything, that creature comforts made up for angry silence and a fear of being tactile with their own children. I'm sorry. There I go again. Please let me know when we can meet. I am so looking forward to it. Meanwhile I will try to take up your suggestion that I go to an open meeting, to give me some idea about the fellowship of AA.

I am writing this to you from the Whiterock Clinic. I had a car accident at night in County Kildare. I'm all right and will be here for another week or so.

Deepest thanks,
Dervla

—◇—

2

Manhattan, June 1988

We got no sleep that first night in Telly's apartment on West Fifty-seventh. You don't when you've got bugs dancing on your nerve-ends, while you curse old-man-Morpheus because the uncaring bastard has left for The Hamptons.

I got out of bed and washed my face. The guy in the bathroom mirror looked older than I'd expected to look twenty years from now. All in all, he wasn't a bad-looking guy, but he looked to me like he'd had something important sucked out of him by the beating he'd been taking from John Barleycorn. I knew that this other guy, the destructive mick inside there had been having his own way a lot lately. The more booze I drink, the more power this bastard has over my life and my thinking, everything. Like this guy knows, Joe Collins is too smart to need this AA shit. Maybe those other people in AA – OK, sure. It's fine if they need all that 'Day At A Time' stuff. But you, Joe! Come on! Come on pal! Give me a break! You've got more smarts than the whole bunch at that meeting tonight.

I threw more cold water over my face, and I said out loud to the loser in front of me, "Don't Think! Don't Drink! Go To Meetings! And fuck you pal! I'm not going down again. I spit in your eye. And I promise you, pal, I won't be taking the first drink today. And you can go and take a flying fuck at a rolling doughnut! Can't you get the message that I'm sick and tired of being sick and tired, wearied by looking at a loser like you in the fucking mirror! So get lost!"

I'm drinking hot-chocolate laced with sugar in the kitchen when Telly comes in wearing a newer version of the dressing-gown he'd given me. He's smiling, and since my expression's obviously shaped like a question mark, he says, "I was lying there in the bed with the ay-em blues going to work on me, when I heard this guy yelling in the bathroom."

He draws on his horrible fucking menthol cigarette, shaking his head in some kind of disbelief. "This guy sounds so tough and so angry, bless him. He was yelling all the words that I needed to hear. I needed to hear them more than any other words I know. Can you beat that?" He reached over and shook my hand. "More and more, I believe we can make it together."

An hour later, with the caffeine kicking in real good, we're sitting under an umbrella of cigarette smoke, talking about booze.

"The first drinks made me feel like a guy should feel like, naturally. I drank and I felt great for the first time in my life. I guess I was hooked after two mixers of whiskey in cider."

The morning was coming alive, another hot Manhattan June day already filled with the promise that it was going to fry the ass off everyone in the city.

"I was tit-mad as a teenager," Telly said ruefully. "Most of us guys were. The Saturday night dances in the school gym, all the girls there in their new brassieres looking like they could poke your eye out." He sipped coffee. "During the week I could talk to them in school, make fun, take-it-or-leave-it y'know? But Saturday night . . . I guess because I wanted to caress those breasts, kiss them or whatever, I was not only tongue-tied but paralysed. No kidding, I couldn't walk two yards across the gym to ask a girl with big tits to dance even though I was aching to feel her wonderful boobies against my chest." His face was a greeting card for disbelief, and this habit he had of shaking his head was really getting a run around the block. "Paralysed is good, just about covers it," Telly conceded. "It was as though my legs were made of stone. Until I tasted alcohol, got that first hit." He smiled a smile that told me life just wasn't fair.

"After that you had tits coming out your ears, right?"

He chuckled at the memories. "Oh man! Beautiful breasts are enough to make a guy believe in God. Any wonder I got hooked on booze . . ."

"I've got a theory," I said. "I think the alcoholic is an egomaniac with an inferiority complex. That's why we have to drink so we can ask a girl if she'll have a dance with us."

Telly was interested. "Intriguing," he admitted. "Tell me about it."

"Those times when my legs were like yours, made of concrete, I believe I was in my egomaniac role. Like, all the guys and gals at the dance, they had dolled themselves up and paid money to attend the dance, right? Well, they weren't there just to have a good time. They were there to look at me. They were there to watch me as I walked across the floor to ask a girl to dance. Here's where the inferiority complex bit comes in. The guy pulls it all together, walks over and asks this Dublin chick 'will you dance?' And she says, 'No! Ask me sister, I'm sweatin'!' And everybody in the ballroom gets to see me get put down."

We both laughed, and then he said, "The booze got rid of all that pain. Three or four drinks and I felt free enough to have asked Liz Taylor for a dance."

"Snap!" I said. "And I'll tell you something else. I laid women in Ireland I would never have made a pass at without booze in me. And I woke up with women who were different to how they were when we were having sex. They'd need drink too, just like me, to get it on with someone they'd just met. Most of them next morning weren't what you could call nice. Like, they regretted what had happened between us. And a lot of the time, I felt the same."

"Until you had a few more drinks, right?" Telly knew this script by heart.

"That's when I started getting into trouble. I drank to do things I couldn't do sober. Later, I started to drink to get over how I felt about what I'd been doing. I drank to kill the shame I felt at my own promiscuity. Till one day the cure had become the first hit, and I was already getting pissed again. It was like the circle had connected totally. There was no gap left to allow you find a way out."

Yes, we talked about booze. And we talked about the sex that went with the boozing. We told each other of career chances missed and opportunities lost, because we chose to drink so that we could feel good. The fact that we kept on drinking, even after we'd been beaten up by the danger-signals at every turn, seemed proof enough that booze made us sick. Now we were willing to believe it was a do-it-yourself disease, and that we were the only doctors who could put into effect the do-it-yourself cure.

Telly and I hit ninety meetings in the first ninety days' off the sauce. After that we got to at least five each week. My buddy and I also talked a lot about booze each day, even when we were working full-blast to earn a living and sign on for some kind of life. I know I repeated the words of the Serenity Prayer maybe fifty times a day, especially at those times when I thought I heard the rattler's tail getting close to the territory I called my life.

I worked a forty-hour week as maître d in Benny's Place on Second Avenue. My seagoing trips as a steward in the merchant marine provided the experience I needed to greet the people on Benny's behalf and keep the bar and restaurant moving along at a steady rate of knots, without turning into some kind of ayatollah.

I devoted thirty-five hours a week to writing. I was writing a book that acted like it had to be written, as though I really had no say in the matter, and I was happier than I had ever been before. Like most first novels it was pretty autobiographical and at times it was pouring out so fast that I knew I had to improve my typewriting to keep up. Other times it was slow, or just asleep so I got no words down on paper for a few days. This is what I mean about the book, the story seeming to be in charge. When the writing was slow, I made love to one of the lovely girls I kept meeting in the restaurant. Benny's Place attracted lots of those young women about town – gorgeous creatures who knew what they wanted. It was one of these that first laid the line "Your place or mine?" on me for the first time.

A little over a year after I quit the booze I finished my book, an autobiographical novel I called *Pity Not The Dreamer*. I got a lot of encouragement from Benny and Dicky Harris, the film star who hailed from Limerick, and a lot of other people that patronised the restaurant. I showed the manuscript to an agent called Lara Lawrence who came into Benny's Place all the time. A few days later she told me she'd handle *Pity Not The Dreamer* provided I signed a three-book contract with her. I was so flattered I agreed right away and by mid-January, we had a deal with Simon and Schuster. Need I tell you that I was in danger of levitating each time I considered how lucky I'd been to get such a break.

I'd already started on a new book and I felt good, thrilled even, that I wasn't a one-book wonder. I also felt lucky that I liked being a writer. I found that the work of writing, the hours at the worktable just made me want to spend even more time doing what I loved to do. I kept the basket full of rejected beginnings – the slips that came back with so many short stories scribbled down during the sober stretches of the last few years of my deathwish drinking. If the ashtray looked like a bomb-site and a health-warning in itself, it was all part of what made for a day worth living.

At this time, I learned to touch-type in one ten-hour sitting by using the *Pitman's Teach You Typing* book. I would type away at my portable, and loved to see the straight lines of print appear as if by magic, decorating the blank sheet of paper with my hopes and my dreams. The stories seemed to come my way, like I was some kind of magnet for the leftovers of writers gone onto another level or something. I certainly never felt that I was actually doing it, doing the writing.

Yes, the overall story would be based on some experience, or dream or wish of mine. Maybe it would get a kick-start from a line in a movie, a newspaper headline, a sliver of conversation overheard while I was working in Benny's Place, whatever. But when the words began to flow, and flow they did, it was like I was just the typist, the guy who tapped out the words being dictated by some invisible scribe who was using me as a channel to tidy up his unfinished business as a scribbler.

Simon and Schuster publish my book *Pity Not the Dreamer* in October. I'm pretty happy about this, especially since their publicity department is fully behind the idea to hold the launch reception at Benny's Place.

Being one very smart Irish guy, my boss Benny Foran made the initial offer to the publisher to help the book get off the ground in his restaurant, at no cost to them.

"Call it mutual publicity, Joe," Benny whispers to me after I've introduced him to the Simon and Schuster publicity guy. "We give them the story you were broke," Benny says, nudging me playfully, which is about the same as getting a punch from a pretty good middleweight boxer. "I gave you the job, then I caught you scribbling here after hours. And after reading a few pages, I was so impressed I cut your work schedule down to zilch. You know the story. The Irish guy who made it – that's me – helping the talented guy on the fringe of greatness – that's you. I say 'I only did it to support his writing talent which is enormous'. I leave out 'like his dick!'" He laughs like a drain. "And here you are, being published by one of the biggest outfits in the world. Jesus Christ, boy! There's a fuckin' movie right there!" He laughs at his own genius. "I'm in the wrong fuckin' business, so I am."

Benny hit the phone very hard in the weeks before publication, filling the bar and the restaurant with actors and television personalities on my big day. Ed Koch was there. Eli Wallach and Ann Jackson, both of whom had encouraged me with my writing, stopped in for a while. Neil

Jordan, always hot, was good enough to show up. Paddy Maloney brought some of The Chieftains along for a jar. The Limerick lads, Malachy McCourt and his brother Frank, dropped in with Dickie Harris, who'd been a mate and a sometime champion to me since shortly after I'd come to New York.

Telly arrives, schlepping his cameras, and a beautiful blonde who looks like she's grown on his arm. He introduces me to Carol Catlin, who is a knockout. Maybe thirty years old, she is wearing some mileage and a whole heap of jewels. Her designer dress in sky-blue silk cost a torso, her very high-heels giving her lovely butt a lift it doesn't need. Overall, Carol is just a bit too brash for my taste. That being said, this is a classy dame.

She is also a book-freak she tells me, her big dream in life being to write a novel. I have to take a rain-check on her story, since there are press guys waiting to interview me. Telly and a couple of other photographers are ready to bang off some pictures.

I'm pretty busy during the next few hours, doubling up as scribbler of the week and maître d, but I can see Carol is sticking to my buddy like honey to a blanket. I notice that she's not drinking booze, which is good, but I've a bad feeling about what's going down with her and Telly. Imagination? Fear? Who knows?

As Telly takes off to process his pictures, we agree to meet at an AA meeting later. I say good-bye to Carol. She tells me she'll be at the meeting with Telly. I give her my shit-licker smile, feeling instinctively that her arrival on the scene is about to fuck-up the rhythm of our lives.

Eddie O'Shea from the *Daily News*, a guy with heart who never quit encouraging me to stay dry and write my book, reckons I've got luck on my side. He tells me, with a philosophical shrug, "Quitting the sauce is something great. I've done it a thousand times. But nobody feels so good, that a bucketful of dollars won't increase the length of his smile, right!"

I see Eddie's eyes following Telly, who is banging off loads of pictures, and Carol who is there by his side all the time.

"It looks like you and Telly have really got a handle on the day-at-a-time routine," he allows, with a nod of encouragement. "And now, our old buddy's landed on a mink runway! And he doesn't even have a plane!"

"Should I know her, Eddie?"

"Carol Catlin. Sutton Place. The Hamptons. European jaunts. Sails out of Martha's Vineyard. Her life's a remake of *Gatsby* with smack! You should know her, Joe. She's heiress to the Styler fortune – major bucks. Her grandfather was a robber baron and her crazy poppa turned Grandad's millions into hundreds of the same variety. So the blonde with the boobs and that incredible ass . . . she's probably going to end up with billions, if she lives."

"Are you serious, Eddie?"

"She's in and out of the club." He was referring to AA. "She's cross-addicted, on and off the smack." He was speaking softly, but he leaned even closer so that I could smell his pipe tobacco along with the whiskey he was drinking. "I like you, kid, and I'm glad you're clean and dry. I'm telling you this, because Telly is taking on a real handful. She's hot stuff. She'll make him smile a lot in bed. But, whether any guy can stay sober around a dame like that? Only a god could give you an answer to that one." Eddie shrugged and finished his whiskey. "Look. I got nothin' against her. She's no kinda bad person, but she's a nutcase and divorced, so

watch out for your buddy. Sampras is one of the good guys."
His grin is the promise of a good write-up. "And there ain't
many of us left."

I get to the AA meeting just as it's about the start, and I find
that Telly is in the chair for the evening. I grab a seat at the
back of the room, a warm glow rising in my chest as I see
him about to lead the meeting. Looking around, I can see
Carol in the front-row. Her blonde tresses are tied up in a
beehive. Her earrings dangle like coffin-handles either side
of her beautiful neck. She looks around all the time, and just
after Telly starts speaking, she spots me at the back of the
room. She practically stands up to greet me with, "hi,
sweetie! Glad you could make it. Congratulations on today."

She turns back to face Telly, gives him a wave and a
"sorry, babe". Then she clams up while he begins to share his
experience, his strength and his hope, with those of us lucky
enough to be present. He says a lot of wise things during the
evening, and I'm so glad to be here while he leads an AA
meeting for the first time. He is so good at it that you know
that the acting secretary to every other meeting in Manhattan
will be seeking his services as a chairman after this one ends.

We dropped Carol off on Sutton Place, but not before she
got me to sign her copy of my book which she'd bought at
the reception. We'd sold more than two hundred books, a
very impressive number so I was told. Shaking Carol Catlin's
hand, saying thanks for being there and I hoped to see her
again sometime, I bid her good night.

"We'll talk again soon, Joe," she said, kissing my face
like she'd known me a long time. "I've a feeling we're going
to be seeing a lot of each other from here on in."

Telly walked her to the door of her building. When he

came back, we decided to walk to the apartment. It was a warm June night, and we needed some air. Telly linked my arm, like he sometimes did.

"She's a beautiful woman, man!"

I looked sideways, to find him smiling.

"She makes me smile like no woman has, in nearly twenty years. Can that be a bad thing?" He sounded like he'd just taken a deep breath of pure ocean air.

"How could it? You're in love. A blind guy could see it. Shit! A really hungry guy could take a bite out of it. So relax, man. It's over a year since we made our deal. No major decisions for a year, remember?"

He nodded. "Sure, I remember. But I've got to be straight with you, Joe. I've been seeing Carol for six weeks. Sorry, sport. I couldn't help it. I was helpless from the first time she looked in my eyes. She loves me so much. Nobody ever loved me like this before. I couldn't walk away from it from the first night. So you'll understand, I can't walk away from it now. Not even if I wanted do."

"Let's keep on going a day-at-a-time. See how the bookie grumbles, OK!" I said lamely, knowing this was no time to send out warning signals.

"Is there any other way?" Telly said.

My book got brilliant reviews in *The Sunday Times*, and the *Daily News*, and it was very well featured on the television book programs. This helped push sales that were already better than average for a book by a new writer, and I was feeling pretty grateful. But I think it was Benny's reception, and the publicity it gathered for all of us that gave *Pity Not the Dreamer* the big push at the cash registers of Manhattan.

I felt good – the book was popular and it looked as

though it was going to earn me some decent bread in the year ahead. Simon and Schuster had already talked to Lara Lawrence about the new book, and she was happy to tell them it was coming along nicely.

So I'm on my way up the career ladder, which makes me one very lucky scribbler. I talk to Benny about writing full-time and I offer him a month's notice. He tells me to fuck-off.

"You're getting famous now, too famous to work in anybody's fucking restaurant, even Benny's Place." He drops a double whiskey like it was lemonade, gasps a bit and puts up his finger to indicate more. Then he tells me, "If you make serious bucks, come back and see me. I'll put the arm on you for ten grand, for the publicity gig." He laughs and hugs me, the way a bear would if he was in a gentle mood. "And if it doesn't work out, you'll always have a job here."

During the next couple of months, I became what you could call a full-time writer. It occurred to me that there was a compulsion in my need to write, and I did wonder if I had just transferred the energy from boozing to scribbling. When you thought about writing and writers in general, there did seem to be a connection between putting words on paper and bending the elbow. I'd heard writers claim they got lonely, that they needed to go out and tie-one-on to unwind after a serious stint as a wordsmith. You could name a lot of writers who died from drinking or from drink-related diseases. But this happened in all walks of life, with famous scribblers getting publicity where an ordinary guy in an ordinary job didn't rate a mention in the press. What did I know?

I knew I was glad to write, happy that it happened for me the way it did. I loved the whole trip that was there to accompany whatever small literary gift I'd been given. It was fun to be fêted for something that had your name on it, and it was a genuine buzz to earn money for doing something you'd done for years without anybody knowing of it, without you ever earning a dime.

All in all, I guess I felt flattered that anybody would pay to read something I wrote. That was really terrific and I was happier that autumn than I can say. At times, I found myself chuckling at the sheer magic that had happened for me in a little over fifteen months. My life was so full. I wrote for some time each day, a terrific therapy for tension. I liked my cool lady friends, and naturally, making love helps you stay as loose as a goose. My scene was *on the level*. I wasn't creating any anxiety or aggravation for myself, and this was something I aimed to cultivate in the belief that I'd had enough drama for a guy my age!

Meanwhile Telly and I continued going to meetings together, but things had changed since Carol had come into our lives. She was a good woman and I liked her. I also liked seeing Telly happier than I'd ever known him to be. He had a spring in his step, his eyes were clear and zippy-looking, and he had started crooning old Bing Crosby songs while he ran an electric razor over his blue-black shadow in the mornings when he was home.

I was bothered that we were no longer talking about booze. Our exchanges in this vital area of our lives had been whittled down to whatever we said at the meetings. I felt it was a mistake to start acting like we were totally normal guys, when we were really just one drink away from another sojourn on 'skid row'. I didn't see that there was a lot I could do. Telly seemed so alive, so light in his heart, and this was good to see. So, I said nothing about the way his primary purpose had changed from staying sober, to being in love.

Up to this time there didn't seem to be any suggestion

that Telly and Carol were going to start living together. I got the impression she was happy enough with their arrangement as it stood. Telly was working hard, attending functions day and night. I often wondered how he could be around all that free booze and not just say "Ah fuck it," and drop a couple before he got time to think about it.

We talked about this, and he was the first to say that without the support we had given to each other, he couldn't have handled the job. "And I'd hate to have to quit, Joe. I love it and I'm actually pretty good at what I do."

"I've always said you're a better photographer than you think. And I'm going to keep on asking you to think again about the book I want us to do together."

Once again, he shrugs at the suggestion that he could ever do more than bang off pictures of beauties, film-stars in low-cut evening-gowns, hot-shots in town for a premiere, or the latest rich divorcée.

"I've got the title right up there on the screen behind my eyes," I assure him in what I hope is an encouraging voice. "It's going to be called *Through A Jaundiced Eye!* We share the credit and the bread, right down the middle."

I confess that I was banging on at him about *us* doing the book together, as a way to stop him putting all his eggs in one basket, a basket-case called Carol Catlin. She was considered risky company, even by people who meant her no harm. All we needed was for this lady to do something crazy, something that could send Telly back on the sauce.

This could happen to Telly, or to me, to anybody with the ism of alcohol in his system. Maybe I was being paranoid, but neither Telly nor I needed another ride on the carousel. We'd spent enough years stumbling around in circles, going nowhere.

The book idea just arose like a burp, after midnight mass in St Patrick's Cathedral last Christmas Eve. Telly got a couple of tickets from a nun he'd snapped for a magazine, so there we were singing along with a whole bunch of people we were unlikely to meet over a dinner table. The show itself was as big, and as sensational as the best Broadway production, which you might well expect when you've been rehearsing it for maybe a thousand years. The grandeur was barely short of awesome, and how often are you surrounded by wealth so daunting that it can't help rolling out into the aisles?

The costumes were Hollywood to the last stitch, the music a magic carpet, on which a female voice caressed Gounod's 'Ave Maria' into a hymn to touch a heart of stone. Meanwhile, there were piles of hundred dollar bills mounted on wooden platters and gathered by ushers, many of them famous names. They were doing their service for the occasion, with suitable expressions of piety and commitment.

Stepping out of the roman opera onto Fifth Avenue, could we get a cab? After five minutes we had to find the subway, just to get in out of the cold Robert W Service wrote about in 'The Cremation of Sam Magee'. I'm talking of that "chilled clean through to the bone" stuff, that makes you wish you were a brass monkey till the temperature moved up a couple of notches.

Another opera was in production in the hot air of the subway entrance. One in such contrast to the presentation at St Patrick's, that my breath seemed alien in my throat, even as the stench of humanity with nowhere to go mugged my nostrils like they'd been hit by the fist of a fighter with something to prove.

Every available coffin of space contained a body that hadn't made midnight mass. All creeds and colours, all persuasions – they were lying around, some of them lying on top of another, all of them wanting to stay warm, maybe even get some sleep.

A lot of them were wasted on booze or junk. Who could blame them?

The subway cast were figures in Dante's *Inferno*, hanging alongside the live painting of *Heavenly Bliss*, in one of the world's greatest cathedrals.

This is how I see this Sewer City Sonata. It was unknown to and unseen by singing barons, priests, bishops, cardinals and famous opera singers chanting for free to the worthy minority that included some of the wealthiest people in the land.

A lone black man, a rastafarian, played guitar and chanted something that sounded like Sanskrit. He was an orchestra of one whose performance brought a gentle wave of peace into the tragic scenario.

The only audience catching the Subway *Late Late Show* were a couple of ex-drunks who made it, only because they needed to escape the pain of Manhattan Christmas night, as it might have been written by Robert W Service.

Telly really had no interest in being part of the book that I had in mind. I wanted to produce a picture book, with me doing the text; a coffee-table tome, showing up the belly and the bowels of his city. I admit there were times when I asked myself what the hell it was going to change anyway. A guy might win a prize for the right picture, even if it depicted poverty and pain, delusion and disease. But, shit, no book of that kind ever caused any radical change in how society deals with and cares for the ones who can't make in it in the script life slapped into their hand. But I won't deny I wanted to use the idea, any idea that would shift some of Telly's juice away from the blonde bombshell with the boobs and the bread, and a double habit that might have killed most people already.

So there I was, seeing the drama that lay ahead for Telly and Carol, ergo for me. I was seeing something that hadn't yet happened, like it was up there on a motion-picture screen fixed inside my forehead. I was like a scriptwriter creating a scenario I really didn't ever want to happen. In a perverse kind of way, it was like coming at "Be careful what you pray for, you might just get it!" from another angle.

3

Dublin, May 1990

Whenever Dervla thought about her husband, Gary, she would find herself wishing that she could love him. Love the poor bastard, even just a little. Other times, she wished he would kick her out, divorce her, anything. Even a divorce Irish-style which she regarded as a joke, would be preferable to the empty luxury of her present existence with a man she didn't even like very much.

She pushed him hard through regular inappropriate behaviour, to help him wake up to the fact that they had nothing in common. "Except booze," she would yell at him during another row, after another night out. "And, oh yes, expensive cars and trendy clothes, not forgetting lots of holidays with friends neither of us like much – people that don't much care for me, because they think I am a bitch to my husband, that very good guy. You know the one! He picks up the bill every time he's in company."

She saw her marriage as a joke, but not the kind of joke that makes you laugh. She resented being married to a man about whom she had no bad word to say. He was something of an English gentleman, well-educated, willing to be nice even when he didn't feel like it. A guy she would never have married, but for her father's insistence.

"He's a great catch, Dervla. You can't allow him to get away," Danny Devine had urged his daughter, his resolve forged of steel. "He's worth millions, and there's even more money coming his way when his old mother dies. You'll never have to think about money for the rest of your life."

She could remember still how his sky-blue eyes had been like lasers while he tried to bore a hole in the power of her resistance.

"Have you any idea of what a luxury that is. To have all the money anyone could ever need. Jesus, Dervla, I came out of Cork without an arse in my trousers. Why do you think I've slaved all my life? So that you and your mother and your sisters would have the things I could only dream about, until I was a grown man."

She didn't expect her father to mention the bank robbery that had helped his dreams come to fruition. Her mother Eithne swore that this was how her husband got the first real stake that enabled him to go into business.

Dervla had no problem believing her mother, a woman who would sooner die than mouth an untruth about anyone. "A bank clerk was killed in that robbery. It was put down to the IRA – and your Da was connected, still is. You wouldn't know the half of what he's up to. His left hand wouldn't let his right know the time of day."

Eithne only ever shared her thoughts with Dervla, the eldest of her three girls, and this happened only rarely, when she was in her cups at a wedding or after a funeral. These were the only times she allowed alcohol to cross her lips, with Dervla being the one to make sure her mother got home to the house on Upper Rathmines Road.

Dervla and her father were alike in many ways, most especially when it came to getting their own way. Danny was the stronger-willed of the pair and more experienced, and to judge by the hints his estranged wife shared with her eldest, more ruthless than anyone she had ever met. He was ruthless enough, she suggested on one of the occasions when she drank too much, to kill someone if they were to get in his way.

Dervla was both scared and intrigued by this sliver of *very serious* inside-information. Coming to her from the lips of anybody other than her mother, she would have taken it with a grain of salt.

"We all do it," she would allow to her reflection in her bathroom mirror. "We 'tell tales out of school' – exaggerate, snog with men we shouldn't, screw people as married as we are even though we're all so very respectable, and never miss going to mass on Sundays and Holy Days of Obligation."

Dervla would laugh at her image at those times, knowing that for all the stuff pushed into her mind by the nuns, she had no faith in God and the accoutrements that were part of that whole story. She would never say a word of this nature to her mother, who had a childlike faith of which she must not be disabused.

Eithne had to be protected from any threat to her picture of 'the next life', if she was to retain even a modicum of sanity. The death of her marriage to Danny had dashed the last of her earthly-hopes. Without her belief in God and the religious ritual she avidly pursued, she would have been a gibbering idiot within a few years.

Dervla felt a fraud when she found herself praying for

help through a seriously bad morning-after. Yet she would resort to prayer yet again when she woke up with another stranger, his come and the smell of him all over her, the taste on her lips and in her throat. Fear that she was losing her mind entirely would force her to her knees by the bed for something more urgent than another bout of fellatio.

At times she felt sad for her husband. "Gary is like my own son, like the kid that loves his mother, although he can see for himself she is a prize-cow. Not that I am actually a bad person." She might allow herself a break, with a shrug of acceptance. "Nor do I set out to hurt anybody day-to-day. I have a short-fuse, sure, and I am moody. I'm a bit like the mercury in the barometer at our house on Shrewsbury Road. Can you believe it?"

The mirrored reflection would shake its head, its expression one of bewilderment. "We have a barometer on the wall, in this day-and-age. That surely tells you the kind of man I married. I will never deny his overall decency as a human being. But you'd understand why I don't have to work myself into a sweat to forget him when I get into my car and drive out of town to work, and to drink, and go to bed with whoever I want."

Her thoughts could pour out like this, in a rush, a small dam bursting all over her sense of wellbeing. When she thought of her 'other life', her life on the road during most weeks of the year, she didn't allow it much purchase on her time. She left it out there in the sticks, meeting it when the mood hit her during most Mondays as she drove deep into the countryside to work her way back towards Dublin during the rest of the week. She liked to work it that way, hating the long *schlep* back to the city from Castlebar or Westport after a week of hard-work, hard-drinking and whatever sexual activities she got herself into as she booked into one hotel after another.

Sometimes, Dervla blamed her father for how she had developed into womanhood. He had told her too much too young; too much stuff about his life and business deals with what he called 'dodgy folk'. Too much about politics and the strokes he'd had to pull to keep his master in power. He never thought of anything he did as wrong; never saw his work for JC as the political chicanery Dervla deemed it to be. She was sworn to secrecy. "You're the only person on earth I trust totally."

Every time Danny said this to her, she wondered was he remembering the biggest secret of them all, the one that nobody could hear about as long as Danny was alive.

"I trust you with my life," Danny reiterated. "You're my own blood. I would give my life for you. And I believe you would give your life for me."

She often felt like telling him to quit being such a humbug. She didn't need all this bullshit to keep her mouth shut about him, his activities, and his use and abuse of her with his secrets and his demands as though he owned her. She had respect for his strength and his inherent resolve to get things done in life, but she thought him all kinds of charlatan, too. She never chastised her father. She loved him and needed him to feel as he did about her.

He attracted her as a man – even now, as she headed into her thirties. She knew she would never again want him sexually, especially after what had happened, but he could make her feel good when he was buzzing in a complimentary mood. Just as he could scare her when he was angered at her 'seeing' someone while he was laying siege to have the richest son-in-law in town. He had set out on a personal campaign for a whole year, to make her see that she simply had to marry Gary. She was ready to throw-in-the-towel months before she finally did just that.

On her honeymoon, she realised that she had never been on a sober date with Gary. Every time they met they started with drinks, then it was dinner with drinks or the theatre and dinner with drinks. The pair of them were inevitably pretty-well smashed by the time they ended up in some nightclub. Then, predictably, Gary would soon be pissily talking big deals with some other money guy, giving Dervla the space to have an illicit snog on the darkened dance-floor with one of the men about town, who were more than eager to swap spit with her and even slip out to have a risky quickie in a car.

"That really was our courtship," she scribbled into her very private journal. "That was the start of this new life my father wants for me, more than he wants anything else."

After their "first-night fuck" – the first time they had actually had intercourse – she lay awake smoking and scribbling her thoughts down to simply stop her thinking about what she had done with her life.

"Men are so silly about sex," she wrote, pausing for a moment to light another cigarette. "They never have a laugh about it for one thing. It's like every ride has to be life-or-death. I'm actually scribbling this on my honeymoon. We're in Paris, which is really like staying at the Shelbourne except the waiters talk funny. Like Charles Boyer, that little French actor, does in all those old movies you see on television. Gary is asleep with the weight of a man who has just had the ultimate experience of his life. So many men are the same. They get laid, and then curl-up into a ball like a well-fed kitten. Gary got a double-ration tonight, even though he wasn't up to it when I climbed on top of him."

42

He was ready for snoozies. His erection was out of sight now, hidden under his foreskin and covering his knob like a Dominican monk's cowl. He slept like a log after his two-minute burst of frenzied humping during which he couldn't even produce a sexy kiss he was so busy fighting for breath. All I could think of was, "thank God for my fucking cousin Eamon, and my other friends in Ireland". A little later, much to Gary's unspoken chagrin, I climbed on top of him. He failed to find the courage to say no, plead a headache, something. The poor lamb is English, of course, and far too polite to tell his bride to fuck off and let me sleep, like a Paddy would. Anyway, in no time flat I had him so rampant you could have run a flag up his pole. As I sat on his washboard stomach – Gary never misses a day in the gym – I watched his gorgeous big brown eyes look as though they were going to go pop. I made a meal of positioning myself, before I embraced his encore. In moments, his eyes almost turned right over in his head while his tongue stuck out like a carelessly chosen tie from Brown Thomas. The poor lamb! I hadn't the heart to tease him, so I set out to give him the time of his life. The sex felt so good, I almost managed an orgasm myself. For a few moments I found my G-spot, which was a bonus I hadn't been thinking about when I set out to blow Gary's sedate little mind.

The G spot is something that poor Gary, and most of the men I've had, wouldn't recognise if you hit them over the head with it. Not that it mattered. I had made my bed, and I would try to lie in it. I had to make a go of it, since Daddy had such an emotional investment in Gary's money. A joke of mine that doesn't make me laugh at all.

I hadn't gone down without a fight though, refusing Daddy when he suggested I use some of Gary's wealth to start my own PR company. "This is where your natural talent lies. Gary has hundreds of millions, and I want some of it for the 'cause'."

I wasn't getting into the 'cause'. Jesus! And I was not touching PR. I hated the spinning and obfuscating, and spreading diseased gossip about those no longer expedient to your needs, and I considered advertising an immoral means by which to earn a living.

I had also told Gary, that I wouldn't change my name when we got married. I wasn't about to become Missus Anybody. Gary agreed to this, only because he knew that if he wanted me to say yes to his marriage proposal, this caveat was non-negotiable. He also acquiesced to my wish to go on working four or five days a week as a sales person, even though we clearly wouldn't need the money.

The job, which I'd had for years, meant that I would be away from home from Monday to Friday most weeks. Gary, a decent man really, was so desperate to marry me that he would have agreed to anything.

So I had gone for broke. I needed the social life I led in my travels about the Irish countryside. If I had to quit that to be the little housewife, I'd go completely crazy. My sisters told me I was mad, that I'd never get away with it. They were as wicked, wild and wayward, and bordering on mad as I was, but they swore they would settle-down after marriage. Angela and Jilly weren't bad as sisters go. They were like big, well-titted kids, really – tons of tit, but not a brain between them. I told them I would sooner die than play the happy-little-housekeeper who made a great apple pie, or a fucking goulash to-die-for. Jesus!"

Despite the kind of nagging agnosticism she had settled into,

Dervla went to confession at Easter and Christmas. She told herself that she did it out of respect for her mother's belief in God. In truth she had no idea why she kept up the ritual. She considered that it was hypocritical to confess that she was heartily sorry for her sins when she was addicted to casual sex. She never asked a priest for his input about her lack of guilt at breaking one of the Church's severest rules. Confession was something long-inculcated into the texture of her existence, initially a week-after-week affair, a habit perhaps by now. She shrugged at her introspection, dismissed it, and put confession away until the next time she spoke to another stranger through a wire-mesh grille.

4

New York, May 1991

I've been 'chairing' AA meetings in the five boroughs, and I'm studying *The Big Book* of Alcoholics Anonymous. Not that I want to become a PhD in 'recovery' or anything like that. It's just that I can't seem to find any emotional depth to back-up my verbal commitment to the twelve step program. For all my good intentions to go to any lengths in search of sobriety, I tend to coast, to skate across the surface taking with me as I go enough to keep me safe-and-sound. Like settling for something good, knowing there is even better stuff waiting for you to go and get it. I feel good and if it never gets any better than it is right now I can have a good life. In a month from now I'll make my third anniversary sober, Telly too. And right now I've got in my hand the dust-jacket of my third book, which is due to be published in September.

Right now I feel the urge to write a stage play. Writing full-time is living a dream come true. I buzz on the thought that this is happening to me, yet again I have no real sensation of doing it, that I am actually writing what comes through. But, I need a rest from book writing for a bit. My sales were good enough for the publishers to urge me on, get two or three books on the shelves and into libraries, get people really interested in my work and have them looking forward to the next novel. What young writer was going to argue with that? Not me, that's for sure. I'm in demand like I could never have imagined, and I like it. And I want more of it. And the truth is, I get more joy from being on my own watching the words fill the page than I do from anything else except great sex. And you know, when you're not drinking like I drank, there is so much time to do what you want. You can work and play and feel good – no more losing days and weeks of your life because you are too drunk to know that you're pissing in the eye of the power that gave you this life in the first place.

Somehow I've managed to keep the females in my life on the same wavelength as myself and the more I see of Telly and Carol, the greater my gratitude that I'm free of such heavy emotional entanglement. I've got too much going on to want to have that scene just at present. I am tight with three ladies I really like. These are women I can have fun with, the excitement of good sex with. Honestly, a guy could marry any one of them right now and probably make a good life. Fortunately, like me, they have come through any immediate need in that direction. So I am fancy-free, having fun and no longer screwing up my life with John Barleycorn.

Alongside all this, I make money doing the work I did for nothing for maybe five years. So you'll pardon me if, occasionally, I knock myself on the side of the head to ask "Is this really how it is?"

I know I haven't chased sobriety as avidly as some other

guys I know, but I honestly feel that if it was any better I could eat it with a spoon.

At this moment, Telly is standing over my work desk with murder in his eyes.

"Carol's in Bellevue. In a fucking straitjacket! That fucking family! Jesus!"

The first thing I tell him is to sit down, while I make coffee. And I need to raise my voice several times to get through to him that going off half-cocked is no way to travel. He lights a cigarette, and I dump the one he's already got burning in the ashtray. He is so angry, so scared, that I'm grateful he's with me. No matter what's going down we need to remember we've come this far through our support of each other.

The story he tells me causes me no surprise. Amy, a friend of Carol's, had arranged that her thirtieth birthday party be a girls-only event. Carol had gone there, without Telly to look out for her, ready to have a fun time with a bunch of her pals. Amy's version of events was that Carol had sniffed a line or two of coke shortly after she got to the birthday girl's apartment on Central Park West. At some stage in the evening, Carol was found lying unconscious on the kitchen floor with an empty vodka bottle by her hand. So Amy had phoned the Catlin home on Park Avenue to ask the name of Carol's doctor.

Within an hour the Catlin's had the situation well in-hand, arranging that Carol be taken in a private ambulance to Bellevue. She was now being held in the hospital, though her mother had used the word 'sojourning' to Telly when he phoned to ask where the hell Carol was.

While Telly's giving me the story, I wonder what Carol had taken before she sniffed the two lines of coke and drank the vodka. A major part of her problem was that after a couple of hits, booze or drugs, she didn't remember shit. So what else is new?

Who could remember how many drinks he'd had after a few? Not me. Not to save my life. Recalling this commonplace state in the quagmire of addiction helped me drop the mood I'd copped by judging Carol. A guy wouldn't want to forget that people in glasshouses shouldn't throw stones!

To crystallise the mountain of pure soap-opera that followed the trip Telly and I made to Bellevue, let me say that my pal was a tiger when it came to dealing with the sophisticated savages, known collectively as the Catlin family lawyers. He was also well able to handle Carol's mother Betsy, a Las Vegas showgirl turned 'lady of the manor', if not the manner. I wasn't surprised to hear her display an alarming absence of caring or compassion towards her daughter. It seemed that Betsy considered Carol a social disease, for which there was no cure.

Basically Telly beat them up. That's right. My buddy took on Betsy and the family lawyers, and he stopped them inside the distance. His insistence that I was present at all meetings and discussions gave me a front-row seat. I had to bite down on many a chortle, as Mr Sampras turned seriously Greek right before my eyes. He seemed taller somehow, towering over the gabardines masquerading as lawyers, addressing all of them including Betsy without fear of stepping on their sensibilities.

Carol's mother and her lawyers simply had no idea what Telly had come through during the last thirty-two months. They hadn't seen him confront and defeat the warriors of alcoholic-thinking, so how could they have known he was going to be the ball-breaker of the decade.

He was more effusive than I had ever known him to be. Without any apparent effort, he created the impression of a wildly-unpredictable character – a guy who might just carry out some of threats he was making. One urgent promise was that no matter what they did to him, he had people on his side who would blow them out of the water if they refused to honour the entitlement of the woman he loved, the woman who would be his wife till the end of time.

He relaxed then, before he slowly turned over his trump card, his 'ace-in-the-hole'. I sat there feeling very impressed. "Publicity is one of the major strings to my bow. It has been said of me – in the media, so you can check it out – that I can shoot out the eye of a bird with the speed and accuracy of my arrows. I'm your actual Robin Hood when it comes to the art of publicity. I want you all to remember that I warned you of this fact when you begin to experience the extent of the intense, unstoppable coverage you are about to have inflicted on your lives. I have a dossier on your treatment of your only daughter, Betsy!

"An alligator gives its young more of itself than you have given your only daughter. One more thing and we're through here." He gave them the giaconda smile then said in a friendly way, "The show-stopper of my campaign is going to be the story," told to him by Carol, "that Daddy Catlin," who wore such a wild beard that he looked like a gopher peering through a privet-hedge, "manifested an ulcerating chancre on his lollipop some years ago. Your husband's pecker, Betsy, made intimate contact with treponema-pallidum – a micro-organism you don't want to fuck with! If you'll pardon the pun! The result of this intruder – syphilis – into Daddy's life rocked the boat containing his jelly babies in a big way. I have the clinical reports which state without prejudice that Daddy believes – depending on which day of the week you pick – that he is either Napoleon or the lovely Josephine."

Cut to the chase. Telly got Carol a hefty guaranteed allowance until she was thirty-five, at which time she would collect big bucks that nobody could prevent her inheriting. The only conditions attached to this apparent generosity on Betsy's part was that her daughter and her new husband Telly must live somewhere that wasn't Manhattan. Somewhere that wasn't in New York State, and for total preference, not even in any one of the United States of America.

While all this wrestling was going on, Telly and I were nursing Carol back to a semblance of health and balance. No easy-trip, no quick-fix. The TLC that Telly and I poured all over Carol needed time to do its work. She was pretty wasted by this recent fall from the shaky grace of being dry. Telly allowed her take some tranquillisers each day and, to my surprise, he finally gave in to her request for a little cannabis. He wouldn't smoke dope himself on pain-of-death, I believed, so he had to square it away in his own mind that it was OK for Carol as a medicinal drug. Emotionally, this wouldn't have been easy for him to do. He was dead-set against drugs, a typical old-fashioned guy. He was a booze hound, retired, who felt that drugs were dirty things to be putting into your own body. I watched him work through this and though I had mixed feelings that anything would really help Carol back from where she been going for years, I admired him for the way he broke one of his own cardinal rules in the belief that it would help his future wife.

At the same time, he laid down the law according to Telly. She could use a little pot, with his blessing. But if he discovered she was into abuse, he would lock her up and keep her locked up until she rediscovered her willingness to be reasonable.

Carol chuckled at him, kissed him in such a passionately loving way. "I need you, sweetie. I need you like I need the air that I breathe. Just hang in there for me." She kissed him then, and I watched him melt in her loving embrace. In a moment, she was looking at him in a way that made me feel as welcome as a ferret in your shorts. I left them to it, giving them the space they needed to make all the noise they wanted while they balled their eyeballs out. I left with a smile on my mouth, as I sort of understood why my buddy had taken on the squirrelly Carol Catlin. She was a nice lady, and she needed him in the way that every guy deep down needs to be needed by somebody.

As I got to our local coffee shop, I had no problem understanding that Telly had to allow Carol some help to deal with her demons. She'd been using, and abusing, for so long that there was no way she could have risked cold turkey, not unless she was keen on having a cardiac arrest or something equally trivial. A month later, Telly and Carol married in Manhattan with Amy as bridesmaid and yours truly as the best man. The next day, the newly-weds and I boarded a plane for Ireland at JFK airport.

Carol was settling in for a snooze as I strapped myself into my seat and I couldn't help thinking how smart that was, if you could do it. As I was opening *The New York Times*, the date caught my eye and I could hardly believe my eyes. It was the first day of June, the third anniversary of the day Telly picked me up off the pavement in Brooklyn.

At that moment, he slipped a slender packet onto my lap. This would turn out to be a beautiful leather wallet, with the words 'Keep It Simple' engraved on it. With that wry grin he was wearing more and more, he said laconically, "Happy anniversary, sport!"

"Jeez!" I shook his hand, speechless, tears closer than I would have wanted them to be. How do you account for a guy like this? We were total strangers – related by alcoholism – when he'd taken me into his home, regardless of the fact that I was nothing more than a stinking drunk alcoholic. He had given me a room in his apartment and a bed in his heart. He had helped me lay hands on things that cost nothing, but were beyond price. The price of admission to the AA meeting where my sobriety started was your presence. The charge for the caring and sharing that went on in that room was precisely nothing. If you could afford a donation, fine. If not, fine. There was no charge.

At the same time, a guy could now come to me on the plane and place a cashier's cheque for ten million dollars in my hand and say, "I'm buying your sobriety." And I would have to tell him, "Sorry pal, I can't help you. It can't be bought and it can't be sold. You can make the cheque for a hundred million and it won't change anything. But, if you attend some AA meetings and do what you're told for a little while you can have sobriety and it'll cost you nothing in terms of money."

This is the absolute truth. I had Telly to thank for the fact I was living proof of it. Sure, I'd only dipped my toe into the stream-life offered to the alky willing to walk the road less travelled, but I was in out of the chill. I told myself I would make more of an effort when I got settled down in Ireland. Life would be less frenetic there, the pace more suited to where I dreamed of being in terms of sobriety. Sure, it was still a drinking culture, but that didn't mean you had to drink. Not me anyway. I was just one drink away from a slow death, and having been there already, I knew it was an experience I'd no need to repeat.

I wondered where I might be had Telly not come to see if was I alive or not, after the two guys had thrown me out of the AA meeting that lucky day on Flatbush Avenue?

Memory slid in on the coat-tails of my good feeling – Telly and me in the gym, jumping rope, punching bag. Running from the sauna to the cold pool – a dying-and-living-and-dying experience, hitting meetings, meetings, meetings, still walking the floor some nights, doubled up with the cramping need for booze. It's purely psychological, so they say, after seventy-two hours. Thanks. Glad you told me that, pal!

Back to the streets through the long days, and the endless nights when you had to just keep moving till you fell down. When sleep was the riches in the other guy's poke, and a still mind was what lurked in the leprechaun's crock at the end of the rainbow!

We shared the sweats together, cleaned the other guy when he fouled himself, as Barleycorn's demons tried to butcher his resolve not to give in. We held each other down when the need to get a drink in was dangerously compelling, when the craving was so terrifyingly powerful and streetwise that your head could flip over in seconds. If that happened to you, all the agreements and promises, all the vows that we had quit could turn into gibberish some other guy had put his name to. Some bullshit promise, but nothing, and I mean nothing, to do with me, pal! Who else could have applied the cold compresses when the other guy was so out of it, so worn by his need for drink, torn yet further by the unrelenting toll that denial made on him in every way. The times when he'd been taken over by some killer-germ that was eating away at the brain, chewing up his mind.

There we were, each of us committed to the other guy. There we stayed, until those days and nights turned into history, so that even talking about them was like rerunning an old *film noir* movie you'd played a part in. I chuckled to myself right there on the plane to Ireland. To be able to laugh at how good it felt, just to have journeyed this far on 'sobriety street'. I was alive and well, and flying home to a new life as a professional writer. So what if the odd horror memory dropped in uninvited? So what? Did any alky ever quit remembering the days and nights when you faced death-in-a-bottle; a slow, lingering fucking dead-life every minute you were awake. A horror show from which the lights-out moment we call death could only be a welcome release.

I longed for the day when I wouldn't be able to remember how rough life had been for the drunk I was. I mean, in an emotional feeling sense. The day when I wouldn't get hooked on the story; the total recall of the good drinking times, before the laughs and the excitement and the feeling of power all dried up in the same moment and you knew you were in for the fight of your life.

I'm not going to go on any more about my personal drinking. No stories of how much I drank, those liquid, long, hard nights. Early mornings when death seemed like a soft option, when the ideas and the dreams and the plans that you had sketched out for your life, forget it . . . Days when the most beautiful and desirable woman in the world couldn't have enticed you into bed, you being too busy coping with veins that had turned into channels of electric impulses like dancing ants with the power to pull out your plug and leave you to eternal dark. This was the stuff of daily existence for long enough. Not any more. So let it lie, and let me see what Ireland the old country has to offer me in the way of a new life; a new life different to the one I had to lead until finally I got out of Dublin in the seventies.

5

Dublin, September 1991

It's hard to believe, but I'm back in the Dublin of my
sorrows. The homeless kid from Kevin Street has come home.
I'm sharing a huge house by the sea with Telly and Carol. And
I'm once more asking myself why do I ever bother to plan
ahead, to sweat and scheme trying to organise the next week
or the next year of my life? Why bother? Things seem to be
taken care of at the behest, even at the whim, of some power
that needs no input from me

Before I can make time to go walkabout on a nostalgic visit
to my old stomping-grounds, I've had a second letter from a
lady named Dervla Devine. I'd planned to see her by mid-July,
and would have done had it not been for a trip to England. I
took the flight to London to discuss a play of mine with my
new agent, Ed Gordon. He saw the work as a very viable and
entertaining money-spinner, with just enough to say without
being didactic. The meeting went well, and Ed said he'd get
back to me within a month. He felt sure he had the people to
back the play which I'd called *Hang in There, Sweetie!*

The letter from Dervla was there when I got back from London to the house in Whiterock, and after a serious welcome from Carol – only slightly stoned – I got a minute or two to chat with Telly. He was relaxed now the packing cases were out of the way. Carol travelled heavy on vacation, so something as huge and traumatic as an actual move to another country naturally cost a small fortune since she brought along everything except the Statue of Liberty. I left Telly with a joke Ed Gordon had told me in London, just glad to see that my buddy was starting to enjoy the feeling of being in Ireland.

When I'd showered, and made myself comfortable in a track suit and sneakers, I sat down to read Dervla's letter. We hadn't yet met each other, but her first letter to me had been so startlingly honest that I wanted to do anything I could to help her help herself out of the hole her life had become as the result of her drinking.

As it turned out, she was writing to me from the Whiterock Clinic which lay about a quarter of a mile from the house I was sharing with my New York buddies. She was recovering from a car accident that had happened late night on her journey home from her working week in the country. As I sat with the letter in my hand I was impelled to go and visit her in the clinic. She had broken ribs, bruises, cuts and the car was a write-off.

Thirty minutes later, I am tapping on the door of a private room in the Whiterock Clinic. The door is opened by a good-looking, well-built guy of about fifty-five who never looked in a mirror he didn't like. If that sounds harshly judgmental, I forgive myself. This guy had a self-satisfied smell about him, like he'd gone and sprayed on an overdose of aftershave labelled 'The Main Man'.

"Joe?" Dervla called out my name as her father and I stood looking at each other. "My God! Welcome. Please, do come in. Daddy, this is Joe Collins."

Dervla's father stood aside, reluctantly I thought, to allow me enter the room. I thought of a young bull, me, walking into this field where the resident older-guy snorted down his nose as he weighed me up for a severe dent or two, in the not-too-distant future.

"It's so good of you to drop in, Joe." Dervla is a stunner, lighting-up the room, even though her smile is sheepish. "Joe, meet my father, Danny Devine."

"How do you do, sir?" I give her father my hand, and his grip informs me that he uses a gym on a very regular basis.

"Nice to meet you, Joe," Danny Devine tells me blandly, like a politician with a lot of County Cork still alive and well in his accent. "Is your accent, do I detect mid-Atlantic, by any chance?"

"That's more than likely, sir. I've just returned to Ireland after quite a while in America." I turned to Dervla and moved over to the bed. As I returned her handshake I said with a grin, "If this was a movie, they'd have to make you down so that you'd look unwell."

She smiled, shaking her head in pleasurable embarrassment; a woman who turned heads wherever she went. The Spanish cast to the shape of her face, the forehead an alabaster curve under a mane of pitch-black hair, eyebrows hovering like dark feathers over wide-set, almond-shaped, midnight eyes – she caused me to catch my breath. No big deal unless you're trying not to let it show. Her tan was drawn tightly over seductive cheekbones and a proud nose. Her mouth was a beautiful, primitive thing, with full lips. There was hunger lodging at her lips; her heart-shaped thrusting chin warning you that this lady would never walk away from a fight.

As we exchanged pleasantries, I got the impression that her father didn't share her good feeling about me being there. I could practically feel the guy waiting for me to depart as rapidly as possible. Clearly there was something going on between them he needed to resolve. I suggested to Dervla that she telephone me when she was ready to talk, shaking both their hands again.

Dervla was surprised when her father, after the briefest pause, followed Joe out of the room with a line thrown over his shoulder to her, "I'll be back in a moment."

She was glad of the respite because, while she was blown away by the visit from Joe Collins, the words of Dr Donovan were replaying themselves across her thinking. He was a young man, a sincere type, with hazel eyes that she found attractive.

"I dropped in to have a word about your drinking, Miss Devine. Your injuries will be out of the way in a couple of weeks, but I have to warn you that you need to quit drinking alcohol. You have some liver damage. I would regard the damage as severe in someone as young as you are. I urge you to consider my warning."

She had been weeping quietly in the wake of the doctor's concern, scared by his warning. When her father arrived he made no comment about the snivelling. He had no time for lots of things, but far and above everything else, he had no time for tears. Dervla watched him flick into his look of concern, his great blue eyes becoming sombre for a minisecond. This helped her feel a little better. Not that he was being real, but it meant he could still be bothered to go through the motions, which was something. His lips on her mouth in a decent kiss told her he wasn't really angry with her.

This was a bonus. When Daddy was mad at her he kept his kisses to himself. He now produced a large box of Belgian chocolates and sat by the open window to smoke a Balkan Sobranie. Smoking was strictly prohibited, but as far as her father was concerned rules like this applied to other people.

"How was Brussels?" Dervla was genuinely curious, relieved that Danny was so tight again with Jay, who was currently leading the government. Jay, the Taoiseach! Jay, the Prime Minister! Who could believe it? My old goat! Horny Jay, take me in the hay! The laughs they had between the long rides he could take a girl on. He was all right was Jay, the fella with the sharp mind and the ever-ready cock. That was Jay in a nutshell, a brilliant mountain goat who could get into bed with a chimpanzee and come out without a scratch.

"Brussels is a sweat shop." Danny flicked his cigarette out of the window and stood up. "It's a perfect venue for politicians to drip in. But I enjoyed it. Talk about wheeling and dealing. Glad that Jay and I are back on track. He climbed down off his latest high-horse when I produced the readies he needs to refit the yacht. No matter what, he's still the greatest we have produced, even if his feet are made of clay."

Her father spoke without irony, like a man who had not been reading the papers in a while. Maybe he had stopped again, as he sometimes did when Jay was receiving a lot of bad press. In the last week or so another scandal of law-bending by one of Jay's oldest and closest allies, Joe Monaghan, had been making the headlines. Another black mark added to the long list of accusations against Dervla's one-time paramour.

Danny came back into the room just moments after he had followed Joe Collins into the corridor. She looked his way, while inside herself she wondered what the hell he was playing at? He had clearly left to say something to Joe. But what had he said?

Danny now got to the real reason for his visit this afternoon. He sat down on the chair that Joe had occupied moments before. He looked at his hands, as though they were worth studying. "I won't stay long," he looked up into her eyes. "I want to have a quick chat downstairs with your new friend." He made this sound like a gentle warning before he said, "Before I go, let me tell you, I was in Avoca yesterday afternoon."

"There is not in this wide world, a valley so sweet!" Dervla quoted, so that she might divert some of the flack that was coming her way about Perry Chance.

"Thomas Moore's words were the furthest thing from my mind," Danny said, giving her a hard look. "Perry looked well, a picture of health and well-being as he got out of his Jag. I'd say he was more than surprised to find me waiting for him in the carpark of his hotel. To cut to the chase, I finally thought it necessary to give him a slap or two."

Dervla hid her astonishment. This was very heavy behaviour for the carpark of a first-class hotel. Her father never considered such things, when force became expedient. She had heard it said of him that when he slapped you, you stayed slapped. There were things she wanted to say, but experience had shown her how unprofitable it was to speak before her father finished his story.

"Perry doesn't like being slapped about. On his own

head! I went to the trouble of telephoning him a couple of times, to warn him off seeing you any more. I told him out straight that if he didn't stay away from you, I would personally pay him a visit."

As usual, her father was perplexed that anyone could ignore a warning that he personally delivered. "I have lads queuing up to do that kind of favour for me. Perry of course is one of our own, a gentleman in his way. He shrugged-off my warning. He now understands that he won't sleep with you any more, that if he does I will break both his legs. At first, he didn't seem to believe me. When I brought him back to consciousness in his carpark, he understood me completely."

Danny took her hand, which looked tiny against his great palm. Legend declared that his fists had done all the talking, in the early days of his journey from County Cork to Kildare Street in Dublin City. She could see the evidence of this in the flat strip of flesh both knuckles had become; the individual bones had been vulcanised into one fearsomely solid mass by constantly impacting upon the bones of other men. His daughter knew that he was, in his own mind, the ultimate pragmatist. "If you need something you have to go and get it, and you let nothing get in your way." How often she had heard this maxim spill from his fleshy lips, her own mouth having been fashioned in the same mould.

She sometimes felt a dart of pride that she was, so he claimed, his first daughter, "my own girl", and sometimes she thought she loved him. But when she sought in her deepest heart the truth of this thesis, it was found wanting so that she didn't know if she loved him or not.

"I'm not moralising, God knows." This, from her father, was a rich admission. In the circles they grooved in, Danny was a legendary lover of other men's wives. "He's a sexual athlete, a fantastic Hammer Man!" was how Jay Charles had once put it to Dervla.

"You will have no more affairs, Dervla." Her father gave her the laser treatment with his ice-blue eyes. "What you get up to here and there, while you're working around the country, alright it's your own business." He glanced away, a habit of his when he was giving people time to let his words sink in. "You will not do anything to jeopardise your marriage. I want your word on this, and I want it now."

"Why do you insist that I have to stay married to Gary?" Dervla sighed in defeat, the answer already chalked up on the blackboard of her mind. "I made a mistake. As a married couple, we are a joke. He's not a bad man and I'm not a bad woman, but we have no future, Daddy."

"I've asked you for your word on something that is of paramount importance to me." Danny allowed his magnanimous side to show, by not chastising her for her lack of respect to his need.

"All right, Daddy," she conceded in frustration. "I won't have any more affairs. You have my word."

"You're my own girl. I know you will honour your promise. Besides, should you go against me on this, the man, whoever he is, will be very badly hurt. I promise you that, and you know I never break a promise. And you wouldn't want that on your conscience, now would you?"

He was so formal that she almost burst out laughing, but the picture he created for her to ponder on ensured that her taut expression manifested precisely how she was feeling at that moment.

Her father got up to leave. "What's the story with Mr Collins?"

"He's written books, Daddy. He's a recovered alcoholic. I want him to help me quit drinking. Today is the first time I met him face-to-face."

Danny nodded, knowing she was telling him the truth. "Drink doesn't suit you, but you wouldn't want to be joining AA or any of that carry-on! God knows who'd see you there, who'd soon be running to tell the town about it."

He took a cigarette pack from his pocket, but decided against it. Becoming fatherly, he lost the relentless look that had embossed his eye while he was bollocking her.

"Should you do anything silly – get in a spot of bother like driving with a few drinks on-board, anything like that when you're out of town, the first thing you do is call me. I want no scandals around you. I want nothing to happen that might cause Gary to leave you. You understand me? I cannot impress upon you strongly enough how important it is that you and Gary honour your marriage vows, till death us do part and all of that."

Again, she felt the need to chortle at the pomposity he displayed, but he was in a very serious mood. All of it, she very well knew, related to Gary's millions. So she stayed poker-faced. In her view, nobody took himself more seriously than her father, except perhaps Jay Charles.

Danny kissed her full on the lips, then the door closed behind him and he was gone, without even an enquiry as to her mother's health. Eithne was currently recovering from her latest touch of depression, her father dismissing this as another example of his wife's hypochondria.

For a moment Dervla experienced a dart of annoyance, but only because she was remembering that people, well-meaning people, sometimes suggested she was like her mother in many ways. Her sister Angela had said one evening, when she was contentedly coked, "Mammy just passed on to you all the hypochondria she wasn't going to need for herself." Dervla had let it pass, dismissing it as a combination of Angela and a hooter full of 'charlie', that was never to be taken seriously.

She got out of bed to fix the flowers her father had moved aside on the window-ledge so that he could throw his cigarette out. As she glanced at the grounds below, she saw her father and Joe Collins meet on the edge of the carpark. She watched as they lit cigarettes.

At that moment, she would cherish later the way it happened, Joe Collins looked right at her as she stood at the window on the first floor. Their eyes met, and she gulped in shock as she realised how impossible it was. Joe could not have known where she was – but, oh God, how beautiful it was. She smiled as he waved his hand at her, and she did nothing to still the delight she knew in the moment.

In the carpark, Joe was smiling as he waved at Dervla. At the same time he was aware that Danny Devine was quizzing him about his role in his daughter's life. The older man was waxing gently, but he was a guy who didn't do casual.

"I imagine Dervla told you that when we met just now, it was the first time." Joe looked into the sky-blue eyes, remembering a great middleweight Art Peters, who could make his baby blues smile as he hit you with a right-hook that could take out a small building.

"She said something about quitting the booze. Does that free you up to tell me what the hell Dervla needs you around for?" Danny was irritated in spite of the effort to hide it. "The reason for my concern is that she is a married woman. I don't want anything, or anybody, not even some new hot-shot writer to turn her head."

"Take it easy, pal." Joe looked the older man square in the eye. "Where in hell are you coming from? I'm here to try and help a young woman, and you're warning me I shouldn't do anything to wreck her marriage. You're way off the beam, pal."

"I didn't say that, Mr Collins."

"I heard you, Mr Devine. I heard what's not being said. What's not said, that's usually what the conversation is about in the first place. And without disrespect to your beautiful daughter, I've got all the women I can handle and most of them quite a bit younger than Dervla."

"If Dervla is serious about giving up the booze," Danny unzipped a glance that said Joe wasn't fooling anybody, with this do-gooder routine. "Isn't it possible for her to get some woman who can help her?"

"That's what I'd recommend should we ever get around to talking things over." Joe confirmed. "It's one of the recommendations of the AA fellowship. The reasons are too obvious to need airing."

"That's good news," Danny said, nodding his head as though he appreciated what had been said. His eyes remained laser-hard, as he responded. "It's just that I'm very keen for my daughter to stay married, settle down, have children, give me grandchildren. Wouldn't that be a treat? And I'll do anything I have to do to make sure and certain that nobody comes along to interfere with a marriage that might have been made in heaven."

Joe resisted the urge to cackle, wondering if this guy knew he was way over-the-top with the Holy Joe-alogue.

"I've got to be going, Mister Devine."

Danny gave him another gold medal handshake. "Is your book, or your books, are they true stories? Or are they y'know, those awful yokes, what d'ye call it, ah yes, fiction, make-ee-uppers?"

Joe smiled openly, surprised by the guy's frankness, his admission, tacit in his play-acting, that he was not a well-read man.

"A bit of both," Joe said. "Think of the truth as the meat in the stew, with the fiction added like herbs and vegetables. Can you handle that?"

"I'm only interested in the truth," Danny assured Joe, as though this particular statement was set in cement.

6

Dublin, early October 1991

I'm on Kevin Street on the fringe of the Liberties, having finally found the guts to come back to my birthplace. I'm walking slowly along the street where I found my mother so very seriously distressed in January 1973. I stop and stand with my back against the security shutter of a store that hasn't opened yet.

Back in January 1973, Ma and me, we'd been estranged for a few weeks. Not the first row in the years since we'd lived together from my father's passing in 1970. My mother was a very judgmental lady, so the fact that she threw a black-and-blue fit of righteous angst when a French letter was found in my jacket didn't strike me like a smack from a passing car. She screamed at me that the dry-cleaner, Lippy White, had found the sheath, and that he had displayed it to her in front of a store full of customers. You'd believe this memory would stay with Molly right up to the moment she donned the wooden overcoat. I could have kicked myself in the head. Knowing what she was like, I owed it to both of us to make sure she wasn't exposed to what I got up to, or down to, when I was having a good time. Fortunately, I'd used the other two condoms, and luckier still I'd thrown away the wrapper from the three-pack. Had Ma found the wrapper as well, evidence that I had used two condoms and proof solid I'd gone 'all the way', my immortal soul would burn in hell forever if I died in this state of mortal sin.

In fairness to Ma, she was just home after another six-week stay in the Adelaide Hospital. Though she put on a sort of a brave face, she couldn't hide the fear that lodged in her heart. I might have done more to help her cope, but the twice-daily visiting had got to me really heavily this last time. She'd been in hospital a lot in the last few years and I was fed-up being her only support, feeling very hard-done-by. So I neglected Ma, just like my father and her husband had done for too many years.

I got hot and cold flushes when I thought again about the chance that Ma could have found the packet of three wrapper. Sweet Holy Mary, Mother of Jesus, and a plethora of other luminaries residing in my mother's heaven, would have been called up for immediate action to save me from committing any more 'mortallers'. Or, my mother might well have taken our good kitchen-knife and performed an ad-lib act of surgery, a cut-and-slice affair designed to eliminate the need for such appurtenances in any future fun activities that I took part in.

In 1973 our rented flat was over Mulvey's the Printers, right on Kevin Street, and as I got closer to the brightly-painted shop-front, my built-in sense of guilt grew muscles and began flexing them at me. Now I was feeling really bad about not going back immediately after the condom row to apologise to Ma. How simple it would have been to say the right things, never allowing truth to interfere with a good story. I could have promised her I'd never use a thing like that again and that I wouldn't have 'relations', well I couldn't possibly say sex or use the term sexual-intercourse, with any other female, until I got married.

Ma had been very sick for a year and a half – cancer had turned this decent woman in her mid-fifties to someone that looked seventy years old. The only guarantee her doctor could offer me was, "Joe, I'd be more than surprised if your mother is on this earth three months from now." In that moment I tried to get this guy, a decent man, to consider euthanasia. The manner in which he dismissed me was about what I expected, so I had no hard feelings towards him over his stance. I was as mad as hell though, angry that my mother who was clearly dying would simply be allowed to wither away in the pain that moved in when cancer took up residence. At times, Ma was in such agony that even the strongest shit they could give her didn't hold it down. She spent much of her time trying not to look like someone who was being tortured to death.

The same doctor suggested I seek out a hospice bed for my mother since she clearly needed more care and attention than I could give her. I went through the motions, discovering that the patient had to be bedridden to be admitted. The other problem was that, even if we'd been allowed a hospice bed, I could never have found the guts to suggest to my mother that she should take up the offer. Not at this time, when she seemed even more scared than she generally did. To Ma's mind, regardless of how the medics dressed it up, going into any hospice was an acceptance of the fact you were dying. And that was something Molly, who'd been giving God a cauliflower ear for most of her life, couldn't hack at any price. So my mother stayed home like a woman waiting for something to happen – not death, because she was not ready to accept she was dying, so what was she waiting for? I'd no idea, but I tried in the best way I could to look after her and make the going as soft as possible down the last furlong of a life she'd found to be a steeplechase with too many fences.

The condom episode was the heaviest thing ever to happen between my mother and me. I ran from it, and the way Ma was carrying on in the days immediately afterwards, it was like I'd added to her personal torture. As I headed for home after nearly two weeks gone – I'd been drinking cider, dossing, and fighting bare-knuckle with these 'knackers' I got along with – I was still trying to dump the shame sitting on my back like a haversack full of bricks. I remember stopping on the street and blowing my nose to try and clear my sinuses. I was OK physically because I'd had enough booze to cure the pains and aches, but I was feeling very emotional as I headed home. I'd needed the drinks I'd had earlier to cure me. Now as I got nearer to home and facing up to my mother, I needed more booze to bolster my belief that all would be forgotten once I gave her a hug and told her I was sorry. I chewed a few more mints to kill any smell of gargle. All I needed was to go in there smelling like a brewery – that would earn a right-hander that could send a middleweight flying across the room. I was kidding myself of course. A hug and "sorry Ma" wasn't going to make things right. To think so was pure horse-shit, and deep down I really knew that. My mother couldn't be bought off whatever petard she had hoisted herself on, not ever. She would hurt, yes, she might regret hanging herself up there to dry in her own loneliness, but you only had to see how her mouth could chomp down on itself to know this lady was not for turning. Molly would die before she could be bought. Neither flowers nor tears, nor any other kind of Irish bullshit could touch down on the runway of her resolve. I pressed on, for I had to make my peace with her. I had to really give it my best shot, even if she ended up spitting in my eye.

Then I see her. I see my mother leaning against a wall at the other end of the street. She is holding on with one hand. Her shopping bag is on the ground by her feet. I start to run, flying up the street to get to her. I know she's in a bad way. The groceries on the ground tell me that.

When I get to her Ma's fighting for breath. Her relief at the sight of me is a palpable thing. She turns away from the wall and throws her arms open to me, trusting me to hold her up. She buries her face in my shoulder, and I hold her as she sobs her helplessness into the tweed of my jacket. I am weeping myself, trying to keep it silent, wishing it wasn't like this. Wishing that she wasn't ill enough to be scared out of her senses, wishing, wishing, oh Jesus, wishing for what? Ma's dying in my arms, and there's not a fucking thing I can do about it. Except hold her up. Hold her until she lets me go.

The fact that I'm there helps Ma gather herself a bit, but it's not of Molly and her welfare she's thinking about. "The few groceries," she whispers through her diseased throat, as though a batch loaf and a half-pound of butter and a few slices of cooked ham matter a fuck. "Pick them up, Joe, please." There is such quiet authority in her stumbling voice I think, stupidly, that maybe she's not dying at all.

Keeping one hand against her hip, I bend down and put the few provisions into her shopping bag. As I straighten up and give Ma my full support, her eyes are glazed as though they're drowning in mucus and there is dribble on her chin. She is having trouble breathing. I give Eddie Mulvey a shout. He comes rushing out of his print shop to help me support my mother, and I hand him the groceries. Still keeping a hand on Ma, I stretch over and turn my key in the lock.

"I'm going to carry her upstairs, Eddie. Stay behind me. Give me a push if I need it."

Eddie nods his dapper little head, a guy of sixty or so with a head of hair that's boot polish black, thanks to black boot polish, applied every morning so that he smells like a pair of well-tended brogues.

I take Ma in my arms, surprised to find her light as a feather. How else could it be? Her body and everything else about her has been ravaged by something the medics don't appear to have any handle on.

Eddie leaves the groceries on the table, tells me he'll lock up the shop and come back to me in a few minutes. I yell at him to call an ambulance. Ma groans in agony, as I place her on the bed. I'm aware of the irony that though we're only two minutes walk from the Adelaide Hospital, where Ma is well-known, we might as well be a million miles away. I'd willingly carry her through the streets to get there in a hurry, but my mother would sooner die roaring than have such a thing happen. I mean, for God's sake! What would people think?

I give Molly a slow drink of water, and I wipe her eyes and her mouth free of dribble. She likes being propped up in bed, so I fix her pillows like that and cover her with the eiderdown, a patchwork quilt she made herself a few years back. She is breathing a little easier, but there's no need to search for her distress. I hold her hand and sit there on the

74

side of the bed. When she opens her eyes she's more peaceful than I've ever seen her be, even in the best and most benign of her quiet times.

"I want you to promise me something, Joseph." Her mouth softens and her hand holds onto mine. I nod my head, incapable of speech.

"I want you to promise me you'll give up the drink."

"That's why I've been missing, Ma." I heard the lie drop off my lips like a bit of spit. "I went down to Mount Mellory in Tipperary, down to the monks in the monastery, and they helped me take the Pledge. I took it, Ma and you know what that means. It means I'm finished with drink, I'm through drinking alcohol. I'll never break that pledge, Ma, I swear to God!"

"You promise me, son?" She grasps my hand the tighter and I feel that my falling tears are helping her believe me. So it's pure good luck I can't hold the fuckers' back.

"I promise you, Ma. One of the monks, Brother Anthony, he gave me the number of Alcoholics Anonymous. I'm going to ring them and join up and go to the meetings, and never put another drink in my mouth again as long as I live."

As all this guff pops out of me, it's like my conscience is on hold, like my thinking has gone into cold storage. Whatever, I'm able to do it without faltering. The unwanted tears are an unexpected bonus I couldn't have dreamed about. In my heart, I know Ma's on the way out so what's the point in making this last bit of her life any harder than it is already? Jesus! When I think of what she's been through in her life!

"Someone was praying for me, Ma!" I say, gilding the lily.

"It was me, so it was." My mother is vehement, though the battery is running low in her voice. What matters is that she has no doubt, no shred of doubt, in her mind – she had got through to God for me.

"It was me on my knees in White Friar Street church, and here by this bed. I blistered heaven with prayers for you!" She lay back on a minor sigh that just might have been contentment. I wiped my eyes, wishing I could pray. Then she was looking at me again. "There's no need for you to worry about me, Joseph. I'll be in God's pocket before you know it."

"What?" The stupid questioning word flew from my lips, before I could stop it.

"I'm dying, son," Ma said.

I sat there in the shock of sheer wonderment. This was some moment – to hear Molly be so together – to witness the last moments of her life as she gets all her strings in tune for the first time. It was something I'd never expected to see happen on this earth. She had been scared of something on everyday that I knew her. She had never seen the world as a friendly place, and here she was, content and seemingly at peace.

I'd later reflect how I had angrily asked her doctor to give her an injection, to put her out of her pain and misery. What ignorance. What a diabolical liberty on my part. To deprive Ma of the time she needed to come to this, this moment where her spirit could go gently toward the heaven she believed in and where she'd surely find a chair somewhere close to the right-hand of her God.

When you think of the mistake that could have been made had my euthanasia bullshit to Ma's doctor been taken on board! I had been sweating that Molly was going to be in severe pain for months, and yes I would have wished to save her that. A noble enough picture, wouldn't you say? Aren't they always noble? Those canvasses we paint to distract attention? I did what I could to try and bury the Joe who had screamed inside, "No, no, no, I can't take any more of playing nurse to my mother. I've had enough of it. I'm going out of my mind."

Ma seemed to go asleep for a minute, and I found myself remembering an article I'd read recently which suggested that we choose our parents, certainly our mother. At that moment, resisting the urge to sling the magazine away, I'd made some bad jokes about my sense of judgement. How smart had I been to pick parents who hadn't a pot to piss in! But as I sat there by my mother's deathbed, I knew without any doubt that if I was to die in the moment, I would go to 'meet the man' with Molly's name engraved on my record as 'mother'. The Ma I wouldn't change, not for anything.

She comes back to me, her eyes open. I can tell that she sees me. I'm talking to her, running off at the mouth really, but trying to keep her alive without having to ask myself why bother?

There's a moment then when Ma tries to take my hand. She has no power to grip me so I wrap both my hands around her fingers. "I love you, Ma." I choke off the sob that's looking for air. The words drown in my fear. The fear is choking my chest and my eyes, and my ears. I'm numbed because I know this is the last good-bye.

"Mind yourself, son. Pray for me." Molly lets go with a sigh that says it all. Passing over in that moment with no fear, no panic, none of the old angers hovering around the bed to hear her so softly take her leave.

I wept though I wasn't quite sure why. Death was a release for my mother, and I hoped that all her belief and all the faith she had shown in a loving God was just now starting to pay off. Then I had the thought, 'It's paid off already. That last sigh said it all. Molly's OK.' Then the same inner voice throws me the question, 'what about you?'

Half an hour later the ambulance guys take my mother's remains down the stairs. About an hour after that, I walk around to the Adelaide Hospital. A nursing sister, a decent woman, takes me by the arm and leads me into this little chapel room where Molly's corpse has been laid out. She is beautiful, the peace she went out on still bathing her face. Her hair has been brushed and in the little chapel's light, it's the colour of corn. I swear to God, she looks like a forty-year-old woman. All the pain and all the fear has shipped out, all the cracks and crevices are gone from her skin, which is as clear now as white marble and as cold to my touch.

I leave my hand on her forehead, hearing this voice softly whisper: "God love you, God love you, God love you." I don't know how many times the prayer falls from my lips, I've no idea how long the tears tumble, but some time later I accept the feeling of release granted to me by the remaining peace in Ma's face. My mother, now free of life's demands, unchained from yesterday and tomorrow is no longer scared of the terrorists stalking the byways of her story. Those saboteurs and killers that ask, "What will people think?" "What'll happen if things go wrong, again?" "Will my son burn in hell for having that thing in his pocket?" "Everything'd be fine if we just had a bitta money." She's free of those malignancies that infect you in the sleepless night, or on the wet afternoon when you can't get the fire lighting.

Within days, I buried Ma alongside my father. In her passing, I was left with the belief that though she might well have been misguided at times, she was usually coming from an inherent wish, a built-in desire that it would be good for me. All simple stuff really. Like, she prayed that I would be a good Catholic, find a nice girl, settle down, have children and never drink again. So I guess you could say she wasn't a lady who asked for a lot! Not if you say it quick! But I felt then in 1973, and I feel it right now in 1991, I'd been lucky to know Molly Collins.

7

Dublin, late October 1991

Having met Danny Devine I checked him out with an old pal who wrote for the *Irish Independent*. Not that Peter Rooney was old. We'd rubbed shoulders a lot back in the early seventies when all we thought about was more money and more pussy, and a one-way ticket to America.

Rooney was a wild-eyed teenager, with a Catholic name and a story stitched onto his innocence about his grandfather or maybe his great grandfather 'taking the soup'. This was the generic term for taking food, or any kind of handout, from the charitable Protestants. These lovely people asked only that the recipient of the charity turn from the Church of Rome to become Protestant. At a time when a lot of people were dying of starvation and malnutrition in Ireland a lot of people 'took the soup', and who the hell could blame them?

Pete was educated at High School on Harcourt Street, which was more Protestant than the Archbishop of Canterbury. As it happened, RCs were forbidden by their church law to go there. The same thing applied to Trinity College. Trinity was good enough for Goldsmith and Wilde, but a Catholic going there was automatically excommunicated from the Roman Catholic religion, his misdeed running a close second to the ultimate crime of marrying a Protestant. Marry a prostitute and the Church would forgive you. Tie the knot with a Prod and you would burn in hell forever. I'd always laughed at this horse-shit, wondering how the Catholic church held Jesus in such high-esteem while they ignored endless opportunities to show the world that they had actually heard of Christianity.

Pete Rooney was now a sallow-faced guy who still liked cigars – he was thirty-six or thirty-seven years old, growing an avocado shape where his six-pack used to be. He'd been a hell of a soccer player, and I liked him as much as I had when we were dreamers together around the city.

When we met in Toner's pub, he produced a copy of the biography *The Indo* had worked up on Danny Devine. All the national papers had a list of prominent people who were written-up like this – connected people who might die prematurely in a car accident, or from a coronary. The guys who knew Danny reckoned he might even make the morgue from an ass-full of lead. This would be provided by an irate husband, as the great whoremaster made his 'exit-stage window' a tad lighter in the sperm-bank than when he'd arrived earlier.

"I've a book I want to write about Danny and his boss, his whores and his heavies. His boss, Jay Charles, JC, gets more pussy than the cat's home all due to Dannyboy Devine. He never gives JC a tart he hasn't tried out for himself. Makes sure the grub's not poisoned, right! Danny is one for the book. The only problem I'm going to have is to make the fucking story believable. Have you heard of Danny's number one buddy, Turk Raymond? Here's a guy who has to be descended from Jesse Fuckin' James. He's so bent they'll have to screw him into the ground after somebody shoots him dead. You give Turk thirty grand he'll sell you County Leitrim, and throw in Achill Island as a sweetener. Danny has all the best strokers and conmen at the end of a phone. Essentially, he surrounds himself with a circle of scumbags – helps him look good when he compares himself to them. As if he would! Compare himself!" Pete laughed. "He thinks he's perfect. Correction. Dannyboy *knows* he's perfect. Chances are he'll put out a contract on me when I write the book."

Pete said that JC admired Danny – "Such a great thief". Loved the elegant dandy, his 'hired gun', admired the cutaway collars, the perfect Windsor knots in the ties. But above all, the Taoiseach was known to revere Danny because of his legendary role in the ongoing revolution down the last three decades. Danny had always been a republican, but as his financial situation improved – 'thanks to that early bank robbery' I thought to myself – he had become a serious player who hovered on the fringe of what was called 'the movement'. He donated a portion of his money and provided valuable connections when they were needed in the name of 'the cause'.

Pete Rooney assured me, that on one of his vacations each year, Danny went training with the secret army. Another story claimed that he had been known to spend nights shooting in Northern Ireland. "And we're not talking about shooting pheasant here, Joe, nor rabbits either!"

Pete sighed reflectively as he finished off another pint. "But even a mongrel like JC – he likes fucking on his desk by the way. Even Jay can't risk having Danny on his team. So he keeps him off the payroll, but on the pad. Some of the rumours about Danny are already legendary. Right now, one of his tricks is 'pee-orring for JC'." Pete sucked some of the fresh pint into himself. "He started a PR company one time, has an interest in it still. Lost interest when he discovered there was more money being a white-collar thief. Danny is the main man when it comes to moving dodgy money around the world so that it comes back to Dublin like it's just been to the dry-cleaners."

Pete chuckled and shook his head in disbelief. "He invites you to lunch to give you a scoop, throws in the gargle. He doesn't have to warn you any more."

"Warn you about what?" I asked, drinking coffee.

"That the story better be published as per the script he gives you. If you let him down, he'll drop in and see you while you're in hospital. And you will be in hospital if you take the liberty of writing up anything he doesn't want featured. Play the game, his game, his way, and there's an extra case of whiskey come Christmas. An envelope too – cash. He's dead easy to handle, once you work from his script."

"Generous to a fault," Pete assured me, "with other people's money. He's copping donations from every scumbag that's got a scam up his sleeve. Guys who've backed Jay Charles since he first came on the scene, paid for his first fucking mohair suit. Danny spends money well, demands results. Not *expects* results, mind you – *demands*! No result? Hospitalisation is guaranteed for the source of his disappointment. To his eternal credit, he never carries a grudge. He punches you out, and he can handle himself, but he'll never say a bad word about you."

Pete laughed raucously, becoming in his own ribald

fashion even more loquacious. "Gas, isn't it? A barracuda in a cut-away collar, never says a bad word about anybody. He's one of the most dangerous cats this town has vomited up in years."

He exhaled a ribbon of cigarette smoke. "Of course, he's not a born Dub. He's a Cork-man. He came to town for the All Ireland Football Final at Croke Park. That same Sunday evening, he threw a rock into the Liffey from O'Connell Bridge. He said to himself, 'If it floats, I'll go home. If not, I'm staying.' He stayed on here, and now he owns half the shaggin' town. He's as rich as O'Reilly and getting richer by the week. And still he'd frame a ha'penny. No kidding! The guy is so tight he has to slap Vaseline between the cheeks of his arse to stop him squeaking when he walks!"

"What do you know about his daughter, Dervla?" I asked offhandedly, though I found myself in that moment hoping for some good positive stuff about the beauty with the drink problem. I'd been thinking about her since my visit to the clinic and I'd read her letters again since then. She had been invading my thinking when I least expected it, and while I did want to help her if she needed help, I had to admit that I was very taken with her as a woman.

"She's a knockout," Pete said with a lascivious tilt to his lips. "Jesus! How could a bastard like Danny and that Mother Teresa wife of his have produced a chick like that? She's so fucking beautiful, and a sexy cow with it. I'd eat chips out of her knickers."

I lit a cigarette while Pete emptied the immediate pint glass just as his next drink appeared on the counter. "Have you met the lady, by any chance?" Even as Rooney asked me the question, he started to smile. "You've met her, you bastard. You've met the lovely piece and you're interested in getting into her knickers." Before I could respond he chuckled. "You haven't changed. Christ! When we hung out together, you were the guy'd find pussy on a troop-ship. And you still have the nose for a softie. You never lost it!"

He drank stout and looked at me with what you could call serious intent. "Listen, I'm not a guy to tell his granny how to suck dick. But, this chick, you don't need her."

"I've only spoken to her once for about two minutes," I said, trying not to sound deliberately offhand, which is such a dead giveaway. "She seemed like a pretty regular young woman."

Rooney choked as he stepped on the need to guffaw in the crowded lunch-time pub. "Correction, Joe." He tapped the counter with his hand. "Correction, *Me Oul' Flower!*" I motioned to him to keep his voice down, his liquid lunch was getting to him now. "The lady is a screaming fucking alky, and she sleeps around when she's had a few. Every time she hits a bar in this town, or one of those fucking kips they call nightclubs, the bird dogs are close by, knowing one of them is going to get laid before the night is out. She has this husband. A millionaire. English. A yum-yum! Old school tie, full of 'jolly good show', and 'right ho old boy' and all that shit. By all accounts, he's a decent skin to work for. Leases out half the cars, corporate stuff, you see on the roads. Old money too, not one of these slags got lucky with some scam. He's blind where she's concerned. Amazing he hasn't had an anonymous phone call, a letter, something, telling him that his wife can't keep her knickers on when she's jarred."

I was remembering giving Dervla my card before I left her in the clinic, whispering so that her father would not hear: "You've got my home and cell phone numbers on there. I'll talk with you any time. Give me a ring." I could still see her, smiling as she said, coquettishly, "Most men want to ring me."

"I'm all for that," I'd said. "But, we're not talking about love and romance and sex here. We may well be talking about your life, and I only know it would be some privilege if I can help you to help yourself." There had been much more I wanted to say to her, but her father hovered like a vulture waiting for the last breath to leave his next snack.

Pete Rooney was about to press on, but I stopped him by telling him I'd run out of time. I asked him if we could have lunch again soon. He nodded, bending his elbow continually to indicate 'as long as it comes in a pint glass'.

"Be my guest?" I agreed. "The guest gets to order what he likes best."

"Give me a bell tomorrow and we'll make a date," he said. "I'll steal some time away from the book. Not often I get the chance to chew the fat with an old pal from the day before yesterday." As I moved to leave, he leaned closer to me. "If you have a spare tenner on you, I wouldn't call the Queen me aunt!"

I slipped him the note with a glad to help gesture and I was about to leave him when he grabbed my arm again. "You're not thinking of getting involved with *your woman*, are you?" His eyes were like boiled sweets, but I knew by his tone that he meant well.

"No chance," I said. "I'm up to my ears in women."

"Yeh. Never doubted it, pal. You don't need her. Not a bad chick, by all accounts. Snotty at times, neurotic some say, and I know a bloke works on the paper says she has the most beautiful tits he's ever come across. So what? She's fucked-up, and who wouldn't be with Danny Fucking Devine for a father. Him and his fucking Windsor knot!"

I made the move to leave, but he held my arm. "Before you go, Joe. You remember Champion? You and him, you had the best street fight I ever saw. You know who I mean?"

"Sure." His question had transported me back to those teenage days, when I was so desperate for money I used to hit another neighbourhood to fight for cash. There were a lot of tough characters around back then. Fellas who would fight anybody provided he was willing to bet money on the result. It was a tough time and fighting didn't seem in any way out of the ordinary. The knackers fought for money on a regular basis, and I'd learned many a dirty trick with those fellas. They fight for real. Even if they'd ever heard of the Marquis of Queensbury they'd have snorted in derision and given him a laughing kick in the ball-bag. You won some, you lost some, but in all truth, I didn't lose many. I almost lost against the guy Pete Rooney was talking about in Toner's pub. Champion was bigger than me – light heavy as opposed to middleweight, a rangy, streetwise nineteen-year-old made of cast-iron. I fought him to a standstill, but he would not go down. He defied me to knock him out. Near the end, I was still hitting him with my best shots without anything coming back at me because he was totally exhausted, but he stayed conscious. I was starting to get worried about the damage I could do to my hands – he was down on one knee, still holding up his arms, his fists like rocks – when I quit hitting him and stepped back.

Pete Rooney had been my 'second' for that fight, and – like the other people standing around us on the waste lot where we scrapped – he was speechless with admiration for the guts that Champion displayed that day. I put out my hand, offering to help Champion to his feet. That he let me do this was a mark of his respect for me. When he was standing, he fumbled in his trouser pocket and found the five pound note we were fighting for, thrusting it at me with a lot of grace for a street guy.

"I don't want it, Champion, OK? I want you to keep it."

His left eye was swollen and shut fast, but his right registered a rising surprise. "We had a fiver bet. It's your money."

"I want you to keep it. You're the bravest I ever fought. We both won this one, and I don't want money to spoil it. OK?"

Rooney was ordering another pint: "He's one of the main men in the city now. Runs most of the northside, imports his wares from Amsterdam." Pete spoke through a bout of coughing and spluttering, amused really by what he was relaying to me. "Constantly referred to as an 'alleged drugs baron', an alleged this and an alleged that, you name it. But because he spreads his bread well among the men in blue, he has never been nicked, not since he became the serious businessman that he is today. That's the bould Champion for you."

Pete's eyes drifted slightly at this point, and I was able to get away without making a song and a dance out of it. I was glad to leave him, relieved to be out of the drinking atmosphere of the pub. As I hurried towards Stephen's Green, I sucked in air laden with petrol and diesel fumes. I told myself I had to get into the countryside during the weekend ahead, get some pure country air into my lungs. As I turned off the little recorder I'd used to tape Rooney's monologues, I tasted the desire to write a book about Danny Devine, and his buddy the Taoiseach. The thought had tickled my mind for a second as Pete shared his version of the two men. When he responded to my question about

Dervla, I realised I'd inadvertently distracted him. Moments later, I needed to shut out things he was saying about her, that I didn't want to hear from him. Like an answer to my wish for an escape route, Kevin Street had dropped into my mind like a lifebuoy, so that I wasn't hearing Pete's voice which I could listen to later on the tape. When I'd shut him out, all the pictures were of my father, my dead father.

8

Dublin, 1970

My father, Tom Collins. He'd been missing for three days before he was found floating in the canal at Portobello. He often disappeared for days, sometimes weeks at a time. Ma had long come to an acceptance of his odd ways. I didn't mind what he did, except I didn't see as much of him as I would have liked. He was a fragile man, and I used to wonder what had happened to break his spirit and turn him into a person who craved alcohol so that he could cope, if only for a few hours at a time, with his inner life.

Ma had to work because Da couldn't work for much of the time. Ma went out six days a week and she cleaned other people's houses, and when she came home she fell into the wooden rocker Da bought her one time, before he drank his entire poke. I used to give her some kind of food in her lap, well, on a plate in her lap, and I tried to keep the place from getting filthy. I never said anything about this to Ma. She was so focussed on the cul-de-sac her life had turned into, that she didn't see the dust, and she could step over a bucket of ashes from the grate like a blind person with built-in radar, or some fucking thing.

The story is I clean the place as best I can. When I say 'clean' I mean I keep the dust from building a body and developing muscles. It wasn't until my mother went into the Adelaide hospital for the first time that I decided to really go for it, go for what they call a spring-clean, even though we're into June. I can remember it because I spent my fifteenth birthday, June twenty-first 1969, alone in our flat over Mulvey's the Printers with Ma in hospital with her throat cancer and Da out there somewhere looking for his own particular rainbow. That's it. I spent the entire day cleaning the flat, all two rooms, wall-to-wall. I threw out two sacks of shite gathered by my mother – old newspapers, abandoned clothes that stank of ailing camphor balls, socks that needed an overhaul, a real pile of worthless stuff Ma hadn't been able to let go of. The place was choking on rubbish. This only increased my determination to create space, give the place room to take a deep breath. This furious energy led me to the big official envelope buried in the back of our solitary wardrobe, a place I would never have looked into had Ma been there.

I take the envelope into the kitchen and empty several old letters out onto the table. Curiously, there aren't any envelopes. At a guess, they hadn't come through the mail. Like, nobody keeps the letter and throws away the envelope, right?

The way the writing paper had faded some at the edges, the ink not as bodied as when the words had been written, pretty much told me the letters had been in the envelope for years. There were five in all, and all written on the same kind of pale blue writing pad. Did this mean they had been scribbled down in a heated rush all at the same time? I'm halfway through reading the first letter when I realise that my father is the author. My intake of breath stops me reading, my heart punches my chest and my throat tightens. I fight to hold back the tears that seem to hover on the edge of my life every fucking minute I think about him. I find I'm holding the page like it's a holy relic, as if I needed any reminder of how much I had loved – love – this man I never even got to know.

This letter is written in a neat hand. It's my first sight of my father's penmanship, and I have to stop reading for a minute. Then I go back to the top of the page and start over. Not one word of the previous reading had registered on my consciousness.

There is no name or address and no date, nothing to suggest who is writing to who, but I focus my eyes and get my brain to start working. It's pretty clear that Da is writing to his parents. I know nothing about them, either, since Da had never talked about them. We had no pictures of anybody except for one Box Brownie snapshot of Ma's mother, so faded you could hardly make the old girl out. I started to read the words my father had written to his mother and father, having no earthly idea of what I was about to learn about these three important branches of my family tree.

–◇–

This is what my father had written:

"Dear Mother and Father, at any given moment I can go back to Glencree. I can go back to the exact time that I think about, like my mind is a camera able to hold the photographs it took all those years ago. I can still hear the sounds of that time, any minute of that time I choose to remember. I still hear the words, the cries and the screams I screamed, like so many other boys that didn't know any more than I knew myself why we were in the reformatory school. I remember Father that you got me there in an ambulance a friend of yours drove us up the mountains in. You gave me over to a holy brother – that's what you called him. When he told me to follow him, I waited a few moments to hear when you'd be back to collect me and take me home. You never said anything, and the brother took my ear and twisted it and I cried out, but when I looked up to see if you were going to tell him not to hurt me like that, you were gone.

"Father, you were gone, and not a word. What did I do? Why was I left in this place, a prison run by holy brothers. I swear it.

"I know I broke a window with a stone I threw at Tommy Carroll, but he was after splitting the back of my head with a piece of slate he fired at me. Oh Father, do you and my mother hate me so much you put me there to be rid of me?

"Brother Benjamin did what he liked with me from the first day in Glencree. He put me in a hot bath, and he washed me all over with soap and he made me stand there in the water, while he played with my privates. I didn't know what he was doing – he smacked me across the face when I asked him. He made me bend over and hold onto the edge of the bath, then I felt the pain of hell go up my back from the inside. When I screamed he stuck a face cloth in my mouth and told me to bite on it, till he finished examining me. I vomited and he put me to bed and I was really sick and he woke me in the dark and sat me on the side of the bed. He told me to shut my eyes and he put something in my mouth and told me suck it, it'd make me feel better. I remember an awful taste then he told me to go back to sleep and say my prayers and be a good boy and that he'd say prayers for me too before he went to sleep.

"I know now what he did to me, and to every other ten-year-old boy in this place. I was always getting hurt by him and the other brothers. I heard other kids crying and screaming from the pain, and I saw lads of ten and eleven just like me with the blood running down the backs of their legs. I knew the same thing was happening to them that was happening to me and though I didn't know how I knew it, I knew it wasn't right. One kid never saw his ma again from the time he was dumped here, and he jumped out the top window one night and died on the spot. God rest his soul, the poor little mite.

"I'm a grown man now father, and I still don't know what I did for you and my mother to put me there to be treated like dirt and hurting all the time from what the holy men did to us. Did you put me there so I'd understand what Jesus meant when he said suffer the little children to come unto me?

"The holy men of Glencree destroyed me father. You died before I got out of that hell. I found your grave in Glasnevin cemetery, but I couldn't make my mind or my lips say a prayer for you or my mother, not even when you were into the ground. God help me, father. Why? Why? Why? Why? God help your son, Thomas."

―◇―

I have to hold onto the kitchen table to stop me tearing the flat apart. So huge is my rage that I feel like my heart might burst at any moment. Then for a moment I am hit in my lower back – a pain so fierce I am forced to my knees to bend over to try and rock it away. Oh Jesus! It's unbelievable. I hear a cry tear itself out of me, exploding like an emotional ulcer, and I involuntarily fall forward onto the floor. I try to drag my sanity out of wherever it's hiding. Jesus Christ! Is it any wonder my father drinks to deaden the pain?

I curl up on the floor, trying to deal with my own stuff without knowing what is going on with me. Whoever said 'nothing comes out of the stones in the road' knew what he was talking about. My self-pity is every bit as powerful as it is in my parents who never feel less than very hard-done-by. Somehow I get to my knees and, lo and behold, there by my hand is the bucket of soapy water I'd prepared to wash the bedroom lino just before I found the letters.

I glance upwards saying 'fuck you' and I go scrubbing that floor like a fella trying to work his way down into Mulvey's the Printers underneath. I focus on my hand as it holds the scrubbing brush, watching the soap do its work. I don't know what I'm doing really, but anything to take my mind off whatever's going on is more than welcome.

The next time I saw my father I tried to engage him in conversation about his life, his childhood and his youth. Did he play football? Oh Jesus! I should have left him alone, allowed him the anonymity he craved. His own identity was a label that was too heavy for him to wear. His shoulders were too slender unless he got enough booze to give him Dutch muscles, the feel-good factor to insulate him for a while from the feeling of worthlessness. Maybe it's the only legacy from his parents who, though long-dead, stoke my anger as powerfully as the unholy men, cleric and lay alike, of Glencree and Letterfrack, and the other hell-holes that should cause our country to hang its head in shame for a very long time.

Can you believe it? Oh! Shame! Shame on you! Shame on you white-collar cannibals handing out penance to some old woman who nicked a can of condensed milk, a kid who had discovered the double-edged sword of masturbation. Shame on all of you who pissed on Jesus himself when you leaked all over his words 'suffer the little children' . . .

My mother was in and out of the Adelaide hospital several times between my finding the letters, and my father's death in the Grand Canal. I was having a tough time, but I held onto the lounge waiter's job I had, contributing almost everything I earned and I kept the dust at a manageable level. I drank all that I could nick in the bar where I worked and I never turned down a drink from any customer decent enough to buy me one. And I ran up a tab in the pub. I wasn't enjoying the drinking, I wasn't going dancing – I was going nowhere, in every sense of the term.

I could get a ride most nights from any one of the lonely women who drank in the lounge and I took advantage of this fairly often. I loved sex, but I wasn't having much fun and the worst part was I couldn't find anybody to blame. I was so full of anger I had to go running and punching bag to take the steam out of the energy that was close, on too many days, to blowing a valve.

One woman, a very experienced woman who could fuck a football team one after the other, told me she got scared one night while I was pounding on her bones. She said I was so violent in my fucking that she thought I'd lost it. I didn't even remember walking her home that same night after the bar closed.

My mother couldn't go out cleaning any more so I had to weigh-in with my pay, and I honestly didn't mind, most of the time. Ma – Molly – didn't have a lot to say. She was a simple countrywoman, coming to Dublin to work as a domestic servant, 'a skivvy'.

"I was lucky," my mother said one time when I asked her about life as a skivvy. "I was only in town a few weeks when your father put his eye on me. Before I met him the Blessington bus was my refuge. I was so lonely that my stomach was very sick a lot of the time. The number sixty-five bus took me out into the country and I said the rosary a lot as I sat watching the fields go by. And I listened to the people talking to each other and with the conductor. I was too shy to hold a conversation with anybody."

I could believe she had been a pretty girl, and I resented the way a lot of Dubs called people from the country 'kulchees'. 'Sodbusters' was another one the Dub used, having picked up the term from a lot of old cowboy pictures. That was about all I could dig out of my mother – about as close as I got to conversation with either of my parents. We talked some about school, the need for a pair of shoes, the weather, something on the radio – that was about it. With me being an only child like my mother, and neither of us knowing whether the Da had any kin or not, we didn't seem to have anything to say to each other. There wasn't even a book or an old photograph album, nothing like that in our home until I started robbing books left right and centre to get my own back for not being able to borrow one from the public library.

A couple of days before they found my father's body, I noticed that my mother seemed particularly low. Putting it down to the cancer, I made her a milky chocolate drink. I made sure it was only lukewarm and I asked her if she'd like anything else. She was lying on the double bed and she turned to me with troubled eyes that weren't thinking about cancer. Nor were they concerned with the fact that she wouldn't have long to wait till she'd be released from a life that had done little but leave her puzzled and scared every day she lived.

"I'm worried about your father." She sipped the chocolate drink carefully while I heard something in her tone that captured my attention in a big way.

"It's nothing unusual Ma. He's only been gone three or four days." I said this like a fella marking time, feeling there was something else she needed to tell me.

"I found him the day before yesterday, above at Harold's Cross Bridge. He had a few cronies up around there, bums like . . ." She stopped and put the drink on the little cabinet beside the bed. "God forgive me." She looked shocked as she said, "I nearly called your Da a 'bum'."

"It's alright. If he was here, he'd say it himself."

"I went looking for him, Joseph." Her eyes were rheumy, old woman's eyes though she was only in her mid-fifties. "I needed to tell him I couldn't go on. That if he wasn't going to pull himself together, to tell me. I needed to know because I didn't want to be waiting for him if he wasn't going to be coming. That's what I said to him."

"Did you mention you're not well?"

Ma shook her head carefully and I found my hand wrapping itself gently around her fingers. She shook her head in bewilderment. "He asked me what I'd do if he couldn't be any different. I told him I knew what he'd been subjected to with the brothers, that I'd read some letters, the ones he wrote to his parents. Some very bad things happened to your father when he was only a lad, Joseph. He never got over it, I'd say." She began to weep silently and my heart went to her. I was now sitting on the side of the bed holding her hand, feeling it was important for her to get this out, relieve herself of the old rusted hurts and the festering pain. "He told me I was a good woman. Said he was sorry he hadn't measured up as a husband or as a father. He said, 'Joe's a fine fella. I wish I'd had more to give him'. And he looked at me, Joe. He nodded his head, his eyes on my face for a minute or more, something that hadn't happened in God alone knows how long. And he said quietly, 'I'll sort myself out in the next few days. I promise you that much, Molly'. Then he patted my hand and I left him standing on Harold's Cross Bridge lookin' down into the water. He was like a small lad's been through a bad time, and I wondered was I ever going to see him again."

The next thing you know, his body's found in the canal at Portobello Harbour. I wanted to tell her she wasn't to blame for my father going into the water. But I didn't. I didn't even want to suggest she might have had something to do with his final choice. I knew I couldn't handle it without cursing the men, the holy ones that had programmed him to go off some bridge somewhere, any bridge anywhere, long before he got even close to his biblical allocation of time.

When Molly died I searched high and low for my father's letters, but they were not to be found. After he died she had clearly burned them, making sure I didn't get to read about what my father had been through. I didn't ask myself whether she had considered the possibility that I'd read them. I doubted she had. She didn't even appear to notice that the flat had been scrubbed, that there was room for her to stash more rubbishy stuff she wanted to hang onto.

I knew that I hadn't known Molly and that I hadn't got within a mile of Tom. After reading the letters he wrote to his dead parents, I felt for him in a way I hadn't known before then. I'd always held back around him, convinced I didn't want to embarrass him by any show of overt affection. The odd time I wondered was it about something else, something that prevented me feeling safe enough to take any risks with my war-torn gentle misfit of a father.

Who knows anything? That's the real question. Who knows anybody? This is one more. Is it even possible to know anybody? Really know them, like? I find myself asking these questions every time I get drunk during the months following my mother's passing. I was something of a solitary drinker, though in the right company I was more than willing to sing a song or two. When I was on the tear, I didn't want to talk to anybody. I sat, and I drank and I went through some kind of manoeuvres in my head. Looking for answers, I suppose, frustrated by the lack of them, despite the questions queuing up to put their spoke in.

Danny Devine came from a different planet to poor, dead, Tom Collins. He was rich, successful and powerful. Could I write a book about both of them? Two guys who were born at the same time in a different place? Maybe I could handle it. But what drove them to their separate ways? Was there anything other than background that the two could possibly have in common?

9

Dublin, early July 1992

I'm lying in bed in need of time out from making love to Jill Clarke. Jill is twenty-four years old, an air hostess who is a genuine high-flyer in the feathers and a creative colleen between the sheets. I like Jill a whole lot. Apart from her obvious charms, that she turns heads like an exciting tennis match does, she's good-natured and easy to be with. She also has a quick mind and is, overall, the kind of young woman any guy would be delighted to find in his Christmas stocking.

Jill has made no bones about liking me. More than that – she swears she is in love, that she wants to marry me. The fact that I am eleven years older than she is doesn't matter a damn to Jill. She even suggests, in her very own devious way, that this is a kind of bonus.

"Women are much smarter than men, Joe." She lays this on me gleefully when I first mention the difference in our ages. "So you'll need to be at least ten years older than me, just to match my emotional maturity, right? Basically, I see no problem at all, thanks to you being as horny as an eighteen-year-old, and a girl can't ask for more than that, right?"

When I got back to Dublin, I was expecting it to be pretty much as it was when I left it in 1973. Was I ever in for a shock? I was almost terminally surprised and I hadn't even caught my breath before I was wondering how Irish guys right now are finding it. Like, had I come home as I was when I left for America, females like Jill would have blown my plugs out completely. I'd have been afraid then to go to bed with a woman who had her own moves, her own ideas and her own demands. If you take the 'on top position' as a pointer, this is like a put-down to a lot of guys, as though the lady's saying 'you're not cutting the mustard in the saddle. I need more than I'm getting to let the steam out of my boiler room'.

I ate up the stuff of women's liberation in the newspapers and the women's magazines. Legal problems and constitutional entitlements, health problems, female and otherwise, were discussed in open forum at the mass media level. And the clarity and openness with which sexual questions were answered by doctors, as well as the usual batch of agony aunts, was pretty amazing.

Jill wakes up like someone emerging from an enjoyable swim, all bright eyed and bushy-tailed with a smile like a gale warning garnishing her lovely lips. She swills the remains of her gin and bitter lemon, takes a drag from my Gold Flake, exhales while she rubs her hands playfully like someone about to start working hard, then she kisses me. And she kisses me in this way she has, which leaves you in no doubt that you are about to get fucked till your eyeballs go pop.

Suddenly I'm not feeling satiated any more so I respond

wholly hormonally to the offer. I mean, what's a guy to do? Just before we join at the hip, the phone rings. Jill gives me a warning look, a glance that says 'don't you dare answer that'.

The clock on the bedside table shows two and I guess somebody's in trouble.

The voice at the other end says "Hi Joe! It's Dervla Devine."

"Good morning, Dervla," I respond in a neutral tone, trying to keep the sound conversational. "Is it my imagination, or are you whispering?"

"I'm whispering," she whispers even softer. "Look, I need your help. Sorry to call you so late." She sounds concerned, but I don't hear sorry. I scarcely know Dervla, but I've already formed the impression that she's not that interested in being sorry about anything.

"What's happening?"

"I just woke up in bed with a guy I don't know. I've never seen him before."

I register the 'blackout', but I don't say anything.

"Thing is, I guess I picked him up somewhere in some kind of blackout, I don't know. I can tell we've had sex. I've no memory of any of it. I need an alibi, if you can help me. I'm not working the country this week. So I was due home for dinner at nine o'clock tonight. Gary sees little enough of me, so he'll be livid. I was wondering? Joe, can I say I was with you talking about giving up the booze? That I got upset, whatever, that it all took longer than we figured, the time just got away, something like that?" I could hear that Dervla was trying to stay cool, but the tremor in back of her voice betrayed her.

I can feel the temperature go down around Jill in the bed, even though she can't hear a word Dervla is saying. This is not something I can bother with, in the moment. When you're dealing with someone as shaky as Dervla is right now, it's a delicate time, a time deserving of your full attention. Really, you need to go softly in what is, in many ways, a negotiating dialogue. It's a situation where one person has to come to trust the other if there is to be any kind of positive result. You have to move with stealth, pick the second in which you make the decisive move. It's the one that will get the reluctant sick pigeon that Dervla is to agree to come with you to that first terrifying AA meeting.

"I'll help you. I'll lie to your husband, OK." I let that sink in for a second before I say: "But you've got to promise me you'll come to an AA meeting with me. And I mean, promise me, Dervla."

"I will, I will," she whispers, urgently. "Oh thanks, Joe. Thanks a mill."

"I'm talking about a meeting tomorrow night. You promise me you'll meet me tomorrow night, I'll back up your story to Gary?"

"Tomorrow's really awkward, Joe. Could we do it next week?"

"You'll be in the country working next week, or have you got another week off?" I'm trying to sound kind of official, hoping my tone of voice gets it through to her that I'm not going to be fucked around here.

Unfortunately, I have no idea if I'm getting this through to her, or not, but I hang tough. This is not the first time she's said she'll come to a meeting. She has promised to call me to make arrangements more than once. Nothing happened. So now it's shit or get off the pot time.

"I could make it Monday next, not go into the country until the Tuesday. Is that OK?"

"No, it's not OK. What's so important about tomorrow that you can't meet me and come to a meeting?"

"I promised a friend we'd go to a movie together. She's part of my social life, you know, and I've let her down twice in the last month."

"You're giving me your social life! I'm talking to you about your life! The one you live in, and breathe in, the one you're throwing away. It's not my business until you come to me looking for an alibi. That makes it my business. So, once more with feeling, will you meet me tomorrow and come to an AA meeting with me? No bullshit now, Dervla. It's a yes or no answer."

"Yes," she gasps on the word, and knowing just what she's going through I sympathise in my heart. This is a seriously fearsome moment in the life of a problem drinker. It's admitting, really admitting you have a drink problem. This means that even if you go on drinking you just know the admission is going to be there, woven for all time into the texture of your future.

"Can you be in the Shelbourne lounge at seven, not the Horseshoe?"

"Yes, I'll be there." She sounds scared, and there's a good chance she's mad as hell with me. I don't care. You can't fuck around with alcoholics when they need help so badly. You have to shove it to them, and hope they don't run away. If they do take off you let them go and you try to remember for your own sake, 'Don't Think! Don't Drink! Go to Meetings'!

I put the phone down, feeling good that Dervla has given her word that she'll turn up. And who knows? Maybe she will. We'll just have to wait and see!"

Jill is as mad as hell. "She doesn't want to quit drinking. She wants to get you into bed." Jill reaches over, helping herself to a cigarette, her hand trembling. I hold the lighter to the Gold Flake and she tries to sound indifferent. "She is a whore, Joe. A notorious whore! She has fucked everybody in town, in the country. Jesus! And now she wants to fuck you because you make the papers, you're on the telly. She's a fucking climber, just like her sisters. Joe, you can't let her get her claws into you."

"I've been a whore myself," I say. "When I was drinking I was as big a tramp as you can name. My only interest in Dervla is to help her to help herself get off the booze and out of the shit-hole her life has turned into. You know that about me. Just like you know that you turning this into a federal case won't change anything. I won't step on your trip, but don't you step on mine."

Minutes later I hear the shower working and I guess Jill is going home in a funk. I get out of bed and go into the bathroom. Telly and Carol are away on a trip to England, so I know I'm not going to discombobulate anybody by walking around in the nude. When I pull back the shower curtain, Jill is uncertain if she wants me in there with her. "Conserve water," I say with a shrug. "Shower with a friend?"

She laughs in a begrudging way: "Fuck you, Collins!" I step in under the jet: "Now you're talkin' kid." I'm doing my Bogey voice. She laughs and hands me the soap.

"Just to show you what a forgiving nature I've got, you may soap me very, very slowly."

"I've got all night, schweetheart! I'm gonna give you bubbles you couldn't find in Dom Perignon." I start to soap her up and we start laughing together. We hug each other in the spirit of mutual attraction and it feels so good to be like this with her that I wonder why I don't grab this girl and go for a real relationship. Any guy with a nickel's worth of grey matter would fight for a female like Jill. This line of thinking, coupled with what Jill is doing with the soap, gives me pause and I have to admit that this is the closest we have been all evening.

Sadly, within a few weeks she will react so strongly against my guidance of Dervla Devine that she will walk out on me like she wants to take the front door along with her. Part of me wants to go after her – she is a wonderful young woman and she means a lot to me – but, shit guys it ain't cigarettes'll kill ya, it's the buts!

10

Dublin, July 1992

There is a mixed crowd in the lounge when I get to the Shelbourne hotel. I reckon, theatre-goers having a drink before heading off to a play. I see one or two affairs – people too mature to be holding hands and looking lovey-dovey if they were married to each other – lovers, risking being together in a public place, lovers, needing to say 'this person is mine'.

We have a few serious drinkers tucked away in the corner down behind the grand piano, which is being tinkled by a lady who works a nice three-finger cocktail programme of Jerome Kern and Cole Porter. I see her accept a drink from one of the guys who prefer her company to the kind of asshole the Horseshoe Bar next door attracts. And I speak as a card-carrying member – three years retired – of Assholes Anonymous.

I sit with my back to the entrance, and I wait. As soon as I see a number of the guys in the room sit up and suck in the gut, I guess that Dervla Devine has arrived. I smile with a glow of pleasure gliding over my heart. I'm smart-ass happy to be right in my opinion, based purely in instinct, that nobody goes asleep when Dervla makes an entrance.

She stands over me and I get out of my chair. We shake hands, and without being romantic or dramatic I feel that I am already in trouble. I shove the thought to the back of my mind. She's lovely, but what she does to me is coming from something deeper than her looks. I tell myself I can handle it. I have to handle it. I'm here to try and help this lady quit boozing and I remind myself that right now she needs a friend. So I give my randy little self the bum's-rush. I get him out of the picture, for the moment anyway. I'll be a friend to Dervla because I know her problem can't be arrested by a rub of the relic.

I hold a lighter to her cigarette and I give her time to exhale before I ask her what she would like to drink. Dervla hits on the cigarette again, like someone who is very surprised. She exhales, "Do you mean alcohol?"

"Sure."

"May I have a large gin and tonic please?" She gives her order to the waitress without looking at the woman who's had a tough day. I give her a smile and ask her to bring me fresh coffee. She hobbles away, my smile having failed to relieve her need for a hot water footbath laced with salts.

I light a Gold Flake and draw deeply, wondering about the best way to open up conversation. Dervla solves the problem for me. "I'm surprised you asked me what I'd like to drink."

I ask her why so. "You haven't quit drinking, have you?"

"I had the impression it had to stop when I came here to talk to you, to go to a meeting of Alcoholics Anonymous with you."

"It doesn't stop. It can't stop. Not until you decide that you want it to stop." This gives her something to chew on. "Have you decided you want to stop drinking?"

Dervla chews on this for a minute or two and I just sit there waiting for her to answer the question.

"God knows I need to quit. God knows that I ought to quit. That it's the sensible thing to do." She smokes some more and I make room on the table so that the waitress can put the drinks down. When she leaves, I decide it's time to get honest. I feel obliged to do this. I know it's got to be done, before we go any further.

"Strictly speaking, I shouldn't really be here with you."

She leans forward impulsively. "What do you mean? You shouldn't be here?"

"One of the recommendations of AA. A guy should not sponsor, that means help and guide, a new member of the opposite sex."

She remains silent and I think that maybe she didn't take in what I said. In time I'd come to know that she never took on board anything that might make her uncomfortable, not if she could help it. Just as I'd come to see that she somehow turned every conversation, regardless of what was being discussed and irrespective of how tenuous was the link, to herself.

"I don't know if I can handle this, Joe." She gives me a very direct look, one she uses when she wants to make a point. Her voice is firm and dry, quietly powerful, so that she never has to raise it in order to be heard.

"Have your drink. Try and enjoy the Gold Flake. They're terrific cigarettes." I hold the lighter for her again. "In a while, see how you feel. If you want to forget this, leave. Whatever, that's up to you. But I won't cover for you next time you get laid in an alcoholic blackout."

"You mean a lot to me, Joe, or I would never have made that phone call." She sips her drink and smokes. "I feel I know you, that I met you, got to know you through your books. I like you and I want to know you. I'm sorry if this is out of line, but Jesus, what time have any of us got? I hate telling lies. I hate the thing of being a fucking liar, even for a minute. I lied to Gary the other night. I brought you into that lie. I did that to stop him feeling like I'd cut his heart out. Those are his words. 'When you hurt me,' he tells me, 'it feels like you have cut the heart out of me.'" She leans on the Gold Flake some more to help her through the moment. "Maybe I'm just deluded, but I honestly think I only ever lie to stop hurting other people." She stops talking and I pour coffee. She hasn't touched her drink.

"Did you hear what I said about breaking an AA recommendation, man helping woman, bad medicine, all that?" I gave her my Indian brave voice, which brings a hint of a smile to her lovely mouth.

"I let it go over my shoulder." She gave me that direct look again. "But, if you intend sticking to that particular rule, I won't bother coming to the meeting. I don't see the point. I've known about AA for three years. I admit to you here and now I've known I'm an alcoholic for at least that long, probably known it since I was about sixteen."

She lifts the gin and tonic and empties the glass, putting it back on the table as though it's very heavy, or very hot. I draw smoke into my lungs and sit there waiting.

"I'm not any kind of joiner, Joe. I'm not a member of anything. I went to an AA open meeting three years ago. I thought I'd puke. I wasn't looking forward to going to this meeting tonight. I came because I thought you'd be taking me there. Without you being involved I've no real interest in trying. Fuck it! I'll do what I do and when the time comes for me to kick the bucket, that'll happen. Does it really matter? Does anybody give a shit? Really, I mean?"

"I care," I hear myself say. This happens before I have a chance to censor my mouth. She takes my hand in her impulsive way and I make no attempt to warn her that this isn't a wise move in such a public place.

"I need your friendship. If I could have that, have you as my friend, I will give AA a shot. I will go to meetings with you. I will take whatever directions you give me about the best way to travel on the dry road." She shakes her head and every guy in my vision seems to move his own in unison. She pulls this amazing drape of blue-black hair back off her face and I have to take a deep breath. "That last meeting, Joe. I don't mean to be unkind, but Jesus! There wasn't a person there that I would have wanted to drink with, never mind try to get sober with. Do you understand?"

I should have levelled with her right there. I should have offered to introduce her to any one of the special women I'd come to know in the fellowship, help her find the right sponsor in that way. That would have been the right way to direct Dervla on her road to recovery, the right way being the only way.

She was close to cracking up. A blind man could have seen that much. I guess I believed that for all her bravado and the strength she dug out of herself to deal with the life she was leading, that she was probably fragile enough to hurt herself in the worst way. I'm not trying to sound like some kind of expert here, but you can only go with what you've got, and that was what I was hearing and seeing and feeling as we sat in the Shelbourne. And if you think this is close to a new high in terms of rationalisation, fuck you for being so bright.

I didn't find the guts. I couldn't find the guts to insist that it had to be a woman sponsor, whether she liked it or not. The logic behind letting the pigeon go is this: 'They have not suffered enough. They need to go back out there, wake up in another gutter, another detox unit. They need to rub their belly in the sand until they bleed. Maybe then they'll throw in the towel and surrender in order to win.'

A minute later, I said quietly, "OK. Let's give it a shot with me as your sponsor. Anybody asks, we say we're old friends and you asked me to take you to a meeting. Let's see how we go with that, a day at a time."

"Will I be asked to speak?" I notice a spot of perspiration on her upper lip. And quite unconsciously, I reach over and brushed it away with my finger. She smiles as though something wonderful has happened. I let it go, and answer her question.

"You don't have to say anything. If by some chance the guy in the 'chair' asks if you'd like to speak, just say 'I'm glad to be here tonight – I'll leave it at that'. You never have to say a word at an AA meeting unless you want to."

"I'll come to the meeting with you. And Joe, seriously, thanks. Thanks for being such a friend. I've no right, I know, but right now I need you and I'm nuts enough to say it instead of behaving like a polite and proper married woman. OK?"

"Afterwards I want to take you to meet a couple of people," I tell her. "Does that seem like a good idea?"

She nods, smiles, looking less tense. "If I survive the meeting, I'm in your hands for the rest of the evening."

When I drove away from that first meeting Dervla was in the passenger seat weeping silently. I was heading for home – I badly needed Telly's input here, but this new pigeon was in need of some TLC. I drove into the carpark by Sandymount Strand, suddenly in need of some time out before deciding whether or not to take her to meet Telly and Carol.

She hadn't said anything at the meeting, but once I parked the car and we got cigarettes going, she began to talk. Dublin was dressed in summer moonlight, great aisles of platinum-like highways from Howth bisecting the surface of the sleepy sea. There wasn't an ounce of wind and I rolled the car windows down. I didn't turn on the stereo. The last thing I needed was late date music.

Dervla stopped weeping and we smoked in silence for a while. When we got fresh cigarettes going, I felt her energy rise, like she was building up to saying something that mattered to her.

"I was surprised, when I phoned you, that you never asked me why it had taken me so long." She was calm now, her inner tension relieved by the flood of tears.

"I was just glad to hear your voice. To know that, despite your situation in that minute, you were still alive and kicking."

"It was because of my father. He extracted, and I do mean extracted, a promise from me that I wouldn't have any more affairs. I tried explaining to him that you only wanted to help me. He didn't believe it, not really, and he saw you as some kind of threat in that area. He's not going to be happy about you taking me to AA meetings. Gary will probably be fine about it, if it means I cut down on the booze. But Daddy – no way!"

"Your father's some kind of control-freak, right?"

Dervla nodded vehemently, her hair huge as it seemed to dip in and out of the moonlight bouncing off the water.

"You're a mature young woman, Dervla. You're entitled to decide what you want for yourself."

"Forget looking for logic where Daddy is concerned. He's a law unto himself and there's only one opinion allowed around him. His – his opinion only." She exhaled volubly as though it had taken some effort to admit this. "I brought this up. I suppose I feel I should warn you about what you might be letting yourself in for. I'd guess he warned you off that day at the hospital?"

"He quit when I told him to back off."

There was a rip of laughter in her voice when she said, "You told him that?"

"Sure. And a couple more things he needed to hear. I told him I was up to my ears in lovely women, that I hadn't come to the hospital to wreck your marriage."

Dervla was evidently impressed. "He's knocked people down for less, Joe. You must have put out a very strong message, even if you didn't know it."

"I knew what I was doing. In your room at the clinic I noticed how his knuckles were a strip of hard meat. Sure sign of a guy who has punched holes in a lot of people. When we were in the carpark – you remember you looked out the window – I let him see my knuckles while I lit a cigarette. He seemed to revise his original assessment of me after that. I'd say the guy is first and foremost a pragmatist."

"You don't have your crystal ball with you, do you?" She squeezed my hand in a show of schoolgirl delight. "Daddy considers himself the ultimate pragmatist." She laughed. "Can I see you knuckles, Joe?"

I flicked the interior light on and held up my fist. Dervla ran her fingers over it before she looked at me. "You were a fighter, Joe. I can see that."

"When I was a teenager, I needed to fight. I didn't know it was to unleash the rage I was carrying around inside me. I used to fight other guys in the street for money. I trained with a bunch of great knackers, learned a lot from those fellas. I put gloves on for a while in the States. It's like talking about somebody else. It's so yesterday, know what I mean?"

I gave her a fresh cigarette. "What I need to know, need to hear from your own lips is this. Do you want to stop drinking alcohol?"

She turned to exhale a ribbon of smoke out of the window. "I know I . . ."

"Hold it, Dervla. This has to be a 'yes' or 'no' answer. So, do you want to quit drinking booze?"

"I have to, so yes, yes, fucking yes. I want to quit drinking booze. Jesus!" She gasped. "I've said it. My God!"

"There's one more question, maybe two. Will you rethink your earlier decision that you will only attend AA if I agree to be your sponsor for now?"

"No. I need you. I trust you. It's you as my sponsor, or I'll forget it."

"You answered both questions right there. I said I'll be your support and I won't back off that. Maybe in time, when you see how wise it is, we can find you an experienced AA female to act as your sponsor. OK?"

She exhaled smoke, but she didn't say anything. I took the opportunity to say, "I'll need to talk to your husband, OK?"

Dervla looked sideways at me. She hadn't expected this. "Is that necessary?"

"It is for me," I told her. "I want to make sure we're all working off the same page."

"I'll tell Gary to give you a call."

I started the car and I felt her withdraw slightly from me, like a child pulling back after a minor chastisement.

"I want you to meet a couple of pals of mine. Do you feel up to it?"

She bounced back with an energetic nod, holding her mane so that it didn't hit me in the face. "I told you, I'm in your hands, Joe."

"You have the most amazing head of hair I've ever seen on a woman."

"I get it from my mother. She's greying now, but the volume is still there," she chuckled. "Mammy had 'big hair' when it first came out." Her tone changed. "That and precious little else. She came from a few acres of land in Monaghan. She worked as a domestic servant in Dublin. Daddy met her at a church social and they married a year later. She never loved him, told me that herself."

"Why marry him then? Had she no hopes of falling in love?"

"He never laid a finger on her while they were going together. He took her to nice places, decent restaurants, and he never kissed her passionately or felt her breasts. She thought he was a gentleman." Dervla was dealing with mixed emotions as she related this to me. She felt warm about her mother's innocence, sardonic about her father not trying to have sex with her before marriage.

"He had women all over Dublin, plenty in the countryside too. He was a womaniser, so Mammy was misled, if you see what I mean. She thought he was a nice man, but he was getting all the sex he needed whenever he wanted it, so he could play the nice guy with her, no problem. Even when they married, she knew nothing about him. He was in business, he had his finger in lots of pies, she said. But she didn't know any more than that. He bought a house, furnished it, took her on honeymoon, and she never had to worry where the food was coming from like she did when she was a young girl."

"They produced three children," I prompted. "They must have come to some kind of loving."

"Not according to my mother." Dervla stopped talking because I'd just driven in through the gates of our house at Whiterock.

"Oh, I like this," she said enthusiastically. "On top of everything, but tucked away. Yes, this is a good place to live."

"I want to hear more about your mother and father next time we meet, OK?"

She nodded her head assuredly. "But let me tell you this just before we go meet your friends. Mammy only ever tells me anything *personal* when she's a bit jarred. That only happens when she's been to a wedding or a funeral. Normally, she's very reserved, shy. But the few jars open her up." Dervla burst out laughing. "A bit like myself," she chortled. "Except, in my mother's case, she opens her mouth to talk while I . . ." She frowned. "Less said, soonest mended."

We got out of the car and stood under the moon and a choir of stars, looking down over the sea from the forecourt of the house. I looked at Dervla and I felt a strong need to embrace her. I drew back from the feeling, walking a few steps towards the edge of the lawn where the garden rolled down towards the ocean.

"I'm still waiting for this juicy bit about your mother," I called back to her, feeling very happy to be in her company, not thinking beyond the moment or daring to go that far.

"Mammy told me, very tipsy she was on this occasion." Dervla came to join me on the lawn's edge, and I felt her hand slip under my arm. "Is it alright to link my hand under my sponsor's arm?" she asked coquettishly.

"It's all right when we're alone," I said lightly. "So come on, the mother, tell!"

"Mammy said that she and Daddy only had sexual intercourse three times in all the years they lived together. She reckons he just did it to have the children, and that after Jilly was born, three girls in a row, he threw his hat at it. He wanted a son, but Mammy wasn't delivering one. So that was that, though she always made it clear to him that she would never refuse him his conjugal rights."

"Did she actually say that, your mother? 'Conjugal rights'."

Dervla shrugged away her own disbelief. "My exact thought when she said it to me. I wondered how they stayed together as long as they did. Poor Mammy! A dote!"

I took Dervla by the hand. "My friends are terrific – Telly and Carol Sampras. Telly's the guy saved my life." I'd already opened the front door, but I stopped and lowered my voice. "She's a good person, but she's something of a flake. I just want to prepare you for that."

"What does that mean exactly?"

"I guess I mean she's a wacko, nuts," I mimed smoking. "She's spent a long time inhaling the laughing tobacco. OK?"

Dervla nodded.

Telly's oil-slick eyes shone the brighter as he saw Dervla for the first time. They shook hands on my introduction, his natural charm winning her over in an instant.

"Jeez, sport! You never said she was the most beautiful woman in the world," he turned to me in complaint. "I'd have worn my lifts."

"And you never told me he was even handsomer than you,

Joe Collins." Dervla's eyes twinkled under his compliment, and I felt good. Two of the VIPs in my life were going to get along. I didn't need to tell him that my pigeon was very important to me. I figured he'd work that out for himself sometime during the next twenty seconds.

He was in top-form, a casual dandy this evening, urbane and sophisticated. His loafers and cufflinks looked great on him and this gentle way he had about him was a hugely attractive quality in Dervla's eyes.

I nipped into the kitchen and plugged in the electric kettle. I heard Telly call up the stairs to Carol. "We have company, honey." The reply he received was pure Carol. "I'll be right down, sweetie. I'm just trying to work out if we left the working mink behind in London."

I met Telly at the foot of the stairs and he said as we walked back into the living-room, "She left it in the dining-car on the train yesterday. I went back to pick it up, but it had already left." He stopped to light one of his fucking menthols. "I figured that since the minks were all dead they would have needed some help to leave the dining-car. Wouldn't you say so, sport?" Telly sounded rueful, but it was throwaway as opposed to aggrieved.

"It's no big deal," I said as we rejoined Dervla. "She has three more in the closet."

Telly shook his head. "You can fall for a dame for a certain reason, sport, and a few years later you can begin to hate her for the same fuckin' reason." He swivelled to include Dervla in his apology. "Excuse my French, my deah."

Dervla looked pleased. "Thank God, is all I can say. I thought I was coming to meet a couple of saints. I'm just so relieved to find that you're all so normal."

"Don't place any large bets on that, deah. Hold the

phone until you've met my wife. And by the way, if this guy, who once saved my life . . . Should he turn out to be a failure as sponsor, I'd be honoured to take over. Meanwhile, I hate his guts!"

Dervla smiled at his New York humour, glancing at me to say, "Is that allowed, sponsor man? Can I change you for another model if you don't measure up?" Dervla was having fun in the moment, and we laughed together. I felt she was doing well, that we might just get her to attend one more meeting, which was all you could hope for with a new pigeon.

Carol arrives downstairs in a Chinese housecoat and golden slippers, her blonde hair fixed in a perfect beehive. She was gorgeous in her own squirrelly way as she was welcoming Dervla and talking to Telly at the same time. "Hi sweetie, you're very welcome. So gorgeous Joe, but then so are you, sweetie. Telly, I'm sorry, sweetie. Guess I left the working mink on the train. How about that! Jeez! You're one gorgeous looking gal, sweetie." She threw out her hand and I saw Dervla react to the length of Carol's nails before she shook it carefully.

"Welcome, sweetie! Tell me your name again?"

"Dervla Devine, Carol. I'm delighted to meet you."

"I'm delighted to meet you, sweetie." However often she repeated her favourite endearment, Carol made it sound like it was your name and that it meant a lot to her. "Now let me give Baby Bear a hug." She embraced me with such passion that I could see Dervla wondering if Carol and I had something going between us. She pulled her head back off my shoulder. "Is Cutie Pie going to be pissed all night, 'cos a girl went and lost the working mink?"

Telly snorted. "I'll make some more cawfee."

I grinned, looking from one to the other. "No, I think Cutie Pie is going to be just fine." I winked at Carol. "That coat was looking pretty tacky, anyway. But don't tell the insurance company that, they might knock twenty per cent off its value."

Carol turned to Telly coming back in from the kitchen. Her slender arm was outstretched, her cigarette holder about a foot long and looking like an extension to one of her stilletto fingernails. "See, sweetie! Joe has it all worked out." Without waiting for a response she turned back to me. "Y'know baby, I'd forgotten the damn thing was insured," she cackled in her throat. "Isn't insurance a wonderful thing, sweetie?" She raised her right hand slightly, using the index finger as though she was trying to draw my name up from somewhere else.

"Joe," I said with a smile, shrugging *I warned you* at a flabbergasted Dervla.

"You're a real doll, Dervla." Carol had turned to give my pigeon some attention. "You're just right for Joe." Her eyes opened in wonderment. "Gee! Think of the kids you guys could produce. Wow!"

"She's Joe's pigeon, honey." Telly cut in before Carol's imagination segued to the rose-covered cottage.

"We're just coming from my first meeting," Dervla told her. "I'm pretty shaky, but I'm glad to be here. I can scarcely believe I'm not drinking."

As I drove her back to her car Dervla thanked me for introducing her to my friends. "I can see why you raved about Telly."

"I won't bring up the sponsor thing any more, Dervla." I glanced sideways at her, resisting the urge to just touch her face. "I've made the commitment to you and I'll honour it.

But you may get some flak on account of it. AA has its share of self-appointed guardians. They mean well. OK?"

"So what happens, now? We go to another meeting next week?"

"Basically, you need ninety meetings in ninety days."

"What?" Her voice was magnified by the shock she felt. The disbelief in that one word was a palpable thing. I said nothing. "Joe, I have a job. I work around the country. I told you that."

"You sound like I'm ordering you to do something." I turned sideways to face her on the bench seat of the car. "I'm not telling you to do anything. I'm offering you another guideline from Alcoholics Anonymous. A meeting a day for ninety days, that's the recommended route for a newly-recovering alcoholic. Some people go for it, some people don't. I've no idea what the statistics are about it. I did it with Telly, we felt so hopeless we were prepared to do anything. I'd have eaten a bag of hay every morning to help me stay away from that first drink. But as my mother used to say 'every cripple has his own way of walking'."

"All right." Recovering somewhat, she said, "As my friend, I'm asking you to tell me straight what you think I should do?"

"I've heard guys in AA say they couldn't give up their job, not even when this was recommended by their sponsor. This guy was running a bar. He'd been doing it so long he couldn't see any other way to make a buck. He was told to give it up, to remove himself from such close proximity to JB – John Barleycorn."

"And did he? Did he give up the job and get sober?"

"No." I gave her a long look. "He was a good guy, but he held onto the job and the booze killed him." I lit cigarettes for both of us, opening the window to let the smoke out of the car. "I've heard guys say I've got to quit drinking because I'm afraid I'll lose my job. They get reminded that if the pressure of the job makes them feel they have to drink, they better quit the job. Like, they'll lose it for sure if the booze kills them."

"This is already as tough as I thought it might be, Joe. And I'm not even into withdrawal yet." Dervla said this carefully, trying not to jump onto the 'I can't handle this' wagon that was lingering at the depot, waiting for her to get aboard.

"It's only fair to tell you, Dervla. If I can help you, and you get a taste for being sober, and if you do everything right for the next year, it's still going to be the toughest year of your life."

"If you're trying to console me, Joe, it's not working."

Dervla is weeping. I know she's genuinely scared of the scenario I've just presented to her. In all honesty, I don't know if she can hack it. From where she is, what we're talking about here is giving up drink forever. I can practically hear her thinking "And all this fucking one day at a time shit isn't going to change that."

"You may get honeymoon periods, weeks here and there. There's the balm of relief we call 'dry'. Relief you're not suffering a hangover every morning. Relief you know where you went to sleep, who you went to sleep with. Relief as you taste breakfast. Relief as ordinary, simple things seem to appear like gifts to people who've fed an addiction for too many years." I pressed on. "The only thing you have to do tonight is get some sleep, if you can," I said, knowing how fatuous this must sound while she was trying to accept that her lifestyle had to change dramatically for her to have any chance of getting sober. "You can call me during the night if you feel you're going to drink. If it's possible for you, I'll meet you at noon tomorrow and take you to a lunch-time meeting." I spoke as gently as I could, wishing, however shameful it was, that I could just take her home with me and hold her in my arms until she went to sleep. "Will you call me in the morning?" I said, my throat so dry it was uncomfortable.

I walked her to her car. I opened the door, but before she got in she turned and stepped into me, her arms wrapped around me, her body pressing against me so that my resistance was under very heavy strain. I didn't move. Did I even breathe, I wonder. The moment passed and she stepped back to get into her car. "Thanks Joe. I'll talk to you in the morning." I stood there watching her drive away. I was bathing in relief, knowing that I should walk away from this scene right now. I decided to sleep on it.

When I got back to Whiterock, Carol had crashed already. Telly was in the living room reading *Newsweek* and smoking a cigarette. I'd been hoping he hadn't gone to bed because I needed to hear what he had to say about me sponsoring Dervla. We were very alike in many ways, so he would know how dangerous it would be for me to be around such a beautiful woman. And how the implications of that could interfere with whatever help I might be able to provide.

"We know there's a recommendation in AA about the 'boy-girl' sponsorship thing," Telly conceded. "And a lotta folks take it very seriously. Me? I see the AA rules more like guidelines." He exhaled smoke. "I'm taking my time here because I'm wondering how I'd feel in your shoes, sport. If this gal came to me and asked me to be her sponsor, if she felt she needed me in that role, what the hell? Who can tell you it's wrong to want to help her? I certainly can't. But, I confess, I'm something of a 'two-step-Johnnie'. I've got the first step down pat, and I'm willing to carry the message to other alcoholics, which is number twelve. I don't need anybody telling me how I should brush my teeth. She's such a beautiful gal and she asked for you." He shrugged. "If it was me, I'd answer the call, but then I'm an old-fashioned kind of guy. Know what I mean?"

11

Dublin, September 1992

Two months after my decision to sleep on my dilemma of whether I should go on being sponsor to Dervla I'm still sleeping on it, sleeping alone on it, night after night.

The truth is I'm not spending a lot of time wondering about whether I should still be there for Dervla or not. She has been dry for two months, she is attending meetings, she has quit the sales job that took her all over the country week-in-week out. Slowly but surely, she is turning onto the 'One Day At A Time' philosophy. She has hope.

She's been under stress at home, all of it predictable and easy to understand from the outside. Admittedly, the stories given to me by Dervla were one-sided, but there was a ring of truth there, now that the madness hit her only every so often. During the first month it had been just about full-time.

On this particular morning, September twenty-first she has a row with Gary that will send him out of the house in such a rage that he almost takes the hall door with him when he leaves.

"It started because I wouldn't fuck him before he went to the office. Trouble is, I can't bear for him to touch me. I thought he was going to hit me. I've never seen him so angry. He's totally disenchanted with AA, and with me and my sobriety.

"'Fuck your sobriety and fuck your sponsor Joe Collins, and fuck you too, Miss Dervla O'Fucking Devine. I am up to my scalp in hearing about you, and how hard it is for you. Your sponsor tells me you're doing ever so well, and that I should be going to fucking Al-Anon meetings to help me deal with my end of the disease of alcoholism. *My end* of the disease of alcoholism! Of all the fucking nerve!'"

"Fuck you, Gary," Dervla shot back at him. "You were the one who kept on, 'Give up drinking Dervla. You'll be a new person'. And it was you, not me kissing Joe's arse when he came to talk to you about being my sponsor. I had resisted giving up the booze forever, but you kept on and on and on till my head almost exploded. Do you hear me? I only gave in because you were driving me crazy. And now, you selfish bastard, because I feel fragile this morning, because I don't want to fuck you or suck your cock, you go crazy. You selfish bastard. Go stick your cock under the cold tap and don't be bothering me with it!"

I could only imagine what she looked like as she made this response to Gary who must have felt he was being mortared by her salvos. And there had been more. But since Gary had slammed out of the priceless house, it was the walls and the delph and the mirrors that felt the force of her madness. Dervla continued yelling at the walls of the magnificent kitchen. All she could see were images of Gary as she vented her spleen, spitting out her confession. "I was bad, I was a total fuck-up if you like, but I was somehow managing my shit most of the time until you forced me to seek help. So, whether you accept it or not, you brought Joe into the picture. And now, here I am, halfway through this month's madness, coping with the crazies that the need for drink dumps on me any time it fucking feels like it. I am weary this morning because I couldn't sleep last night. All I could think about was the moment when I left Joe last night after another AA meeting. We stood so close and I practically begged him with my tits to kiss me, touch me, something – just do fucking something to me. Do you hear this Gary? Mr Fucking Husband of the Year! I was so desperate for him, my body, my head, my legs, every bit of me. Jesus, I was crying out for him in my fucking bowels. It was so bad, so heavy, I would have fucked him in the car, standing up in a doorway, anything."

As I woke up that morning, my first thought was of Dervla, which surprised me. Telly's in the Whiterock Clinic. I dropped him there. He's having some test on his bowel this morning and I went to sleep with his scenario very much on my mind. Yet I woke up thinking of her. It's OK. Telly's cool. It's a precautionary probe or something, so he told me. I don't know if he knows more than he's admitting to me. He looks fine and he's laid-back about it. He's not been tolerant around Carol this past week. She's been wonderful about his bad humour. She puts it down to Telly being scared, and too scared to admit it. He wanted to walk over to the clinic, so I walked with him.

Then I'm walking along Merrion Road in the direction of Shrewsbury Road, where Dervla lives. I'm walking like it's the only place to go. There have been many nights when I thought I would go crazy, nights when I ached from the sheer demand of wanting Dervla. Wanting her in my arms, in my bed, in my life. Not just as a pigeon I'm supposed to be helping, but as a lover, partner, dare I even say it, as a wife, my wife. Jesus! There have been nights when I was hurled back to earth by the reminder that she is married already. Nights when I was within a hair's-breadth of taking her in my arms, moments when I longed painfully for something more than a sponsor's encouraging embrace to his suffering pigeon.

I was well aware that in the role of sponsor I shouldn't be embracing Dervla. You can't embrace a woman who looks like she does and looks at you the way she looks at me, and tell yourself it's all just platonic. You just don't do it. You certainly shouldn't do it, not if you're in my position, which is one of trust, for her care and wellbeing. This is not some delicious piece of ass you've got on your hands. This is a screwed-up young woman in a life or death situation, someone desperately in need of support and protection, not sex.

As I hurried towards Shrewsbury Road, I reminded myself of the times that Telly had talked me through one more unrelenting urge to put a bottle of whiskey to my head. My fear as I stepped up the pace of my walking was that because she's like me, tarnished with the same brush of willful promiscuity, Dervla could be driven by her demons to reach for that first drink. She came close while I was within minutes of ringing her doorbell. She would tell me later how she went about pouring boiling water into a mug. How she dropped the mug on the tile floor of the kitchen. Lucky she had the shakes. Had her hand been steady, had she been pouring full blast, she could have scalded herself.

"The attack was so fast, Joe. Threw me for a loop it did. I was suddenly jerked off-balance. The mug smashed in pieces. I staggered to the fridge, got some chocolate and a glass of milk, sugar to help me stop shaking. I kept repeating the Serenity Prayer. I was desperate enough to ask God straight out:

'God grant me the
Serenity to accept the things I cannot change
Courage to change the things I can . . . and
Wisdom to know the difference.'

"The phone rings. I go to pick it off the wall, stumble and fall to my knees. As I get up I stand on my nightdress, stumble again. I prevent another fall by holding onto the drinks trolley we keep in the kitchen. I miss getting to the phone. And then, Jesus Joe! I'm hypnotised by a fat-bellied bottle of Bisquit Dubouche. I find myself inhaling its bouquet of crushed grapes and wildflowers, savouring again the invasion of pleasure I tasted last time I sipped it from a balloon. I see my hand move as though it is independent of my control. My hand holds the slender neck above the Napoleon belly and I pray for the touch of Joe where the bottle rests against my breast. I wanted to die, Joe."

I didn't know it till that moment, but as I reached Shrewsbury Road, Dervla was going through this torture. I swear, I was sweating and I didn't even know what was going on. I was so anxious that I was telling myself, Hey! Cool down. You're here. You'll be no good to Dervla if you go in there like you're gasping for a fucking drink. Pull yourself together man. Mr Cool! All right!

Dervla is hypnotised by the arc of golden nectar as it comes out of the bottle. She is watching the amber disintegrate as the spirit hits the inside of the balloon glass and bounces around. As she tells me, "My chest seemed to have caught fire. I could hardly breathe. 'Oh dear Jesus!' I was praying, gibbering like an eejit. 'O God! O my God! I'm sorry. I can't help it. I can't go on. I can't live like this, I . . .'"

In that same moment, I hit the doorbell harder than I meant to. It makes a strident shriek in the hallway of the house. The doorbell ringing is like an arrow of cacophony exploding through her brain. It gives her such a shock that the balloon, half-way to her mouth, flies involuntarily from her hand to smash on the tiles at her feet. In a moment she is stumbling up the three steps to the hall, moving as fast as she can to pull the front door open.

When Dervla opens the door with some kind of wild energy, I step backwards as the smell of cognac smacks me in the face. I feel paralysed for the moment. Jesus! If only I'd got here earlier? She throws her arms about me, the joy in her strangled, crying laugh, like a song of release. She kisses my mouth like it's been begging to be kissed from the first moment my eyes rested on her lovely face. Thank God! She hasn't taken the first drink. I'm so aware of her mouth on mine, so taken by her need which is becoming my own need, all my reservations shoved into the back room, away from the light of reason. Somehow I move us both into the hallway and kick the door shut behind me.

"Oh, Joe! Joe! Joe! Joe! Oh God! You'll never know how I needed to find you there when I opened the door."

In the huge front-room overlooking the garden we undress each other with the urgency of people not entirely in tune. I see and touch and kiss this divine body for the first time. Dervla is all over me, and we weep, savage each other's mouths, wanting to be able to do everything at the same time. The emotions that have built up between us the last three months pour all over those first minutes when we jumped up and down on the rules applying to our situation.

All that had been held back was there like some kind of divine madness, as we made love with the driven sexual energy that would always be so much a part of any life we lived. Of course, my heart registered the danger signals, yes my mind sent me a loud and clear warning of how dear a price might have to be paid for this consummation. But I'd already been deafened by my need to be like one being with this wild wanton woman who has captivated me from the first time I laid eyes on her.

Dervla was a very physical lover and I pushed my body to the limit to meet her at every demanding turn. I wallowed in the sound of her tortured breathing as I withdrew almost to freedom, only to plunge deeply again, loving the fractured ululations of muted joy tumbling from her laughing mouth, as she threshed and rose to meet all I had to give her.

When we reached the top moment together, as our cry of relief came as one sound, I felt my tears tumble. I felt myself as I tumbled and slithered down beautifully into the pocket of perfect silence beyond every orgasm. Bliss, broken only by Dervla repeating over and over and over, "I love you," before she laughed and cried out, "And I came, I came, I came. Oh God! I'm still at it."

I lay there mute, stunned, suddenly concerned. I felt guilt at having crossed the line and betrayed the trust AA placed in someone sober enough to know better.

As I moved, Dervla was urgent in her need for me to stay. "Don't leave me, Joe. Let me stay wrapped around you. I love you, Joe."

"I love you." I heard the words that are supposed to change everything. They kept coming to my ears, they kept pouring out of my throat and my mind, and I knew that if I was to die for what was happening there in the moment, I'd say, "guilty your Honour, of being insanely in love with this wonderful woman. I really have no choice. Right or wrong, this is what I want."

Dervla said in a hushed voice, her lips and her tongue at my ear. "There will never, there cannot ever be enough time for this to be stolen from us, no matter what power they think they have over the life I have chosen for myself. That life being Joe Collins and I, living as one, till death or madness us do part. Can you handle it, Joe?"

I rested on my elbows, so attached to her in every way that I couldn't find any shred of resistance to her proposal.

Part 2

12

Lough Dane, County Wicklow, early October 1992

Dervla and I are living in a shooting lodge in County Wicklow, as in 'out of town'. This doesn't alter the fact that we're still getting hit with the smell of the metropolis *merde* coming off the fan in seven sunlit shades of sweet shit-brown. Rumours abound. Gary Lloyd has said he will seek an annulment from Dervla. He will also sue the Alcoholics Anonymous Fellowship on the grounds of 'malpractice by her sponsor'.

A tom-tom beat reaches us on the wind, bringing word of other rumours of a different shade. Gary has spoken to some very heavy people with a view to putting out a contract on my head. This legendary offering turns out to be true in part, but Gary is an English gentleman and he doesn't actually want me pushing up daisies on the mountain where his wife and I are sleeping together. He was interested though, in giving me something much more painful than a bullet in the brain. He was willing to pay some Dublin thugs-for-hire to beat me to a pulp, and to break two or more of my limbs. I took it all with a grain of salt. Dublin was always a mini-capital of gossip and scandal and backbiting, rumour being an integral part of the local wire service, in a village-city forever addicted to small-town talk.

So, there you go. Dervla and I were hooked on each other and totally steeped in what was between us. We felt it was 'you and me, Babe' and then there was the world. This was how Dervla articulated what was going on. We were a very special couple, so she reckoned. We would make our own rules. We would have secrets, she said, things between us that nobody else would ever know about. Our secret songs, she called them.

A few weeks earlier, Dervla had just turned up at the house in Whiterock. "I'm taking you for a drive, if you have the time." I'd sooner have gone to bed with her there and then, but we were worn out sexually from a bliss-filled two days since we had sworn eternal love for each other. I'd no idea where we were going on this drive. Not that I cared.

What was very much on my mind was my inability to bring up an AA recommendation for Dervla's benefit. Do not make any major decisions for a year from the day you put the plug in the jug, or words to that effect. This caveat being intended to include minor considerations such as leaving your husband! I was also crazy about her. I'm telling you, for all my intentions to be the man and lay down some rules, when Dervla breezed through the door of the Whiterock house, I was totally captivated. She was wearing a palm-printed summer dress that was almost see-through and this red chiffon-scarf about her throat.

Just for a laugh I allowed Dervla to blindfold me with the red chiffon-scarf. "I want your mind to be blown when you see my new home for the first time." She sounded so happy, so free of anything but what we were into in those moments. I didn't want to spoil such a luxury either, but I was mollified

a little when she referred to the new pad as "my new home".
Maybe she'd backed off the living together idea herself.

On the short trip up into the hills, Dervla became a
beautiful child, bubbling with whatever she was up to. She
had this trick – when she wanted your agreement about
anything – of turning the situation into something that
would clearly be fun to do, if only you could see it from her
point of view. To assist you in this, she turned those great
eyes on you, allowing a beat or two of time for the effect to
land like a beautiful surprise, until you discovered how easy
it was to let her have her way. Who wouldn't feel terrific
about giving such a gorgeous creature her own way? Weren't
you in her company, in her heart, in her pants, for Christ's
sake? What guy wouldn't die for all that?

When I stepped out of the car and Dervla removed the
blindfold, I shook my head a few times and blinked a lot in an
effort to give the impression I was trying to focus. No way did
I want her to see my reaction to the surroundings and hear the
sharp intake of breath as an icicle of memory pierced my chest.
The pain hit me as I recognised Lough Dane, which I knew to
be just on the outskirts of Glencree village. Bloody Glencree
village, with the tiny church and the hostel for hikers, and the
small shop, and the graveyard for German Air Force guys from
the two World Wars, and the old reformatory. Ah yes, the
reformatory. The reformatory had been turned into a
reconciliation centre. With no reconciliation for me – it was
the reformatory, the scene of my father's personal horror story.
The living nightmare that got under way the day his own
father handed him over to a holy man for safekeeping.

Dervla was already in love with the lodge on Lough
Dane, taking me by the hand, hurrying me through the
rooms and the passageways, gurgling in expectation of the

fun people could have living in such an "amazing house" in an "incredible place". As we stood on the balcony of the master bedroom looking out over the lake and the boathouse below, I saw a herd of goats tailing a fierce-looking Billy along the shoreline on the other side of the water a quarter of a mile away. As I watched the herd begin their climb back up the mini-mountain opposite the house, it was impossible not to concede that this was a genuine beauty spot.

I turn to Dervla and we are all over each other, awkwardly-moving, half-falling inwards onto a freshly-made double-bed I hadn't even noticed when I crossed the room in her wake. In moments she is looking at me from above, beginning to move ever so gently, a smoky smile playing about her mouth as she woos away and screws away any hint of resistance. We make love for an hour, the French doors wide-open, a light breeze coming off the lake, the air refreshing as the sun slips behind the mountain at the far end of the water. We smoke Gold Flake between rides, silent in the silence of the valley of Lough Dane. Then I hear Dervla's dreamy voice, "I'm moving in here tomorrow, Joe. Do you think you could stay just for a night or two, until I get used to the space and the silence?"

"Sure," I inhale deeply to hide my need to smile. I'm finding her incredible. Like, she didn't have to make a decision to be like this. It came to her like breathing, like changing gear in a car, this built-in gift to get her way especially when she sensed there was opposition to her point of view. I guess this was why she never experienced guilt. She never seemed to suffer regret or guilt, unless she brought it on to convince herself she really did care about people.

By the time I got there the next evening, everything was in place and Dervla was buzzing as she showed me what she had accomplished during the day. She had cooked dinner as well, a beef goulash that made your tastebuds purr with pleasure, baked potatoes with crispy skins and horseradish through the pulp, and red and green cabbage touched by a spray of wine. Having a dash of wine in the food was OK for us, since the alcohol was cooked out when the temperature hit boiling point. Dervla produced a baked Alaska for dessert, fresh fruit salad as an extra, and as we sat by the fire in the drawing-room, I relaxed into an old wing-chair thinking 'Shit Man! This has to be the life.'

Within a week my things were brought to the lodge in a hired van. Apart from my large desk, my typewriter, a guitar, two sets of my boxing gloves and too many books, I brought mostly clothes and one steel filing cabinet. I had with me a heart willing to give its best shot as a good partner, and the will to mask any nagging questions like 'are you being a caring sponsor for Dervla?' In a few days I had fixed-up an office with French doors opening out over the lake. The room had amber walls and I knew right away I could work in it. So without delay I got my daily routine underway, feeling light-hearted enough that I asked Telly to keep a close eye on me. I knew that excitement and the kind of bliss you experience in the early days of an intimate relationship can be as dangerous for an alcoholic as the worst scenario in town.

Right away I started getting to know the fifty acres of mountain and lake and timberland that came as part of our rental deal. I climbed the early-morning purple crustacean opposite the house by taking the goat's path, feeling at times that I was floating on air. I used binoculars to observe the game and the birds, fascinated by a hovering falcon, a monarch of the skies; a royal predator who let you know with a raucous cry that he was there, that this was his territory. I always gave him a wave and a huge grin.

After Dervla completed her ninety meetings in ninety days, we committed to three AA meetings a week. If either of us wanted one or two more, the option was there to tag along, but there was no pressure on this. I found AA meetings very helpful, even after they stopped being the dire necessity of those early days when Telly and I first staggered towards 'bone-dry city' back in June of 1988. Basically, I enjoyed being in a room filled with people willing to keep the cork in the bottle.

You have to forgive yourself for having the disease of alcoholism. The WHO, World Health Organisation, lists it in the top five killers of mankind. You have to stop blaming yourself for the sackful of other shit habits you've been *schlepping* around all your life. You've got to forgive you. Only then can you let go of the garbage for good. When you find this hint of tolerance towards yourself, then you can extend it to the pain-in-the-ass guy at the next meeting, even to your live-in partner.

It helps you to develop better feelings toward everyone, but it doesn't mean you're wearing blinkers when your spouse tries to pull a fast-one on you. I'm thinking of the adroit way that Dervla who could read me like an open book, conned me into staying at the lodge that first couple of nights. She admitted she conned me into staying, believing in her heart "and in my knickers" that she had enough going for her to get me to stay on and on, "till death us do part". And of course, the lady was right.

Sitting afterwards in her replete mode, naked on the couch, she told me that her father and Rachel Oakes, the latest in a long line of mistresses, were coming to visit on the following Saturday evening. Telly and Carol would make up the sextet for our first dinner party at Lough Dane.

"It should make for an interesting evening," I said with a nervous chuckle. "Your father's been checking me out."

"Don't I know it?" Dervla drew deeply on a Gold Flake. "He's so mad at me he can't bear to look at me. Rachel and I arranged the dinner without even asking him. I'm sure he cares for me in his own way, but you have to understand that he's been desperately in love with Gary's money since our wedding day. Even though we are a serious item, he hasn't given up that goal. It's not his way to give up, not when he really wants something. He'll blame me for us, not you, Joe. You're not frightened of him, are you?"

"I'm probably a little scared. But I won't be hiding under the table when he comes to dinner."

"It won't be easy for me. He can't bear to be disobeyed. But you know what? I'm with you and I don't give a fuck about anybody else. I'm sorry if that's not the way a nice girl should talk. I'll handle Daddy. However I do it, I won't let him make trouble for us. And I won't let him harm you in any way. He'll have to kill me first."

This woman is inside me, a-thousand-years-a-growing maybe, like the turf on the Featherbed. How positive she is as she sits there in her birthday suit, unaware that she possesses an atavistic streak, some kind of Queen Maeve-gene that turns her fearless when something frightens her enough. I nodded, believing my lovely partner, and hoping she could deliver on her promise. Not very gallant I admit, but I wanted no part of Danny Devine, a guy not to be crossed if you wanted to enjoy continuing good-health.

The very next day I get a phone call from Pete Rooney. He goes cryptic on me and my guess is he's half-pissed. The time is twelve thirty so I reckon he's on the second or third course of his lunch in Toner's pub. The message he gives me while he refers to Danny Devine as "that party we were discussing, the guy who fixes things" is that Danny has been talking to some very heavy people about a problem that has arisen in his life – a problem called Joe Collins.

Beating my way through Pete Rooney's circumlocution, I understand that Danny wants me frightened-off. Pete is convinced the story is for real. The one that Gary Lloyd wanted me broken up was just hot-air. My nemesis is Dervla's father. Danny is for real. He wants me out of Ireland so badly on a one-way ticket going anywhere, that he's willing to lay out some serious bread to hasten my departure. He has said that should this fail, he is in the market for a pro to settle the matter once and for all.

As I listen to this stuff I try to tell myself its just bullshit. As it happens, I get it wrong, and it's a simple stroke of good fortune that comes to my aid.

Fortunately for me, Danny has been directed to my old foe, Champion. These days he is not only a drug baron but your complete career criminal, ergo, a man who can fix just about anything when there is enough money in the proposition to excite his interest. Champion phones me within days and I'm delighted to hear his voice. Of all the guys I ever fought, he was the one I respected most. "I haven't died a winter yet," he chuckled when I asked him how the hell he was. "And I'm keen to ensure that you don't die this winter either." We arranged to meet within the next week and I wrote down his mobile phone number. I was delighted he had surfaced again in my life, particularly at a time when I needed a friend who didn't fight Marquis of Queensbury.

"Before you go," Champion waxes even more confidential.

"Our friend in this situation doesn't fuck around. When he wants something he usually gets it."

"People keep telling me that. I just find it hard to believe that anybody would want someone hit over something like this."

"It all comes back to the root." Champion chuckled. "Everything, sooner or later, comes back to bread. In this case, major-major bucks."

"Are you telling me our friend is so serious about staying close to the Limey's money that he'd put out a hit on a guy getting in the way? Is that really what all this is about?"

"I heard a word or two I'll lay on you when we meet. *Our friend* and this high-powered pal of his with the same initials as Our Lord, they have big plans and they need ten million to give these plans legs. The Limey bloke is worth thirty or forty. With more to come when his old-dear pops her wellies. These fuckers had money when it first came out. Anyway, *our friend* and his pal, they want a real pile. And Joe, make no mistake, they'll do whatever they have to, to get their hands on it. Naturally, the Top Banana won't know the details. But the other guy – it'd take something special to make him back-off. From what I hear, he sees this as getting his place in history."

As I put the phone down I decided I'd say nothing about any of this to Dervla. She had taken the Gary gossip with a laugh, admitting that she felt a bit sorry for him. I went to my office, my mind filled with Champion's revelations, wondering what was to come when we were face-to-face without wondering if anybody was listening in while we talked on the phone. Dervla was just finishing a job she'd been intent on surprising me with, in my office. She wasn't quite through with the work but the surprise part worked, all too well.

My face dropped so fast I didn't have time to pretend that I wasn't pissed by what she'd done to the place. She'd been about to throw her arms around me, but she stepped back as though I'd hit her with a stinging blow on the face.

"Jesus! What the fuck's wrong? These wonderful pictures buried in that grubby suitcase. I thought they would look great in here, bring back memories for you, stories the writer might have forgotten."

I took her in my arms and she surrendered willingly. She would have done anything to shut out what had happened to my face when I came through the door. I felt the same way, and it would have been wonderful to cut the scene right there. But Dervla was due an explanation, even if I didn't feel like giving her one.

"I kept that stuff in the bags because I didn't want it out in the open. I didn't want to hang that stuff on any wall, anywhere."

"You're a winner in those pictures. And the write-ups in the *Daily News* and *New York Post* . . . They said you were the hottest middleweight contender in years. And Jesus! Even I know what that means."

"I blew it. Let's leave it at that, OK?"

She stepped back from me. "This article says you were a great fighter and a very good boxer. Just listen." She had the piece in her hand in a moment. "For a middleweight, Collins can punch like a light-heavy, and at twenty-one he could be set for a serious pugilistic career." She looked at me. "You never told me you were a fighter and a special one at that. I was so thrilled to find this stuff I didn't even consider you might not want me to see it."

I dropped my coat onto a chair and I lit a couple of Gold Flake and put one between her lips. "I have to admit you did a good job. Hanging them like." I sat down and for the first time in three years I found myself unconsciously reaching for a drink, a drink I thought I needed, but most definitely a drink I didn't want. Just like I didn't want to face the demons these pictures conjured up.

"I'll take them down later, OK?" She stood in front of me like a little girl asking her father's forgiveness. I stood up and held her. I held her, not to comfort her but to help me contain the tears I'd held down in the years since those pictures had been taken.

"It's OK. There's no need. It was the shock. Sooner or later I was going to have to look at them again, take them out of the bag, if only to put them back in and throw it on a bonfire." I kissed her face and her hair and put my lips to her breasts under the woollen halter.

"Joe, I love you so much. I'd die before I'd do anything to hurt you. You must know I . . ." I stopped her words with my finger and kissed her lips. Then smiling, I pulled back.

"Have you got dinner cooked by any chance?"

She relaxed and pressed her pelvis into me. "Dinner's cooking, but it can wait Mr Collins!" She could read me like a book. She was smiling now, turning feline, loving the sensation of relief and sexual arousal I could see coursing through her eyes.

I lifted her up and put her sitting on the edge of my desk. In a moment, we had her out of her panties. Seconds later I knelt down, probing as she put her legs over my shoulders. I pulled her thighs against my head, willing to get lost in the bower there, using the taste of her to shut out my senses and my mind. I pleasured her so that she cried out and I pressed her thighs against my ears to stop the sound of my own screams.

13

Lough Dane, County Wicklow, late October 1992

Danny Devine reminded me of an ex-cop I'd known in Manhattan. He was an Irish guy who was connected to the mob, an honour he wore like he'd been made a papal count. Dervla's father displayed this same patina – it's like they know they're special. Guys like this are deluded, but they don't know it and this is part of the delusion trip. They make for bad, mean people, motherfuckers who will do whatever it takes to get what they want when they want it, and God help the guy gets in their way.

Pete Rooney's character sketch backed my gut response to Danny, the guy they called 'the fixer'. Pete talked of Danny with something like awe riding his voice-box and I could understand why. The dossier my old pal had compiled on Danny was scary. This man made up a new rule to fit every desire he ever had, another for every corner he ever cut. People 'in the know' believed he had pulled off some amazing scams while daily wearing a tight white cut-away collar supporting a Windsor-knotted tie. Since he was connected to the top figure in government he had many escape hatches available to him when he came undone in any situation. He dripped charm when it suited him, but he had those eyes that never smiled or seemed to warm up even a little. He reminded me of some IRA guys in the early seventies that I grew up with, guys who became killers of their fellow men.

These guys were different to ordinary people, colder, withdrawn, with no interest in small-talk or joke-telling, any sort of camaraderie. 'Removed' was how I thought of them and I put it down to them having killed people. These were serious revolutionaries, who claimed they were ready to die for 'the cause'. Some of them did.

I was used once to sign my name as a witness to the handing over of a weapon, a loaded revolver, from a quartermaster to a man who was going to use that gun to take another man's life. He did the killing later that same day then returned the weapon like it was a bicycle he'd hired for the afternoon. He had cold eyes, eyes like Danny had.

From the first moments I spent in the company of Danny Devine, I felt that behind the chat which he had mastered with rare skill, he was of the same kidney as the revolutionaries I'd known. He was a man 'removed' through something he had done, like killing somebody. This was just an instinctual thing you understand, not something I could prove. But the feeling was so strong that I had serious cause to be concerned for my own life if Danny genuinely intended to take me out of his path. And it was in this frame of mind that I ushered him and his beautiful mistress, Rachel Oakes, into our victorian drawing-room. I served them aperitifs before a roaring open fire while Frank Sinatra poured some oil on the troubled waters of our situation.

Danny was a well-known wealthy man, but he didn't want it forgotten that he was born tough; a guy who came in fists swinging as he launched himself on his journey to the stars. Somehow, in the course of conversation with him, you were left in no doubt that he was just as tough today as he had been all those years before when he left Cork city intent on getting his slice of the pie known as Dublin.

He was like a sophisticated gang boss from an old Bogey movie. Danny gathered loyalty from seriously-heavy, dangerous dudes, simply because they were afraid of him. You could make big bucks working for him, and wear sharp suits and tear up traffic tickets when you were connected to Danny Devine. Of course, he could wax as gentle as a sleepy spaniel – he invented some of the best moves, was my guess. And I'd have bet money he never passed a mirror without taking a good look at the guy looking back at him. All in all, Danny was quite a man. And, despite his tolerant – 'this is one of those times when it's best to be civil, for now' – routine, you knew he was never going to warm to anybody that complicated his life. This was a guy who didn't like surprises.

Dervla had greeted her father and Rachel, by my side, before excusing herself to check something in the kitchen. So I poured the drinks and tried to keep my eyes off the magnificent breasts of Rachel, who not only knew what her boobies were doing to me but enjoyed the fact that I was so interested in them.

Telly and Carol arrived before I'd actually started to make small-talk and I threw a fast prayer of thanks to St Jude, and made the introductions. I saw Danny's eyebrows shift a shade when he realised because they weren't even offered alcohol, that my American friends were alcoholics and very likely members of AA. And when Carol, who was insecure enough to brag about her family's wealth, dropped the family name and mentioned that they owned blah blah blah, I could have burst out laughing at the expression on 'the fixer's' face. All right I thought, maybe this won't turn out to be a bummer after all.

Danny's woman, Rachel Oakes was stunning. She was a classical beauty with that curvy Reuben's look most men find irresistible. I was very taken with her and excited by her beauty and her body and her brains. At a guess she was forty, maybe a little more. In her case it was a plus and she was clever enough to ride on what she had, giving no time or energy to trying to look younger. She was a lady in the prime of life, a divorcée that had made her ex pay heavily for what she had provided as his wife. She was naturally cool. Her every word might have been chosen with care, but it all seemed to just flow naturally, a generous nature pouring itself out for all to enjoy, while each gesture assured you that the lady knew her way around. Rachel possessed this honey-gold voice that gave most of what she said an import it didn't necessarily deserve. She was an extremely bright and well-read opinionated dame, who would wallow in any polemic that gathered her interest. As I successfully lost the fantasy of falling on her incredible bust, I allowed that she was probably the most sophisticated Irish woman I'd ever met.

Danny left Carol and Telly to interrupt us. He suggested that Rachel might like to pop into the kitchen and see if Dervla could use a little help. To her credit, Rachel agreed whole-heartedly. Danny downed his glass of whiskey in one pop and said to me, "I'd enjoy seeing where you work, if you wouldn't mind a philistine like myself entering such a sacred spot." You had to hand it to the guy. He knew how to get just enough tongue into his cheek. If you took umbrage or backed off in any way, you were the one who wasn't cutting the mustard.

I ushered him down the passage and into my office. The lights were all on, the computer hadn't been turned off, and the printer was churning out some more copies of my play *Hang in there, sweetie!* for my London agent. So the place looked fairly businesslike as Danny viewed it for the first time and I have to say that gave me a buzz.

I saw him react hugely to something before I realised that Dervla hadn't taken down the pictures of me when I was fighting. Along with the framed newspaper clippings from New York, they made the wall to one side of the French doors look pretty busy.

Danny read the write-ups without a word to me, he saw my Golden Gloves awards, checked out the pics of me sparring with Emile Griffiths, one of the great middleweights of all time. By the time he turned to face me, I got the impression he was seeing me in a somewhat different light. He moved across the room and closed the door.

"There are things I have to say to you, Mr Collins. Things that are best kept between you and me." He was already into lighting up a Balkan Sobranie.

"It's cool, Mr Devine. You don't have to beat around the bush with me," I said, smoking a Gold Flake. "Dervla is going to be serving dinner in a few minutes."

"I knew you were going to be trouble when I met you at the Whiterock Clinic." He tapped his cigarette against the ashtray. "I knew it as sure as I knew my own name. Y'know, we should never ignore the gut, the instinct. This . . ." He tapped his temple. "This will let you down, but the gut, never."

"I know you don't want Dervla and me to be together, Mr . . . "

Danny cut me off by raising his hand like it was a weapon. "I doubt you will ever make a more powerful understatement in your life. I remind you again that she is a young woman with a husband she married before the sacrament in the Catholic church. And I'm asking you now – I will not be asking you again – to walk away from this relationship. I'm willing to pay you quite a large sum of money, cover all your expenses. All I ask is that you set Dervla free so that she can return to her lawful, wedded husband, who even as we speak is waiting for my phone call to say that you have agreed to this course of action. The chap is distraught, Mr Collins, and I am not going to stand by and allow this situation to continue any longer."

"I know you've had me checked out, Mr Devine. So you know a lot about me. Just as I, through my own contacts, know quite a lot about you. I tell you now in as civil a tone as I can muster in the face of your arrogance and your astonishing hypocrisy, that I've no intention of leaving Dervla, not now or next week or next year. As far as I'm concerned you can do your worst, try putting out another contract if you wish – you don't and you won't scare me off. Now, do you think we can, as civilised men, go into the dining-room to the wonderful dinner your daughter has cooked for us?"

"I don't care what you think you know." Danny crushed out the butt of the Balkan Sobranie. "You simply have no idea of who you are dealing with. It was not my intention to be so overt, but you leave me no choice. If you don't leave

Dervla, if you don't drop the role of marriage-breaker and get out of this country for a time at least, your days are numbered."

"They've always been numbered, just like your own Mr Devine. By a power greater than all of us, so spit it out. If I don't do what you say, you'll have me taken out. Hit, whacked, snuffed, call it what you like, I get the message. And I'll just say this. Take your head and shove it up your ass. If you weren't Dervla's father I'd lay you out in one minute. And don't bother wondering if you can take me – you can't. There's something else. Between now and whenever you plan to have me hit, you just might have a surprise or two coming your way."

"There's no need for any of this," Danny said, a tiny flame of doubt lighting his eyes for just a second. "If you would just go away somewhere for six months, give Dervla time to get over this infatuation. It's not the first, probably won't be the last. But this, you two moving in together and actually cohabiting, this has to stop before Gary Lloyd throws his hat at his marriage for once and for all. I can't allow that to happen. So, I ask you again as one gentleman to another, back off before it's too late."

"I guess you have big plans for a lot of his money." I threw the line away, but the impact on Danny Devine was immense.

He was stunned for a second, waxed angrily then, all of this bluster designed to deflect my vision of his discombobulation. "How dare you? How dare you suggest such a thing? I am thinking of my daughter's wellbeing, the effect on her immortal soul of breaking the vows she made in the house of God. My God! What sort of a man are you?"

"I didn't come up the Liffey on a bicycle, Mr Devine. And this little chat of ours is over. And I won't tolerate you giving

Dervla a hard time about my stance. She is my partner and I'll protect her, from you and anybody else who tries to fuck up our trip. So, let's see how much of a gentleman you are. Show some form, what?" I opened the door and silently indicated that he should go first. "Age before good looks!" I said this in a friendly party-type voice, naïve enough to think he might have found the gesture amusing. Forget it. It went over like a lead balloon.

Dervla had cooked a wonderful meal, but I hardly tasted a bite. I watched Danny who simply lashed the food into himself with such gusto that he clearly didn't allow his anger or his heavy intentions to interfere with his appetite. I switched my attention to Telly who as always ate as though he had no interest whatsoever in food, which was true of him. He could take you to a restaurant and when you commented that the food wasn't going to win any prizes, he's turn on a slow smile and tell you the décor and the ambience was what brought him back here. Carol was wolfing her dinner down as she always did. When I watched her eat she always reminded me of the poor people I'd known, who gobbled food down as fast as they could in case someone took it away from them.

Dervla was just stunning in a red alpaca knitted dress, a garment which added indecent to sexy, but as usual she seemed unaware of all that she had going for her in the looks department. She was giving a lot of attention to her father, showing him a lot of respect. I felt she had turned her lamps on full beam for the old man, who was in good shape and still a handsome dude in his late-fifties.

I found I was looking directly into Rachel's eyes and somehow I felt she had wished me to turn to her just as it had happened. Fanciful, sure, but what the hell! It was a dinner party. We were supposed to have fun, right! Maybe even flirt a little. This was fanciful too, just me trying to cover up my anxiety since I couldn't shake Danny Devine's warning off my shoulders.

Danny relaxed a little more during the main course, the large whiskies allowing him the release from some degree of the tension he'd shown me inside in the office. He seemed like an easy-going dinner guest, chuckling at Telly's almost languid way with a story and laughing mechanically when Carol came on quirkily funny without knowing it. She was stoned out of her tree, so she thought Danny's interest was genuine. She began making a fuss of him, probably giving him more attention than she ought to have done. When Carol was at cruising altitude on a handful of DF118s, codeine pills that she cocktailed with the best Afghan shit, she was the perfect dinner guest. An hour, and too many pills later, it could be downhill all the way. But that was Carol.

I saw Danny run the rule over Carol. It took him all of three seconds to decide that 'not for all her money in Fort Knox' would he be interested in taking her to bed, not even as an act of charity.

Telly was his usual urbane self, a guy who was always an addition to any moment that needed something extra. He was witty without trying to be funny, full of interesting anecdotes about yesterdays that sounded like a lot of fun. He had been part of the Bogart's circle as Bacall floated in – the most sophisticated nineteen-year-old in history. He had missed being around Bogey and his hot-tempered wife, Mayo, when they earned the title 'the battling Bogarts', but he had stories about his relationship with the man himself. Naturally, we were all of us captivated, and I never appreciated him more than I did that evening.

Some time later, as I head for the downstairs lavatory, Danny stops me for a moment in the corridor. Without any preamble, he tells me, "You have two months from today to make your arrangements. Please do as I have asked." He raises his index finger and points it at me, shaking his hand as though to emphasise the point. "Two months."

I let my memory return to Dervla, to how she looked when she told me she wouldn't let Danny do me any harm. "He'll have to kill me first." The look in her eyes in that moment would light a fire in the most frightened heart.

As I began to get ready for bed, I realised I was scared of what Danny Devine could do. He could have me killed. In the moment, I wondered about telling Dervla what he'd said to me. The threat to my life, the time-limit imposed on me. Maybe we could take off together, just split on a November dawn without a word to anybody. Take it from there. Go with the flow.

I was suddenly aware that Dervla was throwing her clothes about as she got undressed. "My father is a total motherfucker, Joe. Do you know that?" She took up her hairbrush and I could practically see the sparks flying off her great dark mane. "He knows I'm willing to do just about anything to keep him off our backs over fucking Gary and his fucking money. So what does he do? What do you think the bastard says to me in the kitchen?"

"He's so full of surprises, pal. You're going to have to tell me."

"He wants me to go back working with Jay. Handle his personal PR. 'Jay and I would like you to start right away. He needs your help at the present time. It's important to me, Dervla. I'm relying on you to just get on with it.' What a bastard!"

Everything about me rebelled at the thought of Dervla going back to work for Jay Charles, but a tiny bell went off in my head, and I decided to say as little as possible. Danny had just laid a big one on her. To be asked to handle personal PR for the Taoiseach would be some kind of big deal to most people. And Pete Rooney had told me himself that Jay's image had never been as good since Dervla quit on him a few years back. Pete Rooney had also let me know that some very heavy rumours at that time had labelled Dervla and JC as lovers. I didn't care about that, any more than I was concerned they might pick up old threads should she go to work for him. What crossed my mind was that JC was the man for whom Danny was apparently willing to do anything. This could include having me killed, because I was getting between him and ten or twenty millions that he planned to annex from Gary Lloyd. What did he need all that bread for? Surely, it wasn't to buy a new fucking yacht for JC? Rumour suggested an armed takeover of the six counties. I scoffed at this. Even the mercurial man at the helm of the government couldn't be that crazy. I exhaled a sigh even at the thought that it might be for JC's personal use. Come on, it couldn't be. Could it? Time was short, but maybe Dervla could find out from the great man himself if she decided to go work for him as his private PR consultant.

When we got into bed I took her in my arms. "We're not going to go to sleep angry, Derv. We made a deal right?"

She turned to me. "That was between us. It's all right for me to be angry at Daddy when he behaves like a shit." She waited for me to say it was all right. I didn't and she wrinkled her nose at me. "All right, I'm sorry. I'll let it go, for now." She played coquettish. "So, what plans did you have in mind to help a girl get a good night's rest, after an evening slaving over a hot stove?"

"Oh! I dunno. I suppose I could always give you a rub of the relic!"

"Bless you St Joe," she sighed. "My novena's paying-off already!"

We laughed together and drifted into short passionate kisses that got longer as the hunger for each other came into the light. Then she grabbed my hair and gently shoved my head up so that she was looking into my eyes.

"I'm so angry with Daddy. It's only fair to warn you I may take it out on your hide, and your other bits and pieces." Then she said like someone grinding their teeth. "Let's fuck till the lights go out, OK!"

"I'll give it my best shot," I said, wanting her urgently, but wishing I had the power to give her more than good sex.

She responded to my entry with some gentle ululations of her hips, her dark eyes smiling as she drew me deeper. Then she said, "Wouldn't it be great to die in the middle of an amazing orgasm?"

"Wonderful," I agreed. "Like, while you were coming, you'd be going!"

She drew me to her, her eyes alight with good feeling. "Oh take me out to the airport, Joe, and I'll kiss you behind the hangers!" She gurgled then as the ride began, and I forgot everything, except Danny's finger in my face, and his words, "two months".

I didn't sleep that well. As I got out of bed, the black canopy of the night sky was turning salt and pepper and I felt every morsel of my own limitations. I lay for about an hour in a seriously hot tub, drinking from a coffee-pot we kept on a table beside the bath. I knew I was hanging on there in the bath. I kept adding more hot water and salts, pouring more coffee, smoking another cigarette. I was avoiding the simple act of getting out of there, putting on some heavy clothes so that I could get on with what I suddenly knew I had to do.

By the time I was ready to go out into the morning, the light had come up over the lake. October had just gone hibernating yet there was a hint on the wind that we'd see the sun for a minute or two by lunch-time. I wrapped myself up very well for the walk down to Glencree, stashing a couple of candy bars in my coat pocket in case I needed a sugar fix.

Being honest with myself, I knew from the moment my eyes opened that I had to take a walk down there. I was drawn to the bloody place, as though it was a magnet pulling me towards it. I was lethargic and hoping the early morning air would do me good, wake me up properly. I passed grazing sheep, nudging the hillside rising from the twisting ribbon of road, chewing the scutch grass, still enough to be ornaments on the landscape which seemed awesome after first-light.

As I neared the village, I was surprised to find seagulls circling since we were high up and eight miles or so from the ocean. I watched the gulls quit their manoeuvres against the distant canopy of cold-blue sky, admiring the way they dipped their wings to head off in search of something to eat. I wished them luck. This was not a plentiful place, not to my mind, not in any respect. But then it was impossible for me to judge it on its present merits. I was too caught up in its past and what had happened to my father and, as a result, to me.

I'd started going across the Featherbed to Glencree

shortly after my father passed away in 1970. This need to be up there in the hills grew out of whatever happened to me when I read Da's letters to his parents. A part of me had been rent asunder by what I came to call our shared pain. The nights I spent lying up there half-jarred in a sleeping bag did nothing to assuage my anger, but I still returned again and again to the mountain. I could say I went there to try and get in touch with my father, but I honestly don't know. I don't think I believed that Tom could communicate with me from the spirit world by osmosis, or some such thing. I just know I kept going back up, taking the bus to Rathgar, walking the climbing miles after Rathfarnham and up through Kilakee, to go over the vast bogs on either side of the Military Road.

I shudder as I recall the mornings after those cider-drenched nights, seeing a sad fucked-up kid of sixteen or seventeen, not so dangerous with his fists at the minute, dying from a hangover from the bottled scrumpy that hardened drinkers in Wexford Street called Madman's Soup.

The thought occurs that the scenario I was playing in at that time was tailor-made for a guy who liked to get drunk on cider, a kid born with enough anger and madness to give him an edge when it came to being dramatic. I can't say now that I was aware of this at the time. I was so fucking angry I could hardly think, especially when I lay up there under the stars and heard my imagined screams of kids being fucked and brutalised.

The nights before these wretched mornings I thought I was hearing the cries, the cacophony made by young boys in the throes of sexual abuse and mindless brutality. In this madness, I was tortured by the sight of my father as a young lad, his own blood running down the back of his legs. Only later did I realise the cries were my own. I wept like a demented person. I'd say I was mad at times, demented enough to feel imprisoned in the open space of the deserted, early morning mountain and tortured for answers to questions I could scarcely form in my ragbag mind. On my final morning up in the hills, just days before I left Ireland to go to America, I heard a cry of pain unleash itself from my mouth. A piercing stab, like a fierce electric-shock in my lower-back almost threw me across the hillside. It was like the ten-year-old Tom suffered inside seventeen-year-old Joe, having somehow connected with the agony of his father.

Some twenty years later, on this morning in November 1992, I was observing seventeen-year-old Joe back there on the hill. I observed his sad physical state as he released his cry of agony, causing me to gag on my own chronic lower-back pain – some kind of mortal-blow out of nowhere. Taking great care of myself, I managed to sit down on a rock that seemed to grow out of the green mound I'd been standing on. I inhaled deeply on a Gold Flake, staying with the smoke and the nicotine for a full half-minute, before I even tried to work out what was going on.

By the time I finish the Gold Flake the pain has gone and I'm able to lurch away from the spot. I need to lie down really, turn off my head and just chill-out completely, but my mind has other plans for itself. It suggests that the gist of the painful recall is trying to tell me something, help me see something and deal with something so buried I haven't the slightest glimmer of what it might be? I've no idea what it's about, not even today twenty years on, as I walk up the hill away from the reconciliation centre, going home to Lough Dane.

After my father's death, I'd found his birth certificate and I'd used that to help me discover that his parents had both died within five years of his incarceration in Glencree reformatory. My paternal grandparents had become terminal drunks. This fact I unearthed when I found some of their old neighbours in the inner-city. They had been burned to death in a doss-house fire. "You shouldn't upset yourself that they suffered," the old neighbour woman said sadly, meaning well, trying to help me. "They never drew sober breath in their last years, everything they ever had gone on the cursed drink, God save us all. So they surely died without feeling pain."

I try to let it go, all of it, for the present anyway as I set out for the lodge. I drag my attention back to the road under my feet. I listen to the sound of my boots on the stony surface and I count the steps for a minute or two, something I've done since I was a kid as a means of shutting out things that were bugging me.

Last night, I had considered running off with Dervla. Just take off, get out of here, kiss Ireland's November good-bye without a word to anyone. On the mountain road as my legs found their strength after the chronic back-pain, I thought of that nineteen-year-old who ran away and kept running until alcoholism brought him to a standstill lying on a Brooklyn pavement. I stopped and looked down over the valley, and in the moment I knew I wasn't going anywhere. I'd split before to no avail. This time I was staying put. There would be no more running for Joe Collins, the kid from Kevin Street.

14

Lough Dane, County Wicklow, November 1992

Telly's doctor had said he wouldn't need another bowel probe for twelve months, which was very good news. At times though, he seemed dispirited. I put this down to Carol's demands. They were, when she wasn't 'out of it' on cannabis or whatever, incessant. The truth is that she treated him like a servant. She would call down to him when she was upstairs lying on the bed reading the latest fashion magazine, "sweetie, would you bring me a cup of hot chocolate?" Or it might be, "sweetie, would you bring me a pack of those tissues. I think they're in the kitchen." Five times out of ten, as he was halfway up the stairs with her hot chocolate or whatever, she would remember something else she needed. He would acquiesce without demur, but I really disliked how she took advantage of his good nature and decency. I could see that the same thing crossed his mind in recent times. She was too stoned to see it, too consumed with her self to be aware that she was driving him away with her constant demands. I lost count of the nights I sat in the living-room while he went up and down stairs, dancing attendance on her. I felt I would have kicked her arse for her if she treated me like that. I was never a gentleman, you see.

In seeking a way to quit feeling guilty about my growing resentment to Carol, I realised that there had never been enough of her for me to really get to know. The nice easy-going behaviour between us meant nothing. I tried to let go of my resentment. I don't think I made it, though I did spend some moments chastising myself for thinking, "if she was my wife, I'd keep her stoned to keep her quiet. I'd keep her out of it".

Telly and I were having lunch in town. It was an occasion for me really, because I tended to stay up in the hills far from the sadding crowd. He just wanted to talk a bit about booze so that we could remind ourselves where we had come from. I was glad he'd called me. We didn't see enough of each other since I'd gone to live with Dervla, although we did hook up two or three times a week on the telephone.

He'd been great about my leaving the house at Whiterock. My flat was still there of course, since I was a partner with him on the property. Anyway, we were closer than any couple of brothers I'd ever met.

He said he was close to the end of this tether with Carol. She was doing more and more drugs and she was having more and more accidents around the house. And she'd been taken ill in town several times recently. On two occasions he had to take her straight to the drug unit in Jervis Street. Each time she was kept in for several days while they detoxed her. And each time they recommended that she take a full-time course of treatment, in an effort to detach from her addiction. Carol said yes to everything until she got out of there, then she forgot all about the advice and the recommendations. The medics had told Telly that she would die before long if she didn't quit taking drugs. This didn't come as any great surprise to him, but Carol was no sooner home before she was stoned again. Telly believed he had removed every drug that she had stashed about the house, but there is nobody more cunning that the alky or the addict when it comes to hiding their stash.

Telly had found large quantities of shit and grass, several grams of coke, some bags of smack, and endless cardboard drums each containing five hundred DF118 codeine-based pills. "If the cops had raided the place, I could have been arrested as a supplier. Can you imagine? I've thrown out thousands of pills, sport, and I do not exaggerate. I just wish I knew where the hell she gets them. Somebody is indulging in criminal behaviour giving anybody a thousand pills like that at any one time. She never got them on a prescription, I know that much. Paddy Fahy won't give her prescriptions for drugs. He told me himself, she's so into pills that she could get high on vitamins. She's blowing her mind, sport, and there isn't a goddam thing I can do about it." He sounded really down, defeated.

Right there as Telly and I left the lunch table, I decided to ask Champion if he could help me find out who was giving Carol the DF118s. Even if I found out, it could add up to diddly-squat, but I felt I had to do something to help the best friend I ever had. And maybe help Carol, too, though I wouldn't have bet on that.

I'd intended to mention Danny Devine's threat to Telly, but I decided to leave it for a few days. He had enough on his plate right now. When I got home, I called Champion and told him about the DF118 problem. He said he'd get back to me before long.

While Dervla and I are having dinner, she asks me about 'the contract' I was talking about in my sleep last night. She goes on to wonder is it part of a plot for a thriller or something. She is looking right at me and I am so stunned she knows that something heavy is going down and she's waiting for me to give her an answer. I hadn't intended to tell her about Danny's threat, but I couldn't lie to her. She sits there impassively as I tell her the story. "He was probably just flexing his muscles," I say, not believing this for two seconds.

Dervla drank water and took my hand. "He's crazy. He's always been obsessed with this vision of a united Ireland. You know he'd frame a ha'penny right! Well, he'd donate his fortune to 'the cause'. I swear it. Even give his life. He'd give his life to bring about a thirty-two county republic. I'm not waffling when I say he's a madman when it comes to partition. That's why he wants Gary's money. Which he knows he'll never get unless I go back to Gary and stay married to him."

"How do you know this? How long have you known it?" I had to bite my tongue not to ask her, "Are you serious?"

"He's fanatical, and now it sounds like he's crazier than ever."

"You're saying we have to take the threat seriously?"

"Believe it." She ignored her food and lit a Gold Flake. "I didn't want this job with JC. Now I'm going to take it. Can you live with that for a while?"

"Sure, if that's what you want to do? But you make it sound like it has something to do with Danny's threat."

"JC allows Danny to indulge the fantasy in his own mind. He's too smart to get into this shit. JC knows the only solution will be through the political route. He gave up trying to make Danny see this. I'm going to have to get his help here, see if he can get the old man to wise up and back off. I mean, Jesus! If, by some mischance, this madness got off the ground JC would be held responsible. Everyone that matters knows Danny is his number one. It's amazing JC hasn't got wind of this latest episode. He's unpredictable, even irresponsible, but he's not an idiot!"

"I suppose even Danny will listen to the Taoiseach."

"It's like his brain is rotting away or something. Danny's, I mean. Like, this is total madness. You couldn't make it up. And he's serious, believe me. JC can surely get him to back off. I have to give it a try. My God! When I think that he could even consider taking your life. It's mind-blowing."

"I've got an idea or two of my own about how to deal with this. I've got a very heavy friend in this town. So don't you take the job with JC unless it's something you'd enjoy, OK? You're sure JC wouldn't be part of what your father's into?"

"Positive. But, being around him, I can make sure. I can handle him and as it happens, I'm very good at spinning bullshit into gold thread. I want his help. He wants mine. Quid pro quo! Joe, I want this to work out the right way. I once said to you that we'd always be together, even if I had to kill Daddy to stop him wrecking us. God forgive me, I know now that I meant what I said."

"Come on. Don't talk like that."

"I know. It scares me too. I've just called my father a madman for thinking of taking your life, and here I am vowing to do the same to him if he goes on thinking he can rip us apart. I'm as crazy as he is."

The Alcoholics Anonymous meeting at Rathfarnham was just starting as Dervla and I got there so I led the way to the only two empty seats, which were in the front row. I didn't know the guy who was 'chairing' the meeting, but I liked his style right away. He was on the small side, with a weather-beaten face, and eyes that had been there and back. He was neatly dressed and his hair was pomaded to his head, and he had the sound of a guy who was in love with sobriety. His name was Lenny and he ended his fifteen-minute story by remembering his wife, and how she had endured his alcoholism. She had never given up on him, refusing to quit loving him, until cancer took her from him shortly before he found AA and sobriety.

"I remember two things above all else. One morning, I came into the kitchen and I spoke to Kathy. She answered me without turning to look at me, something that had never happened before. I said something else, she answered me and the same thing happened. My wife didn't turn to look at me. I went to her, and I turned her around to face me and I almost collapsed in shock when I saw Kathy's lovely face. It was black and blue in places. One of her eyes was closed from a beating someone had given her. Can you imagine what this did to me? I loved this woman more than anything on God's good earth. I would have given my life that she might live. She was the beginning and the middle, and the end for me, except when the booze got me. I went crazy, wanting to know who did this and demanding to know who had beaten her, swearing I would take his life. Her silence, and the pity I saw in her bruised eyes, stopped my voice. 'It was you, Lenny,' she said quietly. 'You were drunk last night. You beat me up.' She said the words without judgement or anger or anything, and I thought I would choke to death, drown in my own shame and self-hatred."

Lenny paused, and I could feel people holding fast to

tears that needed to flow, as did my own. There were no tears, no self-pity in Lenny's eyes. He lit a cigarette and when he exhaled, he said quietly. "The other time I remember most of all, was when Kathy was dying. We both knew she had no time left. My heart was broken. She was the better part of me." He drew deeply on his cigarette and nobody was disturbed by the sound of women weeping, and men sniffing back the tears in their macho way. "Kathy took my hand and she asked me to promise her I'd never drink again. Which I did, I promised with every ounce of goodwill I could find in myself. 'I'll never drink again, darlin'. I swear it on my love for you.' When Kathy died, I just wanted to die myself. But do you know what I did? I went into a bar for that mythical packet of cigarettes, and I was stinking drunk for a month. I'm here tonight to tell you this much. Knowing what I now know, if I were in that situation today, there is no way I would swear off booze for the rest of my life. Because, if I made that promise today as I did when Kathy was at death's door, I would be setting myself up to drink again. 'For the rest of my life' is too much for an alcoholic to take on. The alcoholic cannot handle it. And mercifully, thanks to what we have learned in this fellowship, we don't have to take on anything we can't handle today. We aim to live without taking a drink just for today. If the thought of a day is too long a time to manage, we can aim to be drink-free for an hour or a minute. We can deal with manageable proportions of time. Why take on any more than that, when there is no need? So, a day at a time, or an hour at a time, we stay away from one drink and we go to these meetings, and we need never again abuse ourselves and our families with the disease of alcoholism. I thank you for listening, and I open the meeting to the floor."

The room was filled with sniffling and coughing, and then by a very un-Irish round of applause, a lengthy appreciation of the speaker for the honesty of his sharing. Applause is the norm at AA meetings in New York, but the Irish in Ireland are very humbled by their alcoholism. They keep their heads down more than you'd believe. So Lenny had touched them deeply for such a spontaneous show of emotion to sweep shyness and whatever out of the road. Nobody said anything for a couple of minutes. The group needed a little time to blow its collective nose, recover from the exposure to such courageous honesty. I felt some movement beside me and I realised that Dervla had raised her hand, indicating that she'd like to say something.

Lenny acknowledged her and Dervla said, "This is the first time I've spoken at an AA meeting. My name is Dervla and it's four months since I decided to give sobriety a try. So far so good, in that I haven't had a drink in that time. By the time I was sixteen I knew that drink and I weren't good company for each other, but I was taken by it from the first jars I ever had. Within a couple of years I wasn't interested in anything unless there was a drink attached. Later, I would claim that I preferred theatre to cinema, as an art form. But the truth was that, well, cinemas didn't have a bar and they didn't have an interval. I became promiscuous on drink – I wrote-off cars and I more or less stopped caring about my mother. I left home at eighteen to go and live with my father – my parents had separated – and I rarely even thought about Mammy. My father was a busy man. He had never been what you'd call a family man, so I could do what I liked provided I didn't get in his way. I've since realised that I moved in with Daddy for that very reason. I wanted to be free to drink and carry on and my mother would not have tolerated that kind of behaviour. That's how much I was hooked into booze and the behaviour that, in my case, came with the heavy drinking. I realise that I am an alcoholic, and I'm very grateful to be here tonight. In particular, I feel very fortunate to have heard your heartbreaking story. You've given me great encouragement. In such a short time, the people of AA have helped me realise so much and I want to say thank you, to all the people in AA."

On the way home after the meeting, Dervla was very quiet and I let her be. I took her hand and she responded with her fingers, and I felt she might have come in a bit closer to the fire. To quit drinking is one thing. To admit your alcoholism is another. To accept your alcoholism, that was the big one. Only time would tell if Dervla had come that far. Later as we just cuddled each other on the way to sleep, I felt closer to her in the heart than I had at any time since we'd been sharing the same bed.

Champion rang me early the next morning to take a rain-check on our lunch-date. "I'm heading for 'the smoke' for a few days. I'll give you a bell when I get back. The face you're after is Aidan Harcourt, known to his intimates as Shivers. He shakes slightly all the time unless he's got a skinful of brandy. It looks like he's shivering, that's where the nickname came from. I know a bird works for him. He's sex-mad so she says and she said he's, is it priapic? I had to write it down. Would priapic be right?"

"It would be," I laughed. "Has the guy got a permanent hard-on?"

"That's it so. He's got 'the popcorn' all day, but she says he's got the same brand of halitosis as the Liffey and no mot'll go near him. Even the brass around the Green won't shag him, so yer woman says. Now, I don't know how accurate this is, but it's the best I can do info-wise till I get back from Stepney."

"You're a gem, Champion. And I'm looking forward to our lunch."

"Nice one! Here, before I split. I kept in touch with your boxing career over in the States. You were lookin' very good there for a while. I thought you were goin' to go all the way."

"Trouble was I got in a fight with John Barleycorn. And I lost. So career prospects went out the window. In a nutshell, I blew it." As I told him this, I realised it was like talking about someone else, or remembering an old movie. It just didn't matter any more.

"The fuckin' gargle! Mr Bleedin' Barleycorn! He's knocked out bigger blokes than us. I'll see you when I get back."

Next morning, Dervla and I drive down off the mountain. She is meeting her father and JC and I'm going to talk to Shivers Harcourt. Shivers works in the Fabulous Farmacy on Dawson Street. According to Champion, word has it that Shivers owns the business, hides the fact because he's scared of being kidnapped by gangsters masquerading as revolutionaries. As you may have decided for yourself, Shivers is not a well man. But when you considered the way Dublin was shaping up, he could have a point.

"It's God's way of punishing him for supplying Carol with all those pills. It's really criminal the way he just gives her what she wants." Dervla was thinking of the drums of DF118s that Telly and I had found stashed in Carol's bathroom a couple of days before. We had thrown out two similar cardboard containers just last week. We knew for a fact that she still carried a heap of these things around in her handbag. During our dinner party as Lough Dane, Dervla picked pills off the floor every time Carol had gone to the bathroom. Poor Carol. She was so out of it she didn't even notice when she dropped ten or fifteen pills every time she took a hit.

"I'd been thinking myself of asking you to go and see Mr Harcourt about this pill thing," Dervla said as we sat at a traffic light.

"Could you say that again?" I was so stunned I got a blast from the guy in the car behind me who thought I'd nodded off to sleep at the green light.

"What?" Dervla wondered what I was talking about.

"Are you telling me you knew all along that Carol was getting her DF118s from Shivers Harcourt?"

"Sure. She told me about it weeks ago," she smiled. "I didn't say anything because I guessed Telly knew where the stuff was coming from. Carol told me yesterday that Mr Harcourt tried to slip her some tongue last week. She said he had the breath of a rhino."

"She told you that?"

"Isn't there anything we can do? To really help her quit abusing the drugs, Joe?" I did well to conceal my surprise. It was the first time in our months together that I'd heard her express any concern for Carol.

"She's been out there too long," I said, trying not to sound like a know-all. "Part of her problem was the money. She always had the bread she needed to buy all the booze and dope she ever wanted. My guess is it's impossible for her to come back in out of the cold."

Leaving Dervla to her fate at the hands of her father and the Taoiseach, I went to the Fabulous Farmacy on Dawson Street and asked to talk to Mr Harcourt. A woman called Angie Parker, her name-tag confirmed she was the manageress, told me that the boss was in St Patrick's hospital with a suspected hernia. I gave her an old-fashioned look and she shrugged 'what can I tell you?'

I told her that her boss had been shovelling pills into a friend of mine. I gave her Carol's name and address. I gave her my phone number – she knew who I was from some recent publicity for the paperback of *Pity Not The Dreamer*. I also told her that unless she confirmed to me that there would be no more pills to Mrs Sampras unless they were on foot of a doctor's prescription, I would create such a scandal that the business wouldn't recover from it. Angie got the message and guaranteed me the matter was over and out. "I'll talk to his wife. She'll put the fear of God up him. He's mad about your woman, Mrs Sampras. She's very nice, but God help her all the same."

15

Wicklow, December 1992

The need to write usually woke me after six hours sleep. I felt so lucky that the scribbling was also my hobby that I usually went to work in a relaxed mood. I just loved being there when the words were coming through, aware that much of what I needed from life came to me along with the pictures arriving through my fingertips. After a couple of hours I'd eat some oatmeal flakes, washing it down with mugs of sugared coffee. I cut a lot of wood into logs for the fire, wallowing in the physical exercise. Initially the early-morning mountain-air caused a tightening in my chest until I got used to it after a few weeks of living in the hills.

I'd take a hot and cold shower and head back to the desk, writing until Dervla let me know she was awake. I'd fix a breakfast tray for her and take it upstairs, glad to do it, willing to help her ease her way into another day without booze.

Mornings gave her a lot of trouble during the first couple of months dry. She could be crazy in an instant, for no apparent reason. It was a very tough time for me. Like a fool, I'd expected that just because we were together in our love-nest at Lough Dane, her trip to sobriety would be a lot less fractious than it turned out to be. Many mornings were so dramatic it was like being in a way over-the-top stage play where the heroine was a mixture of Blanche Dubois and Lady Macbeth. Sometimes, I believed that Dervla's quitting of the booze was just too much for her to handle. She got so upset on this particular morning because the toast was cold or some such fucking thing, that she went into a tantrum and threw some kind of fit that was powerful enough to make her pass out. I swear. She was out of it, her face so pale and still – her lovely face was like a death-mask cast in alabaster. I seriously thought she had died. In that terrifying moment I felt my life had just run out of road.

I believe I was weeping for my lost love when she opened her eyes as though she was waking up from a light sleep. When she saw me she threw her arms around me and kissed me passionately. She moved so that I would lie with her and in a minute we were there again, joined in every way we knew how, grabbing the ecstasy of being alive together, unable to give any thought to the fissures in the structure of our relationship. We seemed incapable of seeing anything that lay beyond the perimeter of lust, laughing like drains after the orgasms that vulcanised us to each other. We were like a couple of drunks who were blind with it.

This scary episode happened about three weeks after she had started working for Jay Charles, but I knew this had nothing to do with the new job. Her road to recovery had, from day one, been littered with irrational behaviour. We had also lived through some minor car accidents, all of them caused by small errors of judgement on Dervla's part. I put all this down to being off the drink. So this latest episode seemed like nothing more than the growing pains of the newly-recovering alcoholic. She was going to be fine. This was my overall response, my hope, and I was going to stay positive, even if it killed me.

At lunch-time that same day, as Dervla was about to head into town for a meeting with her father and JC, came the moment to shatter this perennial fucking optimism of mine. The day had been blustery from first-light, which comes late in the hills in December. Around mid-morning it had developed into a choppy angry kind of day and I felt a storm coming on. On reflection, it might well have been seen as a harbinger of what was to come between Dervla and me.

She was going into Dublin for a late-lunch meeting with her father and the Taoiseach. I was looking forward to a day of uninterrupted work, a day I owed to the book I was working on. A weeding day that I needed to give to the manuscript, which was bogged down by a plethora of information the reader wouldn't need. A barrow-load of unnecessary facts had pushed two of my characters off the board and I was about to tidy up the vegetable patch. When I find stuff like this holding up the story, it amazes me that it has happened again. But then the entire writing process has never been anything but a mystery to me. I've no idea how it happens and I've no wish to find out.

I see Dervla back the Range Rover out of the parking area, glad we have this big four-wheel-drive jeep. She turns the tank around and I see that her judgement is erratic. This surprises me. She's a gifted driver even if she goes too fast all the time. I step out through the French doors to check she's OK. When she sees me at the driver's window she looks annoyed. "What?" she barks, ready to defend her driving.

"I came to kiss you good-bye again," I lie, opening the door. I lean up to her as she tetchily brings her mouth down to mine. I give her a long kiss, a warm and loving kiss, and then I step back and look into my favourite eyes. Right away, I can see that this bothers her. I can also see why.

"What's going on? Why are you looking at me like that?" She gives me a withering look. Is she ever pissed off with me?

"Something's not right." I'm concerned enough that I have to confront her, but I have to go gently here. Dervla doesn't take well to anything that smells of criticism. As I ponder on the best way to answer her, she gets truculent.

"What the fuck, are you suggesting?" Her dark eyes jump from dull to a brief flare-up.

"I don't think you should drive right now."

She wants to slap me, but relents. "OK. I forgot to renew my barb prescription. I'll do it in Rathfarnham. I'll take a couple in the chemist shop and I'll be light as a feather by the time I get into town."

I almost step backwards from the shock that hits me. Barbiturates? In the instant, feeling like I've been slapped very hard, I realise this is how she deals with her painful morning wake-ups. So many awakenings when she faced the day with pain-crushed eyes I'd leave her to her breakfast tray, only to be happily-surprised to find her pretty together within an hour or so.

As I leaned into the jeep, I knew just how she could come downstairs so soon after a deadly wake-up, bouncing and smiling like she hadn't a care in the world. Like ducks eggs and dexedrine, breakfast and barbiturates will do that for you, no problem.

Dervla laughs nervously at the expression on my face. "Lighten up, Joe, it's only a funeral." She sounds light and easy, but it's an act. Once again, I have to take a moment. She gasps with impatience. "What? You look like you've been hit by a fucking train?"

"You're taking barbiturates?" My voice croaks out of me.

"Jesus Joe! What's wrong with that?"

"You never mentioned you were taking barbs. Jesus Christ, Dervla! That's just popping the fix instead of drinking it."

She looks so shell-shocked she just might not have known this. Tears bowled into her eyes. "Joe, Jesus! I didn't know." Fear spread all over her now. "Oh, Jesus. Joe! Don't tell me I have to give up the few barbs." Her eyes roll back to my face, stopping long enough to see the answer right there in front of her. Tears trip off her eyelids. She draws a vicious sniff of air like she's inhaling defiance, shakes the tears away, telling me without the kid-gloves, "No. Fuck it! It's too much. I won't do it. I swore off the booze and I've stuck to that. Nobody ever said anything about having to give up everything. I'm going to town. I've had it, Joe. Sorry. Fuck it!" Her voice rises on an escalator of fear and I know that unless I do something right away, she's going to drive out of there. I lean in and turn off the engine, pulling the keys out of the ignition. She tries to grab them, misses. But she gets a hold on my hand and she isn't about to let it go. "Give me those keys." Her eyes blaze with fury now and her voice let's me know she isn't going to be fucked about here. I pull my hand away and step back. Before I know it she throws herself out of the driver's seat to land on top of me. I fall backwards onto the gravel, providing a nice cushion for my lover, who is anything but loving. She tries to tear my hand open to get the keys.

I throw the keys away from me towards the open French

doors of my workroom, and she makes a move to go after them. I sit up and grab her by the shoulders, willing to give her a good shake to stop her acting crazy like this. She turns back to me so fast I don't see the punch she brings with her and it lands on the left side of my face. She tries to nail me with a left. I parry it with my right hand and I follow through, slapping her hard enough to stop her cold. Her eyes open wide on a cry of anger, amazement making her gag for a second before she yells at me, "You hit me you bastard! You fucking prick!"

She launches herself at me again, but I roll her around and in a moment I'm hauling her up off the ground, ready to smack her before she draws off on me. She kicks me so hard in the shin that I hop on one leg. She kicks my other leg from under me. I break my fall and am up on my feet as she bends to pick up the keys for the Range Rover. I put my foot against her beautiful ass and I push hard enough that she falls in through the open doors and onto the office floor. As I come in she is rolling onto her feet, but I grab her and hold her with my left hand. I stiff-arm her, pulling her this way and that – a show of strength designed to discourage any more of this bullshit.

In the face of my physical strength, her madness wanes. I turn her around and push her down onto the sofa, holding her there. She is breathing like a bull that needs to gore somebody real bad and her eyes look like they're being broiled. She might be coming out of a bad dream. But she's a tiger and I'm taking no chances. I step back.

"You're a tough broad. And you kick real hard. You only get one. After one kick, the Marquis of Queensbury goes out the window."

She glowers at me and I swear to God, she looks more

beautiful than ever. "You fucking hit me?" She is so astonished, I laugh out loud.

"You've got the balls of a rhino. Jesus! I'm trying to save your fucking life here. You drive out of here as crazy as you were just now . . . You hit that mountain road the way you drive, a fucking sheep runs across your path, anything . . . You go off the road at speed. The Rover could turn over ten or fifteen times on its way down."

She gets up off the sofa, a broken-cry tearing out of her. She falls against me, her arms wrapping about me protectively, her tears raining on me, her mumbled words of love and devotion lost in the rumble of her painful sobbing. Her kisses and her sweat and her body are saying it all, without me really hearing a single word.

In a minute she comes to the end of her weeping. I hear the sniffs and the clearing of her throat. Finally she says in a voice shaking with emotion, "Oh God! Tell me I haven't blown it. I love you so much. Jesus! I went crazy there for a minute." I hold her tightly to me, refusing to give way to the inner-voice that's yelling at me "get out of this, get away from this fucking lunatic". I have no defence against the charge that she is a fucking lunatic. But the words "leave her now while you have a chance" fall on deaf ears.

"I'm not sure I can give up everything." Dervla sounds stronger, gathering herself. "I'm close to saying I can't. But I don't know that, not for certain, not for dead-certain. But I am sure, I'm sure and I'm absolutely dead-certain that I can't make it without you." She moves out of my arms while I try to take a time out from the words, and the thoughts, and the aches and the bruises in my mind and my body. She comes back to put a lighted Gold Flake between my lips. The smoke gives my nervous system a reassuring pat. I

watch Dervla inhale, looking for the nicotine hit. She is a
mess facially, but a thread of honesty riding in her eyes
suggests she's not playing games.

"You don't owe me anything. If you have to walk, get
away from the kind of mad-woman I can be, I won't blame
you or try to stop you."

As I sit facing her in my workspace, I'm still recovering
from the shock of her attack, her viciousness in the fight. It's
one thing to talk about someone being wild and impetuous,
even a little crazy. It's something else again when you're face-
to-face with the fear and the anger that has the power to
turn someone you think you know, into a total stranger. I
was in over my own depth, led by the ring through the nose
of my desire for her. But when you boiled it down, I knew
very little about Dervla.

"What you're saying is – you go Joe, if you want. What
you're not saying is that you'll be on the bottle before I get
as far as the Featherbeds." I look at her through a curtain of
smoke and I realise I've never considered her deceitful up to
the moment she laid it on me that she's been dropping
barbiturates from day one.

"You're probably right," she conceded without any need
to waffle on about it. "Joe?" She hesitated, unsure of what to
say next. I was angry as hell with her really on account of the
barbiturates, and for having the sheer fucking effrontery to
attack me and kick me in the fucking shins. This had scared
me badly, reminding me of the damage I did to guys who
wanted to take my head off, in and out of the ring. I
shuddered at what might have happened had I been as out of
control as she was when she knocked me flat on my ass. I'd
been crazy in the past and I hadn't been handed any written-
guarantee that my madness had left town for keeps just

because I took John Barleycorn off my Christmas card list.

"How did you do it?" She spit some tobacco off the tip of her tongue. "I know you've told me. Perhaps I wasn't listening properly. You have to forgive an old tart that falls in love. She's not likely to be thinking of anything beyond getting her guy into bed. OK?" She found a wan smile, her eyes wary as she tried to keep her emotions under control. "What did you hear? What bit of magic did you get touched by that you have come this far – over three years without taking even one fucking drink? Or one poxie barbiturate!"

"This isn't the first time I've quit drinking. That being said, it was Telly. When Telly came and found me lying in the street, it started right there. I was shell-shocked, knocked into some kind of sobriety from hitting the footpath at speed. I could think clearly enough to see – well, I knew then I was a pretty hopeless case."

"But you weren't," she insists. "You're here to prove you weren't."

"I'm talking about what I knew in that moment. And like everybody who says 'I know', of course, I knew nothing. Self-pity is a blindfold, the worst part being that you go and find the scarf you tie around your own eyes. You re-run the hit-and-runs, you go back in your mind to the scenes you ran away from. Like me, back then. I was calling myself a shit because I lied to my mother as she lay dying of throat cancer. You know what an alky can do with that kind of script. Ten, twelve, fourteen days when I was off somewhere drinking so much. I didn't even know I had a mother, let alone a scared, lonely old middle-aged woman who was still alive. Did I care? How could I care? I didn't even know she was there."

Dervla handed me a fresh Gold Flake and I used it to take a breather. "This was terrific practice, a crash-course in the 'poor me' syndrome. It came in very handy when I blew a fight career they said could go all the way. Blew it because I thought I'd have just one drink on the day of my most important fight. Just one I remember drinking. When they found me I was unconscious. I had to be pumped out. I'd taken a handful of sleepers, something I'd never done in my life."

"I wondered what had happened to your fighting career," Dervla said, exhaling smoke. "I think you are amazing. To battle back to sobriety after hitting such a low."

"What's scary is I still don't know why I had to take that fucking-bullshit just-one-drink on that day of all days. I wasn't scared of the fight, of my opponent. You always feel a little fear. That's healthy. I expected to knock the guy out. I welcomed the possibilities a good win could open up for me. I hated pills, still do, but that's the problem with the disease. When you let that madness out of the box you can't legislate to it or instruct it how to behave. It goes its own way. The fact that I took sleeping pills while I was bombed out of my tree proves it to me. That's where the disease directs the action. You can't expect to understand that it's going to shift the goalposts without dropping you a note."

I press on. She has got to be feeling pain, maybe identifying with some of this. I feel nothing that I'm aware of. It's like sitting through another re-run and using the rewind button to help her see just how low she could sink, if she didn't throw in the towel.

"If you don't want to go for it, ultimately that's your decision. But, if you run now your life can go all the way downhill. I've told you this stuff because you asked me how. How did I stay off the booze for just over three years? The simplest answer I can give you is because *I want to be sober*.

I want to have as normal a life as I can find in whatever time is left to me on this planet. If you decide to start over, Dervla, begin by asking yourself 'Do I want to be sober?' If you want it you can give it to yourself. You can't buy it for ten million dollars. But you can earn it without spending any money. It's priceless, but a pauper can have it at no financial cost. Sobriety can be yours and mine. To get it you just have to *want it*."

I need to get a fresh cigarette going. Dervla is quiet, but attentive. So I press on. "'I want' is the fence a lot of us can't hurdle. To actually say 'I want it' – wow! That brings tears to your eyes. All I can tell you is this. I feel I was touched by some loving power, some universal force if you like, in the shape of Telly the Greek who hauled me up off my ass on Flatbush Avenue."

"Recently, you talked about surrender? Surrendering? What was it? Can you remember what you said?" She shrugs an apology for her jaded memory.

"Say for example that you're a hotshot professional boxer." I grin and touch my face where she had planted a good one on me. "And you might just make a good one," I say, smiling at how easily she caught me with that right-hand. "OK. You're now regarded as good enough to fight Muhammad Ali. OK? OK. He beats you up real bad before he knocks you out. You have a return clause and you go in again to fight him. And he beats you up again and knocks you out again. So what're you going to say to yourself? 'This guy is just too fucking tough. There's no way, and there's never going to be a way, I can beat him.' After you realise this, are you going to ask for one more fight with a guy you couldn't beat if he was tied down? I fought John Barleycorn for more than ten years. And don't forget, I was a trained boxer with eight good professional wins under my belt. And JB knocked me out of the ring every time I got in with him. In the end I had to surrender, throw in the towel and say 'OK man! You're too tough.'"

Dervla is not a happy sight. Her face is a broken map of confusion and fear. She draws on her cigarette, but it doesn't get rid of the disbelief in her eyes or soften the reluctance to accept this that rides on her mouth. She shakes her head, exhales in search of relief from the nervous tension that grips her. Her face changes and I realise that she can't actually believe it's possible for her to come out on the far-side of this awful time. I see the girl-child who looks lost and scared in her pre-teen innocence. A young-one with courage to burn, yet scared to immobility and paralysis until the moment when her tears start to slip off her eyelids and she whispers the words, "I want to be sober. Help me to surrender."

I take her in my arms, cosseting her like you would a young person you'd want to be good for in every way. She is inert in my embrace, like someone so bereft of energy they can't move their arms to wrap them about you. "I have to surrender." She sighs, the words barely audible. I hope that this might be a new beginning for her, maybe even a fresh beginning for us as a couple. I hope so, because I know I'm not going to walk away.

16

Wicklow, December 1992

I'd love to be writing that Dervla got the message in block capitals from the day she accepted that you needed to surrender in order to win, but it didn't work out like that. No way. The mood swings through the second half of December, Christmas in particular, were so severe that at times I thought she was going to crack up. I did what I could. I held her when I believed it was useful, I walked her up the hills and down the dales when she was so manic she couldn't sit still. I gave her all the sex she needed, and there were times when I thought, "I can't handle this," which, is some admission for a guy who thought of himself as a sexual athlete. She was insatiable at those times. But worse than that, she was so angry that you felt that in facilitating her need, you were somehow condemning her to more of the same kind of pain.

On manic days she is saying she won't go under, and fuck all that surrender shit. She will beat this the way she beats men, by controlling the scenario. I shudder when I realise that the pattern her sex life had followed was what she intended to use as a blueprint to get sober. I asked myself what lay ahead for us. When Dervla was fucking some guy she was always in control, instructing them when to move faster or slower, or with more power or whatever. Our initial breakthrough about surrender and my ongoing effort to keep this up-front in her mind – all of it had gone for nothing. Her wilful nature needed to feature in everything she did.

Alongside all this aggro, we were somehow living an ordinary life. We shared our home. I did my share of the chores without any bother. I was handy around the house, a by-product of fending for myself since I was a kid. I could cook some, though toast and coffee and orange juice was all Dervla would allow me to play with. She had a reputation as a cook and didn't want anybody stepping on her trip. She shone brilliantly in the culinary department. Every morsel she produced bore the stamp of a real master. And she wasn't drinking.

I forgive myself for getting tense at times, as the date set by Danny Devine for my departure from Ireland draws very near. As though Dervla and her daily dramas aren't enough, I have to put up with this madness from her fucking father as well. By the end of December I should be gone. This is the gospel according to Danny, and I find myself wondering what star I was born under that I have to deal with daughter and father at the same time. Let me assure you, you'd need to be in the whole of your health.

Through Champion I've come to know that no UK hit-man has come to town. My old foe is connected to every major bad guy and villainous family in England. These people don't move into someone else's territory without honouring the code of behaviour agreed between them. Since Champion is the main man in Dublin, he is on top of the real stuff information-wise. Yet, even though my premature demise doesn't appear to be imminent, I'm bothered by the possibility that I could be shot every time I go into Dublin.

As Christmas approaches, I've tried to talk about this to Dervla. She has just off-handedly told me not to concern myself, that nothing is going to happen to me. When I asked for more, keen to know what made her feel so secure, she said she'd tell me in a few days, but meanwhile, relax. I'm still trying to do that, to just chill out and forget about Danny and his latest brainstorm. Meanwhile, it's Christmas so I ask Dervla what's the story with her family about the whole yuletide trip.

"Mammy's going to Florence with my sisters. Daddy and Rachel will be down at his place in West Cork, so we don't have to concern ourselves with family. I thought we might invite Telly and Carol up for dinner on Christmas Day. They could even stay for a night or two, unless you'd worry that she might set the place on fire."

She was referring to Carol's nocturnal habit of falling asleep while she was smoking a joint. Telly was constantly throwing out blankets with half a dozen burn-holes that might well have caused a serious fire in the bedroom. "Let's just offer them dinner," I said, having enough anxiety of my own to handle, despite the good word from Champion.

As my main Christmas present, Dervla presented me with a formal agreement between herself and her husband Gary in relation to a financial settlement on the cessation of their marriage. The sum involved was two hundred thousand pounds and she was suitably pleased at the prospect of such an unexpected windfall.

"What's this all about?"

She smiled at me and mockingly pushed her breasts up under the boob tube she was wearing. "Am I just a knockout? No way. I am a brilliant little minx, not seriously educated but far from stupid. Gary is in love, he wants to get married, ergo he's prepared to collude with *moi* on the story. It's true as it happens, that from day one he and *moi* drank our way through our courtship, that he knew I was an alcoholic, that we were both langers at our wedding, that I was not a fit person to commit to matrimony, etcetera, etcetera, etcetera. This was in the air when I told you to quit worrying about Daddy and his threat to you. Gary had already asked me to help him get our marriage annulled."

I saw a subtle change in her eyes. It was only there for a moment, but it prompted me to ask the question. "How did it feel when Gary laid this on you? How does it feel now?"

"If I was drinking, I'd probably have done a big number with this. I thought he'd carry a torch for me forever," she smiled wanly. "As it happens, I'm getting sober and I want more of the same. All I have to do is find some magic way of handling the mood swings. I'm still assaulted by them. I know I'm going from likeable to lunatic like some kind of schizo. I don't let you see all the stuff that I deal with . . . scared I might send you running for the hills," she laughed. "That's if you weren't in the hills already."

Within days, Dervla confirmed that she'd told Danny the story and shown him the settlement agreement. "He wasn't jumping up and down, I can tell you," she said with a shrug. "But he won't be bothering you about getting out of here. JC says I'm doing a good job for his image, that he wants more of it. He told my beloved father he wants me kept happy. He wants me to stay. And, if you don't mind, the last word was

'Dervla's a better person these days'. Imagine JC talking like that!"

"I told you when you put down the glass – it can only get better. Remember."

She threw a grimace my way. "Oh yes, I especially loved the bit when you said 'when you're hurting you're healing'! That was so comforting."

I said through a grin that wouldn't quit, "You think Danny's going to back-off his need to snuff out my lights? Really?"

"Daddy was pissed-off at having to tell me this, but even he listens when JC tells him, 'I want you to tell Dervla what I said.' Of course it's rough on him – a major blow to his pride that any daughter of his has joined Alcoholics Anonymous. 'Don't you be telling those people your business at those meetings,' he says like AA members are a disease. 'Drink doesn't suit you, Dervla, but you don't belong with a bunch of alcoholics and winos and Christ knows what else, most of them without two pennies to rub together.'"

She made a conciliatory move with her hands. "I'm sorry, Joe, that my father is such a head-banger. He can't help it. Born mad, I think. Obsession and madness beyond the normal run-of-the-mill lunacy you get in this country." She smiled wryly, "Try not to hold it against me." She started to sing with a really cheeky look in her eyes and a leer on her mouth that might have been painted there. "If I said you had a beautiful body, would you hold it against me?"

She had moved from fear that I would blame her for her father's insanity, to a sexy minx who suddenly needed to get laid. It was the same thing, day upon day, mood-swings to scare you and to corrode even the most steadfast resolve not to just run away from it all. An ironic thought, when you consider my resistance to Danny's efforts to get me to split, even when my life seemed to be depending on me hitting the road.

Of course, we attended AA meetings on a regular basis, ate a meal with Telly and Carol at least once a week, went to the movies or the theatre once a fortnight. Dervla brightened many a foyer with her amazing looks and her sense of fashion, which was costing even more money than it had done when her husband Gary was picking up the tab. Without wishing to sound pejorative – she was a high-maintenance broad.

Dervla's thirty-first birthday fell on the last day of December and though I waxed happy and enthusiastic, I really felt that my innards were ageing before their time. Even as I wished her a happy day I was sighing with regret, seriously close to the end of my tether. I was weary from playing leading-man in the melodrama of her battle to get sober. Come on! Nobody in his right mind was going to expect someone as large and as volatile as she was to ever make life easy for herself. But I had hoped for easier.

On New Year's Eve we headed to Whiterock for a quiet birthday dinner and New Year celebration with Telly and Carol. Dervla wasn't happy about being thirty-one years old. She wanted this as low-key as possible. This included the birthday present bit, which had always featured large in her life. All she wanted was a platinum ring, which I'd dutifully provided. Telly had bought her a magnificent scarf and her family would impart their gifts when they all met on New Year's Day.

She was morose, gloomy rather than ill-tempered during the drive down off the mountain through Enniskerry, and onto the main road for a pretty direct run through to

Whiterock. During the afternoon I'd suggested we might go to an AA meeting before we went for dinner. "Oh! For Jesus sake, Joe! It's New Year's Eve." Her eyes registered, 'Shit! What have I said?'

"Holiday times can be tricky for us, especially in the first year or two. The world and his wife are celebrating, which means they're drinking booze, and here we are going to celebrate with people who drink coffee and Diet Coke."

"That wasn't what I meant," she sounded contrite. "It's just that, it's just that life used to be so much fun." She stopped and looked at me. "Oh shit! I'm doing this all wrong."

"No you're not," I said, trying to keep my anger at bay. "Life was so much fun for me that I ended up in drunk-tanks, doss-houses."

"I'm sorry, Joe. It just doesn't seem fair. I'm thirty-one years old and I can't even have a glass of champagne to celebrate it, or drown my sorrows. I don't know which is getting top-billing at this minute."

She remained mercurial for the rest of the afternoon. I heard her singing loudly while she was fixing her hair, but by the time we were ready to head off she was putting out a very heavy vibe. "We don't have to go to Whiterock. They'd understand."

She got into the car without response and I wondered how many young women in Dublin that evening felt down and miserable and even ugly, in a sable coat and a casual party-gown that had cost a thousand pounds. I let her be for the car ride. I felt fed-up, even discouraged, that my aim to help her out of the doldrums had come to nothing.

I parked the car outside the house in Whiterock and headed for the front door. Just as I expected she would,

Dervla tugged at my sleeve. I turned to face her and she said in a quiet voice, "Make me smile as Telly comes to the door."

Part of me wanted to tell her to fuck off and grow up, but she had to be in some kind of pain to need the help she'd just asked for. No matter where we went, it was almost always the same. As lovely as she was, a head-turner in any language, this young woman couldn't relax enough to walk smiling into a room of people she knew.

She hadn't been to the house for a couple of weeks and she immediately noticed the living-room makeover. Carol's larger-than-life rose-covered wallpaper had been traded in for plain-honeyed pastel lining paper with caramel clouds here and there. There was a new off-white sofa with tailored cushions, in pale caramel, the chairs big enough and deep enough for an average person to curl up in. The rugs strewn about the ballroom-sized parquet floor were a mix of the colours already used by the makeover artist, Vanessa, who had been around the place for some weeks making sure the work was being done to the highest standard. Telly had been raving about the lady's talent and when I saw the finished picture of the living-room I knew so well, I had to agree she was a gifted woman.

"I met her while Eugene was coiffing me last month," Carol said in her off-hand way. "Just by talking to her I knew she had talent." She drank coffee with her usual slurp. "I told her on Christmas Eve, 'Sweetie, I just wish you could make-over a New York blonde who's losing out to gravity.'"

"Stop that," I said, being gallant. "You're gorgeous."

"Sure, sweetie," Carol cackled. "Nobody lies like an Irishman." Her face dropped. "Things are going south on me. I'm going to be doing handstands by the hour, at the rate the boobs are heading for Mexico!"

At an early stage in the evening, I went into the kitchen to fetch ice-cubes. I found Dervla taking a toke from a joint of Acapulco Gold – Carol's favourite grass. Carol was well-stoned already since she'd been hoovering weed into herself since we got there. The norm now was that she would have been doing drugs of some kind all day. Willing to appear sophisticated, I buried my fear-driven anger and just got on with the business of getting an ice-tray from the fridge. I was mad, mad at Carol for her part in the scene, mad at Dervla for sneaking behind my back like that and mad at me for, for what? For getting involved with another man's wife in the first place, especially one who seriously needed help. As I put the ice into the bowl on the living-room table, it seemed ironic that I remembered Telly saying something like, "You're free to go for it, sport. Once you're willing to pick up the tab."

Telly was sipping coffee and he looked about as happy as I was feeling. I sat down facing him across the American-style living-room. "OK, sport?" He gave me a wry grin that turned him into the handsomest guy around. He was either fifty-one or fifty-three, he refused to be specific, but he claimed at very regular intervals 'thirty-nine and holding'. For a moment I was tempted to tell him what was happening in the kitchen, but I let it go. Why bring him into it? Why give him any more ammunition to shoot at Carol. He was mad as hell with her at the moment. She was acting defiantly. Carol was normally extremely contrite, but she was into such a cocktail of drugs just then, that she could be mean and hurtful, not at all her natural way. She started dropping remarks that he was living on her money, that he might find a little gratitude instead of 'starring as the fucking master sergeant around here'.

When Dervla came in from the kitchen she immediately came over and sat on the great puffed-up arm of the chair I was sitting in. She leaned in slightly and kissed my head and her fingers were soon on the back of my neck. I wanted to shrug her hand away, but I let it go. In about a minute I realise that she's as loose as a goose, softer than I've ever known her be. She and Telly are dancing to Edmundo Ros records he's loved for thirty years. They're simple songs, easy samba rhythms to service his wonderful dancing.

"Me and George Raft," had been his initial response when I first complimented him on his style. The pity of the moment was that Carol, who loved to dance in her own crazy way, was out of it and already snoozing in one of Vanessa's wonderful creations.

As I watched Dervla slip even more into tune with the fun of the samba beat, I heard her sing along with the sandpaper voice of Edmundo Ros. It was like witnessing the death of the fucked-up young woman who never knew how she would be behaving one minute from now. This newcomer was full of beat, laughing so easily and with such a glow of happiness about her that I had a lump in my throat. Dervla had been going from hot to cold in an instant since early June – one minute fun, the next frigidity, from buddy to bitch, from lover to louse, and expecting me to take it or leave it. A guy would need to be the most selfless saint that ever lived, the original paragon of peace and love and virtue, to go on and on living with this kind of sickness. Even your most charitable heart would surely harden through the fear that you were going to go under, that your emasculation would go all the way if you didn't help bring about the change needed before things could possibly get any better.

As we were leaving, Telly held my coat for me, while

Dervla was using the bathroom. He was working at appearing content. All in all, I felt we'd come into the New Year on a good vibe. When I said this to him he shrugged compliantly, still flushed from the sambas and the rumbas. "And you like Dervla," I said aiming to stay light. "What more could I ask?"

"She's a beautiful gal, sport. A gem if ever I saw one." He gave me another New Year hug. "I love you, you bastard!" He chuckled and punched me playfully in the chest. "You hold onto her, y'hear!" He glanced over my shoulder as though he was making sure we were still alone. "I need to talk. Tomorrow, if you can spare a few hours."

On the drive home, I was feeling peaceful enough, like I was beyond emotions for a while. I felt good as I drove through the village of Enniskerry up onto the winding road to Lough Dane six miles above. Dervla has her head snuggled into my shoulder and seems so peaceful in herself, I don't need to say anything right now.

"Are you mad at me for sharing Carol's joint?" she asks in her 'please don't be mad at me' voice.

"No, I'm not mad." This is true in the moment. I've no intention of telling her how mad I was earlier when I caught her smoking weed.

"I've never felt like I feel tonight, never in my life before." She is curled up kitten-like inside herself. Her voice is tension free, her sound wrapped-up in present-moment bliss, the peace that being good-stoned wraps you up in. "Two or three tokes of American grass and all the pain, all the fears and the hang-ups – all of them – they were all gone in a minute. Surely there can't be anything wrong with having a joint or two a day to help me feel normal?"

She sounds so mellow, her plea for understanding so very

reasonable that I can't argue with it. And in the moment I realise I don't want to argue with her. And I don't want to reason with her, lecture her, guide her, cosset her or save her from the pain she's been standing in line to grab with both hands. I just want some peace for more than a minute at a time.

A blind man could have seen that the joint had helped her have an enjoyable New Year's Eve. Personally, I'd been expecting her to be tight as a drum, trying but failing to lose the resentment she was feeling at having to be dry on her birthday. Instead of which she had, by sharing one joint, been set free of all that was getting in her way. I'd never seen her have such a good time, be so relaxed and, it has to be said, such delightful company. And, my God, even more attractive than she usually was, which was really saying something. I was fairly stunned at the enormity of what had happened and I make no bones about saying I wanted more of how she had been and how she was right there in the moment as we drove up the winding-road towards the moon sitting on the mountain.

There was no denying that, for all my inward protestations at some of and even lots of her behaviour, I was insanely in love with this woman. I heard the word 'addicted' on the fringe of my mind and I had to shuffle it out the door. Let's not dramatise it, I said to the busybody in my head. What's happening here is too good to cast a shadow on. We could have a chance of a terrific life together, I reasoned. A life I want, a life I want living with Dervla if only that can happen without the pair of us killing each other. I want that and I need it because regardless of the madness parading in and out of our heads at times, we are bound together, and I don't just mean at the lips and the hips.

"I know I've been some kind of basket-case for months, Joe. I don't know how you put up with me. No," she stifles my response with a gentle kiss to my hand. "Let me say it. I came to the belief I couldn't do it. Giving up the barbs was just too much for me to take on. And I hated you for insisting I do it. OK? We were doomed, Joe, if I went on as I was. Without you, there is no us, and without us, I wouldn't want to go on. So, not to make a federal case out of it, I want to smoke a little grass. And everything I do, I can only do in comfort if you're there with me as my partner."

In the moment the feeling was that we really were the two halves of one whole. If you ignore the times during the last few weeks when we'd hated each other, we were deeply into a forest of feelings and the stuff that bliss is made of.

"You know I have loved you since I first laid eyes on you, right?" Dervla sounds so laid-back I find myself smiling in quiet joy and glorious, noisy relief.

"I believe every word you tell me. So yeh, I know that." My smile floated onto my mouth, the better to taste since it was free of irony.

"Well, I feel so much love for you right now, it's like I've found a well inside that I didn't know about. Whatever I felt the last time I told you 'I love you', it was nothing compared to this feeling right now." Her head moves off my shoulder and down onto my lap. In moments she has me flying to join the mountain moon as the Range Rover is climbing towards the stars decorating the New Year sky.

As we arrived back at the lodge she embraced me by the hall door. I held her tight, feeling so close, wondering had gods just gone laughing somewhere at the madness of people who can't grasp the simple fact that love never seeks anything, unlike "in love" that does nothing but cry, 'I want, I want'.

Dervla interrupts my philosophising in a quiet voice. "Joe, I hope you still want to help me find the 'terrific woman' you say I can be. I honestly believe we can use cannabis and grass to help me get really healed from this fucking booze thing. I'm not talking about abuse, addiction. I'm talking about two adults using common sense, using the smoke so that we can live together without me driving you away. It's like I've found an answer, a perfect compromise. But it's not going to be any good to me unless you're there with me."

There's a lot I could say to this, a lot I should say, but there is no word, no slogan, no sentence or paragraph I can produce that's going to give Dervla even a hint of the feeling she is filled with right now. I only have to look to where she's at. Where she's at is where she wants to be – her choice. I don't give her any kind of argument because I don't want to. I acquiesce to her proposition, knowing I need to be with her just as much as she needs to be with me.

I can allow that I need her mellow and bliss-filled and warm and loving, as I can admit that I've had enough of her mercurial madness. She has driven me half-crazy at times and that I have had enough of that.

Later, as I get into bed she passes me a joint from her handbag. As she does this she is putting on white stockings and a garter belt. She knows that this sight of her takes all of three seconds to turn my tackle rampant. I can't take my eyes off her elegant hands as she stretches the sheer nylon sheaths over her amazing legs. I watch her slip into a silk gown to sit on the side of the bed. She puts her hand under the covers and gives me a grope, chuckling in appreciation. "Wow! Look what I just found." She laughs incorrigibly and goes to work on me with those pianist's fingers but forgets all about the job in hand when I pass her the joint. She doesn't even bother trying to look cool as she sucks a toke into herself and holds it down like she's been doing it for a hundred years.

She is looking very much her own lady, as though she's had an important new part fitted to her mind. She gives me the roach and I take a deep toke and hold it down in my stomach. Yes indeed. I hold that baby down there, feeling my veins and my nerve-ends sigh with pleasure. My feeling of well-being expands in a nano-second so I don't even wonder if there's anything wrong as we devour that first joint together before we segue into love-making.

As I put my mouth to her, it's like every decibel of sensation is being amplified by the Acapulco Gold. I taste the nectar of her need, feel her thighs caress my face, aware of being one with her in the sheer pleasure of being alive right now – no truck with the past, or the future. And I'm so pleasantly stoned I actually chuckle as I hear in my mind the words 'There is no right or wrong, but thinking makes it so'.

17

Wicklow, New Year 1993

On New Year's morning as I take the breakfast tray up to the bedroom, I tell myself I'm prepared for anything. What this means is that if Dervla has come down to earth with a bang I'll try to help her around it. I won't stand there in judgement laying down clichés and slogans like 'every front has a back' or 'there's no such thing as a free high' or any other useless fucking observation to someone in pain the morning after.

Lo and behold the lady is awake, and showered and sitting there looking forward to her breakfast, her eyes zippy enough to assure me she hasn't had a toke this morning. I play it cool, as though her warmly casual greeting is just like it always is. I kiss her before I head for the shower and she is so responsive and loving, I feel I've been presented with a new Dervla.

So, our first New Year together begins on a warm sexy note, and I'm all for that. During the long morning of beautiful sex she is more giving than I've ever known her to be. She has always been a tigress in bed, but she was too demanding and bossy a lot of the time, always trying to run things just the way she liked them, all of this adding up to 'I want I want, I want it my way'. Now she seemed to have added a bit more *give* to her performance without even knowing she was doing it. And it was pretty damn good from where I lay and by the feel of her, pretty damn good where she laid me. Afterwards, we're very close in every way, wallowing in the convalescence of this gentle togetherness. We share a joint, the sunshine filtering through the curtains on the French doors touching our lives, as I take a couple of beautiful hits.

Telly phones to tell me he's just turning into our driveway: "With fresh doughnuts and Danish, so put the coffee pot on."

I'd forgotten he was coming up to talk so I slipped into a pair of jeans and a sweater, stuck on some loafers and went downstairs to do what the man said. I was in the kitchen when I heard Carol's voice which surprises me. Normally, she didn't put her feet on the ground before one o'clock, but then what constituted 'normal' around her these days, was anybody's guess.

She's still wrapped up in a muff of contented sleepiness to go with her mink coat. She's wearing enough jewellery to buy County Wexford and she greets me with a warm hug. "Hi, Baby Bear! Gimme a sexy hug you big brute. Mmmm . . . Yeh, nice one. That'll keep Baby Doll warm while Grumpy Guy beats your ear."

Within minutes of their arrival she is tucked into the corner of a huge armchair in the living-room before a roaring fire. I give her coffee and Danish, the same for Telly, and I take a plate up to Dervla who pulls a face. She holds the phone out to me so that I can hear her mother's voice firing on all cylinders, the woman hardly needing to breathe.

These mother and daughter calls usually take forever, Eithne Devine being the only woman I'd ever met who could talk the hind legs off a chicken. By the time I get back downstairs, Carol has scoffed her snack and is now beginning to snore gently before the huge fire. I yell up the stairs to Dervla telling her that Telly and I are taking a walk, well-prepared that she might well be still on the line to her mother when we get back. Eithne always brought to my mind that old quip about particularly gabby females – 'She was vaccinated with a gramophone needle!'

Telly and I reckoned we'd settle for an hour's walking in the fresh cold air of the January day. We head down the rough gravel path towards the beach at the inner end of the lake. The water to our left is the colour of oily tin, tumbling hummocks of land to the right of our path supporting birch and beech trees. Closer to the house some tired elms, bereft now of their leaves like distant candles in late autumn, brave the new day of the year with its new wind-chill. It's the harbinger of the snow that we were guaranteed at fifteen hundred feet above sea level.

The land was littered with the droppings of sheep and goats and deer. The mountain might have been throbbing with the slumbering breath of a million hibernating animals. Birds are few around the lake, even in summer. His majesty the falcon's royal presence, no doubt responsible for this.

As I stop to light a Gold Flake, I notice Telly's out of breath even though we're walking downhill. I ask him if he's feeling OK. My guess is that the chill in the air has tightened up one of two of his pipes. It still happens to me occasionally in the early mornings until my pipes get out of bed and realise they are out there on the mountain.

"I'm going into hospital in a couple of days. It's the bowel thing. Another check-up, a set of tests, is all. It's been on my mind for a couple of weeks."

"Fuck you!" I say with meaning. "We have a deal. And sitting on shit like this, if you'll pardon the pun, isn't part of it. You'd be mad as hell if I was in trouble, and I held off on telling you about it for fucking weeks."

"I nearly didn't tell you today." Telly grins and blows some of his fucking menthol smoke my way. I jump back like I'm avoiding being hit by a car. He has a laugh before he carries on. "The doc says it's just a routine procedure, so forget it for now. That's not what I want to talk about."

I stop. His tone has grabbed my attention and he turns to face me. I stand looking at him with the dark mound of the mountain's foot like a bruised tumour looming behind his head. "What the fuck're you about to lay on me? What can be heavier than getting your ass reamed?" He chuckles at my expression and I say: "By the way, if they find my 1954 Chevvy parked up there, turn the radio off and send me the keys." We get a good laugh out of this line and I think that maybe it's our way of dealing with something that could be a very heavy trip, even if the medics palm it off as routine.

We go back to walking down the hill, turning left onto the beach to cross the end of the lake and get onto the path at the mountain foot. It's the one the goats use to come down to the water. Telly stops to grind out his cigarette underfoot and he says, "I'm in love, sport."

It's all too clear that he hasn't rediscovered his original feeling for Carol – this much I knew for sure. The way they've been behaving towards each other the last few months had been reading like the writing on the wall for the Sampras marriage.

"I kinda hope you're kidding, but I know you're not." I

light a fresh cigarette, looking down the lake. It was starting to wrinkle as the mountain drew some wind down from the peaks above. "And whether you know it or not, you make it sound very fucking serious."

"That's because it is serious, very serious."

"You're not sleeping with Rachel, are you?"

"I'm flattered you think she'd give me that pleasure, sport." He reflected on this for a moment, like he was enjoying the fantasy.

"So are you going to tell me who it is?"

"It's Vanessa."

I go 'Vanessa' several times in my head before I remember. Vanessa's the interior designer, the makeover artist. I'd met her a couple of times, just saying hello, while she'd been giving Telly's pad a facelift. She's about forty years old and attractive, if you like demure. Would you believe house-wifey? And the very last dame on earth I would have thought likely to get into an affair with Telly. I'm astonished that someone who looks like a future president of the Irish Countrywoman's Association has that much gall.

"Jesus!" The exclamation just jumps out of my mouth. "The makeover woman. I thought she was married with four or five kids."

He throws me an old-fashioned look that says he doesn't need a comedian right now. I hold my hands up in apologetic surrender.

"Her husband's been gone three years." He lets go more smoke. "She's never heard a word from him since he went back to Pakistan. Her two eldest boys are teenagers. They'll be off her hands in a few years. The other two are all right kids." He stops, like he's realised he's trying to sell me the story.

"Can we back up here?"

"Nothing's going to change the way Vanessa and I feel for each other." He gives me a heavy look to go with the verbal warning. "I expect you to understand."

"Just hold the phone a minute, will you? I'm just getting over the shock here."

"I wasn't looking for this to happen, sport."

"Yes, you were."

"Now wait just a goddam minute."

"Nobody's saying it's crazy for you to be in love with a grass widow with four kids, even if it's fucking off-the-wall-bananas-and fucking cream-crazy. What really scares the shit out of me is what're you going to say next."

"You know something, sport? Just for a second or two you sounded like you did at that first meeting in Brooklyn – all piss and vinegar." His hand shakes some as he gets another cigarette going.

"I just wasn't expecting this. I'd no idea you were having an affair."

"It's not an affair. Don't call it that."

"Oh, pardon my rhythm! It's not an affair." This was about as bad as it could get. Meanwhile he's murdering the cigarette while he stifles the urge to murder me.

"May I ask? Are you and Vanessa into fucking yet?"

"We don't fuck. We make love."

I thought 'Oh Jesus! This just gets better and better!' What I said was, "OK, sorry. Let me just check I've got this right. You are 'making love' to a woman who is not your wife. At the same time you are still living with the lady to whom you are married. Pardon me being so precise. I just don't want to tread on your sensibilities, OK?" He snorts down his nose.

He wants badly to punch me out. I take a deep breath. "You're in a relationship with the lady, OK. Is it your intention to keep things as they are?" A negative answer to this question is my big fear and Telly doesn't keep me waiting for his response.

"I'm going to leave Carol," he says it real short. "Not today or tomorrow, but I'm going to go. I've taken all I can, and I feel entitled to a little happiness."

I make inroads into my cigarette. I'm giving myself time to take this in. I have to think about what I'm going to say next. In thirty seconds I'd moved from 'I hope this is as bad as it can get' to 'Jesus! Where the fuck is this thing going'?

"Will you do something for me?" I ask.

"You ask me to walk away from this, I can't do it."

"Come on. What do you take me for?" I lie. Would I ask him to walk, run, ride a bike? Does a fish swim?

"What I'm asking you to do is take a time out – no major decision for three months. Just put 'I'm leaving Carol' into cold storage for three months. Create a little space for both of you. We can keep talking about it. And maybe we can get back to talking about booze more than we have been the last few months."

"I don't know if I can do it." He kicks a stone in anger and for a split second a destructive flicker distorts his eyes, something I'd seen many times in the long months we spent staggering along our own highway of busted dreams.

"I just don't think you can do this to Carol. Not right now," I say calmly, knowing that I'm talking bullshit. You couldn't blame him if he rolled up his tent and ran away from her this instant. For months I'd spent some time every day wondering how he put up with her incessant demands and even worse, the zeal with which she worked at wiping herself out. When you considered that Telly was a huge part of the world she was trying to escape from, wasn't that some kind of statement about their marriage and their life together?

"Listen, sport. You and me not talking about booze like we used to, it's not all my fault." He sounds hurt, and I feel guilty.

I'd always considered Telly and Carol as a couple, they had each other. But thinking about it there by the lake, it struck me that there wasn't enough of his wife in place for her to be any kind of real partner. Carol coped because she could afford to support her needs. However you dressed it up, Telly was an appendage to the unreal life that had become real to her – the life where the next hit was first choice and in the crunch, the only one.

"I didn't mean to sound like I was blaming you, Telly." I faced him straight-on, wanting him to see that I meant what I said. "Jeez! I'm so jammed into this relationship that's part magic and part fucking-madness. Talk about the agony and the ecstasy. My head's been so gridlocked with emotional stuff, I can hardly hear Socrates any more."

"Snap!" Telly said, the disdain in his voice directed at himself.

This thing with Socrates, it had been a just fun thing that helped us now and again. The idea was that guidance was coming from the great spiritual misfit who died because he stuck to the truth, appealing to the romantic in a couple of drunks. We had identified the great gadfly as the sound within. He'd had this voice that told him, ergo us, when a certain thing ought *not* to be done. Sure, we're talking here about the gut feeling that never lets a man down, even if he has trouble walking and talking the truth, like chewing gum and clapping your hands at the same time.

"Hey! Come on, sport. Don't go over the top on me. We have feelings, we have needs. Some guys, like you and me, we maybe need more than most guys, whether it's booze or broads, or whatever. It's not a criminal offence to fall in love." I say nothing and his voice flipped its shoulders in a shrug of admittance. "Sure, I accept that if you want something you gotta give something. And if you want to hold onto something you gotta let something else go. Jeez, sport. Any guy with a pair of balls would be willing to let go of everything else for a gal like Dervla. Most guys would give their life for a woman like her."

"I'm not saying a word against her, or against you," I assure him. "I'm not putting myself down, either." I hammer the point home. "But you and me, we made a deal, a pact, and it got us to a place we thought we weren't fit to reach. However we staggered, we made it to an oasis of sobriety in a Sahara of fucking pain and fear and delusion. We got a miracle is what we got. And we'd hardly pitched our tent before we start falling in love. It was like we couldn't wait to jump back into the 'I can't live without you, baby' script, while we're still in diapers AA-wise."

Telly didn't speak, so I pressed on. "And here we are facing a new year and stepping into the fourth year of life without fucking booze fucking it up. We're both in pain, sweating shit and bricks to try and keep 'the relationship' going. Jesus! We have to come up against a crisis like this to remind ourselves how long it's been since we just talked about booze, which is how we got sober in the first place."

Telly let go a long conciliatory sigh, "It's not a crisis, sport. Is it?"

"Not yet it isn't. But it will be if you don't listen to me. You leave Carol right now and we'll be going to her funeral long before you can start waking up with Vanessa every morning."

I lit another cigarette while I tried to act more upset than I was actually feeling. Anything to shift his attention however slightly, get him to disentangle himself from what he wanted for a few moments. I was hoping he would get back to seeing the bigger picture, which would include all that he had to lose.

"I know what that would do to you," I said flatly. "You're too good a guy, too big a man to walk away from that one without wishing you were dead yourself. Jesus! Sure, Carol is a fucking nut, but we've always been there for her. We can't pull that rug out now. I believe she'd kill herself." I stopped, scared to go on, but then I got an urge from somewhere and I heard the rest of it come through. "Think about it, man. It's only three years or so since you were so in love with Carol that you took on the barracudas Betsy Catlin called her legal team. I was there, man. I saw and heard you walk all over those motherfuckers and that fucking mother. What was it about Carol inspired you to act like that on her behalf? Whatever it was man, surely it's not gone up in smoke and disappeared forever? It can't be. It was too powerful to get lost because a little time has elapsed and you're so resentful of her, you feel entitled to go elsewhere to sink the log."

"You're wrong about the sex thing. Jesus! Of course I love the love-making I have with Vanessa. I might have blown eighty fuckin' million brain cells with the booze, but

I'm not short of hormones. But it's not just sex, I swear it."
Telly threw away the butt of his cigarette. "I feel so good, so
fuckin' tender about this woman. I just, well, fuck it, I just
want to make her life better, and it is better when we're
together. She tells me that all the time."

"I remember you telling me the same thing in Manhattan.
Back when you fell in love with Carol. Shit! Why else would
you have gone to war with those fucking lawyers?"

"You're forgetting, sport. There was a hundred million
bucks or something they were trying to screw Carol out of.
And that just didn't seem right to me."

"So you wanted to make her life better by helping her get
what she was entitled to?"

"Fuck you, sport!" He looks mad as hell.

"Our vines have tender grapes," I say. "And you look mad
enough to try and kick me in the *cojones*."

"Let's walk." He turns and starts to go on ahead of me.

"That's the same as running away from what you don't
want to hear."

He turns back. "You're always so great with fucking
questions and the fucking assessments, sport. This time, can
you let me hear what you think the fuckin' answer might
be?"

"Who knows anything?" I say with feeling. "But here
goes. When you were fighting for Carol's rights, you were
seeing her in a certain way. You never kidded yourself she
was related to Mother Teresa and you knew she'd been
around the block on the 'Bob Hope' scene."

"She was like a wounded bird," Telly tells me though I'm
not sure he heard it himself. It was like a wisp of memory
sliding silently out of him, a sigh of chagrin for the loss of

something beautiful, something that didn't seem to be around anymore.

"You wanted to protect her rights, look after her. Personally, I thought she was too big a flake for any guy to take on. But when I saw you two, when I saw the love that was there between you, I would have fought for your right to be together. You had that to offer on her behalf and she had the need of you. How do you think you're looking at her these days?"

He turns to look at me and I can tell by the little turn-up at the corner of his mouth that despite his discomfort, he's glad we're having this talk. "I come out here for a walk in the fresh air and I end up on the fucking rack!"

"Just answer the question. How are you seeing Carol these days?" I stand there looking at him, until he finally releases his resistance, slips into a rueful grin.

"Come on," I urge him. "Quit fuckin' around. Answer the question."

"You could get a shingle as a shrink in Manhattan, you know that?"

"I'm in no hurry here," I say. "I've got the time and I'm a patient guy."

"I'm seeing her as a major pain-in-the-ass. I am sick to the teeth with her."

"In this clinic, you get to say that. So, don't stop now. It's just me and the mountain listening."

This gives him pause, but he slowly starts to nod his head – the suggestion seems like a good idea. "Let's walk a bit, sport. Not up the hill."

"It's not a hill, it's a mountain."

He gives me a hard look and I say, "OK! It's only a little mountain."

"Let's go," he says.

We walk along the narrow path that runs around the lake by the water's edge. I'm just a couple of paces behind him and he starts to talk. "Carol was never a bad girl – she was crazy, a flake from day one, but she was fun and she was manageable. She's become a fucking monster, sport. She is so consumed with me, me, me that she doesn't know if anybody else has a need or not. She doesn't know and she doesn't give a flying fuck. She is killing herself with drugs. There's no doubt in my mind about that. And all the caring, all the love I've shown her, it isn't enough, sport. It isn't anything like enough to make her even try and keep it down to smoking weed. You told it like it was. I loved her, wanted so much to protect her. Shit! I'd have killed those fuckin' lawyers. And fuckin' Betsy too! The mother from fuckin' hell! Callous bitch! I took Carol on when no guy in his right mind would have touched her with a forty-foot pole. I gave my life over to being there for her, making sure nobody ever tried to do to her what those *mothers* in Manhattan tried to pull. To put her away, Jesus! Keep her locked up so she couldn't embarrass them." He stopped and he was full of hurt. "She pisses in my eye every day of the fuckin' month."

He stops because he needs to regulate his breathing and I can see that regardless of the chill wind coming off the lake now, Telly is sweating. I stand there close beside him, supporting him with my every heartbeat. We've come to the end of the lakeside path, and I wait until he's ready to move on. We step over a little wooden footbridge that takes us out onto the Military Road. He takes my arm and away we go, nice and easy, and he starts talking again.

"No matter what I do, it isn't enough, nothing is ever

enough. She treats me like a butler who gets to fuck her when she feels she should act sexy for eight minutes, between hits. Like she's married right? And the guy, me, should get his ashes hauled, she should melt his fucking butter or he'll go get pussy somewhere else. She doesn't want me. She doesn't want anybody. All she wants is another fucking hit, and I'm not even blaming her. How could she want anything else when she's been a fucking junkie since she was sixteen years old? But I have had about as much as I can take. I want, I want, I want, is all she can hear in her fucking head. If I outlive her, I'll put that on her fucking tombstone." He stops, looks a shade embarrassed. "No, I won't. I was the schmuck thought I could make a difference because I offered her love. She was already beyond feelings in that sense. Drugs wipe out the whole fuckin' switchboard when you've been doing them as long as she has. Maybe she'll blow her fucking fuse box right off the wall with the next hit. God forgive me, but I won't shed any tears. It would be like she was doing me a big fuckin' favour."

He finishes with a sob that rips a hole in me. He stands there weeping with pain and frustration, and I take him in my arms. And I hold him while his guts spill out of him, listen to him as he releases the reiterating incoherence that is the by-product of self-criticism. I let him go, get a cigarette going, holding the light cupped in my hands to his menthol job. "I still don't know how you smoke those fucking things."

He exhales volubly and spits on the sand. "I started because I thought I wanted to live longer." His short cough condemns this idea to the rubbish bins. "Jesus, sport. I feel pretty weary right now."

216

"That was good, what you did. It took guts and you'll feel the better for it."

"So what're you saying to me, sport?"

"You did good."

We turn back on the mountain road, and in a minute we're walking back up the drive towards the lodge. The falcon comes into view gliding high on the wind, his span like an aircraft against the noon sky. He turns from tawny to black against the pale blue chill-filled umbrella over his head, wisps of cloud like a great chorus of diaphanous nymphs gaze on his passing. He unleashes that cry of his, and I laugh at the bastard. It's like he's showing us how free a guy can be if he keeps his zipper closed, and I brandish my fist at him and yell, "You're right, you fucker! You're right. This guy and me – we're fucked because we think we have to fuck, or we're nothing. We're cock-led and pussy-whipped and . . . ah fuck it!"

I watch him go and Telly smiles with that sardonic twist to his mouth. "I heard shrinks were crazy. So tell me doctor, what am I to do right now?"

"Do nothing. Say nothing. Make no promises. Make love, not promises. And just try going back to that place inside you where you were in love with Carol, you know, before you started judging her. Let's face it. She hasn't changed. She was a ball-buster from the day you met her. You thought it was cute then – now it's a pain in the ass. Well, it's like piles. It's a bother, but you won't die from it. And you're a big guy, you've been around, you know you can survive this. Just promise me that if you get into a hassle with Carol, and you feel you're going to give her both barrels, call me and say let's talk about booze. I want you to promise me that before we go back inside."

"OK, sport. I promise." He gives me a hug and I sigh with relief, letting him go on into the house ahead of me. I make a big deal of scraping my shoes on the metal rug outside the door as I shake my head in disbelief. It seems incredible that Telly hadn't even considered what he would live on if he left his multi-millionaire wife for a dame who makes over other people's houses, when she is not up to her ears caring for her children. Telly spends more on magazines and parking-fines, and lunches for him and Vanessa than most guys take home in their monthly pay-packet. I laughed critically at myself. What did I expect? Wasn't my beautiful buddy 'in lurve'?

Part 3

18

Wicklow, April 1993

Dervla had decided at some stage that she would take the 'fifth step' in the AA recovery program one year from the day she put the cork in the bottle. As her sponsor, and despite the fact we both smoked a little grass, I'd encouraged her to get into the twelve step program. I encouraged her to read the steps, even study them a little, with a view to giving her a serious focus point, as if being off the jar wasn't enough to handle.

As we went to sleep one night at the end of March, her last words to me were "I think I'm ready to tackle the fifth, Joe. Can we do it tomorrow?"

I mumbled, "Sure. If that's what you want, let's do it."

So there we were ready to rock the next day. I stalled about mentioning that it was the first of April – April Fool's Day – just in case this put her off. She seemed so gung-ho to get on with it that I didn't want to be a wet blanket.

The wording of the steps one to five were as follows:

In step one you had 'Admitted we were powerless over alcohol – that our lives had become unmanageable'.

In step two you 'Came to believe that a Power greater than ourselves could restore us to sanity'.

In step three you 'Made a decision to turn our will and our lives over to the care of God as we understood him'.

In step four you 'Made a searching and fearless moral inventory of ourselves'.

In step five you 'Admitted to God, to ourselves and to another human being the exact nature of our wrongs'.

The fifth is the first step in which the alcoholic has to enlist the aid of another person, usually their sponsor, to whom they divulge their shit. So it's easy to see why just about everybody would sooner sit in a dentist's chair. Dervla was no different to most of us, and I regretted stifling my initial urge last night to suggest that she make a final decision in the morning.

By noon we were set up, the drawing-room windows open to the morning sunshine and the shimmer of breeze coming off the lake. The forecast promised a warm-to-hot day, which I considered a good omen, until Dervla got cold feet. She came into the great Victorian room looking like she'd just had minor surgery, and I guessed she was having a tough time. "I don't think I can face it yet, Joe."

"You don't have to do it," I quietly reminded her. "Some people take years to get to the fifth. Others find a way to stay comfortably dry without ever getting beyond the first three. And others take just steps one and twelve, go to meetings and never drink again."

She drew heavily on her cigarette. "When I'm stoned it's as though I'm talking about somebody else. I can rattle off the list with the best. It's like it's all fun-and-games, and what harm in having a laugh about what a bold bitch I was, you know. But, to do it straight, to sit here and lay it all on you in cold blood, Joe . . . I'm really sorry, I just can't." She was close to weeping and I relented on my earlier judgement. Obviously, she was upset, but she was trying to stop the fear taking over completely. She left the drawing-room and I waited to hear if this really was her final decision for now.

When she came back in she was dressed for a walk outdoors. She put three leather-bound books in my hands. "I've put bookmarks in some pages you should read. Give you some idea of what I have to reveal. I'm going for a walk, hoping you'll still be my partner when I get back. I'll be about an hour." She kissed the top of my head and I let her go, because I didn't know what else to do.

I light a cigarette and opened the first journal. She had marked this one. "This is where it all started, really. I can't blame Dara. He was just a horny young guy. I led him on or it would never have happened."

◄○►

June 22nd 1977

"Dara Keely couldn't have had his langer between my legs if I hadn't given him a lot of encouragement every time Daddy told me to go in and help out in our shop in Rathmines.

"Dara's good-looking and he knows it. Whenever we worked together he was all over me with his eyes. My best friend, Janice – she is English, though her family live in Limerick, God knows why – Janice says all guys are the same. She'll be a doctor one day, I swear it. She reads and studies everything to do with our bodies and she knows just about everything about sex, though she hasn't been fucked yet.

"In the shop Dara touches me pretty much as he likes. He never says anything about this and neither do I. I like him touching me – his fingers passing over my bum while I'm serving a customer; the way he brushes his chest against my tits when he could easily get by me without it happening. It excites me when he does it and it excites me that he wants to do it. Like, no matter how I wish things were different, I am still a schoolgirl, even if I have been getting my periods for two years already.

"Imagine Mammy has never said a word to me about sex. She would have a fit if she thought I was even thinking about it. She's behind the times. Not her fault. Like, we all know what Ireland was like when she was growing up.

"On the particular morning I'm writing about, Dara pressed past me while I was stacking a shelf – we hadn't opened the shop yet. He had a hard-on and I didn't tell him off or anything for rubbing up against me.

"So part of what happened was my fault. He told me to go down to the storeroom and bring up a box of Kit-Kats. I went downstairs taking my time about it because I felt that something was going to happen. My throat was dry and my nipples were standing out in my bra, and I had just taken the box from a shelf when Dara was behind me. I dropped the box when his arms came around me. Then he was feeling my tits, like he wanted to be doing everything at the same time, and my heart was pumping and his hard-on was there like a rock at my behind. He had me so curious that when he turned me around I was wide open to him even though my legs were still tight together. He kissed me, and the thrill I got made me dizzy. Gradually, he worked his tongue into my mouth and I loved the feel of it there. In a minute it was halfway down my throat and I actually pulled him against me so hard he looked at me like he'd found a fiver. Then he was rubbing his prick against me and I was gasping for breath even while he was kissing me.

I was nearly weak at the knees, but I wanted him to keep on doing what he was doing. A part of me was reminding me we should have the shop open, but I wanted more of what was happening to happen and I didn't give a shit about opening the shop. It's easy to say now that Dara should have known better than be snogging with a young-one who wouldn't be fifteen until the end of the year. But, in fairness to him, I didn't feel fourteen-and-a-half and I was as hungry as he was to do what we could in the few minutes before we had to go upstairs and unlock the front door.

The thing is I had never been kissed like Dara was kissing me. What he was doing with his lips and his tongue, not to mention him rubbing against my crotch . . . Well, you could see how it could make a girl want to go all the way. In all honesty, I can say, hand-on-heart, that nothing up to that heavy-petting session in the storeroom with Dara had ever affected me in so many ways at the same time.

"Lads of my own age were eejits where kissing and groping was concerned. Most of them didn't know what their langer was for – so Janice says anyway, and I agree. Lads all wanted to get into your bra in the Stella cinema and grope your tits and maybe try getting a finger in down below. But they hadn't a clue, and though I tried really hard to get some kind of thrill from the snogging and the petting at the pictures, I never felt the slightest reaction down below.

"Whereas with Dara, well, he had started a circus of tingling down there with his first kisses and the way his fingers played with my nipples. So it seems reasonable that when this gorgeous fella of nineteen was interested in kissing me, I wasn't going to run away from the opportunity. The idea of trying to stop him never even entered my head. He had me held so tightly in his arms and his lips seemed big as chipolatas against mine, and his tongue was like a piece of velvet in my mouth. He was kissing me as if his tongue owned my lips and I got a huge thrill when my own tongue was responding to his. God, that first totally real snog. It was wonderful, and I felt such a sensation in my knickers that I gasped when he let me come up for air. Then I lay back as he pushed me gently against the wall, ready to go along with whatever he wanted to do next.

"His hands went down behind me and he was pulling me into him so that he was like a rock against me and he was rubbing against me and I had to fight for breath. Then I felt him fumbling down below and then his hand lifting my skirt and in seconds he made me open my legs so that he could slip his langer into the gap between my thighs. It was as stiff as a bone wrapped in something soft. It was there then, between my thighs, rubbing against the double gusset of my fucking school-knickers. Nobody will ever know how much the likes of Janice and me hated those fucking knickers with their double gusset as if you were going to wet yourself or something and you old enough to have periods. The shagging nuns . . . No, I'm not going to go there.

"Dara was so mad with the horn, that I don't think he noticed my double gusset. He pulled his tongue out of my mouth for a second, and he had my knickers off me in a flash. Then he was back thrusting his langer between my thighs, and I know I wanted to come off like you do on the finger. I was going so mental to come off that I heard a roaring in my head. I felt Dara's fingers down there, and the next thing I knew he had me open, trying to push his langer into me and me doing nothing to try and stop him.

"I had to be very far gone mentally, because I didn't even hear Daddy on the wooden stairs down from the shop. The first thing I knew about him being there was when he ripped Dara off me. He punched him, sent him flying across the stockroom with blow after blow, the poor fucker getting no chance to fight back. Going backwards, he raised his hands to ward off Daddy's attack, his langer gone limp, rapidly.

"I ran upstairs to the washroom at the back of the shop, rinsed my face and combed my hair, waiting until I heard Daddy throw Dara out onto the street. I heard him slapping him a few times by the door first, telling him he would kill him if he ever laid a finger on me again. 'Make it your business to keep out of my way,' Daddy said as though he was offering Dara good advice. 'If you see me coming towards you on the street, my recommendation would be to cross the road. If you so much as look at Dervla again, I give you my word as a gentleman. You will end up in hospital.'

"The door of the shop slammed shut. Then I heard Daddy open it again to start the day's business. I took a few deep breaths thinking 'here goes!' Daddy looked at me when I came into the shop, and he asked me if I was all right. I said I was and I saw a change come into his eyes, like he was seeing me for the first time. He told me then that I was growing up. 'You're no longer a child, Dervla. You'd want to be very careful not to let lads take liberties with you.' He asked if I knew what he meant. I nodded my head carefully, not wanting to seem too knowledgeable. If only he knew what girls were like these days, he'd have a seizure.

"Daddy said not to mention this to my mother – are you kidding me? He gave me a pound note to go and get my hair washed and dried, urging me to hurry since he had to meet some upcoming politician. Jay Charles, I think his name was.

"Luckily, Doreen Ryan who Daddy called 'the best shop assistant in Dublin' was coming in, so I knew there was no need to panic. She gave me a wink, the look of her telling me she'd met Dara on the street. I threw her a smile and she winked at me again, knowing well that I'd tell her everything that had happened, later."

―◇―

The entry closed here, and I shut the book. I was moved by Dervla's hunger, which was as virile as mine at the same age, and equally secret. The country was so closed down you couldn't discuss sex except with someone chosen with great care. A journal wasn't a bad idea, provided you could be sure the wrong eyes didn't read what you'd put down in it. All in all, I thought Dara deserved a good beating. Had Dervla been my daughter, I'd have given him something to remember me by. Sure she enticed him, but the guy shouldn't have let his randy nature get the better of him. Not with a fourteen-and-a half-year-old girl.

Putting down her journal, I rose and closed the windows. One of the local farmers was driving a lot of sheep up onto the free grazing on the hillsides around the lodge. I put a match to the fire I'd set earlier in the morning. The weather guy hadn't got it quite right. His 'warm to hot' day was not making it. Not a bad day for the first of the new month, with Al Jolson's 'April Showers' already moving in before a breeze snappy as an ageing corgi.

I sat there smoking and thinking about Dara and me. It's not all that far-fetched. He should have looked after the girl, used his common sense to deflect the desire that had dismantled her common sense. 'Like you did, when you became her sponsor, Joe?' The sentry is sarcastic today, and I try to ignore him.

The next journal entry she had marked could only be called a tabloid editor's dream. It was dated July 1989, and related to a sexual event and a political event, both of which involved Dervla and the man who was then Taoiseach – Jay Charles. This is what she had written.

–◄○►–

"Jay and I woke up at the same time and he had an erection to die for. 'Look at that, Dervla,' he said, practically grinding his teeth in delight: 'You could use that to whip an ass out of a sandpit.'

"I embraced it, loving the feel of it in my fingers. I gave it a good squeeze and I said, messing, 'As long as it's not all wee wee', knowing by the feel of it that it was the Real McCoy. 'I'll soon show you, my gerrel,' he waxed country, his accent of the bogs and the mountains, rather than the peaks and valleys of politics. He was chuckling as he came to lie between my legs, while I could hardly wait to welcome his massive prick into me again.

"We had fucked beautifully before sleep last night, but Jay wearing bravado like a new after-shave was something I recognised. Anyway, I knew why his adrenalin was rushing to a peak this morning. So, though I longed to feel him inside me once more, I wanted this particular ride to be the best we'd ever had – for him.

"When he left me he was going to face the mob. Not a mob of common riff-raff, not a march by strikers, nothing so manageable. Today's mob was comprised of the shaven and the shamed, the talced and the traitorous. I could just see them right now, many of them tanking-up in a private-room at Buswells hotel, fortifying themselves to cast their vote. They knew that no matter how badly many of them wanted JC gone from the helm of the party, they were taking a desperate chance in denying him their support. Like Lazarus, Jay was uncommonly gifted in the process of resurrection.

"'Brace yourself, Bridget,' he smiled at me as he pressed his magnificent limb into me. I wrapped my legs about him, opening myself in every way I knew how, wanting all of him, every breath of him, caring for him in a way that was beyond the dolling out of sexual excitement. He was a bastard, a charlatan some said, an opportunist, a white-collar criminal, said others. He was called a scumbag by some, who knew from the inside what that word really meant. He was labelled a serial womaniser, a lecher, an awkward and difficult man, a chauvinist of the old-school, tender only when under pressure and afraid. He was a brilliantly-talented fellow who had done much good, doing all the unnecessary harm to himself through his waywardness and the manner of his lifestyle. He was a married man who became single every time he left the family home. And he was a man I liked more than I liked many much more presentable specimens, if you accepted the yardstick polite society operated by.

"Lo and behold! All lovers should be scared for their life when they make love to their ladies. For, never is a man more likely to offer more of himself than Jay did this morning. Oh, God! How he pleasured me. How he caressed me with that great knob, how he abused me with it, plundering me and sundering me so that I wondered if parts of me might drop off and be lost and gone forever. How he stretched and extended me, drew me and slew me, annihilating my earlier determination to give as good as I got. He rendered me helpless and compliant before he drove me off the edge of the cliffs of Moher, to tumble and rock and roll and scream and shout, and laugh and cry. I wondered how it was I didn't die from the sheer ecstasy engendered by this insanely-gifted hammer-man.

"As JC left me he was smiling. No bad thing in a man facing the end of his political dream. He was still the party leader, but he was not the Taoiseach, at this minute, having failed to get enough votes from his party members to retain the job. Many wanted his head and wanted his job. Some said he was 'forgotten but not gone', that it was over for 'the great chancer'. Some had bet money that he was through.

"He was without doubt, a rogue and a rascal. If the real truth be known JC was a revolutionary mix of the best of Padraig Pearse and Michael Collins, ergo, a doubtful candidate for a step-aside role in public life. Jay, my lay, was bully boy and bastard, friend and fucker, pal and parasite. And possibly the last of the great political survivors. I hope you fuck every last one of them.

"Jay blew me a kiss by the door off the palm of his hand. 'I'm a long way from dead Dervla, and they can kiss my arse. Let them ceilidh on someone-else's coffin.' Then he was gone, the door slamming behind him.

"One question before I finish this entry. Will he survive? Can JC pull it off again? Time will tell."

—◄o►—

As I finished reading this episode in the journal, I remembered that a 'ceilidh' was an Irish dance, and I found myself smiling at JC's 'never say die' attitude. I couldn't remember what had happened to him in the days following his departure from the bed he had shared with Dervla through the night before the 'morning of the long knives'. I'd read the Irish newspapers in New York. The internecine warfare within Ireland's oldest political party made good copy for ex pats, but nothing arose in memory. I turned a few pages of the journal until I found the recorded notes that proclaimed:

‒‹○›‒

"He's done it again! The master-stroker has bamboozled the political circus by forming a coalition with his arch-enemy, Shamey McMaster. Shamey's not the worst. He tried and failed to shaft JC in that memorable leadership battle. He wasn't quick enough, ruthless enough with the blade as my good-looking-goat of a friend. After this knockout, what did the bold Shamey do? Fair play to him, he left the party and formed a new one of his own. He has balls. You have to give him that!

"PS Shamey, like JC, never to be confused with a nice man, is probably our most successful failure in the political arena."

‒‹○›‒

Before I can give it any more thought, Dervla comes back from her walk. Her complexion looks fresh, quite peaches and cream for her. "Are you still talking to me?" she asks, like someone not at all sure about the answer they're going to get.

I stood up and hugged her to me, suggesting gently that she curl up by the roaring fire in the giant grate while I brought her a cup of coffee. She smiled at me, relieved that I wasn't clambering onto any moral-high-ground. I left her there, glad of the few minutes I could spend putting the coffee together and needing the time to collect my own thoughts.

"You write very well, do you know that?" I said, passing her a joint of home-grown along with her cup of coffee. I was hoping she would respond to the ease with which I'd welcomed her back from the walk, that she was feeling freer, that she might be able to make a stab at the 'fifth step'. It didn't have to be signed, sealed and delivered in one hit.

I see her relax after a couple of tokes and I throw another log on the fire.

"I know I wouldn't have come this far without you, Joe. You know that too, so there's no need for us to labour it. That includes you bending the rules to let me have a few joints. I know you like it, too. At the same time you'd never have introduced dope into the scenario if I hadn't convinced you it would help me." She pauses like she expects me to say something. I stay quiet, giving her all the space she needs. "I was so relieved," she admits. "You agreeing we could do a little smoke every day. I was in such a terrible place just before Carol gave me that first toke. I was in such a state. I know I'm a bit of a drama queen." She smiles ruefully, her look asking me to make allowances. "If you had put your foot down. If you had said 'No way, Jose!'" She shakes her head in utter disbelief. "I can hardly believe I'm saying this. I was so crazy, Joe, I think I was just crazy enough to have dumped you."

"I know about that one. I'd have driven a car over anyone trying to stop me when I was desperate for booze. It's OK. You just do your own thing here. Whatever goes down today, we're going to be having dinner together tonight. The last words you'll hear from me before I shut my lamps will be 'I love you'. I love you and I ask you to give yourself a break here." I get another joint going and pass it to her.

She sits silently and I go down to my office, coming back with Collins' English dictionary. She responds with a quizzical glance while I rifle through the pages. "Listen to this. This is a definition of the word 'sober'. Sober, an adjective. 'Not Drunk. Not given to excessive indulgence in drink or any other activity. Sedate, rational, a sober attitude to a problem.' If you're talking about colour, 'plain and dull or subdued'. Back to people now. 'Free from exaggeration, speculation' as in 'He told us the sober truth'. OK?"

I allow a breath or two for this to sink in. Then I venture on, hoping this isn't driving her nuts. "Now, here's what's on offer in relation to the word 'sobriety'. 'The state or quality of being sober, refraining from excess, the quality of being serious or sedate.'"

I close the book loudly in an effort to lighten things up a shade. She finds a wan smile, but she isn't having the best of times, so I say, "I can vouch for the fact you're not drunk. That you're not given to excessive indulgence in drink or any other activity, with the exception of incredible sexual fucking, sucking, humping and bumping. Have I left out anything?"

"Fantasising," Dervla says, willing to sound brighter, coming back in from the cold with an amused response to my wickedness.

"You did say fantasy?" I play at checking her out. She laughs at the surprise in my voice. She's vaguely nervous then, or maybe excited, as she exhales smoke to tell me, "Sometimes, I get into fantasy. I didn't plan it. It just started recently. Well, sometime in January. I got a memory-flash of myself and Janice in school. She was my best friend, a year older, from Limerick. She was what guys called luscious. She sort of dripped with sexual promise, high breasts that seemed too much for her skin, beautiful and firm, huge nipples. She only had to touch them while she was washing to want to come off. She was crazy about me and once we started slipping into each other's bed in the night, I fell for her like a ton-of-bricks. She was what kept me sane the last couple of years in that school."

She is reliving the memory, her eyes full of those moments, as she relates the story. When she finishes she looks at me directly, assessing my reaction. Obviously I've taken things in my stride because she continues. "Janice talked of us living together when we were older, and when we were touching each other in bed, when she drew my lips to her breasts and I went to her with a kind of hunger I didn't understand. I didn't argue," she smiles ruefully. "I get very turned-on at the picture of you in bed with both of us, you riding Janice from behind while I kiss her nipples and feel her mouth and her tongue on mine."

"We can't have that for a carry-on." I say this like an old fusspot, losing my loafers and my pants while Dervla undresses like her clothes have caught fire. I move closer and she comes to me, gift-wrapped.

"Your man is only bursting, Joe."

Afterwards, I lie still inside her, my mind still turned-on by the fantasy she had described earlier. She opens her eyes in something like relief, smiling in a knowing way. "Right now, Joe, I feel pretty sober. Don't you?"

"We're going to stay that way. No booze. A little dope seems OK. We go to meetings. We talk to each other about booze and we deal with whatever comes off the fan. We do whatever it takes to hold onto what we have here. What I feel when we're fucking – forget it! Something happens and it's starting to happen again right now."

She laughs shortly: "If AA had a rule that you had to give up sex I'd go to bed with a bottle of pills," she laughed shortly. "And a vibrator."

I slide into her and she quits the small-talk. I begin to move gently, watching her eyes turn opaque, thinking that this might be the best time ever for a guy to die. To ride off into the sunset on the sheer pleasure of us, totally immersed in the consuming joy of our sex life. What could be better than that?

I hear nagging. All this love and sex, all very well, but . . . It's dope-fuelled, the by-product of a recalcitrant philosophy that states the rules are too heavy – we're doing our best.

19

Wicklow, May 1993

Despite my belief that it didn't matter a damn, knowing that Dervla and JC had a sexual history didn't do a lot for my peace of mind when she went working with him again. Like, how could they be around each other without remembering how it was when things were good and hot between them, between the sheets as per some of the entries in her journal. I could only judge it from where I stood, and I knew that it would have been tough on me being around a woman I'd had such good sex with, without wanting more of the same. I know that most women think differently than men do about sex, but Dervla liked it more than any woman I'd ever met, and according to her journal JC had balled her eyeballs out. The two of them working together wasn't a scenario I'd have suggested, even though it was a great connection, and we could use the money she was earning, so I had to live with it. She was back in Kildare Street working with the main man, and by all accounts, doing a very creditable PR job on his somewhat tarnished image. I just couldn't find what was needed to tell her to quit so I just had to hope she had found enough in our relationship, that she didn't have to kick-start something that had been over for some time.

Dervla and I had a lot going. She had gone against her father over our liaison, which was a major statement about where we stood together, but I found myself wondering now and then just what was it that we did have? Like, did she fight Danny because she had to have me, or was it just because she'd had enough of the bully-boy bullshit that was his stock-in-trade? I'd no idea.

We had fallen in love, that's for sure. And we had a close relationship in that we liked a lot of things about each other, but I didn't doubt there were times she wanted to strangle me just as I could have choked the life out of her. Overall, we were friendly towards each other, but I'd come to realise that I didn't think of her as my friend. At that time I couldn't see myself being in love with a friend. Pretty immature in hindsight, which is always 20/20 vision. But just then, that's how it was with me.

That being said, I would have done almost anything for her and I know that when things were at their best between us, none of any day's dreary happenings could tarnish the good feelings that lit me up inside. And I'd risk the view that she felt like this too at those times when we scaled our mountaintops together.

Meanwhile, I find myself listing as a bonus the fact that our fantasy scene was helping us both to new heights of sexual sensation. Janice, the school friend Dervla had been in love with, had been joined in our imaginings by Rachel of the magnificent flowing breasts, and one or two other females that we'd come to know in the past half year. I felt that the togetherness needed to make our fantasy-life work was in itself a kind of friendship, a trust, something between us and a secret that we wouldn't be sharing with anybody. Paradoxically, though other people were sharing our most intimate sexual experiences, we seemed all the closer for their imagined company.

Adding all these positives together, I felt pretty good about our chances of going on together indefinitely, give or take the odd day of madness when you wanted to run a mile. There were times I thought I'd like to marry Dervla and she sometimes suggested, while stoned, that she'd like to have my baby 'because the father would be the most wonderful man that ever lived'. I didn't argue with her taste. It was only expressed so hyperbolically when the dope was the very best, but I had no doubt that the idea of marrying me had crossed her mind. I hoped this was true since, if she was in this frame of mind, it was hardly likely she was going to get into an affair with her boss. She was earning excellent money working for JC and we needed it since dope cost an arm-and-a-leg, and we lived very well. The cost of living soars when you're supporting two automobiles, cigarettes, dope and dinner parties that cost real money because Dervla ordered everything top-of-the-range. And the wine our guests drank had to be the most expensive, even though she and I drank Diet Coke or sparkling water. It was as though I was printing my own currency.

One of the real killer's bread-wise was Dervla's inability to pass up a bargain. She was one of those women who get a buzz from buying a coat they don't need simply because it has had three or four hundred pounds cut off the original price. From the moment she woke up in the mornings until she closed her beautiful eyes last thing at night Dervla never did one thing that I knew of to relieve our financial situation. Not entirely true. She bought her own clothes, which helped a lot.

We weren't broke, but money was becoming tight by the time she took the job. I'd been keeping my financial statements to myself, since I wouldn't have wanted her to see that I was just a little way from going into overdraft. I told myself it was none of her business, but this was a euphemism for my need to appear well-off in her eyes. I felt that much of my appeal for Dervla was my mini-fame, coupled with her belief that people who wrote books and appeared on television were all loaded with dough.

Recently, the news that the film of my novel *Pity Not the Dreamer* had been postponed yet again had prompted her to ask me did this cause a headache for me financially. I'd played this down, minimising the delay without having any actual knowledge of how long the picture would remain on the back-burner. For two years I'd received pretty decent option money, and it was very likely there would be a third option bought. The producers had sunk a lot of money into the project – two screenplays had been commissioned, one of them written by me, and so on. I remained positive that the film would start shooting shortly. On that magical day when the director called the word 'Action!' for the first time, I would be paid a very tidy sum. I called it 'end of the rainbow day'. I couldn't wait, but I had to learn to do so.

In this way I kept Dervla ignorant of our financial situation, believing in my own madcap optimistic way that everything would work out for the best, simply because I was me. It was hardly surprising my movie was called *Pity Not The Dreamer*, a title that she liked, though she never said why.

Since she now worked in town three days a week and

handled things from home the rest of the time, I was seeing less of her than we'd become used to. This worked out fine. She stayed with Rachel in the Ballsbridge penthouse. Her father was there at times though he didn't live there.

Since I liked to spend a lot of time alone, the arrangement suited me just fine. By the time I saw my lady again, I was as rampant for sex as she always seemed to be, even though she was in a demanding and stressful sort of job.

I'd expected her to be tired when she got home after her three-day stint in town, but once she'd had some hot food and a couple of joints she was her luscious, randy self, so that our honeymoon just went on and on. I began ditching the part of me that could wax critical of her, to find within a short time that I was falling in love with her all over again.

All in all, life seemed pretty good and I was content with my new novel *None But The Blind*. My agent, Ed Gordon, was hot about it as he waited for me to deliver the last couple of chapters. As soon as I e-mailed the pages to Ed, I put on my walking shoes to go for a stroll in the noon air. I was on my way out of the lodge when the phone rang. I felt what you might call replete in the wake of typing those magic words 'The End'. I didn't need anything, but I couldn't resist picking up the receiver.

It was Barry Lane, a senior editor at Hodder and Stoughton in London, inviting me to lunch with him in Dublin in two days' time. Barry is responding to a proposition I put to him at a launch party in London earlier in the year. I'd followed this up later with a five-page outline for a series of books in which he'd expressed interest. Now he was ready to talk a deal. Barry Lane has a warm voice, his accent like something they inject you with when you go to Cambridge. "Joe, hello. Sorry to take so long to get back to you. I finally got around to reading *Pity Not the Dreamer*. Wonderful read, Joe. Yes indeed! Well done, old boy."

Over lunch a couple of days later, Barry tells me, "Very keen on a natter about your series of easy-to-read novels. My boss loved your description 'a Forsythe saga with cleavage'. We see it as a classy soap-opera, which I believe is what you had in mind?"

I told him he had it right, and over lunch in the Shelbourne Grill he made me an offer I couldn't refuse. It was for a six-book deal, with a seriously possible television tie-in. The books would be published directly in a top-quality paperback format. I'd suggested this myself, since I thought hardbacks far too expensive and I resented the fact that the less affluent had to wait maybe a year before they could buy the cheaper, paperback edition.

Everything was just the way I'd laid it out in my proposition. Though I didn't agree money, deciding to leave that to Ed Gordon, the initial ballpark figures that Barry mentioned sat well on my Chateaubriand and my glass of Evian water. The publisher would give me a six-book deal. As soon as the contract was signed, I would get a third advance on each of the six books. So, within weeks, I would receive a very tidy sum, a real sweetener designed to bring a large smile to my face in the upcoming early days of June.

I would receive the second part of the advance on delivery of each manuscript and the final part on the publication of the book. Since they wanted to publish every six months, I was guaranteed a financially trouble-free existence for the next three years. Since you had no guarantee about bread in the writing game, you could say I was more than happy about this. With the business done and dusted, I drove back to Lough Dane singing country songs and laughing at the afternoon.

Two weeks later I receive the first cheque from my agent, and I drive into town to lodge it with my bank. After this I expect to have a cup of coffee with Champion, who is finally free enough to give me a little of his time. I'm on the way in from Lough Dane when I get a call on the mobile from Dublin's biggest outlaw. "I can't make it today, Joe. A colleague of mine contracted a bit of lead-poisoning last night and I have to deal with the fall-out. Let me ring you the weekend and we'll rearrange it, OK?"

Leaving the bank later I go for a ramble around Dublin, and wouldn't you know where my feet take me? I'm standing facing the spot on Kevin Street where I lived for my first nineteen years. Mulvey's the Printers is no more – the old buildings are gone, but I need to be here. I need to tell my parents, 'I'm doing OK, still thinking of you'.

The moment clouds as a couple of guys in their late teens come staggering down the street, dressed like they've just escaped from a wedding party that was going nowhere. They're little more than kids, but seriously drunk, particularly when you consider it's just three thirty in the afternoon. One of the guys falls against me as he passes me, and I bang my back against the lamppost I'm leaning against. The guy staggers away having no idea that he has even bumped me, but I'm in grievous pain. My lower back is on fire. The awful sensation is a red-hot assault of such severity that I have to clamp down on my need to cry out like a young boy in agony. I'm shattered by whatever's happened, sensing the past in the pain and wondering what's going on. I'm feeling as though someone is trying to tell me something. Or maybe I'm just going crazy. I don't know. All I know is pain that almost deprives me of my senses.

I have to buy pain-killers in a nearby pharmacy. I sit in a

café sipping coffee until the pills kick in, then I walk slowly back to my car and begin the trip back to Lough Dane. I drive carefully since I feel, even yet, like I've taken a good kicking in and around my kidney area. I remember nothing of the drive over the Featherbed, no memory. It's something I haven't experienced since the blackouts quit after about a year of living booze-free.

At home, I smoke a joint and take a couple more of the painkillers, wondering what the hell is going on. I sit at the typewriter to see if I can put something down on paper. I hit a blank wall and I let it go. I sink into a hot bath laced with Radox crystals, and I'm sound asleep when Dervla calls. She tells me she's staying in town to work late, that she'll sleep over with Rachel. She mentions that Danny is in the West Indies this week. I have no problem with any of this. I feel so bruised, so abused really, that I need to just hit the hay, escape. I seem to smell anger, serious anger sitting on the edge of my mind. I can't get in touch with it, so I have to let it be. I roll another joint and I smoke it. I get into bed, and the next thing I know is the cacophony of sheep baa-baa-ing by the lodge in the morning light. A couple of dogs are making sure that they don't loiter, or become wayward along the way to the grass at the far end of the lake.

My back still hurts and I decide on another hot Radox bath. There is no way I can sit at the keyboard in my present condition, and I wonder am I coming down with a heavy dose of haemorrhoids. The Chalfont St. Giles, piles, is something the alcoholic drinker is heir to. I let the thought go, deciding to have a week off work before I start the first of my six books for Barry Lane. First I need to get rid of the pain, get it to move out of my lower back. Until that happens, I'm staying up to my neck in hot water. I close my eyes and let the heat and the power of the Radox crystals have their way with me. I allow the Serenity Prayer we use in AA to run across my mind, remembering how often it seemed to hold me still at those terrifying times when I wanted to run to the nearest drink. I let the words come back again, giving them time to ramble along the pavements of gratitude they helped me build out of the emotional quagmire I was drowning in when I took my last drink.

'God grant me the

Serenity to accept the things I cannot change

Courage to change the things I can . . . and

Wisdom to know the difference.'

By noon the next day I'm fit and well, so much so that the entire Kevin Street back injury episode might have been one of my rich imaginings. I've had Telly on the phone and we talked a bit about booze. But really he wanted to talk about Vanessa, and he was wondering why I hadn't been to the house in ten days. I explained about finishing up the novel and agreed to get over for dinner on Saturday evening.

"By the way, sport," he said as he was about to ring off. "Are you all right for dough? Are you earning money these days? I've got a few grand stashed in the little brown jug."

"I just signed a six-book deal that'll keep the home-fires burning for the next three years and maybe more. Got the first cheque yesterday."

He was delighted and I found myself telling him that I'd taken another walk down memory lane by going back to Kevin Street for a few minutes while I was around town, but I didn't mention the pain in my back. He had enough on his mind with Carol spending a fortune to get 'out of it', as in out of their life together. Meanwhile, Vanessa was doing novenas to get into it. My buddy was stuck in the middle, waiting for something to happen that would help him make up his mind about exactly what he had to do.

I'm in the drawing-room sitting at the old piano I bought a few weeks earlier. I've been developing a very simple system for playing accompaniments to my own singing and it's a lot of fun. It's also the best way I have found to unwind from the scribbling and to let go of your latest story, if you possibly can.

I hear the engine of a motorbike come along the drive from the mountain road and I get up and walk out the front door. I have a soft-spot for motorcycles and the heroes that ride them. I don't use them to travel on any more – not since the night I came off one and ploughed into a privet-hedge that saved my life, if not the only sports coat and pants I owned at that time. This motor-cyclist arriving at the lodge is not a hero but a heroine, an immensely lovely girl who is knocking my eyes out from the moment they land on her. I go to greet her in the warm afternoon sun, willing to not look over-eager. She stands there smiling, taking off her helmet, her demeanour suggesting that she knows me, while all I can do is forgive myself for having lived this long without ever seeing her before.

She really is a golden girl, gorgeous and sunny as this beautiful day in June. Her complexion is peaches and cream and she simply shines under a waterfall of honey-blonde hair. Her eyebrows are darkened to look like wings over orange-flecked light-green eyes, the dark-brown pupils encircled by broken golden-rings. Her magnificent mouth is like a blessed-wound harbouring beautiful teeth whitely shining between pink-red lips that seem to invite bold and hungry kisses.

"It is you. Hi!" She gives me her hand and I take it with genuine pleasure. "My name is Annie O'Reilly. I know you from your pictures in the papers, and I saw you on *The Late, Late Show*. I'm intruding, I know, but I wanted very much to meet you."

"You want to come in, have some coffee or what?" I'm waxing casual, but I'm intrigued.

"I'd love some coffee. I'm disturbing you, I know, but I'm trying to write and I just felt you were so nice on the show that you might just give me a few minutes of your time." She let the words flow as they arrived, making no effort to sound this way or that, free of concern as to how she came across to others. This was all so evident that even I could see it, and in time I'd come to believe she was one of the most natural people I'd ever met.

"Oh, you're disturbing me all right. The two hormones I have left are going crazy. Come in, anyway. I'll give you coffee and you can tell me everything."

"Can I use a bathroom first? Wash my face, that kind of thing?"

I point the way and she is gone. Moments later I'm in the kitchen making coffee. I find myself laughing because I can feel my heartbeat running and jumping in glee, like the ticker of a sixteen-year-old thrust into the presence of this amazing girl who comes winging to him on a petrol-driven charger.

When she comes back from the bathroom, I have coffee ready on a tray and we repair to the table and chairs overlooking the lake. She walks ahead of me with a plate of buttered brack and I find myself smiling again. This is a lot of fun, the only way to spend a summer afternoon in the sun-drenched mountains.

Sipping coffee and smoking one of my Gold Flake Annie sighs at the beauty of the surroundings. "And the peace of it all," she is impressed. "What a perfect place for a writer to live in." I sit there trying not to look spellbound, not needing to say anything, just perfectly happy to let her say whatever comes into her mind, while I simply look at her thinking heaven could be like this, if it's all it's cracked up to be.

"I liked you enormously on the *Late Late*," she spoke frankly without having to change gear to do so. She was like clear water, she had no act, and I was falling in love with her by the minute. "And I knew you were the man I needed talk to about my writing."

"I'll be honest with you, I promise you that much," I told her. This was intended as a warning, but she found the positive in what I said.

"That means you will read something. Oh, thank you, Joe. May I call you Joe? It's just that, well, seeing you on television during your long interview I know lots about you. And I've read your three novels. I can't wait to read more. And if I'm overstepping the mark, just tell me off and I'll be as good as gold. Is that fair enough?"

"What are you writing, Annie?"

"I've written enough short stories for a book, that's if they're good enough to be published. But someone told me it's difficult to get a book of stories published. Is that right?"

"Pretty much. But tell me why you write, Annie? Is it just to be published?" I lit up a joint of grass, had a toke before offering it to her. She reached forward eagerly, smiling as she took it from my hand. "I just knew you'd be cool." She closed her eyes as she drew the smoke in.

"I write because I get a kind of push from somewhere. I don't know if you'd call it a need, but it's kind of like that. I have something to say and it needs to be written down. I haven't really thought about it that much. I just do it, and I like what happens when I'm doing it."

"Are you writing about the people and the things you know about?"

"Yes. That's all I'm capable of so far. Me and my experiences – stories about a girl who is bi, how she has adjusted to her duality, sexually, and about her parents and how they came to terms with the lifestyle she has chosen for herself. You know. The stuff she can only deal with in terms of her personal experience. But I have big ideas for big novels. Big dreams."

I was remembering how she looked as she walked towards earlier. No feminine undulation, her gait not designed to add to the beauty of her body, her incredible natural endowments worn like her complexion, unconsciously. "Did you bring some of your stuff with you?" I ask as I retrieve the joint from her fingers.

She shakes her head and the sun seems to bounce and sparkle off her golden hair. "I didn't want to assume. But, I could come again if you'd have the time to talk to me, read something and maybe give me some advice. You're the writer I admire most."

"If I can help you, I will. Why not come back on Saturday, any time after noon. Dervla will be here. She'll love you and I know you'll find her terrific. Bring some of your stories and I'll let you know what I think, on one condition . . ."

She throws a quizzical glance my way and I tell her. "Just as long as you understand that it's just this guy's opinion you're getting. And I know very little about writing. OK?"

"I should know so little," she smiles and I know I'll remember how she's lit me up again in this moment, while I dismiss a flash of she and Dervla embracing each other. She is so lovely, this twenty-two-year-old woman. who might have been conjured up by the force of our fantasies. Dervla herself might have willed her to appear to us. Maybe she even prayed for a golden girl, without remembering to mention it!

"Before I leave," Annie stands up, gathering the coffee cups and the cake platter and stashing them on the tray. "Could I just see whatever you're working on right now?"

"I've just e-mailed the last pages of a novel to my agent in London. I've printed it out. I do that for safety, just in case anything goes wrong with the computer. I like to have the pages by me. Come on, I'll show you."

She takes the tray through to the kitchen and washes the cups and the plate before she's ready for me to lead her down the passage to my office. I'm smiling. What an amazing girl? I stand and watch her as she reads the first few pages of the new book. In a minute she turns to me. "I love it already. Maybe when you get to know me better, you'll let me read the manuscript?"

"Come on Saturday. Let's take it a step at a time, all right?"

She put the pages down on the desk as though they were very precious. "I'd love that, Joe. I really would."

I felt that she was inviting me to touch her and I was sorely tempted. But I didn't want her just for me. I wanted her for Dervla and me. And I knew that when I introduced them I needed my partner to know, which she would do in an instant, that I hadn't had sex with Annie. She would resent anything happening that she hadn't OK'd first and I didn't want anything to get in the way of the trio I'd been visualising since Annie had ridden into our lives.

There was something else to be considered, too. I didn't

know Annie at all, and while I had good instincts about people, anybody's protective equipment could be thrown off course by exposure to this golden creature. I wanted Dervla to meet her, feel her out, employ her feminine intuition as she listened to Annie's sound. Much as I wanted this girl to play with us, I wasn't making any kind of serious move until my partner gave me the nod.

Annie and I agreed that she would come to lunch on Saturday. Before she left we shared a hug of amazing promise, and I was relieved as I let her go. Saturday, she arrived bearing wine and fruit, and when she had changed out of her riding gear she was wearing a boob tube and a short skirt and sneakers. At the same time Dervla in a T-shirt and hot pants and walking shoes, came up the slope from the lower part of the lake. As they saw each other they seemed to stop for the split of a second, like they were frozen in time. Then they were eagerly shaking hands, Dervla so welcoming, the golden girl alight with pleasure in those first early moments between them.

Dervla looked stunning, her dark mane held behind her head in a pony-tail and Annie responded to her as though she was under her spell. It was a beautiful way to spend an afternoon, under a blessing of blue sky and sitting in the company of two such beauties. I was sensing we were heading for an adventure that would send the three of us into orbit.

Annie had a degree in horticulture. She had two brothers and one sister who were living in America. She had lived in Manhattan for a year but, "I needed to find myself here at home, and I feel I made the right choice." Her family home was in Ranelagh. Her father managed a bank. As we prepared lunch, Annie said she had to leave in the late afternoon. Her mother had a heavy dose of summer flu and she was playing nurse for the weekend. Dervla invited her to come back anytime from Thursday onwards, since she would be working Monday through Wednesday the following week. Annie said she'd phone before coming up the hill, and she thanked me again for agreeing to read some of her work. As I watched Annie ride away with an over-the-shoulder wave, I could only wonder if my partner was ready to handle it, now that the word was made flesh and dwelt amongst us.

That night Dervla and I shared a moment after love-making – we were smoking a joint and just chilling out perfectly. She looked me right in the eye and said in a nice and easy way, "If you have to take Annie to bed to introduce her to the idea of a trio, that's OK with me. I could see she's already crazy about you. And you're so good at sex it could be the perfect way to get things started."

This blew my mind. It was like I was walking a high wire. My breath turned into a fist in my chest and then it was normal again. The moment was 'green for go' in terms of the pictures flashing through my mind. And as soon as we began making love again, my incredible partner was urging me to tell her how I would make love to Annie when I had her for the first time. Just before we finally surrendered to the overtures of old man Morpheus, Dervla asked how I felt about what she had said.

"I don't know," I said, being honest. "She's very loose about being bi. And she was just as much in love with you as she was with me. My feeling is you should let it happen between you two, then invite me in."

"I'd want to kill you if you cheated on me," she said this as though she was reading my mind. "But, God, this is so exciting, breathtaking in its way. I want it very much, if we can have it together, make it work for our relationship. There's no crime in wanting to make love to a beautiful girl, surely?"

We went to sleep on that note, my last lingering thought not in keeping with my earlier contentment. I actually wanted her to make love to Annie before I did. That way, should anything go wrong, she could never accuse me of orchestrating the whole thing. Even though I grudgingly admit that I had just done that very thing.

20

As I drive into Dublin on the Tuesday following Annie's first visit to Lough Dane, JC is being interviewed on the *Pat Kenny Show*. I smile. The great man is giving Kenny, one of the sharpest minds at the national radio station, a good argument on a couple of issues. Strong stuff which leads into a gentler second phase with a good few laughs between the two heavyweights and I can feel Dervla's touch all over what is basically a good performance by her boss. The weekend papers had been full of JC. Here he was in Sligo opening a new home for old people. He was seen on the television news cracking jokes with pensioners in County Tipperary, even rattling out a few bars of 'Paddy McGinty's Goat' along with a toothless old guy who would die happy now that'd met 'the great man himself'. JC was back in the saddle – hopefully not with Dervla, I thought – with the renewed faith of his party which was settled solidly behind him now that he had scared the shit out of a whole heap of them. By the sound of the guy, the only thing he was not going to do for the country was build a wall around it. You couldn't help liking the guy and I found myself chuckling at some of the stuff he managed to say while keeping a straight face. He was a guy with greatness thrust upon him who seemed determined to be more of a character than the politician the country had hoped for. It was just an opinion. What did I know about anything?

I hit the tape button to fill the car with Billy Eckstein and Sarah Vaughan. They were singing 'Passing Strangers', one of my favourite love-songs, and I couldn't help thinking 'aren't we all?' When you boil it down, what do any of us know, really know, about another person? So much of what we put out is simply behaviour, the way we're conditioned to be about life generally. But how much of it is in any way real? I let the thought go, turned off the sound and sang every Hank Williams song I could think of that had the word 'heart' in it. I've always loved Hank, who added a whole new dimension to the notion of self-pity.

When I got to Toner's pub, Pete Rooney had a fresh pint of stout arriving on the counter. He ordered black coffee for me and though he seemed genuine in his offer to buy this round, I put a note on the counter. He'd called me earlier because he had something I needed to hear, something too hot to mouth over the phone. It seemed only fair that I should buy him his lunch.

As soon as we met, I could see that Pete was in some difficulty. He had something to tell me, but he was having trouble getting to it. I've never thought of myself as particularly prescient, but that lunch-time he sipped stout, lit a cigarette and generally seemed to be stalling. I heard myself saying to him in a fairly casual voice, "If it's to do with Dervla working with JC . . . It's OK, go ahead and tell me."

As soon as I'd said it, I realised I'd known something was out of whack from Dervla's earliest days working for the Taoiseach. I sipped the coffee, needing a few moments to get used to this uncomfortable feeling of being vaguely clairvoyant. This mind-trip started because Dervla had surprised the hell out of me by coming home from work as horny as ever I'd known her to be. Before she had taken to staying in town three nights a week, she had come home from work, showered and had something to eat. Then she had screwed me with such energy, with a kind of angry passion, really. It was like she was trying to make up for something awful that she had done. As it turns out I'd been right on the money.

The word among those in the know was that JC was having an affair with Dervla. They had been caught *en flagrante* by an aide. The guy swore she was sitting on top of JC on his desk for a purpose not dreamed of when it had been designed. Pete felt I should know. He didn't want guys sneering about it without me knowing what was going on. And he wanted to give me the option to do something about it. It was so crushingly obvious. She had been assuaging her guilt in the early days of her return to Kildare Street through her amazing sexual assault on my body. I'd been the scrubbing brush she used to rub away the guilt stains, after she had been hard at it during the day sitting on JC's cock.

Fidelity had never been my strong point so I had a lenient attitude overall to Dervla wanting to screw someone else, but I hated the idea of being used like a toilet brush. She could have told me what was going on. She had reason to believe I'd be cool about her having a fling with an old flame. But then she wouldn't have been in control and that would have hurt her. In just the way it hurt me that she hadn't – for want of a better term — asked my permission. Creating aggravation comes so easily to control-freaks, doesn't it?

I left Pete Rooney to head for the john; I needed to harvest some common sense from somewhere. Shit! I was mad enough to spit bile. I rinsed my face in cold water. I took deep breaths. But the anger wouldn't quit, distorting my mirror image until I had to get out of there. I'd had this idea that I was Mr Cool, but underneath the bullshit I found I possessed the heart of a guy who didn't like being cuckolded. I was mad and pissed off enough at Dervla that I couldn't make allowances just because she and JC had screwed each other before. But, I also knew that she had only taken the PR job to find a way around her father's threat to my life. In Toner's john, I wondered had she considered that she couldn't be around JC again, without wanting to lay him. I'm not saying she was some little innocent, forced into some form of slavery by her dastardly parent. Dervla had too much mileage on her to offer this kind of defence. But she was very susceptible, very likely to be turned-on again by the idea of banging the Taoiseach. She wasn't the first woman who took off her knickers when such power came a-calling.

When I left Pete Rooney I found I was storming towards South King Street where I'd parked my car. At the top of Grafton Street I found Rachel, laden with bundles and trying in vain to get a cab to take her home. I was so relieved to be distracted that I immediately volunteered my services and she was only too happy to accept my offer of a lift. Her purchases from Brown Thomas were unloaded onto the back seat of my car, and a few minutes later we were driving towards Pembroke Park where she had an apartment.

"I was very surprised to see you in town during the working week." Rachel touched the back of my hand in an intimate way, somehow giving me the feeling that she was chastising me for not having called her. A bit fanciful, maybe, but I was remembering how her eyes had lit up when we bumped into each other a few minutes before. "Dervla tells me you have some kind of iron discipline when it comes to your work."

"The only way to deliver the stories is to knuckle-down, punch in the hours during the working day. I don't know any other way to help it happen." I glanced sideways at her and her eyes were all over me.

Rachel really was a terrific-looking woman. Her skin was flawless under a light tan, her splendid breasts designed to take a guy's breath away. Why else the hint of *décolleté*, the top buttons of her lightweight denim dress undone. I wasn't sure about this. Rachel hardly needed to be obvious. Men gazed at her longingly wherever she went. Even as I'd met her, I could see guys taking a second look. She was just that kind of woman, a woman that guys went for regardless of what she was wearing. And here she was being intimate with me, definitely. As though we were old and trusted friends or lovers – in just two or three meetings, yet there seemed to be some kind of unspoken bond between us. Maybe we both felt that however tight we were to Danny and Dervla, we would always be outsiders where that crazy family was concerned.

She touched my arm again in the car and when she spoke, I glanced long enough to see a hint of amusement like dots of flint in her agate eyes. "Are you happy enough about Dervla and the job, Joe?"

I glanced at her again, before making a left to head for the canal bridge at Leeson Street. "I know why she took the job. I have a pretty good idea of what the job entails," I said evenly, wanting her to know that *I knew*. "I don't own her, Rachel. Nor do I want to." We were stopped at the traffic light, so I had time to give her my eyes and observe her reaction to my tone. I didn't want the hurt in me, the anger and the hurt that was making me want her, to interfere with the signals I was sending.

She brushed something invisible from the pleated skirt of her denim dress, and she turned to me. "It's a cliché, I know, but I think we have to grab any moment that is likely to give us what we want. Dervla is really a terrific lassie. Her father's told me that had she been a man, they would own half of Dublin between them. But she's been doing her own thing for a long time, Joe. And since being 'in love' lasts for only so long, it's not unreasonable to assume she will revert to her old ways when she feels the need. If you can accommodate that, you two might have some kind of future."

"I thought Danny owned half of Dublin anyway," I said, not giving a damn what the guy had. I just didn't want her talking to me like a fucking agony-aunt.

"He's a wealthy man, Joe. You can be sure of that. But between us, he'd frame a ha'penny. We don't live together, you know. I couldn't bear the penny-pinching he goes on with. But he can be fun and he likes to do things, go places, which suits me at the present time. We have no future together, though. He's tight with himself too, you see. I want a man who will give me all of himself, before I get too old to attract any man at all."

I stopped outside the entrance to Ardoyne House. "Park just there, Joe." She pointed at one of the very few empty spaces in the large carpark. I did what I was told, grabbed some bundles from the back seat and followed her into the elevator. At her behest, I dropped the packets on a bed in a spare-room, before I followed her into the huge living-room. A giant picture-window allowed a magnificent view of the south city in the summer afternoon and I thought of James Plunkett's *Strumpet City* and Rashers Tierney, before I responded to Rachel's voice.

"I know you don't drink, Joe. Would you have coffee or something?"

"Is Danny likely to be joining us?"

"He's out of action until tomorrow morning. He's with his lawyers, something big going on. And I won't tell, if you won't," she smiled. "Like some coffee, Joe?"

I said, "No thanks, Rachel. I don't want coffee."

She stood looking at me for a few moments, brushed something from her skirt again and smiled like she understood exactly what it was that I did want. As she walked towards me I noticed how tanned and how smooth her gorgeous legs were. Then she was taking me by the hand and I allowed her lead me into the bathroom. Rachel undid her button-down-the-front dress and it dropped to the floor. Without taking her eyes from my face, she reached into the shower and turned on the water. I knew I was undressing, but I didn't have any real notion of how it was happening. All I could do was allow the magnet of her eyes, coloured now like brandy and soda, to hold mine. Her bra fell to the floor and I touched her breast. So magnificent, flowing like a woman's breast should, the nipples like lush raspberries. Her kiss was so gentle, her lips soft and fleshy. The lightness was almost unbearable even as she gave me her tongue. There was no violence in her need, no demanding tone in her movements as she dropped her hand to touch me and stroke me as though she had wanted to do just that for a long time.

She took my hand and led me into the shower and we

embraced under the powerful jet, kissing and washing and embracing and stroking with no suggestion that we were going to 'get it on' right there. I was hungry for her kisses yet I found myself restrained and gathered to her needs without a word being said. In a moment she slithered down my body and filled her mouth with me, staying there until she drained me dry, for the moment.

We spent much of the evening making love. The truth was that I couldn't get enough of her, and she made no bones about enjoying being wanted in this way. At some stage my insecurity kicked in and I asked if there was any other way I could pleasure her. She looked at me and laughed out loud. "Oh Joe, you're the best time I ever had." She drew my face down to her mouth and kissed me long and lovingly. I pulled back, trying to hide my sad and devious curiosity.

"But I thought Danny . . ." She hushed my mouth with her fingers, moving her hips and guiding me back to where she wanted me.

"He's too selfish to bother learning any tricks."

This time I made love to her to the point of being brutal, trying to scale new heights. I wanted some little bit of her to belong to me from here on in. I relished the pleasure of knowing I was a better lover than Danny Devine. My sexual athleticism had been powered by the news of Dervla and JC fucking on his desk without even bothering to lock the goddam door. I tried telling myself it didn't matter, but this was bullshit. I tried to let it all go, to just empty my mind. I hoped that Rachel hadn't sensed my anger, the kind of anger that could drive you to kill someone.

I was still mad inside on Wednesday morning so that when Annie called me at noon I told her that if she was free she could pay me a visit. She wondered had our plans been changed. Was Dervla having the day off? I said no, that I was alone and would be until at least midnight, when Dervla got home from dinner and a show with her mother.

"You're sure it's. OK. I don't want to interrupt your work."

"Of course it is. I'd very much like to see you."

"I'll be about an hour," Annie said.

When she turns off the engine, takes off her helmet and comes towards me, I go to her. I know that my eyes and my smile and my body are saying 'welcome, welcome'. Her nearness makes me feel so good that I'm sure she cannot see any evidence of the anger I'm still feeling towards Dervla. I take Annie's hands and draw her to me, to embrace her with a loving hug that she responds to without any resistance. She kisses me then and there is incredible heat between us.

"God, it's good to see you." Taking a breather, we stand at arms-length, holding hands, her eyes all over me. I want to inhale her, inhale all of her.

"Your timing is perfect. I've just started *Family Affairs* for Barry. The first novel of the six-book deal."

"Can I see it? Hold the pages? Wish it luck?" Her eyes melt with excitement.

"Follow me." I head through the French doors.

I light a joint of grass and sit watching this beautiful creature as she avidly reads the first pages of the opening novel in the series. A minute later, Annie is kissing me. I step back to place the joint between her lips. As she takes the hit she looks like someone who's just had a brilliant idea. She presents me with a big bright smile, her tone casual and sort of bursting with fun. "Are we going to fuck sometime soon?"

"You're the most wanted woman in Ireland at the moment. Does that answer you?"

"Let's get it on, then? I can't wait any longer. Let's fuck. Let's do it right here on the desk?"

I'm aware of the irony as I take off my shirt, watching her pull the top over her head. Naked she takes my breath away. She comes to me and I bend my head to kiss her dark nipples, feeling that my eyeballs are in danger of melting. I push files and stuff out of the way, some of it drops onto the floor and I don't give a goddam. In a minute I am lying on my back with Annie above me. She straddles my thighs, guiding me inside her. I sit up some to meet her mouth coming down to mine. Her tongue gently caresses my lips and my tongue, until she takes her mouth away to lift her perfect breasts to my lips. All the while she's moving, gently moving, gently rising and falling a few inches, our breathing turned to one force when her lips come back to my mouth and her tongue finds mine again.

I guess it's not unreasonable of me to say I got more than my fair share of women right from the early days of my sex life. I can also admit that I had some strong feelings for some of the women I made love to over a period of time. And I say without shame that while I was in love with one, I could be with others in promiscuity, one thing having nothing to do with the other. I guess that most people compartmentalise their lives to some degree in the sexual area, and I became fairly adept at keeping apart things that oughtn't to meet.

Allowing all of this, I have to say that before Annie and I made love that day I'd never felt that it was possible for me to be in love with two women at the same time. But by the time my golden girl and I were luxuriating in a bubble bath, I was as crazy about her as I was about Dervla. In the moment, I was so relieved and so content, I felt like I'd never hurt again. I quite naturally began to tell Annie about the fantasy Dervla and I had created, of the three of us in bed together.

Annie splashed water all over the floor as she was coming up out of the bath, unleashing a joyous whoop as she moved to sit on top of me again and kissing me with the same demanding passion. "You'll never know how I've dreamed of making love to you both at the same time." She was laughing incredulously as though she couldn't believe what I had just laid on her.

"OK. Here's the thing. From here on in, we share everything with Dervla. But today I want for us, for you and me. I want to keep it locked away between us. I want it to be our business and nobody else's. Will you indulge me in this? It's very important to me," I assured her, ignoring the sentry chiding me for getting my own back. Annie didn't need any explanation and she wasn't being offered more than I had already said. She just nodded her head, her expression suggesting that my request was cool.

She began to gyrate gently on my stomach and I said, "The first move should come from you. Can you handle that?"

"Sure. I fancy Dervla like mad. She is beautiful and I can't wait." She leaned into me and kissed me passionately.

Later I said, "Before I send you off into the night, I'm asking you to please come on Saturday. Let's get our trio together?"

"I'm going to blow your mind." She was laughing as she kick-started the engine. I watched her ride off into the night and I went straight to bed. I didn't hear Dervla slide in beside me and I was up and about with an hour's walking behind me before she surfaced for coffee and toast.

She was in mixed form, but said she was relieved it was Thursday, that she didn't have to go to town today. She responded quietly, like something was on her mind, but I could see she was more than interested when I told her Annie had been by and that she was coming to visit on Saturday.

"If you had to make love to her to introduce me into the picture, it's OK. I told you that, right?" Dervla was buttering toast as she spoke. I was watching a smoke-ring from the Gold Flake I had on, but something in her tone made me glance her way. I noticed that her hand was clasping the knife with unnecessary force as she cut into a loaf of bread.

I wanted to ask her what was wrong, but I said instead, "I didn't have to do anything. She's cool. And she thinks you're about the most beautiful female on the planet. Let's just play it by ear. See how it works out." I stood up to leave, getting no joy from the thought, 'two can keep secrets'.

"We talked about her doing some landscaping outside. And, maybe we could give her a few hours' work a week as my secretary."

Dervla threw me an appreciative glance, her voice sounding a bit jaded as she said, "Putting the cover-story together already, Joe? I like that in a man. Means you think we've got a very exciting summer ahead of us." She drank her coffee and accepted a Gold Flake. "You're not rushing off anywhere, are you?" Her change in tone was at once playful, relaxed. Too relaxed if you considered how distracted it had been just moments earlier. "If you have the energy you can come in here and we can play 'mammies and daddies'!" The sense that she was trying to cajole me, if you like, brought my anger up onto its hindlegs. I told her I had to go and write. I didn't hang around to see if she liked this or not. But I heard her call out, her voice gone flat again, "We need to do grocery shopping."

At one o'clock we were driving over the Featherbed to the supermarket in Rathfarnham when the news headline came on the air. The lead story gave me such a shock I had to pull the tank into a lay-by and for a moment I couldn't look at Dervla beside me.

"Taoiseach's special assistant, Danny Devine, in money-laundering scandal! Authorities allege serious charges of fraud and financial irregularities."

I lit a Gold Flake and passed it to Dervla. She was the colour of putty or so it seemed and she just leaned forward and turned off the radio. "I'll tell you about it. Did you bring a joint or two?"

She didn't say anything else until she had depth-charged a couple of decent tokes. As she passed me the joint, she said, "I knew about this when I came home last night. That's why I didn't wake you. There was no point in disturbing your sleep. I know how hard you've been working on the new book." I gave the joint back to her and she took the last hit from it, while I thought 'if only you knew'.

"How come you didn't mention it when you woke up?" I said, letting my own stuff slink off to the sideline.

"Because I was so pissed off. I thought, fuck it! I'm sick and tired of warning him he'd come unstuck. He knew better. He always knows better. I could see this coming a mile off, but his fucking ego wouldn't allow him listen to me. If I'd been his son instead of his daughter, he might have paid attention to the warnings. He might have missed this opportunity to go to jail, the stupid asshole!"

She angrily pulled a couple of Gold Flake from a packet and gave me one. When she was smoking she smouldered angrily, not hearing how she was repeating herself even if the language was different. "It's been coming for ages, inevitable. I saw it, warned him. Most people would probably have seen it and backed off, even for a while. Not our Danny! Not him and his fucking ego. Oh no! He could get away with anything because JC was his pal." She was smoking violently. "Well, not any more. He's finding to his astonishment that Mr Jay Charles is no longer his buddy. He is no longer special assistant to the great motherfucker. He is not only gone, he is forgotten! And I am to work from home for a week or two, do all I can to divert attention from this story and keep the fall out to a minimum. After that, it'll be 'bye-bye sweetie, it's been nice, but you're related to a leper, didn't you know!'"

"You'll get fired," I said, glancing at her to see how this landed.

For a split second, her eyes were flashpoints of anger. She exhaled, simmering down. "I won't *get* fired. I *am* fired. The words have not been spoken to me yet, but the message is loud and clear. In a few weeks I'll get a polite note thanking me for all the good work, that it was wonderful having my talent around and all good wishes for the future. And kiss my fucking ass! You're out dear! So be a good sport and help your Daddy realise he deserves a long and happy retirement, *or words to that effect!*" She turned to me, a wry smile on her lovely mouth. "I'm OK. Really I am. I half-expected this. Daddy has been flaunting the international currency laws, as though he was daring the authorities to do something about it. He took me down to the Caymans once. I met the guy he did all his transactions with. The hair stood up on the back of my neck around the guy. Daddy just laughed when I said 'don't trust him'. 'I have him over a barrel,' he said. 'He's a married poofter and I have pictures. When I say jump, he asks 'how high?' Besides which, he is making a heap of money.'"

"So what's happening to Danny right now?" I get a joint going, like this is hardly the time to start getting sensible.

"He's been charged this morning. He'll get bail, but it won't stop him having a very heavy weekend."

"You're saying JC won't be returning his calls."

"JC just may stop short of sending a wreath and a mass card. But I wouldn't bet on it."

"Friends in high places, right!"

"There are no friends in high places, Joe. Only contacts, fellas that will work from the old pal's script when it's expedient. I wonder if the 'big guys', the guys that go all the way like JC, have got any feelings of their own. Or do they just become convinced that what they think is how they feel? With enough practice, you can rationalise feelings right out of the picture. Language allows us to keep talking about feelings, but when you knock on the door, nobody's home."

I started the engine and gently took the jeep down the hill towards Kilakee.

"How come you knew what your father was up to all along?"

"I knew everything," Dervla said. "Since I was nineteen, I've known every dodgy move he made. He needed to tell me his most dangerous secrets, and he needed me to stay married to Gary's money. He had plans for a truckload of Gary's bread. After JC warned him off the six counties takeover bullshit and threatened him with the total chop if he ever mentioned it again, Daddy went on wanting Gary's money. He had earmarked maybe twenty million he was going to get from Gary. He wanted it to buy land that was due to be rezoned, he being one of the exclusive club that knows all about this rezoning ordnance. That land would be worth ten times its original value to a man with the right information and the money to act on it. And people in high places who are desperate to help him because of what he has on them. Are you getting the picture?"

"So he quit being a revolutionary?"

"I don't blame you being sarcastic," she said, shrugging her face. "The thought of making, stealing a hundred million or more gained his full attention. He's still convinced he'll have Gary in the deal as a silent partner though he may have let that fantasy go since he got arrested." She half-smiled, a grim compliment to Danny's madness. "Though, knowing him, he won't be sweating over this. He knows where all the bodies are buried. Too many people in high places owe him big time. He's probably calling in markers even as we speak."

"And none more than JC himself," I said without even having to think.

"Believe it. There were times JC survived at the helm only because of what Daddy knew about some of the guys who would have voted him out of the party altogether."

"Has he made things cool between himself and the provos?"

"According to himself, he has. He goes back a long way with the older guys. I'm not so sure about the new kids on the block. But you know my father. He can handle anything, right!"

"I often wondered why he didn't he ask the provos to waste me when he wanted me out of your life?"

"He would never have done that. It wasn't political and he wouldn't ask 'cause' guys to do a criminal act. He's always had a real poker up his arse about the purity of revolutionary action, and whatever you're having yourself."

"Now I forgive you being sarcastic."

"He drives me crazy with his phoney idealistic shit. You watch, the chance of a hundred million and he'll have a memory lapse about his political affiliations for the last thirty years."

"He really should be the Taoiseach. He's got all the qualifications."

"Not enough money in politics for Daddy. He's been busy setting up a string of phoney companies to front what could be the biggest scam ever pulled in this country. There's big bread involved in the laundering he's involved in, but it's only coffee money compared to what he expected from the rezoning scam. The success of the scam was all about timing. It's beginning to look now like he's run out of time."

"The thing I don't understand is this need to tell you everything. You might have cracked up from drink. You might have let something slip without knowing you were doing it. Just having it in your mind could have helped you to a nervous breakdown."

"Sounds crazy I know, but it's true. He has a great street act, but with me he came bare-assed to the table. He felt that he had to share his secrets with me, because he carries the guilt of the night he came bare-assed to me in my bed a long time ago." She lowered the window beside her. "Joe, can we stop a minute?"

I said nothing. The implication of what she had just said shut my mouth. I took the elbow bend above Kilakee, pulling the jeep into a lay-by a little way down the road to Tibradden. Sitting there behind the wheel, I toked on a large bone of home-grown and passed it to her.

She took a serious hit so that it was a few moments before she said, "This is not an easy thing to admit to, Joe. But I enjoyed it, that my father was a powerful guy – well-off, self-made, arrogant. And he's always had style by the bucketful. He's always been a dandy and I liked how people looked at us when we went to a function, or some dinner-dance for charity or a fundraiser for the party. He was a jumped-up bastard with attitude, I was a jumped-up bitch. Or as Eamon my cousin christened me 'a meadow lady', a cow!"

I knew some of the story already. How Dervla and her father had moved out of the unhappy family home. "Finally moved," was how she put it. "Mammy and Daddy were incompatible. She told him a dozen times before to just get out, and this time he did. I went with him knowing Mammy would never stand for the carry-on I had in mind for myself." She shrugged philosophically, "Drink and sex couldn't happen in Mammy's house." She passed the joint back to me. "Daddy was like something let out of a cage. He was out every night. All of this was right up my street. He was so busy playing Jack the Lad he never gave a thought to what I was up to. I could even bring guys back for the night, once I made sure they were gone before he surfaced in the morning. He took me to a lot of places at that time. He was very proud of me, referred to me as 'my lovely girl, my beautiful daughter'. And I loved it, Joe. I loved being his lovely girl. God, at times it was like I fancied him. Only it was ridiculous. My own father, for heaven's sake!

"Sometimes at some function or other, when it was late and we were having a slow waltz together I felt him get a hard-on. I honestly believed he didn't know. He was pissed, getting randy with some woman was what I thought. But I wouldn't have minded if he had known he was leaning in to me. It made me feel closer to him and I liked that.

"On the night I'm talking about, I brought a guy to the

house, but my father was already home. I knew I couldn't sneak the guy in. Daddy was jealous of me with guys, and I sort of liked that too. The guy and I got laid in the back of my car. Then I drove him to a cab-rank.

"I was still half-jarred when I got back to the house. Daddy was fairly well-cut himself and we had a drink or two together. At some point, just for a bit of a laugh, we had a slow waltz together with the stereo playing the right kind of music. That was the last thing I remembered till I woke up the next morning.

"As I came to, lying naked on my own bed, my father was crossing from the bed to the door and he was as naked as I was. I called to him, but he waved his hands in despair without even turning to look at me. I heard a broken cry tear itself out of his throat. 'No Dervla! Oh my God! Oh Jesus help me!'" She took the last toke out of the joint, the telling of the story causing her to perspire. "Then he was gone out the door, slamming it so hard after him that it hurt. I got up off the bed. I was shaky on my feet for a few seconds, badly hung over and feeling very upset by my father's total rejection of me. I thought of going after him, but I was bereft of what I might say. It had just landed on me, the possibility, Jesus! I can hardly believe I'm saying this . . . I was asking myself was it possible Daddy and I had fucked each other in a drunken blackout?

"All I can manage to organise is a hot bath, a bottle of Drambuie and a glass. Then I slip into the hot water and I sip the liqueur. I'm trying to drag up some memory of what happened when we started to have the slow waltz in the living-room. But there's nothing there. I could remember what had happened just before that, without even trying. I could visualise fucking Terry Davis in the back of my car, driving him to the cab-rank. It's as clear as a bell, even down to the smell of the Brut aftershave he wore. I remember we had no condom and I said 'ah fuck it, let's do it'. But from the moment I took that first or second drink with Daddy, it's all a big blank zero.

"I was tortured at the thought that I might have shagged my father. It could have happened. I found him so attractive and I admired so many things about him. Yes, we could have got it on. The thing is I'm lying in a bath of water, drinking, and I don't know. I don't know if my father has fucked me and then walked away from me in disgust. His disgust and my horror join forces, and with a few more Drambuie's inside me my misery is choking me. I see the glass coming full to my mouth, feel the heat of the stuff going down my gullet. I watch the bottle flying out of my left hand, and I hear the glass break as I bang it against the edge of the bathtub.

"The next thing I know I'm in a bed in the Whiterock Clinic with my left wrist bound up, my arm in a sling and my heart like a broken glass. All I'm remembering is Daddy slinging his hook, going out the door of my bedroom asking Jesus for help and leaving me with the emptiness that hasn't gone away while I was out of it.

"The story is that I cut my wrist with the broken glass. I know nothing of this until I'm told about it. Lucky for me, so they tell me, our cleaner arrived just as the Drambuie bottle crashed against the bathroom wall so that she came to look for the source of the racket. She saw the blood coming out of my left arm. She let the water out of the bath, dragged me out, bound up my wrist and phoned emergency. I don't know how I didn't just expire from the pain of my father's rejection. We were so close, and he had turned his back on me. I felt like I like a common little whore.

"When he came in to see me a few days later, he was still in bits. Not that he'd let anyone see that, but I knew him too well for us to pretend he was as right as he made himself out to be. I got stuck into him without a hint of fear in me. I was so angry I could have punched him. He took it, because he was as mystified as I was as to what had gone down. He'd had an alcoholic blackout just like me, been having them for years. He felt bad, bad that I was so hurt. He tried being macho, but I told him to fuck off, and I warned him not to start giving me any lectures about my bad language.

"He was mortified. The total loss of control blew him away, and I didn't doubt he was desolate over what could well have happened. I couldn't tell him for sure because Terry Davis had come inside me in the back of the car just before I went into the house and started drinking and dancing with Daddy. 'It must never happen again,' he said, like he'd been whipped or something. 'Whatever happened, it must never happen again. My God! I nearly had a heart attack when I woke up and saw where I was. It has to be our secret, Dervla, you understand that, don't you? Nobody else can ever know about this.'

"'Do you think I'm going to be blabbing about it? Do you really have to be so fucking patronising? Am I supposed to be sorry I'm just a female, that I'm not the son you wanted? Well fuck it, this is me. I am what I am, and you know I've been whoring and drinking my loaf off, but today that's me. You either have to put up with it or just fuck off like you did in my bedroom without a single thought about how I might be feeling.'" Dervla spoke in a harsh voice, reliving the pain of that attack on her father.

"I was crying like a baby by this time, Joe. I was shattered and I didn't give a fuck if I lived or died. He was so pathetic

I stopped berating him. I hated seeing him in pain. So, right there in my room at the clinic I felt sorry for my father for the very first time in my life. He was devastated by my attack, shaken so badly that for a minute he looked like an old man. He swore that I was all that mattered to him on this earth, that he would not have swapped me for five sons. He swore he hadn't meant to reject me, he was just so ashamed of what might have happened between us and it would all have been his fault. I told him we had to share the blame, that it wasn't all his fault. He hugged me then, swore he'd always be close to me. And that he'd make sure nobody ever gave me a hard time about anything. I knew what a scary guy my father could be, but that day he was so scared himself that he started to tell me what he was into with the money-laundering. From then on I heard about the other scams he was running and I wondered how long he could get away with it.

"Being Daddy, he reckoned he could get away with his stuff forever. It was all down to connections so he said, and he had plenty. Plus a little moolah goes a very long way, he assured me, rubbing his thumb against the first two fingers of his right hand. He always claimed money was the key to everything, Joe. That is his life-long mantra. From that day I was my father's confidante. That's how I know all about this shit that's going down at the present time."

I flip my dog-end out the window. I can hardly breathe, some memorised residual hurt making me feel that I want to break Danny Devine's head open with my fists. In the same instant I lurch out of the cabin, catapulted by an unmerciful pain. A second or two later, I throw my breakfast up into the ditch at my feet. I hear Dervla get out of the tank as I'm gasping, taking in the mountain air and trying to use my willpower to rid my lower-back of a fresh pain attack.

In a minute, I light a Gold Flake for both of us and draw the smoke in. Dervla looks at me as we stand by the grass verge. "I'm sorry for laying it on you like that. You're the only one I could ever share it with."

I exhale smoke and nod my head gingerly. "It's OK." We sit down beside the road and I take her hand, bring it to my lips. "No matter what comes and goes, I don't think anything can ever change how I feel about you. Now tell me the rest of the story."

"Naturally, in time, his old arrogance came back." She smirked like she couldn't help admiring the bastard. "He would kiss me on the lips the odd time, letting others see that he was the main man, if you like. I could handle it because I knew that behind all the bravado he was a scared man who was beholden to me for my ongoing silence. So I got the stories as they were in the making. And believe me, some of it you couldn't imagine."

She took a smoke from my cigarette. "This Cayman island thing – I'm only surprised it's taken this long to hit the media. He's been stupidly arrogant about his power. It's all happened now because that devious bastard of a bank manager has finally come out of the closet. He's made a deal with the authorities. He's not going to jail and he's free to sell his story of Danny's dealings to the highest bidder. In this case, that's an agency of the government. He's been paid well, and they intend to see that Danny picks up the tab for everything. Whether he knows it or not, he could go to prison over this. And the country is full of people who will be quaking right now. The carpetbaggers are heading for their comeuppance. They know that if Danny goes down he will be taking a herd of ex-ministers, backbenchers and county councillors along with him. He's probably cooking up a deal with the law right now."

We sat on the grass verge in the midday sun. Way down below, Dublin came and went at the whim of a diaphanous mist.

"What does this do to us, Joe?"

"It's yesterday's bus tickets," I said quietly, though I still wanted to break Danny's head. "And y'know, if we carry on sifting through your shit, remember there's no blame. Sure, we have to take responsibility for some of the stuff that happened in the past, but there's never any blame. The angers and the resentments and all that stuff, the judgements we made about people . . . This is the stuff of your 'fifth step'. The sex and how you were sexually, that's just one thing. And sleeping with some stranger to help you make it through the night, what is that compared to judging someone without knowing what's causing their behaviour? The stuff behind the drinking and the fucking, that's the nitty-gritty that we have to face and deal with, sooner or later."

"So you're not going to leave me or anything?"

"Right now I just love you. Is that OK?" She nuzzled against my shoulder for a little while and I let her be. When I felt the change in her as she let go of the debris of the story, I stood up and took her hands. As I pulled her from the grass verge, I said, "Now let's go and get the groceries. We might stop off somewhere and have a snack. I just lost my breakfast."

21

Wicklow, June 1993

The revelations about Danny Devine were building up on Friday. *The Irish Times* carried a front-page banner: 'Aide to Taoiseach surrenders passport'.

In the same paper, the leading article questioned the relationship between Jay Charles and Danny Devine. The alleged charges brought into question the 'need-to-know' loophole used by presidents and prime ministers when their closest associates were accused of unethical practice. This was something which no leading politician should ever countenance on behalf of his government, or indeed himself.

The *Irish Independent* demanded that "the Taoiseach should, even at the risk of creating a precedent within his party, do the honourable thing and resign without delay. As for his erstwhile aide and confidante, Danny Devine – *a man you would not buy a second-hand car from* – the authorities are correct in confiscating his passport. Just in case 'the fixer' forgets his court date while sunning himself with his crooked bank official pals on Grand Cayman. Dannyboy has been flaunting the law for two decades. The financial irregularities and the charges of money-laundering will, before long, be seen to be merely the tip-of-the-iceberg. Reliable sources inform us that charges in connection with the rezoning of land, both for residential and business development, are imminent. We also understand that at least two other individuals, both acolytes of the Taoiseach Jay Charles, are to be indicted with a matter of days. Let us hope they enjoy their roast beef this weekend, lest before long they have to make do with porridge."

The build-up to the weekend editions was obvious and I could only imagine what the tabloids were going to do with this gem in their 'Sundays'. It had been a quiet week from a news angle, so Danny's tribulations were manna from heaven to every editor in town. The television news featured some of the facts. The in-depth stuff was meagre and the padding was all about personalities, in particular, Jay Charles and Danny Devine. There was reference to 'lavish lifestyles' and monies donated to the party being segued into numbered personal accounts in the Cayman Islands, to rapidly appear 'as if by magic' back in Dublin in the personal bank accounts of people yet to be named.

On Friday afternoon when Dervla talked to Danny at Rachel's penthouse, he was about to leave for a trip to West Cork. "I'm attending my reformatory school reunion," he said with such gusto that she burst out laughing, delighted that he wasn't feeling down over the media onslaught he had been through during the day. And his last words to her, "It'll take them years to get me to court. And you know, a lot of people get a change of heart when a thing drags on for years and years. Some of them even have memory losses. And as nature takes its course, some of them even pass away. So it's a long way from doom and gloom. Now I'm off to the south with my lady Rachel, and my best to you and your scribe."

Dervla laughed at his incorrigibility, and though I believed the guy was a total slimeball I had to tip my hat to his flair and his style. In his eyes, the rules that society laid down were there to be used or to be broken as he saw fit, without any suggestion that he might ever have to pay a price for doing things in his own sweet-street way. In the crunch, Danny didn't bend the knee to any rules but his own.

Annie phoned late Friday afternoon to check if Saturday was still on. Dervla took the call and came into the office to tell me what was going down. I took a break from the keyboard, planning a long evening on the book I was finishing for Barry Lane at Hodder and Stoughton.

"Annie asked me if I'd like to meet her in Terenure, catch a movie. She thought she might cadge a lift back with me and come up tonight instead of riding up on the bike tomorrow. How does that sound?" She was standing in the doorway in a light cotton dress and slingback shoes, her hair like a great force lying on her shoulders. Her stance suggested she was excited and I held out my hand. She came to me, her body against my shoulder and we were very close. What we'd come through was more than enough to bring people closer together.

"It sounds perfect," I said. "I have an evening's work ahead of me. I have to get these pages together, especially as I expect to have the entire weekend off. Enjoy yourselves. Maybe bring back some M & Ms?"

Dervla went smiling and I was content to see her go. I thought this was a cool move on Annie's part, suggesting a movie together, nice and easy. It seemed like a perfect way to get our weekend on track. I went to work in a contented frame of mind and got a full quota of pages written. By the time the tank bounced up the drive at eleven thirty, I was fresh out of the shower and drying my hair in our bedroom overlooking the lake.

It was a bright moonlit night and I lifted the lace curtain on the French doors to the balcony, intending to go out and shout a welcome to the two beauties. I saw them get out of the jeep. They stood there close, their foreheads touching, and I forgave myself for wishing I could hear what they were saying to each other. They sauntered, arms about each other to the lodge. Dervla looked up to the bedroom and called my name. I opened the door and stepped out onto the balcony. Laughingly, she and Annie said almost in perfect sync, "Stay where you are."

I heard their excited laughter as they hurried steps up the stairs, the door opening wide as they came together to me, embracing me. They tore the towel from around my waist, warning me I was 'in for it'. In this way our *ménage à trois* took off beautifully, with me hoping that it wouldn't sometime crash-land about our ears.

Within days, Annie moved in. Ostensibly, she was going to redesign some of the landscape by the lodge. She would be a part-time secretary to me, working for an agreed salary with a signed agreement to maintain our fiction. We were happy as humans could be in those first days, seeing no reason why it couldn't be like that always.

In mid-June we learned that Danny's first court

appearance would be in October. It took some kind of special session to get this arranged so quickly. Danny was more than surprised, and admitted to Dervla, "The bastards are really out to get me."

We were driving to town with Annie when Dervla told me Danny wanted to see me. "He just asked if you could make some time to talk to him for an hour."

"He give you any idea what it's about?"

"I didn't ask. I know what he's like. All that 'never say anything you don't have to say' stuff. He invented all that."

"I'll call him tomorrow."

"You don't have to see him on my account. You owe him nothing." She quit playing hardball. "All the same, thanks."

I left the girls in town and finally got to have that cup of coffee with my one-time foe Champion. As I passed through the revolving doors into Smarts Hotel, it occurred to me that I hadn't any idea what Champion looked like. He was a step ahead of me, this well-built guy in an expensive dark-blue suit. I didn't put the street fighter of my memory together with this truly elegant guy who was very much at home in the plush surroundings of the new hotel. He came to me, his enormous hand outstretched, a genuine, old-fashioned grin on his mouth. His immaculately tailored frame was in peak condition. "I had the advantage, Joe. I saw you on television a couple of times, and I guessed you'd show on time. I'm really glad to see you again."

Champion was a handsome guy when he smiled, but later I noticed how cold his eyes were. They were shards of ice as I heard him dealing with someone on his mobile who wasn't delivering what the man wanted. He came and took my arm, and diplomatically ushered me into his private office. He owned Dublin's latest grade A hotel, along with two others, and at a guess, about half the northside of the city.

"I'm into lots of things, Joe. Little bit of this, little bit of that. You've made a great success. And your stories are terrific. I've read them, honest, without moving my lips." We shared a laugh and I was in awe of life's vagaries as I looked at this guy. He had pushed his way up out of the concrete sewer he'd been born into, like some kind of wild flower appearing between the cracks in a paving stone. I smiled inside. 'A bit like meself', I thought.

He poured coffee for both of us. "You gave up the jar, fair play! I never got into it myself. Saw what it did to the oul' lad."

We drifted quite naturally into talking about the past and I found myself liking him. This said something for his natural charm since his reputation suggested he could be a monster when it was called for.

"I never forgot you, Joe. You were unique, d'ye know that? You're still the only really decent guy I ever met. What you did the day you licked me fair and square, you insisting I keep the prized fiver, it was unbelievable. It somehow gave me a bit of faith. I can't explain it, but I found I didn't have to be hard as nails with everyone. Some people you have to be. Some people don't know about fair play, that kinda thing. But you saved me from being a total shit to everybody I met. I've been a bold boy all my life. Still, there are a few people around who think I'm OK, and I'm not talking about the ones who'd say that because they're scared of me."

"Even though I wouldn't have known what you looked like by now, I never forgot you either," I told him. "I fought pros in the States, serious fighters who didn't have your heart. And I'm glad to see you. I hope you stay ahead of the posse."

He gave me his approbation with a wave of his hand. "You understand the street. The life. I did what I had to do at first. By the time I didn't have to do that any more, it was too late to stop. If I stopped right now, I'd be wasted in no time. They wouldn't believe I was retiring. They'd have to waste me to feel comfortable on my patch." His smile was a sad one.

"You OK with 'the fixer', Joe?"

"Yeh," I said with a laugh. "We're pals now that he's up to his neck in shit!"

When we parted company that day, I felt good about meeting Champion again. He might have been a crook and a gangster like they said, but he'd lost none of the grit he manifested that day all those years ago when he would have died before he'd roll over just to avoid further pain and punishment. We said we'd meet in a month or two, maybe catch the fights together at the National Stadium.

A couple of days later, I told Dervla that I was meeting Danny in his club on Stephen's Green after the weekend. I'd no idea what it was about and I was prepared to leave it at that. She was standing at the window in the drawing-room and when I joined her I saw that she was watching Annie, who was building a rockery close by the house.

"Have you ever seen anything more beautiful than our lovely girl?" She took my hand conspiratorially. "I never dreamed I could feel such happiness. Do you think we can hold onto the bliss? Does anybody get away with being happy all the time, for years and years?"

"I'm a day-at-a-time guy, you know that."

"I'm glad we've come this far." She turned to me and I caught a spark of real excitement in her eyes.

"What?" I said.

"I've got some news for you." She was giving me an enigmatic smile that made me wonder about this upcoming revelation.

"Are you sure I'm ready for it?" I said, willing to be light.

"I don't know, really. How do you feel about me being mother to a child of yours? Like, I am some kind of flake, right?" She hugged me for a moment. Then she said, "I went to see Tony. He confirmed I'm seven or eight weeks pregnant."

I reacted big, big and happy and delighted for her with hugs and kisses and the right noises. A blind man could have seen she wanted the baby though a child was the last thing I needed in my life right now. And during the weeks that came after, nothing happened in my mind to change how I was feeling about becoming a father. In my mind, I had instantly considered that the baby might belong to Jay Charles. Leaving this possibility aside for a moment, I hadn't thought about having children with Dervla, no more than I had felt any pressing desire to marry her. She'd mentioned marriage before, especially after Gary got inside information that their annulment would be granted within the next six months. She felt her mother would accept me if we were married. 'Great!' I thought. 'If we get married she might even pay us the honour of coming to dinner!'

Above all, I wanted to write. And I don't mean to just write snappy stories that could provide me with a luxurious lifestyle. Inside me there was a voice asking 'when do you get to the Real McCoy?' There was stuff inside me in need of a ride to the fingertips. I'd no idea what it was, but the nagging voice didn't just hit me once and go away – it was there a lot of the time. Even if this caveat to the notion of married bliss hadn't been there, I didn't know if I wanted a serious domestic scene with kids, mortgage, all that stuff. Even as I was thinking this, I was staring the whole fucking enchilada in the eye. I was already into the two-car trap, and the fucking mobiles and whatever. Marriage and a kid, and a nanny or an au pair and all that went with that whole trip. I didn't think so. I just couldn't and I wouldn't allow my work to be pushed into second or third place on my list of priorities.

She gets a joint going and we go together into the kitchen to make coffee. Annie is bound to be ready for some java. She's been redesigning the garden area to one side of the house, and she just seems to float through four or five hours of what I'd call strenuous work when she's doing her thing. She's been writing some, but we're still in the throes of each other's magic, wallowing in those early days when you can't wait to get back to what you love best, which is making love. After a couple of serious hits, I pass when Dervla offers me the joint again. I'm hearing the voice of the sentry I live with, with his smart-ass question, 'so whatever happened to social smoking?' I tell him to fuck-off, refusing to consider his suggestion that I'm sucking this shit into myself just to help me make it through the night. But I'm stoned as I sip the coffee at the kitchen table. So that when Dervla comes back in, having given Annie a cuppa on the hoof, I hear myself saying, "I suppose you'll have to ease up on the fags and the 'Bob Hope', now that you're going to be a mother."

"Why on earth would I do something like that?" She sits

down on the pine bench to face me across the oblong kitchen table.

"I imagine you'd do it for your health and for the baby's health. It's the route the medics recommend, or am I deluded?"

"I don't smoke many cigarettes. And we're just social smokers when it comes to dope. Not enough to harm a fly, never mind a child."

For some reason her tone needles me. "We quit being social smokers a while back."

"Oh come on, Joe. Don't start. Don't make a federal case out of it."

"I'm telling you. I know how much we're smoking. I buy the stuff. I know how much we're spending on it. And all I'm doing is suggesting that you cut down. Did you tell Tony how many fags you smoke? How many joints you get through in a day?"

"You're really pissing me off," she said. "I mean, I tell you some good news. We have Annie in our lives. We're OK for money right now. And you dump this shit all over the fucking afternoon. I mean, do we really need to hold a fucking tribunal over smoking a bit of fucking dope and a few cigarettes?"

"You're smoking thirty Gold Flake a day."

"Don't talk such fucking rubbish." She slams her coffee mug down on the table like she wants to break it over my head.

"And we're smoking a couple of ounces of grass a week, plus a fair amount of hash when we can get decent stuff. And you've been popping the odd Ritalin from the bottle I keep in my office drawer. I use it to get me an extra few hours work when I need it, you shouldn't be taking it just for the hit. It could be addictive."

"I've had enough of this bullshit." She gets up awkwardly in a rage and bangs her knee on the table. She gives a yell and throws the coffee mug against the wall. "Now look at what you're after making me do, you and your fucking lecture." She starts to storm out of the kitchen, remembers she has hurt her knee, and drops into a half-limp like her leg is only broken in a couple of places.

"Call Tony, he's the medic. Tell him what you're smoking. Even if you cut it down by half, he's going to tell you to start easing up." I raised my voice so that she would hear it in the drawing-room. "And I'm asking you, as a personal favour to me, don't drive the jeep when you're stoned. You could have a bad accident." Oh dear, oh dear. From the mouths of babes and scribblers such wisdom flows. And may I never again say anything I wouldn't wish to see realised.

I sit in the kitchen remembering the bliss of the previous night. Dervla is sitting astride me while Annie takes a shower. I'm answering her question, "Are you happy, Joe?"

"Happy wouldn't cover it. And I've never loved you more than I do this minute. A great thing's happening here. We're all opening up, letting go of the catechism thinking, and the 'ten commandment' minds."

I get up from the pine table and pour myself another cup of coffee. I'm thinking of how we're keeping the trio motoring along nicely. Like, it was a fantasy come true, and we were all having a great time with it. Yet, an ordinary everyday thing like asking your partner to cut down her smoking now that she was pregnant and not to drive the jeep stoned could erupt into a three-act drama. I'm so taken by memory, I'm careless enough to spill some of the hot coffee on one hand. As I'm looking for some aloe vera gel in a kitchen drawer, Annie comes in and gives me a quickie good-bye kind of kiss. "We're going to Enniskerry. She needs to talk to me. We won't be long. Are you all right?"

"Just ask her to hang on one minute. I'll be right out."

I find a tube of gel and I'm actually rubbing it onto the coffee burn as I come through the drawing-room to the front of the house. As I open the hall door to go and talk to Dervla, she takes off and I'm left standing with a mouthful of dust from the sun-dried gravel. "Jesus!" I yell. "Fucking women!"

Ten minutes later, I get a panic phone call from Annie. They've had a bad accident about halfway down the twisting hill to Enniskerry. I clamber into the old banger I use as a spare car and take off down the drive at about half the speed Dervla used earlier. The car won't go much faster, and anyway one smash in a day is enough for any family. At the scene of the accident, Annie rushes to meet me. Dervla is being stretchered into an ambulance. She's unconscious. Her face has been banged up. "She hadn't the seat belt fastened," Annie whispers in my ear. "She was going too fast. We came around the bend. There was a lorry coming at us – it was over the centre of the road. We had nowhere to go to get out of the way. It's a miracle it wasn't worse, Joe."

"You go in the ambulance in case she wakes up. I'll follow on behind."

Annie nods and I see her talk to the paramedics. They allow her get into the rear of the ambulance. I lock up the jeep which isn't badly damaged and minutes later I'm following it as fast as my old banger will go.

Dervla came back to consciousness a couple of days after the accident. Her fractured ribs were strapped up. She hadn't fastened her seat belt and it was a miracle she hadn't been killed. She had a black eye and the other bruises and cuts, but in time she would make a full recovery from her injuries. When I asked about the baby, the doctor told me that Dervla had miscarried. Four days after the accident, the medics felt they could tell Dervla that she had lost her baby and that in order to save her life they had to perform a hysterectomy. They didn't ask my permission for this procedure since she and I weren't married, but Dervla would remind me more than once in the months ahead that I should never have let them do the operation. As usual, I thought, somebody has to get the blame when you fuck up.

Initially, I was sad that Dervla had lost the baby. Who wouldn't be? But there wasn't a thing I could do about what had happened. And sure, I felt bad that she'd had to face a hysterectomy. But in the cold room where reason allowed you a little space from the force of emotions, I reckon God got that one right. Dervla as a mother was not likely to be any kind of good idea. When I thought about it, all that came to mind was 'God help the poor kid' because knowing her as I did, there was no way I could see Derv beaming with motherly love. And God help the father who would, very likely, end up playing both parents – and the guy's name would be Joe.

Ten days later, I drive back up towards the lodge. In the back seat, Dervla's head rests on Annie's shoulder, her arm across the golden girl's breasts. Annie is supporting her, minding her. I'm amazed yet again at the maturity, the confidence, of my favourite twenty-two-year-old. She has been a rock throughout the ten days we've been living together, the pair of us ensuring that Dervla had everything she needed to aid a speedy recovery from her injuries while we were bathing in new shades of sensation and comfort.

Dervla had a long history of hospitalisations, a lot of them for imaginary illnesses. She'd had more than one head-to-toe testing process and each time there had been nothing to suggest that she was physically ill. Her sister Jilly, laughed when we talked about Dervla's health. "She's always been a hypochondriac. Like everybody in our family, including me, she can't get a headache or a cold. It's got to be a seizure or a brain haemorrhage or pleurisy or pneumonia. When Derv gets a pimple she goes for cancer right away. The Devine clan don't touch for 'mickey mouse' diseases!"

As I drove up the drive to Lough Dane, Dervla was already stoned. In the clinic she had not been allowed cigarettes, and of course dope-smoking didn't even get into the frame. On her release she was still somewhat sedated on doctor's orders, and she was to take some tranquilisers and pain-killers for the next seven days. Despite being somewhat sedated, all she wanted when we drove away from the hospital was a joint, and make it fast.

It was very clear that she was happy to see Annie. The ordeal she'd been through hadn't changed the way she felt about our golden girl. With me she was cold and polite, but way out there somewhere, too far out for me to make any real contact with her. As I carried her bag into the house, Annie was helping her upstairs to the bedroom. I was staying back, deliberately taking my time so this could happen without any awkwardness. When we were picking her up at the clinic, I got the vibe that she wanted Annie's arms as her main support. I was relieved, still mad to the teeth for the recalcitrance that had sent her out in the jeep minutes after I'd talked to her about not driving it while she was stoned. She might have been killed, and she might have killed Annie at the same stupid fucking time.

While Annie attended to Dervla's needs, I cooked dinner. I tried to focus on what I was doing, but the question, 'what happens now?' wouldn't let me be. When I took up her dinner tray, Annie was brushing her hair. To the manner born, Dervla was wallowing in such loving attention. I almost burst out laughing. She was like some fucking princess, with a beautiful handmaiden waiting on her hand and foot.

"Could I ask you to bring Annie's dinner up here, Joe?" she said as though it was obviously the right and proper thing to do. Annie shrugged and I indicated that it was cool. There was no danger of Dervla seeing my reaction since she was sucking the guts of a joint into herself.

"No problem, darlin'," I said with a conspiratorial wink at Annie, pulling a funny face in acknowledgement of the fact that marriage to me wasn't at the moment top of Dervla's agenda.

Annie said, "I'll eat downstairs, Dervla. I've got a thing about grub in the bedroom."

I left without waiting to see where this first small disagreement travelled to, and I was putting my own dinner on the table when Annie came into the kitchen. She came to me and embraced me. I held her fast and tears came to my eyes. No matter how uncaringly she behaved, the cow upstairs was my chosen life partner. Though I could shrug for Ireland, it hurt that she had shut me out so forcefully.

Feeling my tears on her face, Annie took her head back and planted small kisses all over my wet skin. "I want you to know I will always be there for you. Dervla is pretty sick right now. She's dealing with all kinds of shit. We have to make allowances, right?"

I nodded, sniffing back the tears and she kissed me again. There was no more talk and I let her go happily up the stairs to Dervla. A minute later I took up dessert and tea and I left them there, like patient and nurse. A few minutes later, Annie came down again.

"She wants me to sleep with her until she recovers some more." Annie relayed the message without inflection of judgement. That was her way, to come straight out with what had to be said, not getting bogged down in explanation or apology. Especially when it was someone else's message she was delivering.

"It's OK, Annie." I looked at her and she answered my unspoken question, with a huge grin climbing all over her sunshine face. "You just try and keep me out of your bed! As soon as the sleepers knock her out, I'll be in to climb all over you."

The picture of Annie dolling out the prescribed sleepers introduced a small nag in my mind about drugs. While I felt sure the medics knew what she needed to deal with her injuries from the accident, I wondered had Dervla mentioned her addiction to booze. I was suddenly so pissed off with the way she had treated me since we picked her up at the hospital, that I really didn't give a shit. The impact of this thought stopped me dead, and suddenly I knew how Telly felt about Carol. I could actually empathise fully with my buddy, since I was working from the same script. He put in all he had to give and was found wanting. He tried and tried and then one day he said fuck it, I've had it – which was exactly how I felt at that moment.

I was saddened by what had happened, but Dervla had written that script herself and it wouldn't be long before she accused me of ensuring that she would never have a child, by not blocking the hysterectomy procedure. I knew this was total horse-shit, but it broke my heart some, and I knew that I needed to straighten her out on that one. Thankfully I'd heard Annie's plea of tolerance for her, listened well to the wise counsel of the golden girl. Dervla had just been through hell, and my saying that it was her own fault wouldn't aid her recovery one bit. She was the one who had to climb up the mountain of her miscarriage grief, and the ego pain she had to be going through. Whatever else might be said about her, nobody could accuse her of being stupid. She'd know she had to pick up the tab for the crash. Not that this would stop her dumping as much shit as she could all over me.

During the next three weeks, I spent a lot of time at the desk and I delivered the first of the six books I'd contracted to write. Barry Lane came back to me very quickly, well pleased with the writing. This was good news, a harbinger of good things to come between the publisher and myself. The thing is that I never really know if the thing I've just written is any good or not. You hope. You might even pray about it when the thing is done and dusted. There are better ways to spend your time than rewriting, but when you scribble full-time you probably spend half of your life cutting and rewriting and polishing. Like, you can't just deliver a shitty, shoddy manuscript and hope your agent or your publisher is going to be jumping up and down with glee.

I'd already outlined, in a general way, the next two books. I began the second by outlining several of the early scenes, and I was more than happy with how I was working day in day out. I was even happier when the cheque payable on delivery of the accepted manuscript came to me from my agent Ed Gordon. I was feeling better about myself than I had in a while. I was sticking to my allowance of three joints of grass a day, and twenty Gold Flake, tops. Sometimes when I needed another two or three hours work, I'd pop a solitary Ritalin to help me fill a lot of pages. But I was very careful with this shit. You had to be or you could soon be starring in a remake of your booze story, and that was an experience I certainly didn't need to repeat.

22

Wicklow, early July 1993

As Dervla came out of the dark, as her genuine wounds and bruises and cuts cleared up, she was a little easier around me. There was, though, no suggestion that I come back to bed with herself and Annie. I don't know if she ever considered that golden girl and I had our moments together after she went to sleep. I didn't care what she thought, so it never came up. Then, to my surprise, she accepted an invite from Danny to join himself and Rachel down at his luxurious farmhouse in West Cork. What amazed me was, not that she could leave me, but that she could consider being away from Annie for three weeks. She was now pretty obsessed with my writing student, who week by week was tapping out some good short stories.

It didn't surprise me that Dervla was so intense in her relationship with Annie. She had been like that about me for a good while. With her you never knew the moment when that button might get pressed once more in her head, and you'd be the top banana all over again. She didn't discuss any of it with me, but before she left she thanked me for all the caring. I said nothing. She seemed very sad as she hugged me briefly, and I thought maybe she was coming in out of the cold. Maybe everything wasn't lost, though our relationship was definitely in bad shape.

An hour after Annie came back from dropping Dervla at the airport she came to me in the office. I looked up from the page as she closed the door behind her to find her standing with her back to it wearing the silk dressing-gown I'd bought for her birthday.

"I hope you're not too tired or too busy, for this." She wore that wicked smile I'd come to know and love, as she undid the tie of the dressing-gown. As it dropped to the floor, she stood there with her arms as wide as her giving smile. My blood pressure went up several notches. She wore sexy knickers and a bra above white stockings that rode high on her magnificent thighs. Her high-heels made her as tall as me when I came out of the chair like the house was on fire. Laughing happily, she said, "No matter what happens, I'll always love you. And I wanted to give you a little surprise after what you've had to put up with the last few weeks." She held me at bay for a moment. "Do you like what you see? Do I please you?"

"You're amazing!" I croaked. "You make my heart sing. And you make the rest of me throb. Christ! Just looking at you my whole body's gone hard."

We devoured each other before she mounted me on the desk. She rose to the occasion, you might say. And I joined her, breath for breath, move for move, stroke for stroke. It was arguably the most fulfilling sex we'd ever shared. And not once during that blissful hour did the name Dervla cross my mind. As we finally went up the stairs with nothing but sleep in mind, we were closer than ever with the glow of all she was to me lighting me up. Before we lost it to sleep, she told me, "If things crack up or break up, you know. If the three of us has to stop because Dervla doesn't want you back, I want to be with you. You've given my life a meaning it didn't used to have. I come to the new day now with my whole body smiling and that's down to knowing you, being with you, being loved and fucked by you."

"This is wonderful for a guy to hear, especially a guy heading for the big four O. But right now, I'm giving you an order. Go to sleep."

A few days later, there was a phone call from the Taoiseach's secretary asking if she might speak with Dervla. I told this very nice woman she was not home, that she was recovering from a bad car accident. The woman was gracious, but I could hear disappointment in her voice. During the next few days, I understood precisely why they'd come calling for Dervla's services. They needed her talent to counteract the negative publicity and the numerous demands for the Taoiseach's impeachment.

The government is supposed to be on its summer vacation. At a guess, very few were on holiday. The honest people in Kildare Street, civil servants who do all the real work, are very likely working long hard days to stop the rot that's eating the government. While a lot of politicians walk the floor at home as they wonder will JC survive and will their head be next to roll.

I can't help smiling as I put the phone down. Without being fired in any official way, Dervla had been dumped from her job, and from the fucking desk of JC. But now when they were up to their necks in umbriago and deep in the shit they came without a qualm to assure her that she was needed desperately at government buildings. Scumbags!

Telly drives up to see us, bringing Vanessa for a cup of coffee. They are a serious item now and there's no doubt in my mind that he will leave Carol just as soon as he can create a viable situation. I say very little, allowing that Vanessa is an OK person. I don't really know her, but I have been reasonably tight with Carol over the years and I feel disloyal if I give Vanessa anything more intimate than common courtesy. I leave her with Annie who gives her a real welcome, having blessed Telly with a hug that took years off him.

We take a walk down the hill to the lake and we light up cigarettes and start to shoot the breeze. Out of the blue, Telly says to me, "You and Annie, you look and sound like an item. Or am I imagining things? And if by some chance I'm not imagining things, has Dervla's absence any special significance, or is she really just on vacation with her father in West Cork?"

We're clambering over rocks to find a place to sit by the inner end of the lake. It's a fine July day and when we're comfortably seated, I tell him the story.

"We are an item, Telly, have been for some time. As a matter of fact, and you're the only one outside the three of us who gets to hear this – we've had a *ménage à trois* going up here for a while now." I spoke low-key, trying not to smile as he reacted to what I said. I look down along the lake as I speak, trying hard not to smile in advance at the look of disbelief that was by now surely bending his features out of shape. I hear no sound of the lighter in his hand as I turn away from him. I give him a few more seconds before I can turn to look at him. I'm so desperately in need of exploding with laughter that I could pee myself.

His face is a bountiful blasphemy, a mix of criticism and admiration, a kind of benign wound though his eyes are flinty with envy. He finally inhales a deep drag from his stinking mentholated cigarette. When he has unleashed a long tail of smoke he finds his voice. "You're telling me you make love to those two beautiful women at the same time, night after night after night? Is that what you're saying to me?" He sounds like he's being tortured, but just too proud to cry out in anguish. "You're the only one knows. The only one I'd ever tell."

"Why the fuck did you tell me? You want to drive me fuckin' crazy in my middle-age?"

"You asked. I could have admitted about Annie and me. I just didn't want you thinking I was cheating on Dervla."

He sucks smoke in and exhales as though the smoke is burning his mouth. "How come you can walk around, work, climb this hill and 'get it up' one more time? I think I'd die after one minute in the feathers with Annie and Dervla."

I laugh. "You'd be surprised what you can get up to, or down to, when you're watching two women make love."

He exhales again, looking fed-up with life. "I guess when you're being kinky as a couple the scene needn't damage your relationship. I mean, if you and Dervla want to have another woman in bed and it's in situ, presumably you all can handle it?"

"I'll keep you posted," I said, wanting to change the subject. "Meanwhile, what's your story?"

"That's what I came up here to talk about. I'm leaving Carol and I'm going to live with Vanessa." He said it complete with a built-in warning that I shouldn't question it. I shrugged and told him I'd still be there for Carol, when she needed me.

"I was banking on that," he said. "She'll go bananas when I lay it on her."

"Have you decided when you'll tell her? And, forgive me asking, but how are you going to live? What're you going to do for bread? Vanessa's not secretly rich is she?"

"I was about to tell you. I made a deal with Betsy for some money of my own. She knows I've kept Carol alive, she even told me on the phone I'd earned every penny she was giving me. I've got enough dough to live good for whatever time I've got left. And if you need some dough, I've got some for you, too."

"That's terrific. And she's right. No money could pay you for what you've put in where Carol's concerned. Chances are, no disrespect, Carol won't notice all that much. Without you though she's going to need a paid companion, a live-in nurse, somebody to make sure she doesn't torch herself while she's lighting a joint."

"I'll organise it before I leave." Telly sounded like he had it all worked out. "And I'll go by the house a couple of times a week to make sure she's being looked after. I just won't go on sacrificing whatever time I've got left to her obsession with wiping herself out."

Hearing this I was tempted to talk about Dervla and me, but I had something important I needed to ask him. "What's the story with your health? Where are we with that one?"

"More tests next week. I screwed up the last one by not

attending properly to the stuff they give you to clean out the bowels. They didn't get as clear a picture as they need so we do it again on Wednesday. By mid-afternoon they should know what the story is. Even if I need surgery, I may be at home for a few days before I go back in for the knife."

We moved on without any further talk and I was thinking just how terrific he was. So brave in his own low-key way, the last guy in the world who needed to talk about himself. His last words to me before he drove off that day were, "I always dreamed of two women, not hookers, two women who were in love with me and in bed with me at the same time. Jeez! It's actually happened for you and you're alive to tell the tale. I love you, Sport!" He gave me a grin, shaking his head like I was the coolest guy on the planet. "I fuckin' love you! You know that, don't you?"

I stood watching him drive away, remembering how he'd hefted me up off the pavement in Brooklyn. I thought of the quizzical shape of his Ivy League demeanour when I asked him, "If those guys are bums and assholes like I said, and they throw me out, what does that make me?" I went back in the house, telling myself we'd get over this latest episode, just like we had come through all the others.

In the middle of Dervla's second week in West Cork I get a telephone call from Rachel. When I hear her voice I think something's gone wrong, but she hastily assures me that Dervla is in fine fettle, "making a full recovery physically". I get the implication of this, but I let it pass on. Then she comes to the point of the call. "I'm truly very fond of you, Joe, and I hope that what I'm about to tell you won't in any way interfere with us being close in the future. Anyway, here it is. Dervla spent the night with a Spaniard, a young guy, a waiter, good-looking, something of a stud by the look of him. We go, quite a bit, to the restaurant where he works. I've seen him after work squiring various types of woman in the night-clubs Danny takes me to. I'm telling you this because this chap gets around so much he might be carrying something you wouldn't need in your life. So, at the risk of offending you, please ask Dervla to have a check-up or something when she gets home. I don't know how you can manage that, but if you have to, you can say I told you about her and your man. That's how strongly I feel about this. You shouldn't be put at that kind of risk."

"I appreciate you calling me, Rachel. Thanks. I'll find a way, and I won't forget the risk you took here. I think of you as a good friend. And we'll get together after you come home, OK?"

"I'll look forward to it, Joe. You take care. Bye."

I put the phone down, saddened by what I've just heard. Not that it's the end of the world, Dervla needing to get laid. Maybe she was trying to blast herself out of the dark hole she's been in where men are concerned. Then I wondered if maybe that just applied to me. Then I said "Fuck it, I don't give a shit!" But I did. I hurt that Dervla had gone back to screwing-around.

Dervla is due back from West Cork as Annie has left for an overnight stay in Galway, but she hasn't called asking us to go and get her from the airport. I think maybe she's going to stay on a bit longer. When I get back from dropping the golden girl at Busaras in the late afternoon there she is, Dervla, standing on the balcony overlooking the lake. My throat constricts some when I see her looking very well and absolutely stunning. I give her a wave and a fairly cheery, "Hi!"

She asks me, "Where's Annie?"

"She's on the way to Galway. Be back tomorrow night. And I'm feeling OK, thanks for asking." I go into the kitchen feeling decidedly snotty and I start putting coffee together. I know better than to be mad right now, but nobody's home when I reach for a friend in my head. Then Dervla comes marching into the kitchen.

"One of you might have let me know she was going to be away when I got home." She throws this down like the head-mistress of a school for arseholes who don't know their good manners from their elbows. I take a deep breath knowing I have to tread softly here or I am likely to wreck the kitchen just for the hell of it.

"I know West Cork has its problems," I say slowly, pacing my words to fit with a slow breathing pattern. "I didn't think that lack of telephones was one of them." I lit a Gold Flake and I didn't offer her one, pouring the boiling water on top of the ground coffee, determined to be Mr Cool.

"There's no need for sarcasm, Joe."

"Don't tell me what there's a need for you fucking cow!"

She looks at me with a hint of alarm in her eyes. "What the hell's the matter with you? Jesus! This is some home-coming."

"Fuck you, you stinking fucking whore. Got well fucked, did you? Was Raoul the waiter a great fucking lay? Did you check him out before you sucked his cock? Make sure he didn't have VD? And I'm not even going to go the AIDs route. My mind boggles at that one. Or didn't you think of any of that when you were taking your knickers off?"

"Jesus!" She looked like I'd just slapped her around the face. "Joe. Oh Jesus! I'm sorry, I really am. I was trying to feel some kind of normal. I've been out of my mind since the accident, the hysterectomy. Raoul – it was, I was, Jesus. I was trying to get back to a man, in the hope I might be able to get back to you." This left me lost for words and she said. "I don't blame you for anything you say. But that's the truth. I know how cruel I've been to you, a man I swore to love till death us do part. The finest man I ever met. Jesus! I've been out of my mind, and I couldn't even get you to help me because I'd shut you out so completely." She needed to shed tears, but somehow she held onto them. "I couldn't get down off my fucking high-horse, turn to you, the one who risked everything, broke the rules and risked your life with my fucking crazy father. I turned away from you. That alone should tell you how demented I've been. How demented I am. A sane person would never have done that to you, to anybody."

My hand was shaking as I poured two mugs of coffee. "You'd do well," I said quietly, not attacking her at this moment, "to go and see Tony and get him to check you out. You might have picked up some kind of dose. By all accounts, your pal Raoul puts himself about quite a bit. In addition to whatever else he was offering, he could have given you a present to bring home."

"I made him use condoms, Joe."

I handed her the coffee. "You even managed to control a Spanish waiter who'd fuck a chicken," I laughed. "You're amazing. What did you do? Make him go out and buy French letters when you got to the fucking stage?"

She held the coffee mug as though her hands were cold.

"I bought them. I knew what I had to do. Who the guy was, was pretty immaterial, as long as he didn't smell too much. I was just using him, whether you believe it or not."

"I need some air," I told her, heading out of the kitchen.

She followed me into the late-afternoon. I heard her come across the gravel to where I stood watching the lake flatten as the sun sank behind the mountain.

"Is that it? Is that all we have to say to each other? Have I been dropped for being crazy after the accident, the baby?"

"Don't forget to mention the hysterectomy," I said, wishing I had bitten off my tongue before allowing this cruelty to tumble from my lips.

"I'm sorry for blaming you."

"I've never heard anybody get so much fucking mileage out of the word 'sorry'. Do you never get tired of hearing it out of your mouth?"

"There's no need to be a shit. One shit in this family is enough, Joe. I am sorry over everything. I swear that's the truth." I couldn't find anything to say to her and she cried out, "So what the fuck am I supposed to say? What do you want me to do?"

"Maybe you should just shut the fuck up for a few months. Listen to the stuff you lay down. Hear yourself. Hear the way you blame me and me and me, and anybody else that's handy for your fuck-ups." I finished the coffee and I found myself turning towards the boathouse down to my left by the water. I watched the mug go flying from my hand to smash to pieces against the old stone wall.

"I really have blown it with you, haven't I, Joe?" She sounded desolate, but I wasn't feeling in the least angelic so I couldn't say one word to comfort her.

"You're wasted in PR. The way the words just trip off your tongue. To be able to think on your feet the way you can, you should be in politics. As a matter of interest, were you ever going to tell me about fucking JC?" I was looking at her as I said the words, watching with some kind of sick fascination as I got ready to deliver the knockout punch. She was reeling in what I could only describe as a welter of shame even before I said, "Were you ever going to tell me how you got caught sitting on his dick on the Taoiseach's desk?"

Without moving an inch, she was like a woman being driven backwards by a combination of blows to her face and body. The coffee mug fell from her hand and, had I not moved as fast as I did, she would have crashed onto the gravel in front of the lodge. I hefted her into my arms – she was out cold. I took her up to the bedroom and lay her down. I pulled a cover over her and I went into the bathroom and found smelling salts. I ran hot water into a plastic basin, and found a face flannel. I went back into her where she lay supine, completely out of it. Carefully, I held the smelling salts under her nose and as she started to respond, I wiped her face very gently with the warm face flannel. As I did so, I was remembering the times before we started driving into the cul-de-sacs we create for ourselves. Times when we washed each other with warm flannels, rubbing oil into our skins, so in love that we used every chance available to touch and be touched. There was so much love between us that our angers, and our tantrums and our fears and our madness couldn't fuck it up.

Dervla opened her eyes and closed them again, as though she couldn't bear the gift of sight for a moment longer. I asked her would she like a hot drink and she shook her head from side to side, without even opening her eyes. I headed for the door and she called my name. I turned around and she pushed herself up onto the pillows against the headboard of the bed.

"Apart from whatever else may be wrong with me, I have my father's real sickness which is this fascination with power." She reached over to the bedside table and lit herself a cigarette. Exhaling she said, looking directly at me. "I found you so powerful I fell in love with you at first sight. No matter what you think right now, I still feel all of that." She drew on the cigarette and I waited. "I'm trying not to say I'm sorry, Joe. No matter what you think of me, when I agreed to go back working with JC, I swear I believed I was completely beyond having sex with him again. I would never have gone, but I wanted Daddy and his stupid fucking threat off our backs."

"I know that," I said. "You don't have to explain it to me."

"Nevertheless, I'd like to get it out of the way, regardless of what's going to happen to us. I accept full responsibility for what happened. He was always the same around me and I thought the effect he used to have on me wouldn't cost me a thought. I wasn't working for an hour when he came to my office. He welcomed me, embraced me. I put my arms about him and then he simply devoured me. And Joe, I have to be straight with you, I didn't object because I couldn't. Once he exposed himself to me and all the rest of it, I didn't want to put him off. It was like my head had turned right over. One moment I knew that nothing could possibly happen between Jay and me, the next I was wrapping myself around him, holding him like I wanted every shred of him inside me. After that he had me any time he wanted. He did what he liked with me and I welcomed it. And the day we got caught on the desk was not the first time he fucked me there. That's the story. If you wash your hands of me right now, I can't blame you. If it was the other way around, I don't think I could live with you."

"I think we should take the weekend, not make any major decisions tonight. If you agree to that, we'll see where we go in the morning."

She looked somewhat relieved and she said so. "Of course, I agree." She started to get off the bed. "I need a shower. Thanks for picking me off the gravel. The other way around and I'd probably have left you lying there." She began to unbutton her blouse. "I'm here if you need to talk more tonight."

I shook my head. "I've been working my ass off on book two for Barry Lane. If I get a good weekend's work, I could be e-mailing it to him by Tuesday. I'd like that a lot."

As I turned to go she said, "Are you still happy about Annie and us?"

"Sure I am. Annie helped me stay sane the last three weeks."

"Did you tell her about Raoul the waiter?"

"No. She's cool enough to handle that, but I didn't see the point. You enjoy your shower."

In the office, I went to work and except for rising to make coffee I beavered away until three in the morning. The work had gone well. I was more than pleased when I counted the number of pages that had come through for me, even more grateful for being as preoccupied as I was with the book.

That night the work was a lifebelt and I willingly gave it all my attention until I climbed the stairs on my way to a much needed night's sleep. As I made my way down the passage to the room I'd been sleeping in while Dervla had shut me out, I heard her call my name. I went to the door of our bedroom. When I pushed it open I found her sitting up with a book that she was putting down on the duvet cover. "If you want, you can come back to your own bed."

I stood there looking at her, glad she seemed easier in herself. "You look lovely, and more importantly, you look very much better. I still hope we can come through this, but I don't know what's going to happen."

"Come into bed." She said it as though she thought I would, provided she asked me in the right way and played her cards right. "Let's put it all behind us. It was all just the games people play. Compared to where we've come from, none of it seems real."

In a way, I felt she was right, but in that moment I was the one couldn't get down off his high horse. "I'm really tired, so I'm going to go down the hall. I need to be on my own, let things sift through, see where we are after the weekend. No way can I sleep in there with you, without wanting to fuck."

"Is that such a crime? Come on, Joe. It's not like you to hold a grudge."

"That's not what I'm doing. We'll talk in the morning. 'Night."

I turned away, unconcerned about the longing in her eyes, the hurt around her mouth as she realised she wasn't getting her own way tonight. The truth was that, for all my cool, my heart felt bruised enough to be broken, and I didn't want to use a fuck to insulate me from whatever I had to go through.

"Goodnight Joe," she said, like someone believing they'd lost something of great value.

I had to steel myself to keep going, to not turn around and go back and take her in my arms in our bed and make love to her. In a while, outside the room I was in, I heard Dervla begin to turn the door handle. Then she stopped, and I almost said a prayer of thanks out loud. I leaned against the door for a few seconds, as though that would ensure it couldn't open again for the rest of the night. I sighed in relief when I heard her close our bedroom door. I guess I just didn't want to take any more anger into our bed, though I ached to have her. She was my woman after all.

'Enough shit', I heard myself yell in my mind, knowing that just this once I didn't want to hide from what I really felt by burying myself between her legs. I want to stay at the coal-face, face up if you like, sort out some of the shit that's clogging up my head. I wasn't going into our bed to hump her. No way. I knew that if I did I'd be there to hurt her physically, which part of me wanted to do.

Somehow, the ache in my mind seemed to travel south. A minute later I had this dull ache in my lower-back, the same feeling I'd known previously, only not so strong. As the back-pain hit me, I felt angry. I was angry at the way I'd let things slide, mad that I hadn't protected my ass, meaning Dervla and me. I should have said no, fuck it, to the idea of her going back to work with a guy she'd had such a great time with in and out of bed. My attention had been in the wrong places when the job suggestion came from Danny Devine. I'd been looking at how much she could earn, at the amount of work I'd get through if she was out of the house a few days a week. The implication of herself and JC in a close working relationship had been ignored, because at the time it suited me to overlook it. Letting her go back there, even though she was responsible for herself, was a stupid and careless mistake. And there was no accounting, even leaving out the ache in my back, of how much that whole trip was going to cost Dervla and me.

Meanwhile, I'm in need of help. Since I'm not going to get it through hiding in hot sex, and I can't seriously start praying to a God I've derided since my teen years, I do what I should have done in the first place. I head for the stairs, intending to go down and phone Telly. What else does an alky do when his shit is bouncing off the walls? He phones another alky, and they talk about fucking booze.

As I head along the passage, I hear what sounds like mumbo-jumbo. It's coming from our bedroom and I tiptoe to the door. As quietly as I possibly can, I turn the handle as silently as I can. I see Dervla on her knees by the bed, her arms raised and wide in what I'd call the crucifixion mode. "For all my sins and transgressions, for the sins of the flesh with which I know I offend thee, O lord. Help me get through this night without causing you further pain. I am heartily sorry for all my sins; through my fault, through my fault, through my most grievious fault."

I quietly step down the stairs, my heart limping along with me. I have to steel myself to keep going down, to not go back and take her in my arms with promises of undying love.

Downstairs, I rang Telly's number three times. It wasn't that late and I'd have been more than surprised if he'd gone to bed by now. I didn't expect Carol to answer the phone since she was totally wiped every night by midnight, getting carried to bed by Telly more often than she got there under her own steam.

I thought of the clinic, rang the number and talked to the night guy, Jimmy. I'd given him a signed copy of one of my books and he was a fan. He told me that Telly had been kept overnight for further observation. According to the nursing staff, he was fine, but some small irregularity had presented and they were just being thorough. I put the phone down, relieved that the news wasn't any worse than it was. Then I made some coffee and I sat and went into the memories of a lot of good times – attending a lot of AA meetings in Manhattan, branching out into the five boroughs, going to hear new voices, meet new people, every meeting another step towards sober thinking. Unless you were doing anything to get in the way. Like falling madly in love, like smoking dope. I quit the thought as quickly as I can. I had enough to deal with for one night.

23

Wicklow, late July 1993

Annie gets back from Galway tonight and we're driving to Harold's Cross where we'll meet her at an AA social evening. Dervla is beside me in the jeep, but we're not jumping up and down. She is a bit remote, but her vibe is gentler, a lot of her anger gone with the wind. She has come in a step or two from the furthest fringe she could find away from me. I don't mean to be critical here. She was doing the best she could. It was just that there had been too much pain hurled at each other, too much choking off the good stuff that had been there between us. It had to be there still, even after the trauma when she got back from West Cork and I went for her over her shag with a Spanish waiter. I reasoned that all we'd found together in the turmoil and the agony of trying to get sober couldn't just have disappeared in a puff of smoke. In a nutshell, so much of the behaviour and the repeated shifting of emphasis and blame added up to one simple thing – a dry drunk. A dry drunk means you are pissed in your mind– though not actually drinking booze at the time, though you are behaving like a guy who has a bunch of mean fucking devils partying in his head. This realisation was, in itself, a sobering experience and I was feeling a lot better as I parked the jeep at the Harold's Cross venue.

As we went into the hired hall I could hear dance music that wasn't half-bad. Dervla whispers to me, "Make me smile, Joe, please?" I was glad she was well enough to say please. This was a first and I chose to see it as a harbinger of better times ahead.

I said *à la* Carol, "You ought to remember my face, sweetie! You sat on it often enough!" Dervla burst out laughing, and that was the first sight of her that our AA acquaintances got on that Sunday night. I saw Telly across the room and raised my eyebrows as Vanessa came to him with a glass of orange squash. I smiled as they touched glasses and said to myself, "What difference? It's all just one big soap opera!"

Telly told me later that Vanessa had come to the dance by herself. She was attending Al-Anon meetings now. Al-Anon is the fellowship for people affected by the alcoholism of a significant other. I was relieved that he wasn't going public about their affair. All in all, we had enough on our plates without creating any more flak. There were AA people at the gig that never spoke to Dervla or me. These people had taken a stance about us. I heard of one stalwart, a big bluff type who said, "I talk to them to remind myself I'm in AA", which I thought was fair enough. At least the guy was trying to let go of one judgmental attitude.

I found a couple of seats at a table and we sat listening to the music, which was ordinary but acceptable. At least it was live and not so loud you could mistake it for another D-day landing. Dervla smoked a Gold Flake and I brought soft drinks to the table. She looked lovely and I knew part of me was going to be broken up if we couldn't survive the aggravation we'd been generating in recent times.

When I saw Annie come into the hall, my heart lit up. She was untying the belt of a new lightweight raincoat and when she took it off I'd hazard a guess that every guy in the place gasped audibly. She was wearing a skin-tight red woollen dress and I guess that was about it. I felt like giving her a standing ovation. She was so alive, so wide-eyed and open to whatever came her way, so free.

"Annie's arrived," I said quietly.

Dervla brightened up and grabbed her handbag. "I'll just be a minute."

As she headed for the ladies' room, I went to greet Annie. When she saw me, she shook her head in playful delight, her honey-blonde hair flying loosely about her shoulders. She threw herself into my open arms. Then, before I had time to decide whether or not it was a smart move to be seen kissing her in public, Annie planted her lips on mine. I managed to cut it short, having noticed the smallest trace of white powder around her nostrils. Golden girl had been sniffing coke.

The music started and we began to throw some shapes. Right away, Annie was having a great time. After a minute I opened my arms, indicating that I wanted to dance closely. I leaned into her, whispering "Lean into my shoulder and rub your nose against me. You've got a bit of Charlie showing." She did what I said and pulled her head back to whisper her thanks. I winked my eye. "Be careful, Annie. We're getting a lot of attention that we don't need."

She nodded, simmering down a bit, but only a bit. She was bubbling when she told me in a happy-go-lucky voice that she had met a guy, a black guy that Dervla and I would just love. "I managed to get him to bed, we hardly slept." She was shining on whatever had gone down, with a little help from the Charlie. But she wasn't slow about giving me an old-fashioned 'what do you take me for?' kind of look when I said, "Please tell me you used condoms."

Annie galloped on, the whole story delivered guilelessly, the sound of the pleasure she'd experienced honeycombed through her voice. She brought her friend, Jenny, into the action. It had been a long time since they had any kind of sex scene together. She prattled on, full of her dreams and the future adventures she wanted to have happen to her. "Could we invite Jenny up to Lough Dane sometime? She's a riot, game for anything."

I made the right sounds, surprised at how hurt I felt that Annie had just gone off and got laid. I didn't let her see this. I was playing Mr Cool to the hilt, ignoring the need to say what I felt. I didn't want to risk any division between Annie and me. I had enough of that going full-blast with the other woman in my life. As Annie and I stood waiting for the band to play the next encore, Dervla was beside us on the dance-floor. Her eyes were all over Annie. I put them together saying very loudly, "I need to strain the potatoes!" as though I was the comic turn.

Dervla coming onto the dance-floor to take Annie in her arms was something I hadn't expected. But overall, I was glad. I mean, it was a far cry from asking me to "make me smile" as we came in the door. Change could only be for the good, or so I thought in my own ingenuous way.

I stepped outside into the noise of Harold's Cross and smoked a Gold Flake, wondering if we could go on as a trio. When we started out it was pure Hollywood, every day a happy ending as we went to sleep entwined and in love. In those early times I could never have imagined it turning into anything like kitchen-sink, but it wasn't technicolour any more, that's for sure. I heard the control-freak in my head moaning that if only people would listen. That's where the trouble comes from. Everybody wants to have their own agenda. Why can't they just listen to me and we need never have any aggravation. I shut the guy out, choosing to remember things that weren't going to bring me down. I saw myself back there at lunch after the trio had spent its first night making love. I was smiling. My ladies were so much in love with each other, both of them in love with me. What more could a guy ask for?

"Annie wants to come and stay, Joe. Move in, OK?"

We're all agreed that Annie should come and be with us at the lodge, it's just a matter of creating the cover-story. By the end of lunch, Annie is my part-time secretary, given room and board and some money and the facility to get on with her own writing, with some tuition for me. In addition to this, she volunteers to do some landscape work around the house. And so we had started out. That was the beginning of a new level of sensation in our lives and I never once thought that it would end. We were so happy so much of the time that the idea of it finishing just never entered my head. Even when the cracks started to show and Dervla crashed the jeep and got swallowed up by her pain, I avoided any notion that a moment would arise or a time would come when it might very well end. I wanted it to go on and on. I knew I wouldn't do anything to break it up. I never had an inkling that when it did come apart, the break-up would be between my two lovely ladies, with me playing the role of innocent bystander.

Shortly after we leave Harold's Cross for Lough Dane, my

ladies are tight in the back of the jeep, which is really a Range Rover. They're wrapped about each other, and by the time I drive up onto the Featherbed, the vibe is so coated in good feeling it's a crime that a guy couldn't take a picture of it.

I went straight to the spare-room, pretty sure that Dervla wouldn't be calling me back to our bed tonight. I didn't mind. I was tired, and I knew that Annie would come to me at some time during the night. I went to sleep right away, but it wasn't long before I woke up with a start at the sound of the door being torn open. I blink and shield my eyes against the light that has been turned on by a half-crazed Dervla. She's wearing a nightgown that cost me an arm and a leg in Brown Thomas and I notice she is gripping it in her two fists like she's afraid her insides could spill out onto the floor. Her eyes are shattered and I move to get up and take her in my arms. "What happened? What's going on?"

"She told you. She told you and you said nothing. You let me give myself to her after what she did and you said nothing," she ranted in a strangled voice. No screaming and yelling, not yet. I shook myself, fully-awake by now. "You allowed me put my lips down to her, knowing she had sex with some black guy she never saw before last night. How could you? How could you let that happen to me?"

Suddenly I was mad. "Get the fuck outa here. I've had all I can take of you." I got out of the bed and just shoved her out of the room, sliding the little bolt across the door. She began pounding with her fists and kicking to be let in. I wrenched at the door, forgetting the bolt and I felt for a moment that I'd broken my wrist. When I got the door open I was so angry that I smacked her across the face. She fell back against the wall of the landing, probably too stunned to yell, and I walked past her without saying a word.

Annie was sitting up in the bed and I went to her. She was sobbing her heart out. "She said it's over, Joe. She called me crazy names, said she'd never speak to me again. Joe, she went crazy, and all I did was share what happened with Laurie. I thought she wanted to know everything. Oh shit! I fucked it up." She released a groan of despair. "I don't know what I'm going to do without you. I love you so much."

I kissed her forehead, waiting while she started moving back from the hurt. "Give me a second," I said, going to the door. Dervla was still lying back against the wall, as she had been from the moment I smacked her. I went to her and I lifted her face up off her chest so that she was looking at me.

"I'm getting into bed to comfort Annie. I'm asking you to drop this, to come and be part of us again. I love you. And maybe we all need to comfort each other as opposed to any of us blaming anybody for anything that's gone down. It's already in the past. So, come into your bed. Come and let's all help each other to simmer down?"

She looked at me like I belonged under a rock. "I can take the smack. You owe me more than one. But if you put a finger on that dirty little tramp, you and I are over and out. I mean it, Joe. That's my final word."

I let her see my shrug of resignation, and I watch her as she peels herself off the wall to practically hurl herself into the spare-room. She slams the door shut and I stand there for a few seconds. As I hear her get into another crazy praying trip, I shake my head in resignation and I leave her to her God.

I go back to Anne and I lie down beside her and put my arm about her shoulders so that she's able to snuggle into me. Then I have to get up for a second to lock the bedroom door. The way Dervla is behaving, I'm not taking any chances tonight. In a little while, as we both drift off to sleep I'm thinking I don't want any more of this Dervla shit. No disrespect to her. Let her be any way she wants, or feels she needs to be. I don't give a fuck. I believe it has to be possible to live in some kind of peace on a continuing basis. That's what I want and somehow I have to find a way to make that work for me. Dervla doesn't want to know right now, and though this creates a nagging in the heart region, it doesn't bother me enough to keep me awake.

When I woke up at seven thirty, I made Annie lock the bedroom door behind me as I went downstairs to get some food going for all of us. I half expected that when I took Dervla a cup of coffee and some hot toast smothered in butter and marmalade, she'd have forgotten the madness. I didn't really believe this, not this time. She had said some pretty wild late-night things in the past, but I'd never seen her quite so pineapple as she'd been over Annie and the black dude she laid over in Galway.

To my surprise, she joined me in the kitchen as I was putting a pot of coffee together. I wished her a light-hearted good morning, willing to at least attempt to get off on the right note. It didn't work. She came marching into the kitchen with her sergeant major's stride at full-stretch and wearing her very own storm clouds.

"Sorry for the smack, Derv. But you were going crazy."

"I want her out of my home. Now. Today. If she is here past noon I'll be the one to leave, and you will never see me again." Her voice is so tight, so controlled I fear she might crack into little pieces right there before my eyes. I butter the toast, trying not to lose my temper. She can't be well to be talking like this.

She stormed out of the kitchen and I called after her, "Say something, even if it's only good-bye!"

As I took a tray upstairs for Annie, I repeated the vow to myself not to get involved in this shit. I gave Annie coffee and toast, heading down to my office to see if I can find anything in Dervla's journals that might throw some light on this need to pray like she's being tortured. On the landing, I stop outside the spare-room. I hear more of the mumbo-jumbo sound come through the wall and when I open the door I see Dervla is at it again, kneeling by the bed with her arms wide in supplication to 'the man above', her rosary beads wrapped tightly around her left hand. Her desperate pleas for forgiveness were accompanied by tears that tumbled off her eyelids like rain bouncing off a windscreen. Her voice, normally quite dry and firm, is coated in phlegm and might belong to someone I've never met. ". . . for all my sins and transgressions, for the sins of the flesh with which I know I offend thee, O Lord. Help me get through this day without causing you further pain. I am heartily sorry for all my sins."

I close the door. To find her like this makes me sad. It happens sometimes and it bothers me because she sounds crazy when she gets into this sort of frenzied praying. It can happen for a day or two or, can you believe it, the seven weeks of Lent?

Leafing through her journals in my office, I found that this 'holy mary' role had puzzled the hell out of her cousin Eamon for years.

◄◦►

"My poor fucking cousin Eamon is mesmerised yet again this year, when I refuse to fuck him during Lent. Eamon's willing to settle for blow-jobs so he assures me, his face dropping like a stone when I tell him there's no way. He simply can't understand how someone like me, he means a nympho like me, can just shut up shop for seven weeks. So poor man, born with a hard-on, has to go to hookers, which has its own buzz, so he assures me. But it is a dangerous thing for a guy in his position to do, with so many 'tabloid toe-rags' as he calls reporters lurking about in the dark sniffing for a story, that will get them a banner headline come Sunday."

◄○►

To help me keep my head together, I get into the great escape of music. It helps me when I need a break from work, and it's a great antidote to the very heavy vibe running through our great old shooting lodge at this very moment. So, I'm at the keyboard in the drawing-room working out some chord structures, when Dervla appears. She's wearing a black track suit, her hair drawn back behind her head, her face bereft of make-up. She is beautiful and my heart lurches for a moment at the solidity of the distance between us. Her perfect eyes, dark as grapes, are like badges of pain. My heart goes out to her, but I know this is no time to try to help her to a better place. For now, she has lost all trust in me. It's no surprise that Dervla blames me for not telling her about Annie and the guy in Galway. It's a rare situation in which she can't find somebody to blame for whatever she doesn't want to face. Right now, with her black track suit and her dark demeanour, the vibe suggests she is about to lay down some new by-laws she has designed to help me deal with my end of our situation.

"You understand we are finished with that cow, don't you."

"Annie's a great friend. I won't be deserting her, not for anybody. I guess you've already done that."

"No! Not just me. Us! We, we are finished with her." She seems to catch up with what I've just said, and this stops her for a moment. I see the fear double up in her eyes. She grabs a quick snatch of breath before she can tell me, "She's out of our lives. Or I'm out of yours."

"OK," I said. "Let's run them up the flagpole. These serious problems you have in your mind. But first get it straight in your mind that Annie, who's been a real pal and by your own admission 'a most generous lover', did nothing wrong. She got a bit pissed and she finally got some black ham, a guy she wanted to fuck. It was her idea of fun at the time, and I see nothing wrong with that. No! Just listen a fuckin' minute. For you, the problem with the scenario is that Annie didn't ask your permission to bang a black dude she fancied. That's all. You couldn't control the situation. So, now I'm warning you. I won't turn my back on her, and you have no right to expect that me to."

"We gave her everything – a home, money, trust, friendship, love. And you think it's all right that she went off and fucked a total stranger?"

"Did you ask her if you could fuck Raoul down in West Cork?" The question hit her like a blow, but it didn't stop me finishing what I had to say. "I don't give a fuck. But I find your self-righteousness nauseating. I mean you're the same lady sits on Jay Charles' cock on the desk in the fucking Taoiseach's office. For Jesus sake, Dervla! Just listen to yourself. You've over-reacted here. For fuck's sake! For everybody's sake, hold your hands up. Let it go. Get down off the pulpit before it's too late."

I walked outside into the morning. It was turning toward

noon, the sun was high over the lake and it seemed like a perfect August morning of the kind in which everyone ought to know some degree of happiness or contentment. My glorious falcon was up above the lake somewhere, but I was in no mood to look for him. His latest cry seemed to carry the ring of loneliness in it, and I had enough of that to be going on with down here.

In that moment Dervla is right by my side. "I can't believe it," she gasps fearfully. "I thought she had self-respect." She speaks so quietly I wonder have I heard her right.

"If we go on talking like this I'm going to say a lot of things I'd rather not. But I have to warn you about people in glasshouses! You mention self-respect, Jesus! You have balls, or maybe it's just blindness. The blindness you share with your pal, Jay. I don't give a fuck that he has no self-respect, it's OK with me. I don't have a problem with that. I do have a problem with his lack of respect for the office of Prime Minister of the Republic of Ireland. Consider the air of corruption he spawned even before he became the main man. Nobody but JC would have been seen dead around Turk Raymond and your father. But they stole money donated to the party, nicked it for him and for themselves. 'The Mohair Men' – the Mohair Menace more like. And what about the allegations of gun-running, how he's fuelled the rumours and the gossip that turned him into some kind of folk hero, though 'fuck hero' might be more appropriate. And while your father is 'doing the laundry', what's Dervla doing? She's working on Bullshit Boulevard glossing the motherfucker's image, and oh yeh, she's banging him at the same time!"

She was stunned to muteness, but I was barrelling on

anyway. I couldn't hold down the build-up I'd been sitting on for weeks, not any longer. "All the shit that goes on. All the criminal fucking scheming so this asshole, this motherfucker, can get big enough in his own imagination that he can haul his ashes on the Taoiseach's desk. It's unbelievable. Seriously, you couldn't make it up. To not have the wit to lock the fucking door? Or did he want to be caught? That's it! Fuck me! He wanted to add another stroke of colour to his already technicolour image. And he used you to help him do it. So you go down in history as the whore who sat on his dick while drug barons are shooting each other all over the country, and there's more police corruption than at any time in our history.

"And he's happy because they'll be talking about him fucking, not only in his office, but on the fucking desk if you don't mind," I stopped for breath, but not for long. "So be careful how you talk to me about self-respect. Can't you see, fucking you he was fucking Ireland by depriving her of his real talents, his god-given abilities. And he was fucking the faith and the hopes of the poor fish that elected him in the first fucking place. Don't you see, he was fucking everything and everybody whenever he stuck is cock into you."

I turned around to find Dervla weeping silent tears and I heard myself saying, "God help me, because for all the shit that's gone down, I love you. And I care deeply about what's going to happen to you. But you're not going to stop me seeing Annie. I love her too, and I care about her future. I can't flick a switch and stop loving Annie just because your ego is in a sling or you've got a broken-heart this morning."

Anger flared again in her eyes, her tears were brushed aside and she said with self-righteous defiance. "And I know I can't bear the thought of you going off to be with her. I can't take that. And I won't." She was looking at me as though she needed help.

"So what're you saying? You are absolutely totally saying that unless I drop Annie as you seem to have done, you and I are through. Have I got that right?"

She nodded her head, and her tears began to flow again. It was awful to watch. I'd never seen anything take hold of her the way those fear-filled moments did. "Something terrible is going to happen," she said, like someone observing an inevitable disaster. Then she turned and went back into the lodge.

A couple of days later, Dervla is still in residence. As yet, I've not made any move to get Annie out of there. Like a kid, I'm hoping that things will just come right because that's what I want most of all.

Telly gets admitted to the clinic, and I talk to him and he's OK about his scene. I'm not so sure and I'm trying to get more information from him when he asks me to hold on a second. I hear some murmuring and then I find myself being addressed by Telly's chief medical guy. He tells me that since Telly has arrived into the clinic with a slight chill the proposed surgery is on hold for a few days. "We want him in top form before we do the procedure. Mr Sampras has already given me signed authorisation that I am free to talk to you about his condition, Mr Collins. Otherwise, we could not be having this conversation."

I told him I understood and I asked him could he tell me any more.

"Only that we expect Mr Sampras to make a full recovery. He's told you about the colostomy bag. That will be in place for perhaps six months, just part of this particular surgical procedure. It has become fairly routine. At this time we see no major reason why Mr Sampras won't be up and about within two weeks."

I felt some relief to get the word from the main guy, and I went upstairs and told Dervla who was moping about in her nightgown. I noticed signs that she was setting up to leave the lodge, but I didn't say anything. She thanked me politely for letting her know how Telly was, and I left her alone.

I told Annie that I'd be driving her down to the house at Whiterock within a few days, hoping meanwhile that Dervla came to her senses. "You'll be staying in my flat, sleeping in my bed, some nights with me. How does that sound?"

Annie took a drag from my Gold Flake and gave it back. "No matter what happens, Joe, I'll make no demands on you. I love you, and I always will."

I left her then and I went looking for Dervla. I had to give my appeal for reason just one more shot. Maybe she was scared enough to listen, to simmer down long enough for commonsense to tell her, don't wreck your partnership over this. If we could get to that point, maybe then we could talk things over and see if we could rescue something that had seemed indestructible. I didn't get to talk to her that day. As I was coming downstairs to see where she'd gone, she took off in the Range Rover. I came running out of the lodge waving my arms and yelling at her to wait a minute. If she heard me, she didn't react, and if she saw me in the rear-view mirror it didn't help her hit the brake and then she was long gone.

I can't remember when I last felt that sad. I tried to let her go emotionally, but all I got was a spaghetti-like twist of hurt and the kind of inner turmoil that can make you dizzy. The thought that we really could be over sent infantries of fear coursing through me and I actually threw up on the gravel. Some deep breathing later, I felt a little better and I went to my office. I needed to write. I had to get on, do the work. No matter how badly the shit was hitting the fan, I had a delivery date to honour. There was no way I'd ring Barry Lane and ask for more time. I always felt that when you've been paid an advance, you leave your shit outside the office door and you deliver on time.

Later in the day, I get a call from Champion. He's been off-side, he tells me, keeping a low profile. "A misunderstanding with some heavy revolutionary types," he explains quietly. "Nothing I can't sort out, but it means you let things slide. So, now that I'm back on the front burner, how about you bring Dannyboy to see me the day after tomorrow? I own a café, two doors up from the Bad Ass. Daisy's Diner, half three sharp, OK?"

I say thanks for calling me back, if only because it'll show Danny Devine I can make something happen. Champion had refused point-blank to meet him before because of his threat to me. "He's got a big fucking squirrel in his head," Champion had told me without rancour. "Corkmen are like Mexicans. Bananas from living so far south! Anyway, I'll see the prick because you asked me to."

I left Annie to unpack her stuff in my flat at the house in Whiterock and I went looking for Carol to say hello, see how she was doing. I found her lying on the bathroom floor. She was unconscious. Her pulse was so faint it took me a while to find it. I knew the drill by now. I called her doctor Paddy Fahy and told him the story. He asked me if the pulse was steady and I confirmed that it was. He said he'd be there within the hour. I put Carol on her bed, told Annie to keep an eye on her, that I'd be back as soon as I'd made a quick visit to Telly in the clinic.

He was sitting up in bed reading a copy of *The Long Goodbye* by Raymond Chandler that I'd left with him a few days earlier. He and I were Chandler freaks, and we regularly talked about the characters as though they were in our circle of acquaintances. I gave him a hug and he held me tight for a few moments, which told me something.

"I guess it's been a scary time for you," I said. "You're not alone on that one."

"I've never been scared of dying, sport," he ruminated as though he was thinking aloud. "I am scared of pain though. Be glad when it's over. And I'll wear the bag, OK? Sorry for making a movie out of it."

My grin of relief was my answer to that one. "I know," he allowed. "'I'd sooner be dead than have to dump into a bag.' Hey! Did I really say that?" I got his five thousand dollar grin. This was what his last set of caps and some fillings had cost him before we left Manhattan. "I've had a change of heart, sport. I want to live, and I'm gonna do whatever they tell me. They say six months or so, I can have the colostomy thing reversed. I'll be able to do my number twos just like regular folk."

"How's Vanessa holding up?" I asked. "I've had some problems so I haven't been calling her."

"She's OK, sport. She's a tough lady, knows how to roll with the punches. These problems of yours — are we talking about you and Dervla? And Annie?"

I spent a few minutes telling him what had gone down. "Hit a pile of meetings, sport, top up your bank-balance, sobriety-wise," he advised me.

"I aim to get one tonight," I said honestly.

"Make sure you do, sport. Don't Think! Don't Drink! Go To Meetings!"

"I hear that. And thanks for reminding me. It amazes me that I can forget. Without the slogans and the meetings, Jesus man, where would we be?" I shook my head. "I'll tell you one thing, this sobriety ain't for wimps!" He smiled at my cornball accent.

"Being a stinkin' drunk ain't neither!" Playing along, he gave me a grin.

"Listen, just in case she comes to see you. I love Dervla. They were my last words to her. A lot of shit went down. She took off. I've let her go to see if she wants to be reasonable. I can't do any more than I did. I promise you that."

"Sure." His dark eyes were rheumy looking. They were what I'd call 'kinda old eyes' in someone else, but I didn't want to think of him in that way. There were lines in the irises, each one like a sliver of pain or disease. The picture disconcerted me more than I wanted to acknowledge. I was suddenly weary, admitting to myself that I was harbouring a nagging worry that my buddy wouldn't come through the surgery. At the same time, I honestly believed he would. Next thing, I'm dumping on myself for being judgemental about Carol, who had been so busy trying to kill herself for so long that she didn't know any other way to be. All of this shit clogging up the head while I'm asking my best buddy if there's anything he wants me to bring in next visit. He makes no mention of Carol so I let the hare sit. We're both preoccupied with him, which is just as it should be.

I got back to the house as Paddy Fahy, the doc, was arranging for Carol to be taken to St Pats to be detoxed. He looked at me and gave me his old-fashioned look, the one that said it was a waste of time. "She needs the detox unit.

She'll be out of it for a few days. No need to worry about her. She won't be going anywhere."

In a way, I was glad she was out of things for the moment. The truth was that Carol was in a lot more danger than Telly. Every minute she was allowed drive her own scene she was putting another nail in the coffin of her life. There was no way, short of having her committed to a locked-in, drug-free unit, that Telly could stop her from doing dope. She was, quiet literally, doomed to die by her own hand, even if she wasn't actively trying to commit suicide. It might have been a kindness to have just allowed her go on lying where she had overdosed. But we had to go on drying her out, having her detoxed. She might wake up one day and know that it was time to get clean and dry, and see about making some kind of sense out of the rest of her three score and ten.

I got to Daisy's Diner at twenty past three. There was no sign of Champion, but Danny Devine's limo driver dropped him off with a minute to go before the half hour. He greeted me with a handshake and a murmured word of thanks for fixing up the meeting. I offered him coffee. He declined and lit himself a Balkan Sobranie without offering one to me. I got a Gold Flake going and then Champion came out of the kitchen. He sat down beside me and facing Danny. He was handed a slim leather briefcase by one of his minders. They were heavy-looking dudes, guys with short foreheads and eyes you wouldn't want to see looking your way. They sat at a table between Champion and the door. I couldn't swear to it, but by the shape of their fairly shapeless jackets, I thought they were tooled up.

"OK," Champion said. "Before we start, Joe, take this with you. Don't open it till you get home." He slides the case to me on the tabletop. "Really, there's no need for you to be here beyond this point. OK with you, Danny?"

Danny nodded and Champion stood up and shook my hand. "We'll grab a bite soon, OK." He raised his right hand, pointing the index finger at me, like he was saying 'and you make sure you get there'. I nodded to them both and headed for the door.

When I got back to Whiterock, I phoned St Pat's and heard that Carol was out of the detox unit. I left a message I'd come by later. I hit the answering machine hoping for some word from Dervla, but she hadn't called. Annie arrived in from a run she'd taken along the shore and while she was in the shower I flicked on the television news. The lead story brought me out of my chair with the shock before I fell back again, so stunned I almost blacked out.

Champion and Danny Devine had been shot dead in Daisy's Diner just minutes after I'd left the table. Two guys in balaclavas had come in through the kitchen, one keeping the staff quiet, while the second stepped into the café. He disarmed the heavies, made them lie face down on the floor before he shot Danny and my old friend with a machine pistol. Then he walked back out through the kitchen and, according to an eyewitness report, the pair rode away on a motorcycle, removing their balaclavas as they went. The hit had been claimed by a breakaway, provisional IRA group, the speaker giving the registered password for the unit. As a shy garda inspector appeared on screen, delivering the usual waffle about following a definite line of enquiry or whatever, I hit the remote button and the screen went dead.

I lit a cigarette and inhaled about half of it into myself before I could even let my mind go to what might have been had Champion not ushered me from the scene when he did.

It was the strangest feeling. To think I could have been lying dead right now just because I was in the wrong place at the right time to die, doing a favour for a man I had absolutely no respect for.

The case against Champion as anything other than a career-criminal who had done it all in terms of breaking the law precluded the possibility of me seeing him as some kind of public benefactor. I did feel a hint of sadness though, over his exit. I liked Champion and I felt a lot of gratitude to him. I loved being alive far too much to be blasé about the fact that I was still here. I wanted the day, no matter what was going down in scenario.

I remembered the briefcase Champion had given me. When I opened it, I found a large sheaf of typewritten pages covered with dates and numbers. It turns out to be a record of Champion's life which even at a glance read intimate and dangerous. There's a short note covering the information with the initial C being the only clue to the writer's identity. The note said 'in case you ever decide to write a book about me'. There were a few handwritten scribbles as Champion had attempted the opening of a book. And there was a plain envelope with a key in there that looked to me like a safe-deposit key. The accompanying note stated, 'If anything happens to me, you'll get a letter soon. Then you'll know which hole to stick this key in. Good man! C'

The tone of expectancy that something would happen to him brought tears to my eyes. What a way to live. For all the power, all the muscle he had around him, nobody had been able to keep him alive when somebody thought there was a good reason why he had to be wasted. Champion surely knew his time was up – he'd had enough warnings. In making me leave the café he was getting me out, just in case someone came gunning for him. It moved me that Champion had entrusted me with his story. I was smiling then as my few tears rolled off my eyelids. "You were one great fucking scrapper, baby. I'll never forget you."

Annie came in from the shower in time to hear my good-bye to Champion. She lit cigarettes and I began telling her the story. When she realised how close it had been for me she gasped from shock. "Oh my good God!" Tears seemed to leap from her eyes as she gave a short cry of joy. "Oh God! Thank you, God, for sparing Joe!"

She was wrapping me up in her arms, kissing my face and my head like she was trying to set a new world record. Her tears fell on my skin, soft warm tears washing away the thoughts of what might have been, making space for love-making so soft and gentle and fulfilling that afterwards I felt renewed.

We ate an early supper and Annie came with me when I went to see how Telly was doing in the clinic. He was all bright-eyed and bushy-tailed, relieved that he had been given the all-clear for the surgical procedure which was happening in two days' time at something like seven in the morning. He hadn't caught the early evening news, so I told him about the death of Danny Devine and Champion. He immediately thought of Dervla, something I hadn't done up to that moment.

"Jesus, sport! What's this going to do to her? She adored her father."

I shuddered to think what Dervla could do with something this big. Telly was right about the way she adored Danny, and I knew from the way he'd spoken that he was afraid she might go off the deep-end. I mean if ever an alky was presented with the perfect excuse to hit the juice, this was it. As if she wasn't rocky enough already with what had gone down from the time Annie came back from Galway.

"I don't even know where she is, Telly. She took off without a word."

"Don't worry about it," he said confidently. "The minute she hears the news she'll be on the horn to you." Without deference to Annie, he continued, "What you guys have got hasn't gone away. It just got bogged down somewhere."

Telly was right about the phone call. It came at midnight while Annie and I were watching a video of *Casablanca*.

"Do you know what happened?" Dervla's first question landed on me the moment I said hello.

"As it happens, I do know. I was there with Danny and Champion minutes before the shooting."

"Jesus Christ!" She gasped and I could hear her hauling deep breaths into herself as she tried to remain in control. "So you could have been taken as well." She began to weep and I stood there holding the phone. I waited, saying nothing, giving her all the time she needed to unload. I was staying free of her emotions. Taking her shit on wouldn't help me to be of any use to her.

"I'm coming home," she said finally. "I'll be back at the lodge sometime tomorrow afternoon. Can you be there?"

"Sure. I can meet you there."

"Joe, tell Annie I'm sorry for the things I said. See you tomorrow."

Dervla calls again at about eleven o'clock the next morning. I'm out taking the air along the seafront so I get her message off the tape when I get home. Some kind of a go-slow at Heathrow meant that she couldn't get a flight until tomorrow lunch-time. She said she'd call me when she got to Dublin. The Range Rover is in the carpark at the airport – she'll make her own way to Lough Dane.

In one way I was glad she'd been delayed; my mind was full up with Telly and the surgery in the morning. I went walking and got into a litany of affirmative thinking, so that my mind wouldn't start writing any Hollywood dramas to drive me crazy.

24

Wicklow, August 1993

Telly looked tired during my mid-morning visit, so I cut it short, telling him I'd be back in the afternoon. "Just in case there's anything you might need that I can get for you." I heard my own nervousness. "Shit!" I was cackling now. "You'd think I was the one . . ." I stopped, waved my hand ineffectually. "Don't mind me, deah!" I said, "It's just that time of the month." Telly nodded patiently, giving me the smile that said 'thanks for warning me'!

Regardless of what was on your <u>mind</u>, you couldn't avoid the media coverage that turned the twin killings of Champion and Danny Devine into a circus. The suggestion, as I read it between the newspaper headlines, was that the killers were the same guys Danny wanted wasted by Champion and his crew. Danny had never said anything about killing anybody, but putting two and two together you just had to come up with four. The provo group that had claimed responsibility produced a press release that the dead men had been mishandling funds intended for 'the cause'. Proof was at hand to support this statement. In addition, there was further proof that Danny Devine and some of his close government associates had been siphoning monies donated to the political party into offshore accounts for the last several years. Full details were to hand and would be presented to the authorities in due course.

Nobody mentioned that the meeting in Daisy's Diner was only the second time the two dead men had spoken to each other, but now the press had stuck a label onto Champion by association. Through the meeting I'd arranged, he was placed inside whatever scam 'the fixer' had going, the scam that had cost both of their lives minutes after I'd left them at the café table.

The afternoon edition of the *Evening Herald* had reliable information that both men had ignored opportunities to refund the stolen monies. They had been warned, they had ignored the warnings and they had been executed. You could interpret this any way you liked, but since no amount of thinking and interpreting was going to bring Champion back, what was the point? Danny Devine, one-time republican, being shot by provos over money had an ironic sheen to it – who lives by the lie, and all that. When you're morto, does it matter whose lie you fell on? I don't think so.

In the evening I went into the clinic for the last-before-op visit with the guy I owed my life to, even if he denied it and claimed that the reverse of this was the truth. Telly didn't have much to say except that he'd forbidden Vanessa to come back in to see him again this evening. She had been there in late afternoon and he'd promised her he was going to come through this, and that as soon as he could walk properly they were moving in together. And that was final.

I felt it only right to tell him that Carol was in St Pat's. He smiled grimly, nodding his head like a wise old guy. "I made a call there today. I had this goddam feeling that Carol was due another detox. The word is she's recovering, going to be in there for another week. She's promised to go to Coolmine House for a year." He pulled a face. "She keeps giving them that same script and they keep on believing it just might happen."

"Maybe this time she'll do what she says. I was pretty hopeless when you hauled my ass off the pavement on Flatbush Avenue," I remind him.

His eyes drifted off for a few seconds and he turned his head away from me slightly. There was a faraway sound in his voice. "You get outa here now and hit an AA meeting, for both of us. I'll see you when I see you, sport."

I got up without a word. As I moved away I heard him say like he was just thinking aloud, "Don't Think! Don't Drink! Go To Meetings!"

Later that evening, at an AA meeting in Dun Laoghaire, I stepped in for the visiting chairman who hadn't shown up. I spoke for a little while. I tried to make room for everyone in the room to speak then as time ran out, I gave them some memories of Telly and me. I asked them to think of him this night as we recited together,

'God grant me the
Serenity to accept the things I cannot change
Courage to change the things I can . . . and
Wisdom to know the difference.'

I was at the clinic at ten o'clock the next morning expecting to hear that Telly was already out of the operating theatre and in a recovery-room or whatever. This wasn't how it was, and I began to feel serious concern for my man. As the day went ticking by it became more trying to be gracious when reassuring sounds seemed very lame. By three o'clock my serenity had well and truly left town and I was feeling very aggravated when the main man finally came out and told me. "Your friend, Mr Sampras has passed away. I'm sorry, Mr Collins"

I thought I'd pass out. Had Annie not been supporting me with her hand very securely wrapped around my arm, I swear to God I could have fallen down.

The operation on the bowel had been what they deemed 'fairly routine'. A small aneurism located in Telly's genital area had burst, and though they fought to save his life he never regained consciousness. They fought for seven hours to keep him alive, but Telly never regained consciousness.

I knew I was walking away from the guy who was still explaining things. It was like I was following myself, trying to catch up with Joe. I only just managed to get into the car before the driver's door slammed shut. He was like someone trying to get away from himself and what was tearing him apart. I don't know how long I sat there mute behind the wheel of the car. Then I felt Annie get out of the car. She came around and opened the door, nudging me over into the passenger seat. On the short trip back to the house I didn't utter one word. When Annie stopped the car she turned to me and I buried my face in her shoulder. And then I began to weep.

For what seemed like a long time Annie held me in her arms, encouraging me to let it flow, her hands so gracefully gentle on my head, her fingertips touching my temples. Her patience was like some kind of blessing as grief rendered me pitiful in my unmerciful loss. Her caring helped turn the flow back into the boundless love I'd felt for the Greek who came bearing gifts. I buried myself in her arms, giving way to the wanting and the needing and the pointless wishing that I would wake and find it was just a nightmare broken by a phone call from Telly. A while later I was able to go into the house, my spirit crippled. I thought of Telly, my some kind of angel who'd been hanging out at the Brooklyn meeting when I needed him as badly as my next breath.

I took a shower and afterwards Annie poured coffee. Dervla came through on the telephone to check that I was meeting her at the lodge. I said I'd be there in an hour. When I got to Lough Dane there was plenty of light left in the evening. I gave a shudder as I drove past the reconciliation centre, knowing I wouldn't be coming back to live by the lake. No matter how idyllic it could be, it was just too close to too much pain relating to my father.

The Range Rover was there when I got to the lodge. I went into the kitchen to make coffee, and in a few moments I heard Dervla's footsteps on the stairs. I turned to face her, more than surprised to see that she was OK. Hurting sure, but her shoulders were back in an easy posture, suggesting she wasn't cutting herself up over Danny's demise or the likely passing of our relationship. As a guy who cared about her, I was relieved to see her on top of things. She wore a black raincoat that had that chic Brown Thomas stamp about it, over tan slacks and boots. Her hair was tied back and I bit down on the wish that things between us were different.

She only had to look at me to know that something was very wrong. I saw her eyes change gear as she stopped playing it safe. Then after she'd taken a needed breath, she asked me, "What's happened?" I told her the story, and she came to me and she put her arms around me and she held me like someone she needed to protect. We stood like that with only the force of shared grief holding us together. When the pressure eased we were able to let go of each other. I lit a couple of Gold Flake.

"You give great hug," I joked. Then I gave her coffee, asked her about her plans. It seemed amazing to me that neither of us had mentioned Danny. I'd left it to her to bring it up if she needed to talk about him, but it never happened.

She said she wanted us to have a six-month trial separation. She talked as though we were married, and that made me feel good for a second. She was going to the States. She had already organised to stay with her cousin who had a serious apartment on Central Park West. "I've got to get myself off the hook that men and sex have become for me. From Daddy onwards, I've always been looking to some guy to make it right. You were the latest and the greatest, the man I like most on earth, even after the shit we've been throwing at each other. I hope we can come out the far end. In going, I'm doing the biggest thing I've ever had to face. A few weeks back I felt I'd die if we broke up. And here we are on our separate trips, and I'm not going to die. I'm going to use this pain to drive me in the right direction. Tell Annie again, I'm sorry. I didn't mean any of the shit I dumped on her, or on you. Or if I did, I don't mean it today. I fell for her like a ton of bricks and I was so unhappy about that without being able to share it. I thought I was a lesbian and I know now that had that been the case, I'd have killed myself. I've nothing against gay people, but I couldn't have lived as one. And if that needs looking at, I won't run away from the challenge. I've got an appointment at Hazelden in the States. I'm going for 'reality therapy', even if it fucking kills me." She found the gist of a rueful smile. "A few months back you said we both needed reality therapy."

She shrugged. "If they take me at Hazelden there's a chance I'll be a better listener, OK?"

"I've got an appointment at Rutland in a few days. I need help too, Derv. It's tough, six weeks of intense therapy, a live-in community, everyone off the wall for the first few weeks."

"I'm glad to hear it. You'll come through it, I know you. I need a break from Ireland, so Hazelden is killing two birds with one plane flight." She nodded her head. "You saved my life, Joe. No matter what's gone down, that's the truth. I love you and I'm going now. Anything I've left behind, please find some charity to take the clothes. I'll call you and give you numbers as soon as I'm settled in Manhattan. I presume you'll want to talk to me, at least meet me for a meal if I survive all this 'reality therapy' stuff?"

"If I survive it myself," I said truthfully. "That's if they'll take me into the Rutland. Paddy Fahy got me the interview. He says they don't admit just anybody. After us, Telly being gone, I've got to sort out my shit." I felt very sad that I didn't have much more to say. I'd run out of road. Grief had stunned my ambitions and they lay comatose in the deep well of my heart.

I thought Dervla was great as we stood there in the Lough Dane kitchen. Then she said. "I'll survive Daddy's death. But honestly Joe, had you been shot to death along with him, that would have been a bridge too far." She gave me a tiny wave of her hand and I followed her out to the Range Rover. She was loaded and ready to take off. "I'll leave the jeep with Eddie at the Berkeley Court. He'll keep it safe until you pick it up. And by the way, if you need some money, I've got bundles." I let her know I was OK financially and I didn't move as she got into the Range Rover.

She drove away fast and I had such mixed feelings of sadness and relief that I looked for the falcon as though he might help me get some idea of what the fuck I was going through.

A few minutes later, as I stood smoking a cigarette on the fringe of broken lawn above the lake, he flashed across the sky, like he had come through for me in answer to my unspoken thought. In the instant, I knew where I had to go and what I had to do. I didn't know why, but something made me get into my car and a few minutes later I parked it by the roadside down at Glencree. I felt compelled to climb the hill to a point where I could see the renewed buildings that had once housed the reformatory where my father Tom Collins had been so brutalised. I stopped at a given point without conscious awareness of why I'd been brought here. I sat down, shrouded in some kind of interior mist. It was as though my own body was trying to hide whatever I felt was here to be discovered. Sounds fanciful perhaps, but that's what was in place in those first moments on the hillside.

In a little while I felt the urge to ask for help, pray for help to understand whatever was going on with me. I found that this offhand application for divine assistance brought Telly right back onto the screen of my eyes and tears were close behind. As I wept over the pain of his going, it seemed to dovetail into the pain of my father's death. What torture must he have endured to drive him to such an extreme act? The two men who had figured most in my life were there together, framed in our shared pain. All I could do was wait until the tears quit so that I could gather myself and see what had drawn me back here once more.

Suddenly it was here again, the cry of a boy in pain. For a moment, I assumed it was my father. But no! It wasn't him. It was Joe Collins, aged about ten or eleven years old and in the moment a very confused kid. He didn't like what was going on. I heard him talking then, his voice running scared as he stands still in a tin-bath of warm water before the dead fireplace in the living room above Mulvey's Printers on Kevin Street.

"Da? No! I don't want you to examine me. I'm cold. I want to put me trousers on. Da? No! Don't! No! No, I don't want. Da? You're hurting me."

I hear Joe scream again, the same hell-bent sound that seems to come out of the depths of the hillside itself. I see blood trickling down his leg and I fall backwards off my hillside seat as the pain in my lower-back engulfs me.

I land on a flinty limestone rock and I hear the lad weep. He's lying on the bed now. His father is heading out of the bedroom, almost running to get to the start of his long walk, the journey of his lifetime until he found his only escape hatch at Portobello Harbour. Having rejected himself and the abuse of his young son he's running scared, running to lie still in the waters of the Grand Canal.

On the hillside above Glencree, I hear a voice mumbling. It's my own voice, the voice of Joe Collins, thirty-eight years old making a phlegm-filled protest. "You'd no right, Da." I hear my own sobs and I bite into the back of my hand to stop me screaming. This is some form of catharsis, but I can't get to the part where you feel you've vomited up whatever's fucking up your life. "God help you Da, I love you." I hear these words and they seem to suggest I've forgiven Tom for what he did to me. No way. There's nothing in me leading me to fucking sainthood. I'm so ripped up with fucking anger, I want to lash out and hurt somebody. Oh Jesus! Is that what it's about? Had Da's abuse by the holy men of Glencree so angered him that he used me to rid himself of some of the lifetime pain?

Now I'm looking at stuff I can't identify. Like the cause of me being an alky or whatever. Da was an alcoholic misfit, a guy who'd been fucked by the guy in charge of him in the reformatory. Years later Ma leaves me in Da's care while she's in the Adelaide hospital, and he does the same thing to me. I'm sobbing again. It's like a shower, a cleansing rush of water or something running through me and setting me free to some extent anyway. I hear my breathing turn towards normal. I'm leaning against the car as I gulp the air into my lungs and then a minute later I'm smoking a joint in the last of the evening light. And then the rain comes down the way it can out of the blue in those hills and I sit there getting drenched to the skin without the slightest need to get up and into the car out of the sudden downpour.

"Are you OK?" I ask myself finally. I hear a sigh released, a sigh that sounds a thousand years old. "Better than I was." Slowly I get up, get into the car and drive down the hill past Glencree village knowing that I will never again travel this road.

Six days after my catharsis on the hillside, I carry out Telly's wish by having his body cremated. I still wept every time it hit me that he wasn't going to be around any more. Carol didn't make the cremation service, having been transferred from the detox unit to the Mater general hospital. She was so severely run-down that she was actually in danger of losing her life. Some of her organs were so damaged she might never make a recovery worth having.

I spent a few days putting all of Telly's wishes in order. Vanessa inherited whatever bread he had left and I was happy about that. She had gladdened the last months of his time with us – her contribution was priceless. Playing executor kept me from thinking about my decision to go into the Rutland Centre. The closer my interview date got, the more my interior critic questioned my sanity. "You don't need that shit, Joe!" I shut him out knowing I needed all the help I could get.

Before I left for New York to further carry out my duties as executor to the estate of Telemachus Sampras, I discovered Telly had signed over his half of the Whiterock house to me. Carol would most likely get this. But the apartment at Fifty-seventh Street and Ninth Avenue in Manhattan had been mine for the last year, even though the bastard hadn't bothered mentioning it to me. He'd handled this outside of his will, his lawyer Gerry Dolan smiled when he told me. "He wanted to make sure the estate couldn't touch the apartment." I was pleased to have such an intimate reminder of our first years off the sauce, glad to know the apartment was there when Manhattan beckoned me back.

I flew to Kennedy and drove in a hired car to Flatbush Avenue in Brooklyn. I stopped on the way for food, dawdling until the sun went down. Telly had said in his will that, "as the executor of my estate, please scatter my ashes on the pavement in Brooklyn, on the spot where we first met"?

Hearing Gerry Dolan read those words out of Telly's will, I was back there in a second, experiencing some kind of concrete rock-bottom before this classy guy helped me up off my back so that we could start a new life.

He had also suggested, "You shouldn't get to Flatbush Avenue before dark. You don't want to end up in court for fouling up the neighbourhood with a handful of ashes!"

As I watched the ashes become part of the Brooklyn night, I smiled grandly. I saw the Greek bastard with his crooked five-grand grin pulling me up off the pavement before he took me down the block for a cup of coffee and a trip to die for.

Epilogue

Annie takes the car into the grounds of the Rutland Centre and drives me to the front door. The place looks like an old person who is not too far from falling down. I can't take any of it in because whatever powers of observation I normally possess have left town, just as the withdrawal symptoms are in full-swing. If an aching wound could walk and talk, it would look and sound like I do at this killing time in my life. At least part of me is dying, and there's not a thing I can do about it.

What do I know? I know its Friday lunch-time, that it's a lovely afternoon. I feel like I missed the good time to die, back behind me somewhere. I am humiliated to gagging point by the disgust festering in me, that I have come to this. Annie puts two suitcases at my feet. She is cool, but a little withdrawn, looking decidedly unhappy. How could she be happy? Annie is hurting maybe just as much as I am. I'm going into a fucking treatment centre for a six-week course in 'reality fucking therapy' and she needs to get away so that she can smoke a joint on her way back to Whiterock.

"This is as far as I can go today. They have these rules here." She is tearful and I have very little to give her. I shrug and nod my head, empty of anything to say. I'm busy coping with the grieving need for a joint, something, anything, to help me through this heavy withdrawal. I press the bell and I hear the car door closing as Annie gets ready to leave.

At that moment, the door opens and I find Winona Merry looking at me as though I've just crawled up out of the toilet. "What're you doing here?" she says with that superior look I got to know for a while in the States.

"I'm not here for fun. I was assessed here for admission three days ago. I got word to be here right now. So I don't need any jokes, Winona. I hate to admit it, but I need help. That being said, if I'd known you were a patient here I wouldn't have joined!"

"So you finally got smart, Joe. Nice one!" Her mid-Atlantic drawl hasn't changed a bit since I'd last seen her in Manhattan. The sneer stitched onto the hem of her bottom lip was still there too.

"Can I see one of the staff, a counsellor, somebody?" I say with a phoney grin, my defences slamming down like steel shutters.

"Follow me," she orders bluntly, turning away.

When I come into the office she shuts the door and I put the cases down. "If you feel like you look, you should sit down." This is totally impersonal, thrown over her shoulder as she goes behind this desk.

"I can stand," I say, remembering how she had disliked me intensely while I was drinking in Manhattan. Back in the days when she had to serve drinks to me because that was her job. Days long lost and gone, during which I never quit telling her how I could have her climbing the walls in sexual bliss. All she had to do was get down off her fucking high-horse. How little we know. At that very time Winona was just off the booze herself, going to an 'after care' group and attending AA meetings and just trying to stay away from the first drink, just for today.

"Can I take it you've been 'clean and dry' for the last three days?"

"It wasn't easy deciding to come in here. I'm only here because I'm scared of what will happen to me if I go on as I am. So yeh, I've been clean and dry for three days. Only God knows how."

She looks at me as though she's seeing all kinds of stuff I'm not aware of. "OK, you go down the hall into the dining-room and have your lunch. I'll have your cases checked by the time you finish. I'll come down there and show you where to go."

"What do you mean, my cases checked? Checked for what?"

"Booze, speed, smoke, a few valium tucked into a sock. Maybe booze in the aftershave. And who knows? You might have come up with a new stroke. Coke dressed up as talc. You wouldn't be the first." She looks half-amused as she lays this on me.

"I don't want any lunch, thanks." I throw in the word thanks as a 'please give me a break' gesture, and she jumps on it with the subtlety of a linebacker who'd love to kill a couple of running-backs.

"Excuse me!" It's like the crack of a whip. "Did I ask you if you wanted lunch?"

"Ehm, it's OK, Winona. I'm not hungry."

"Pardon me, you fuckin' asshole! I don't give two fucks whether you're hungry or not. And I didn't ask you if you wanted lunch. I told you – watch my lips carefully now. I told you – go down the hall into the dining-room and have your lunch. Got it?"

"But I don't want."

"Shut the fuck up, will you. In here you do what you're told. Even assholes that're regarded as great and famous, they do what they're told. That includes you."

"Jesus, Winona! Do you have to be so fuckin' heavy? I'm in pieces here."

"Just shut it, Joe, and listen." She looks at me in a baleful way. The vindictive bitch, she'd love to punch me in the mouth at the minute. "Here's the story. The fact that we know each other means nothing in here. There'll be no turning to your friend Winona for guidance or whatever. We are not friends, we never were, and my guess is we never will be. I don't like you, I never did. I can't stand men who think they're God's gift to every woman they meet. That's for openers. Now, hear the rest of it. In here you do what you're told when you're told to do it. Do you understand that?" I nod, sniffing back tears that I hate. I hate the fuckers letting me down in front of this fucking nazi.

She throws a box of tissues on the desk. "Help yourself." She sits down to look up at me. "If you don't do what you're told, you can fuck-off. You can fuck-off at any time, or you can fuck-off right now. We don't actually need you in here. We are up to our armpits in assholes just like you. OK?" Winona waits while I give her another nod of acknowledgement. Then she says: "OK. You are free to leave here any time you take the notion. The gate out there is open twenty-four seven. But, and this is for real, if you step outside that gate you don't come back in. Are you clear? You go out, you stay out. There are no second chances here."

She pauses and my tears come in an eruption. They just burst out of my eyes, eyes not yet ready to register the extent of my powerlessness. Jesus Christ! What did I do that was so fucking terrible? Do I really I deserve this?

"You have to want to get well so badly, Joe," Winona weighs in again. "You have to want it as though your life depends on it, which it does really. You need that kind of motivation." She stands up and I shudder at the idea that I once fancied this chick. Of course, I'd no reason to know she had a mouth on her like a blowtorch and I'm not talking hot fellatio. "Now, for the last time, go down to the dining-room and get your lunch."

I hold up my hand in a conciliatory way. "Can I ask you a question?"

She sighs like she's having one of those days. "What now?"

"I just want to know, can I bring brown rice in here."

She looks like I've hit her across the forehead with a shovel. "Can you what?"

"Can I bring brown rice in here?"

"Get one thing straight." This is as direct a warning as a guy could wish for. "You'll eat what everybody else eats, and you'll fuckin' lump it. Or, as I've already told you, you can fuck-off right now. Jesus!"

"It's just, I need it, Winona. If I don't eat some brown rice every day I suffer with piles."

She releases a kind of twisted exhalation. "Let me lay it on you for once and for all, Joe. You get your head right, and your asshole will take care of itself! I have one further warning for you. This is about as easy as it's going to get. We don't call it 'tough love' for nothing. Probably it'll be tougher on you than most guys, you being famous and all that. OK, so you haven't had a drink in years, but you need to be here because your enormous fucking ego thought you

would hit the dope trail and not end up in the shit you're in."
Winona stands there beside me and I feel she is reading my
mind. Then she tells me, "Believe it or not, I know what
you're going through."

"Are you telling me you've been though this 'reality
therapy'?"

She nods a little, not making a big deal out of it. "I did it
in the States. That was before they toned it down, softened
it up for the Irish," she is laughing at herself here. Then she
says, "The thing is, you're not OK, even if you didn't take a
drink today. You're all fucked-up right now, and you need to
be here. If you didn't need to be here, Joe, we wouldn't have
admitted you. We don't take just anybody."

"Who do you turn down? Hitler? Joe Stalin?" I give her
an apologetic glance and she lets it go. "Can I smoke?" She
nods and I get a Gold Flake going. "I'm sorry. You're right,
I'm all fucked-up. I hurt so bad I can't believe I'm still
standing."

"Stay with it. Don't try to blot it out. Just let it be. In
here, if you stick the course, you'll feel sore like you can't
even imagine. It takes some kind of dynamite to shift you off
your shit. We're all the same when we come in that door."

"I'll stick it," I say, my pride rearing its head.

"Maybe you will. If you do, you can make a new start.
You've got a hard road ahead of you. Now, go on down and
get something to eat." I nod my head, accepting that I have
to do what I'm told without questioning it.

I step into the hall, the first step towards going to the
dining-room, to do what I've been told. I find I'm glued to
the polished wooden floor, watching myself go out through
the gate, flying in case I lose the courage to run, glad they
don't let anybody back in for a second shot.

Winona comes out of the office and she stops for just a second. "The local cab number is by the public phone on the wall by the dining-room." She passes on then, leaving a scent of perfume behind with her belief that I am already leaving. I want to call her names, tell her she's a fucking bitch, but I can't deny that she identified my vibe. I pull it together enough to walk down the passage and into the dining-room.

There are about thirty people sitting at four or five long wooden dining-tables and though I'm blind with self-pity, I can see some reaction to my arrival. It's something I was getting used to since I'd been making regular appearances on television, and at the same time it was something I never expected to really get used to.

There are serving tables on my right and I look at the food. I see some tasty-looking lamb chops, lots of vegetables, gravy boats. I know I can't eat, but I put something on a plate and I walk down to an empty table and sit down on a wooden bench. The truth is I can hardly breathe and I push the food to one side because I have to drop my head onto my arms. I cannot bear to blubber in front of all these people, I have to try and hide some of it. I am sobbing and it's like my heart and my other vital organs are trying to leave town. I seem to be on the verge of vomiting them up onto the table and I am truly desolate. The sobs quit after a while and I rest my head on my arms. I become aware that somebody is touching the fingers of my right hand. I move to look up and there is a guy standing there, a big rough-and-ready guy.

He is giving me a friendly look that tells me he understands just what I'm going through. I watch his working-man's hands as he drops a boiled sweet into my hand. "You'll be all right, pal," he tells me. Then he leaves me alone.

I put the sweet in my mouth and I feel my Paddy come up.

I get some saliva going in my mouth and I vow to myself: "OK. You blew it again. But you're going to beat this sucker."

"OK, sport?" I hear Telly's voice and I'm seeing the wry grin. "We let a couple of things get in the way, so what? Just go for it. You can handle whatever they have to throw at you in here."

His ashes may be dust now on Flatbush Avenue, but he's as real to my heart as ever he was to my eyes.

"You're doing the right thing, sport. You need help. Let these guys do their job and you'll come up roses."

I lower my head and I hear myself praying. "Hey, Jesus! You're my man. I'll listen to these people, but I'm asking you in all humility, for fuck's sake, mind me?"

I sniff back tears that want to get busy again. I see Telly sitting across the table from me lighting up a stinking menthol cigarette. He grins at me, nodding his head in that familiar way. "You did good, sport!"

The End

Also by the author

Fiction

Goodbye to the Hill
A Bed in the Sticks
Paddy Maguire is Dead
Does Your Mother?
Ringleader
Ringmaster
Requiem for Reagan
Hell is Filling Up
Trials of Tommy Tracey
The Corpse Wore Grey
Midnight Cabbie
Day of the Cabbie
Cabbie Who Came In From
the Cold
Virgin Cabbies
The Cabfather
Maggie's Story
Big Al
Harbour Hotel

Non Fiction

Sober Thoughts on Alcoholism

Stage Plays

Goodbye to the Hill
Return to the Hill
Does Your Mother?
Busy Bodies
One Man's Meat
Only the Earth
The Full Shilling
Tough Love
Bless Them All (One Man Show)

Co Adapter/ Director –
Plato's Dialogues.

Television

Only the Earth
No Hiding Place
Callan
Vendetta
Troubleshooters
Wednesday Play
Weavers Green

Radio Plays

Whatever happened to you,
Mick O'Neill?
Tough Love
Aunty Kay
No Hiding Place
The Pot Wallopers
Only the Earth
Kennedys of Castleross
Harbour Hotel
Konvenience Korner
(2,000 scripts in all)

Film

The Pale Faced Girl
Paddy
Wedding Night
Goodbye To The Hill
Do You Remember Bray?
Riley's Bonfire

MA Honours Screen. IADT.
June 2004